Falling Apart, Falling for You

ENDORSEMENTS

A witty novel featuring relatable characters and surprising twists—everything from sharing shame-filled secrets, hobbling through grief, growing a fledgling faith, and the joys and trials of enduring friendship. *Falling Apart, Falling For You* will capture your heart and encourage you that it's never too late to make a fresh start.
—**Sarah Hanks**, author of *Mercy Will Follow Me*, *Mercy's Song*, and *Mercy's Legacy*

You'll want to gather Suzanne, Rachel, and Marla into your arms for a group hug as you cry about their past heartaches, then cheer while they embrace challenges, victory, and the promise of love to come. A celebration of old friends, fun times, and a faith-filled future!
—**K.L. Gilchrist**, author of *Thick Chicks* and *Engaged*

Three close high school friends find each other after forty years. Three very different women, three types of families; gut-clenching challenges and fun; sorrow and hope. And reblossoming faith. All wrapped together in a delightful fortieth high school reunion. This story will tickle your spirit and touch your heart.
—**Kathy McKinsey**, author of *All My Tears*, *Millie's Christmas*, and *Gifts of Grace*

Falling Apart, Falling for You

Chris Posti

COPYRIGHT NOTICE

Falling Apart, Falling for You: Real Life and Romance for the 50+ Woman

First edition. Copyright © 2022 by Chris Posti. The information contained in this book is the intellectual property of Chris Posti and is governed by United States and International copyright laws. All rights reserved. No part of this publication, either text or image, may be used for any purpose other than personal use. Therefore, reproduction, modification, storage in a retrieval system, or retransmission, in any form or by any means, electronic, mechanical, or otherwise, for reasons other than personal use, except for brief quotations for reviews or articles and promotions, is strictly prohibited without prior written permission by the publisher.

This is a work of fiction. Names, characters, businesses, places, events, locales, and incidents are either the products of the author's imagination or used in a fictitious manner. Any resemblance to actual persons, living or dead, or actual events is purely coincidental.

Scripture taken from the New King James Version®. Copyright © 1982 by Thomas Nelson. Used by permission. All rights reserved.

Cover and Interior Design: Derinda Babcock, Deb Haggerty
Editor(s): Cristel Phelps, Deb Haggerty

PUBLISHED BY: Elk Lake Publishing, Inc., 35 Dogwood Drive, Plymouth, MA 02360, 2022

Library Cataloging Data

Names: Posti, Chris (Chris Posti)

Falling Apart, Falling for You: Real Life and Romance for the 50+ Woman / Chris Posti

346 p. 23cm × 15cm (9in × 6 in.)

ISBN-13: 978-1-64949-563-1 (paperback) | 978-1-64949-564-8 (trade paperback) | 978-1-64949-565-5 (e-book)

Key Words: Romance, Mature-Age Readers, Friendships, Humorous, Small Town, Divorce, Widows

Library of Congress Control Number: 2022937133 Fiction

DEDICATION

To my husband, Dave Walls, with appreciation for your support, encouragement, and love.

ACKNOWLEDGMENTS

Thank you, Lord, for blessing me with a love of language and writing, for giving me every word of this story, and for occupying my mind with something challenging and constructive during the pandemic.

I thank my longsuffering husband, Dave, who encouraged me to keep at it and tolerated many hours of silence as I wrote, and my daughter, Elizabeth, who brought my grandsons for weekly visits, blessing me with joy and much-needed respite.

Many people chimed in with their writing and editing expertise, which I appreciate more than any of them realize. That includes the awesome "Scribes" critique partners at ACFW who encouraged and instructed me even as I made baby steps. Special thanks go to "Little Loop Ladies" Diane Samson, Jamie Ogle, and Kristine Delano, and to early readers Elizabeth Mazzei, Marion Kusajtys, and Kim Hohman.

I thank the Lord for guiding me directly to Elk Lake Publishing and its powerhouse owner, Deb Haggerty. When I learned we share an April 29 birthday, I knew our relationship was meant to be.

My sincere thanks to other talented people who have helped me along this path—editors Karli Jackson and Cristel Phelps, cover designer Derinda Babcock, and website developer Bill Weil.

I love you all.

CHAPTER 1

SUZANNE

"A change?" Perspiration prickled Suzanne Fleming's skin as she struggled to grasp her boss's message. "You need to make a change?" A sudden heat radiated from within. She spread her elbows onto the arms of the conference room chair. *Shouldn't have worn the new silk blouse.*

Every April for the past nineteen years, the airline's training director, Noreen Vale, had conducted a perfunctory meeting like this with Suzanne. In less time than it took to board a 737, she'd thank Suzanne for being a dependable trainer, assign her a fresh topic, and hand her a new annual contract with a three percent increase.

Today, though, Noreen wasn't following the script.

Suzanne curled her manicured fingers and toes as she clung to a sliver of hope the "change" Noreen referred to merely spelled a new training topic. She'd all but memorized her current program, "Sexual Harassment & Sensitivity." Spending months on a dry subject like that bored most trainers, but she'd made a habit of injecting humorous anecdotes into her material, which energized her and kept her audience engaged. She'd gone above and beyond—they owed her something for that.

Looking at Noreen's demeanor, though, Suzanne suspected the "change" portended something less benign than a new topic. She tucked a stray tendril of platinum blonde hair into her wavy up-do while straining to read the documents spread out on the other side of the table.

Noreen fingered the papers while peering at Suzanne over top of black-rimmed reading glasses. "Yes, a change." She cleared her throat. "You've been a reliable contract trainer for us, but we've learned when our employees see someone over and over, they tune the person out. So, we've decided to make some changes to the training staff and increase our online training too."

"Is—is that so?"

"We'd like you to finish your remaining sessions here in Las Vegas and a few other cities, but unfortunately, we won't be renewing your contract. We'll pay you through the end of June, even though you'll complete your sessions two weeks before that. Here's a list of items you'll need to return." She slid a paper toward Suzanne.

"Is it because I'm too old?" Suzanne blurted. She'd heard stories of others around her age being let go, and the words tripped out of her mouth before her brain realized it. She did that sometimes now.

"Not at all." Noreen deadpanned. After all, the woman was notorious for terminating longstanding employment contracts. Trainers were easily replaced in a glamorous industry like the airlines. Just another item in their spare parts inventory, like a wing or a window.

"So—are you saying this is it?" Now barely breathing, Suzanne clenched her entire body.

"Next year, we'll move on to some new programs." Noreen tapped her pen on the laminated tabletop, as if bored by a conversation she'd often repeated. "We can talk about it then, if you're interested in being considered." She lifted her papers and wiggled them until they stacked together. She slid a paper clip on the corner and inserted the documents into an expandable folder. Typed in a large font, the tab read: "Former Contract Trainers."

Seriously? Even her ex-husband Mike, a pilot who'd attended many of her classes and relished pointing out her perceived flaws, had always said that even at five-foot-three, she knew how to command a room. Now, at fifty-seven, she was far more experienced, confident, and capable than ever. *My age has got to have something to do with the decision.*

"All right, then. Do you have any questions?" Noreen placed her hands on the edge of the table, readying herself to stand.

"No questions." Protestation would be pointless. Suzanne worked as a contractor, not an employee. No redress available for spare parts people.

Noreen stood and extended a rigid hand. "We wish you all the best, Suzanne."

I'll bet. She rose for a one-pump handshake, her sweaty palm a stark contrast to Noreen's dry fingers. "Thank you," Suzanne replied, with the warmth of an icicle. In Alaska. In winter.

She snapped up her purse from the chair beside her and stumbled into the empty hallway. A large vent on the wall blasted cold air on her as she passed by, causing a shiver to dance up her spine. She backed up, put her hands on her hips, and did a slow three-sixty in the hope that, at the very least, her silk blouse could be salvaged. She forced herself to breathe slowly. Deeply. *Lord, it's been a while since we've talked, but I need you now.* A wave of guilt washed over her for thinking about God only when a crisis arose.

And this was a crisis for sure.

Her jumbled thoughts darted to Adam. These past four months, they'd established a pleasant groove of texting throughout the week and spending weekends together. The ease of their relationship had taken her by surprise, even generating in her an unexpected tug to return to the altar. Men had always been her undoing, and since her divorce, she'd trained herself to avoid anything more than casual dating—easy to do when your job bounces you from city to city.

Adam, though, offered potential as the perfect mate. But could their budding relationship withstand a jarring development like this? *What'll he think? That I'm a loser, incompetent at my job? That I'm looking to him as my retirement plan?* She was *this* close to hitting her retirement target—but if she stayed jobless for long, her IRA would take a hit.

Blouse still damp, she kept rotating. *Would this situation become another point of contention with her daughter?* Ever since Jill and Drew had gotten married, Suzanne could no longer do anything right in her daughter's eyes. It had to be Drew's influence. He never said anything directly to Suzanne, but his body language spoke loud and clear, even pursing his lips dismissively, just like her ex used to do. The first time she met Drew, when she asked him what he did for a living, he raised his chin an inch before responding. "Finance." Whatever that meant. She never broached the subject again.

Finally, with her blouse dry and emotions under control, she marched to her assigned meeting room. Suzanne was nothing if not self-disciplined. Poker face in place, she delivered the training to thirty ticket agents—even got them to laugh at some of her stories—then caught a flight home to Pittsburgh.

As the plane was full, Suzanne thanked God for the aisle seat. She crossed her legs, allowing her skirt's short slit to expose a triangle of well-toned thigh. *Will my muscles turn to blubber now that I won't be using hotel gyms every night?*

A beefy, handsome, forty-something man, dressed in expensive business casual and wedged in the middle seat, struck up a conversation. At first, she assumed he'd ask to switch seats, but he surprised her with his knowledge of travel, international politics, and natural health. Their lively conversation rejuvenated her, even made her wonder if he had an interest in her. But when he needed to pass her to use the restroom, he said, "Excuse me, ma'am."

FALLING APART, FALLING FOR YOU

Ma'am? Suzanne stood in the aisle to let him out. *That settles it. I guess I am old.* She sank back into her seat, wondering if her gray roots, laugh lines, or something even worse had given her away.

Suzanne clunked her cinnamon bagels and a pint of strawberries onto the grocery's checkout counter. "Happy Saturday, Dorothy." She smiled at the wizened old woman, a comforting staple of her weekends home in Pittsburgh.

"Home for a couple days?" Dorothy glanced at Suzanne while ringing up the items on an ancient cash register.

Suzanne nodded. "I had to come back—I couldn't take all that sunshine in Vegas." Pittsburgh, with its many rivers and lush rolling hills, ranked behind only Buffalo and Seattle as most overcast city in America.

The woman winced as she placed the items in a plastic bag.

"Arthritis acting up?" Suzanne tipped her head in sympathy. Dorothy's gnarled hands reminded Suzanne of her mother's. Some days, the poor woman could barely open a jar.

"Yeah." Dorothy rubbed a knuckle. "Must be the damp weather."

Suzanne clucked her tongue. "Spring in Pittsburgh—if it's not raining now, it's gonna." She scooped up her bag of groceries. "My mom swears by some cream she uses. When I visit her today, I'll find out the name, and I'll bring you a jar to try."

Hiking back to her condo, she stopped at one of the sidewalk observation decks overlooking downtown. Even through murky skies, she easily picked out Adam's penthouse among the glass towers. No wonder. The architecture of his building stood out from the crowd—just like Adam did.

She set her bag on the damp cement and rested her elbows on the metal railing. Ever since her days as a flight attendant, heights had helped her figure out anything on her mind. She scanned the budding trees on the steep hillside below, then watched a flock of swallows zooming overhead, seeming to have no goal other than flying like dive-bombers. Waiting for inspiration, she followed their antics. But this morning, her mind remained as foggy as the sky.

When the dampness increased to rain, she flicked her umbrella open and made her way back home. After a quick breakfast, she headed to her mom's. Only forty minutes south of Pittsburgh, entering sleepy little Port Mariette comforted her like a warm hug.

Her mother pushed the screen door open, her eyes registering concern. "Everything okay?" Her brow furrowed as she examined her daughter. Normally, Suzanne visited on Sunday afternoons—never Saturday mornings.

She broke the bad news as soon as she stepped over the threshold.

"Aw, what a shame, Suzie." Her mother circled her arms around Suzanne and patted her on the back.

Suzanne couldn't help herself—she sobbed like a child.

They plopped onto the worn sofa. "Have you told Jill yet?"

"I called her last night." Suzanne sniffed. Jill worked grueling hours as a pastry chef in an upscale New Jersey hotel, which apparently made her too busy to produce a grandchild, or even be available for regular conversations with the woman who brought her into this world. "She thought it was crazy they'd let me go. She agrees it could be age-related."

"You're not old." Suzanne's mom shook her head with vigor. "You barely look fifty."

"Thanks for the boost, Mom. But Jill did remind me I still use paper handouts. These days, no other trainer does that." She rolled her eyes. "I do despise technology."

FALLING APART, FALLING FOR YOU

"No sin in that." Her mother chuckled as she inclined her head toward the beige cordless phone perched on the end table.

Suzanne had to admit she'd been slipping mentally too. Last month, while loading suitcases into her rental vehicle, she'd put her cellphone on the roof of the car, then driven off. A driver approaching from the opposite direction beeped, jabbing his finger at the top of the car until it dawned on her to rescue the phone.

"Jill said losing my job might turn out to be a good thing." Suzanne shrugged. "Like she said, I'll have more time for Adam, at least until I land something." Thank goodness her call with Jill had ended on such a positive note. Not all their conversations went that well.

"By the way, at the hairdresser's yesterday, I overheard two women talking." Her mother raised a finger as she recalled the details. "They said something about your class having a fortieth reunion. That oughta be fun."

Just what she needed, an occasion to tell her former classmates she was divorced, out of work, and didn't have one single grandchild. She hadn't seen any of these people since graduation—why now? Still, she'd love to know how her classmates had turned out. Rachel, her friend since kindergarten, had stayed in Port Mariette, but her other close friend, Marla, had moved back to New York.

"How 'bout Adam—have you told him yet?" Her mother asked in a tentative voice.

"Not yet. We're going to *Carmen* tonight. I'll tell him then."

"An opera?" Her mom scrunched her face. "I never knew you enjoyed that kind of stuff."

"I don't, really." Suzanne lifted a shoulder. "The sets and costumes fascinate me, though."

"You always did like anything artistic."

"And Adam needs to be there for his bank. They're a big sponsor of cultural events."

"Sounds like things are getting serious with you two. You've been dating him longer than most." Her mother raised a thin eyebrow. "Since around Christmas, right?"

The ends of Suzanne's mouth curled into a smile. "Uh-huh." *Exactly four months today, in fact.* "But with my schedule, we aren't able to see one another all that much, so it's hard to say." A couple weeks previously, she'd tossed out a trial balloon, saying she'd consider not renewing her training contract if she had a reason to stick around in Pittsburgh. He'd acted intrigued, but their conversation went nowhere. What would he say now, when he learned she'd been let go?

"Such a shame about your job." Her mother shook her head in slow motion. "You really seemed to enjoy that kind of work and all the travel. But maybe God has something better in store for you." She looked up, eyes bright. "Like, remember when your dad and I sent you to visit your cousin in London right after graduation? After that, all you could talk about was getting a job with an airline."

There she goes again, acting as if Dad participated in our lives.

"You bet I remember." Suzanne recalled the terror she felt leaving tiny Port Mariette all by herself. She'd always dreamed of leaving town, but when it finally happened, the reality threatened to overwhelm her. Changing planes in New York, she'd misread the ticket and gone to the wrong terminal in JFK, nearly missing her connection to Heathrow. Once she made it to London, though, traveling took root in her soul, crowding out all other interests.

"Anyway, Suzie, maybe there's something else you're passionate about you've neglected all these years of flying all over the place. Maybe—maybe it's time to settle down."

Suzanne couldn't have put it better herself.

FALLING APART, FALLING FOR YOU

According to Adam, who was quite knowledgeable about all matters cultural, *Carmen* had a reputation as the sexiest opera of all. *Oh, goodie. Nothing sexier than telling your current beau you've just lost your job.*

She pulled from her closet a dazzling red dress she'd picked up in Chicago last month. The dress, sleeveless with a filmy and flowing short skirt, yet cinching her waist to emphasize her figure, would turn heads.

A few hours later, just as she zipped up, Adam arrived at her door looking dashing as ever but flushed. As a senior bank executive, his schedule could be taxing.

"Sorry I'm late, *mon petit chou*." Adam had also taken French in high school, so they sometimes dropped a phrase of *français* into their conversations. He'd chosen "my little cabbage"—loosely translated as "my darling"—as his term of endearment for Suzanne. She took it as a sign of his growing affection.

"I got caught up on a call." He leaned over and pecked her cheek, avoiding her dewy red lipstick. "Sorry."

The call, he said, was an urgent one, and ironically, dealt with a sexual harassment charge against someone reporting to him. "Pretty confidential. I shouldn't talk about it."

At dinner, though, as they sat side by side in a plush leather booth sipping cocktails, he raised the subject again.

From only a few details, Suzanne gleaned the gravity of the situation.

"Tom's my top performer—he'll be impossible to replace." Adam took a gulp of Scotch as he ran his hands through his short sandy hair.

"I remember meeting him at some event you took me to." Suzanne tilted her head. "I think it was a hockey game. Seemed like a nice guy." She shrugged. "But I guess I was wrong."

Adam nodded. "I hired him myself. We've worked together for years. This is going to do his career in. He's never going to recover financially. He'll have to move to another city where the scandal's not common knowledge."

"I can't believe he was dumb enough to have an affair with a subordinate." She paused. "It could cost him his *marriage*." She loved dropping that word into their conversations just to gauge his reaction.

Adam's eyes bored into his drink. "And then he wants to get her fired because she wasn't doing a good job?" Adam blew out a breath. "His testosterone must have affected his brain. Anyway, this is the part of my job I absolutely hate." He took another gulp of Scotch. A big one.

Adam drank, but never heavy like this. To shift the mood, she poked his ribs and said with levity, "That's why they pay you the big bucks, banker boy!"

"You are so heartless, Suzanne," Adam chuckled. Turning serious, he planted his hand on hers. "Thanks for bringing me back to reality. I needed that."

She did feel bad about Adam having to deal with the situation. Yet she didn't want Tom's bad behavior to ruin the night with Adam. She decided to delay talking about her own career crisis until they got to her place at the end of the evening.

The opera? Oh, yeah. Sexy indeed. Those richly colored flamenco skirts and castanets created a sultry mood, and when she and Adam returned to her condo, she felt closer to him than ever. Adam, ever the gentleman, always respected her boundaries. She was no saint, but she did have a few lines in the sand. He knew her beliefs prevented her from having a sexual relationship outside of marriage, and Suzanne loved him for not pressing her on it.

But tonight, she had a need for some serious hugging. As soon as they reached her condo, Suzanne let out a groan. "Oh, I can barely breathe in this dress!" The cinched waist had been boring into her tummy for hours. She disappeared into the bedroom and changed into soft, figure-hugging loungewear.

FALLING APART, FALLING FOR YOU

When she returned to the living room, Adam's eyes widened. He patted the cushion on the sofa. "C'mere."

As he raised a muscled arm to embrace her, she nestled in next to him.

And then his cellphone rang.

The caller spoke in a loud, urgent voice.

Adam's brow furrowed. "Yes, Mark. I see." Mark Lawton was the bank's president.

"I'll get right over there." Adam put his phone in his pocket as he stood. "I'm sorry, Suzanne. I have to get to the hospital." He blinked a few times, as if trying to get his bearings. "Tom tried to commit suicide. They don't know—" Adam choked up. "—if he'll make it."

CHAPTER 2

RACHEL

Rachel Baran knew all three thousand residents of Port Mariette, Pennsylvania, could not squeeze into her home, even with some of them spilling over onto the wide wraparound porch. Not everyone showed up, of course, but boy, oh boy, it sure felt like they had, as they ebbed and flowed throughout the afternoon of her husband's wake. Too bad the morning's April shower hadn't continued. Might've thinned out the crowd.

Every possible expression of sympathy passed from their lips to her ears, with "I'm so sorry for your loss" and "What a blessing he went without suffering" being the most popular of all conveyances.

Through it all, Rachel pasted a fake but brave smile on her puffy-eyed face as she stood by the living room fireplace dutifully receiving her guests, shifting her weight from left foot to right, thankful she'd remembered to wear the flats with arch support this time. After all, she'd gone through this only a few years prior for their son Brian, and before that with both of Stan's parents, and before that for her own father.

Déjà vu all over again, she knew the drill well. Everyone felt sorry. Everyone appreciated the delicious food. If she needed anything, she should call them. But she wouldn't. She couldn't. No one could understand. No one could help.

Yes, she knew God could help. She remembered that much from her parents, her church, and most of all from the devoted nuns of St. Cyprian's Academy. But right now, she didn't feel it. In her heart, she felt all alone.

Stan wasn't a perfect man or a perfect husband, but he'd been serviceable. She'd miss his companionship.

Serviceable! What a word to describe your just-deceased husband. Maybe that word came to mind because Stan owned the town's service station. Regardless, it fit him well. Stan had been indeed durable, useful, and easy maintenance.

All the locals called him "Stan the Man," a natural nickname for a fellow who'd captained both football and basketball at St. Cyp's and had broken more sports records than anyone in local history. When they were young, he was Port Mariette's number one catch, and Rachel couldn't believe her good fortune when Stan broke off his engagement to Charlotte Housmann the day before Rachel stopped by for a fill-up. Turned out Stan had gotten wind that Charlotte wasn't the virgin she'd claimed to be.

"What's a pretty little lady like you doing all dressed up tonight?" He teased Rachel with his smiling blue eyes. "Goin' to a party?" As if he didn't know. Everyone knew everyone's business in this tiny town.

"Tonight's Tammy Suber's graduation party." Rachel beamed as Stan grabbed onto the roof of the car with his burly fingers.

Providentially, Rachel had dressed in her most flattering outfit, one purchased to match the school's maroon and gold colors. The gold accentuated her long, corn silk hair, and the maroon cast a pink glow on her porcelain skin.

"I'll be closing up here around ten. Wanna meet up at Ruby's for a game of pool after the party?"

A few hours later, Rachel sashayed around the pool table and capitalized on her unexpected opportunity. As a just-retired majorette, her body was fit and firm, and she possessed a smile worthy of a toothpaste commercial. Her efforts were soon rewarded with a ring and a wedding date.

Over time, Rachel bore Stan four healthy boys, and the natural events of small-town family life occurred—sports, church, meals, holidays, and then, Stan's transition from being the gas station owner's son to being the owner.

By Port Mariette standards, it amounted to a very good life.

"Too young, Stan was too young!" Sandy Roczinski, Rachel's longtime bingo companion, waved some tissues about, then blew her nose. Rachel nodded, but she also knew that only God got to choose the day and time we are called home.

"Tell me, Rachel, what can I do for you here?" Sandy leaned forward and squeezed her friend's arms.

"Could you check on my daughters-in-law? They're a little lost in the kitchen." Rachel gave a quick roll of her eyes. The three women had offered to help with heating and serving the mountains of food Rachel had prepared, along with the baked goods her cousin Bernadette had brought. However, judging by their pained expressions, the task seemed more than they could manage.

"I'm on it!" Sandy marched to the kitchen.

Looking around the living room, Rachel felt encompassed by the loving concern of the people in this town. Everyone knew her situation—Stan gone, their son Brian with him in heaven, three other sons planted in cities far away, her widowed mom in Florida, recovering from shoulder surgery. Already, a few people had asked if she thought she'd be staying in this big old house or remaining in town at all. She responded pleasantly to such questions—except when Mary Frances, her high school classmate who had become the town's aggressive real estate agent, made the inquiry.

"I have no idea what my plans are." Rachel brushed Mary Frances off with a curt reply, even though being brusque didn't fit Rachel's style. Ever since Mary Frances had somehow finagled a date to the senior prom with Tony Mastriano, her best friend's boyfriend, Rachel had never been able to feel love in her heart for the woman.

That prom date remained one of the mysteries of her senior year. The other was a note someone had passed around school claiming Rachel was "easy." If there was ever a virgin at St. Cyprian's Academy—and, of course, they were legion in that place—Rachel was surely one of them, right up to her wedding night.

"I think they need you in the kitchen for a moment, Rach." Bernadette steered Rachel away from Mary Frances and in the direction of the kitchen.

Bernadette's family owned the local bakery, and she often told tales of Mary Frances inquiring about deaths, divorces, and such in order to increase her real estate revenue. A demanding woman, Mary Frances had a well-known habit of arriving at the bakery late in the afternoon, hoping for a discount, and if they were out of jelly donuts, she'd vociferously complain. Rachel had heard Bernadette say more than once, after the door had closed behind Mary Frances, what that woman could do with her next jelly donut.

"Thanks for rescuing me, Bernie. My nerves are frayed, and I might've regretted continuing that conversation."

"Any time, Rach. It's always a pleasure to thwart Mary Frances." She gave her cousin a loving hug. "I'll go keep an eye on her, maybe give her a jelly donut."

Frank Sowak, Rachel's widowed next-door-neighbor, eased himself out of a cushioned rocking chair and sidled up next to her.

"A good man, your Stan. We'll all miss him. If you need a friend, someone to talk to, a shoulder to cry on—I'm right next door. You were so kind to me when Wendy died. Let me know what I can do for you now."

"Thank you, Frank. That's kind of you." Rachel looked at him with appreciation, noting the sadness in his dark eyes and a slight slouch in his posture. She was only a few years younger than Frank. Were her losses taking a physical toll on her too? She forced herself not to glance at her reflection in the picture window.

Frank shook his head. "What a pity none of your boys are here to run the service station." He massaged an ear lobe as he paused before speaking again. "If you're looking to sell, I suspect one of mine would be interested. Not Joey, of course, but the younger ones."

To others, Frank's inquiry about the service station may have seemed inappropriate and premature, but unlike Mary Frances's question, it didn't offend. Selling the business to a family she trusted—*well, except for Joey*—would be a simple solution to her challenge of now being the sole owner.

"I'll give that some thought, Frank." Heading off further discussion, she added, "Be sure to take some of Bernadette's nut rolls home with you. My hips sure don't need them." Frank's belly didn't need them either, but he didn't seem to care as he gleefully packed close to a dozen assorted into a Styrofoam container.

Her husband, Stan, had suffered a massive heart attack, ushered in by her cooking. Half Polish, half Italian, the mother of growing boys, and constrained by a tight budget, she made meals of pierogies or pasta out of necessity.

"I'm heading out now." Sandy circled her arms around Rachel. "The leftovers are all packed up in the fridge."

"Thanks a million. You're a doll."

Rachel scanned the emptying room. At last, the remaining vacillating visitors hugged their goodbyes and drifted down the rickety wooden porch steps.

Her daughters-in-law picked up a few errant napkins while her grandchildren stared into their cellphone screens, thumbs whizzing on the keyboards.

Pete, her oldest, spoke up. "Dad would've enjoyed hearing all the nice things people said about him."

Rachel smiled. "Father Obringer did a good job in his sermon at the funeral mass too. He sure knows how to tell a funny story." Rachel, of course, had fed the priest plenty of material.

The other sons nodded in confirmation. When it came to communicating, they all took after their father. Rachel smiled as she remembered a long-ago Fourth of July celebration. She and Stan had invited both sets of parents over for a bash, and Rachel had wanted to impress. She'd gone overboard with the menu—Delmonico steaks, homemade fries, warm cornbread, fruit salad in a carved-out watermelon, and buttery corn on the cob. After Stan had finished his third serving, he stretched up from his chair, patted his stomach, and announced with a straight face, "That corn was good."

After that, Rachel didn't waste any time expecting compliments.

"Grandma, your clock's not working." Her youngest grandson, Caleb, pointed at the stately grandfather clock in the foyer.

"So it seems, buckaroo." Rachel stared at the motionless pendulum.

Pete jumped up from the rocking chair to restart it.

"Don't bother, Pete." Rachel raised a hand. "I never liked hearing those gongs anyway." The room went silent. What other changes would she be making?

Pete's wife, Marianne, filled the void. "It's a beautiful old clock."

"Yep. Sure is. Maybe one of you boys will want to ship it to your home someday."

No one responded, so Rachel moved to a new topic. "What time do you have to be at the airport tomorrow?" They'd all flown in for the funeral and stayed at the nearest hotel over in Lyondale. Pete had told Rachel they'd be staying there "to give you some peace and quiet." More likely, her sons didn't know how to deal with a widowed mother. On top of that, her daughters-in-law weren't close enough to care, and the grandkids yearned to play in a pool.

In any event, Rachel didn't want any of them eating a stale continental breakfast. Tomorrow, she'd send them off with a hearty meal—eggs, toast, pancakes, sausage, and bacon.

Exhausted, Rachel pushed herself up from the lumpy sofa, signaling the end of the day. Her family members rounded up their belongings and headed toward the door. After goodbye hugs, she locked the door and turned, absorbing the moment. All alone—except for Cinders.

Willing herself into motion, she meandered to the kitchen and scooped a cup of dry food into the dog's metal bowl, then shuffled to the living room and once again sank onto her side of the sofa. As she lifted her throbbing feet onto the chipped coffee table, she took care not to crinkle the crocheted doily. The table had been her mother's, so by now it no doubt qualified as an antique. *Just like me.*

From her pocket, she pulled out a wooden-bead rosary, caressed it, crossed herself, and prayed aloud. Her mind drifted from God, to Stan, to her current situation. She'd spent her whole adult life taking care of others, but what now? From today on, it would be just her and a dog.

The aging black Lab mix waddled into the living room and sat motionless in front of her, staring.

She looked into his big, brown, comprehending eyes.

And wept.

Cinders continued to eye her while she cried her way through several tissues. "Now what, buddy?" Not waiting for an answer, she turned on the television and vacantly flipped through the channels in a vain attempt to focus.

Hours later and still unable to unwind, she propped herself against a large sofa pillow and fed herself cheese curls out of the bag. She'd just won another hand of Solitaire on her cellphone when an email popped up from Herbie Herbinger. *Strange. He usually sends his pizza shop ads on*

Mondays. Herbie had inherited his family's businesses in the middle of town. Rachel knew him from high school, where he'd served as both class clown and senior class president.

She clicked the email open. Turned out Herbie was offering to chair their fortieth high school reunion, and he needed a few classmates to help. Rachel shook her head in disbelief at how the time had flown—yet what a thrill to have such an unexpected distraction. Gaining some fresh energy, she lumbered down the wooden basement stairs and unearthed her musty senior yearbook.

Oh, how Rachel cherished her school days. She loved the stability and the sameness of St. Cyprian's Academy. The nuns, the classrooms, the chalkboards, Mass every Friday morning, and art the last period of every week.

Poring over the yearbook photos for the first time in who knows how many years, she floated into her past.

During their senior year she and Suzanne had befriended the new girl, Marla. In Port Mariette, a new classmate was a novelty, and at first, everyone wanted to be her friend. But she came across as prickly and arrogant, and the boys ignored her because on top of that, they all agreed she was not very pretty.

On their class mission trip to an orphanage in Guatemala, though, Rachel and Suzanne warmed up to Marla. Their mission at the orphanage sounded pretty simple. They were to pour out their love, like Jesus, on the sweet little babies and toddlers. As Rachel and Suzanne huddled in the nursery hoisting babies high in the air, they noticed Marla leaning over a crib and sobbing as she reached for a black-haired baby with a soiled shirt. Her compassion melted their hearts. They took her under their wing the rest of the school year, calling Marla their "Plus One" friend. The nuns had taught them there could only be one "best" of anything. Naming her their "Plus One" friend solved this grammatical dilemma.

FALLING APART, FALLING FOR YOU

Rachel flipped through the pages. Ah, the memories that surfaced from the old photos. There she sat in home ec, next to Marla, licking a mixing spoon. On the next page, she and Suzanne struggling to write pen pal letters in French Club. Suzanne, painting a mural in the art room. The two-page spread of the mission trip to Guatemala with a photo of the three of them cuddling babies. That's the page where Suzanne had written in Rachel's and Marla's yearbooks, "May this circle of friends never be broken."

But right after graduation, they all went their separate ways. Suzanne, who'd always dreamed about leaving town, launched a career in the airlines. Marla, as expected, immediately whizzed back home to New York. Apparently, a single year in Port Mariette was more than enough for her. Only Rachel had stayed behind, planted in Port Mariette, the one place where she felt comfortable and content.

Would a fortieth reunion bring them together again?

CHAPTER 3

Marla

Marla Galani had reviewed the numbers, compared the pros and cons, and analyzed every nit-picking detail. Now, the moment had arrived. It seemed as surreal as the Salvador Dali prints on her office walls. On this sunny April afternoon, she'd sell her business.

Dreamlike, she floated into the glass-walled conference room to greet the buyer, Jason Spencer, and a phalanx of suited lawyers. Marla's long silver-blonde hair glistened under the bright halogen lights. Her white silk suit fit so impeccably one might think a tailor had made final alterations right outside the conference room door.

"Good afternoon, everyone." Stepping around the table, Marla flashed a controlled smile as she acknowledged each person's role in the process, leaving behind a whiff of her presence after shaking each person's hand. *A pleasure to see you again, Jason. Thank you for your patience yesterday, Dean. So kind of you to take our call the other night, Paula.*

"Well, shall we get to it?" Jason Spencer waved a hand at his lawyer.

Everyone in Manhattan is always in a hurry. What's the rush? Marla shook her head at her unexpected annoyance.

The attorney snapped to attention and seized the stack of documents in front of him.

Marla's longtime lawyer, Warren Hartley, displayed no emotion. Following his lead, Marla sat stone-faced, hands folded in her lap. *Would her loud heartbeat betray her poised exterior?* She crossed her legs and hugged one knee under the table to calm herself.

Warren must have noticed—he slipped her a quick and comforting wink.

The buyer's lawyer ticked off the main points of the sales agreement. The documents had been painstakingly edited and reviewed by both parties, making comments more of an opportunity to grandstand than a legal necessity.

"Everything looks in order." Warren nodded in Marla's direction. "Ready?"

She toyed with the gold-plated pen he'd given her for the occasion. *Am I being shortsighted? Did I make the right decision, or merely an expedient one?*

Warren cocked his head and arched an eyebrow.

She dropped her train of thought and signed. The process was over in minutes. He'd warned her New York lawyers are faster than most.

Warren pushed his chair away from the table and strode to the credenza. Grabbing hold of two magnums of champagne chilling in buckets of ice, he popped the corks with more abandon than one would expect a lawyer to muster. But Warren was unlike most lawyers—she had to give him that.

Marla lightened up to match the moment, pouring champagne like an enthusiastic game show hostess. Amid the laughter, she reflected on how fast the deal had fallen into place.

A recent article in the *Wall Street Journal* about her Gemstones Gym fitness centers had set off the firestorm of interest from potential buyers. Marla, with her gift for marketing, had dreamed up a unique spin on the otherwise mundane and cyclical business of fitness centers, which had caught a business reporter's attention.

FALLING APART, FALLING FOR YOU

Marla's private instructors taught clients proprietary facial exercises so effective they staved off dreaded plastic surgery, and her state-of-the-art tracking technology motivated clients to exercise. Anytime someone attained a milestone level of anything measurable—number of reps, miles run, inches lost, or any of a host of other accomplishments—she'd earn a new gemstone to add to her bracelet or necklace. When Marla's clients paraded around town flaunting their jewelry, they unwittingly served as her crack sales team. Topping off her techniques, Marla knew her clients well enough to help them mingle with their peers, all of which made for fun, effective, and high-profit fitness centers.

Marla was in the throes of opening another location in Florida when multiple buyout offers materialized. The legal wrangling culminated in a multi-million-dollar sale to the nation's largest chain of fitness centers.

"Congratulations, Marla." Warren hoisted his champagne flute high. Much clinking of crystal ensued, followed by sips and smiles, then briefcases were snapped shut, and at last, a rush of happy handshakes and goodbyes.

Warren was last to leave. He gathered the reams of paperwork and hugged Marla—unnecessarily long, in her eyes—to congratulate her one more time before strutting off in triumph.

Marla sat alone, except for her office manager, Deanna, hovering a few feet outside the double doors, waiting for an invitation to enter.

"Deanna, I know you heard every word, so come on in and have some champagne with me," called Marla.

Deanna dipped into the spacious room, a grin on her face, with her long arms bouncing toward the ceiling in a victory pose. "I knew you could pull it off!"

Pull it off, she did.

"I've finalized the announcement from you to all employees, and one for our vendors too. Everything's sitting on your office chair." Deanna had a valuable habit of anticipating needs and resolving problems before Marla had even heard about them.

Marla poured champagne for Deanna and slid the glass her way.

She took a tiny sip, then set the flute aside. "I'm so happy for you, but I'm sure gonna miss working with you." Deanna fidgeted and took a deep breath. "I know we talked every day, about everything from my sick cat to your latest marketing idea, but this seems like the right time to tell you the things we never talked about—like how much I respect and admire you and appreciate all the opportunities you've given me." She smoothed her skirt, even though it didn't need it. "I know sometimes you didn't have much choice, being so busy and all, but you trusted me with more than I ever thought I could do."

Her eyes welled with tears. She brushed them away with an outstretched forefinger. "Because of you, I'm a different person today."

The heartfelt words—so rare in Marla's world—moved her. Her eyes misted, yet she forged on. "Thank you for saying that, Deanna. Without you, though, this business wouldn't have succeeded. You're a take-charge gal, and I could always count on you to handle snooty clients, problem employees, and unreliable vendors."

Marla didn't say it, but the fact was, few would dare to tangle with this sinewy, five-foot-ten black woman with exotic brown eyes. If they'd known the real Deanna, with a heart like a ball of fur, Marla would've spent far more time resolving everyday problems instead of focusing on strategy, marketing, and growth.

"I want to show you my appreciation." She slid a check toward Deanna.

Glancing at the amount, Deanna burst into tears. "I'll be able to pay off my mortgage!"

"And remember to donate to your church." Marla laughed, knowing Deanna would surely give away a large part of that check. The woman served as a deaconess in her Baptist church and devoted much energy to Christian causes, chief among them evangelism. She often tried to persuade Marla to come to church with her.

"I'll tithe, I promise!" Deanna squealed. She sounded like a little girl boarding her favorite ride at an amusement park.

How wonderful it would be if I felt the same joy about the remaining millions.

"Now you go home before you get drunk on that champagne," Marla chortled as they hugged. Without a doubt, this was one of the very few times alcohol had touched the lips of this devout Baptist.

As Deanna bounced away, Marla grabbed the champagne bottle and a crystal flute. She flicked off the conference room lights for the last time and strolled to her corner office with its panoramic view of Central Park.

Her cell showed three texts and a voicemail message, all from Todd, her current love interest. *Give it a rest, Todd.* And then her phone rang, Todd on the line.

"Congratulations, baby. Let's celebrate!" Todd owned a limo service and knew all about partying.

"Thanks. We've already polished off a few bottles of champagne here."

"How'd things go? Any surprises?"

"None at all. Except I was shocked how fast those lawyers finalized everything."

"Well, you know they want to be paid, honey. Glad it's over, and now, we can have a night out on the town to celebrate. What time d'ya want me to send a limo over?"

Marla hesitated. Seeing Todd right now didn't fit her broody mood. He was all about having fun, nothing more. "You know what, I'm exhausted. I'd just like to go home and lounge in my whirlpool a while. Soak this experience in for a few hours."

"Alone?"

"Uh-huh."

Todd replied with a note of dejection in his voice. "Okay, I get it."

"We'll have a big night out soon," Marla said, in her softest voice.

"Oh, I love it when you purr with that voice of yours. It's like melting chocolate."

Marla let out a short laugh, too tired for banter. "Let's talk later."

"Okay, babe."

"Thanks for understanding, Todd."

Champagne flowing through her veins and playing tricks on her brain, Marla peeled off her white suit, ascended a few marble steps, then steeped herself in the warm waters of her twelve-jet whirlpool. She let out a lengthy and sincere sigh as she allowed her thoughts to float.

What now?

The sale had happened like a whirlwind, allowing Marla no time to ponder what she'd do next. Now, with time, talents, and piles of money, she couldn't fathom a purpose for any of them.

Over the years, she'd learned the best predictor of future success was prior performance. So even though her mind was blurry, in the hope of coming up with an idea for what she could do next, she decided to mull over her life to date.

Generally, she avoided thinking about her past. Hers wasn't a happy one, but rather, rife with painful lessons. Busy, arguing parents. A teenager who learned how to party at a tender age. A night to remember for all the wrong reasons. A pregnancy at age sixteen.

And then, a dramatic change of life as she knew it.

CHAPTER 4

SUZANNE

Suzanne heaved a wet load of laundry into the dryer, slammed the metal door shut, and smacked the start button with her fist. *I can't believe how I behaved with Adam last night! What if his phone hadn't rung?* She shook her head hard, as if to shake away the memory. *I tried to seduce him!* Jimmy Carter had been ridiculed for saying he had sinned many times because he had "lusted in his heart." Last night, she had gone a lot further than the former president.

A text from Adam interrupted her mental lashing. "Back at the hospital. Last night was tough. Looks like I'll be tied up a while longer. Sorry."

"Thanks for letting me know," she replied. "Keep me posted." *Was Tom still alive?* Suzanne didn't dare ask. The situation was difficult enough for Adam without her bugging him. Yet she did need to talk with him about her contract being terminated. She'd be flying to Phoenix in a few hours. There'd be no time to meet, even if he left the hospital soon.

Suzanne glanced at her inbox. A lone new email—from Herbie Herbinger, of all people. Hadn't seen the guy since high school graduation.

You're Invited to St. Cyprian's 40th High School Reunion. She let out a long, slow whistle. Forty years since Tony dumped her right before the senior prom. She blanched just thinking about her childish behavior back then. If they both showed up at the reunion, she'd have some apologizing to do.

Last night, her behavior with Adam had been childish too—at least from a spiritual perspective. She'd abruptly stopped attending church when she went to London forty years ago. Then, after her divorce, during a rough week in Atlanta, she cracked open a Gideon Bible in her hotel room and had a spiritual wake-up call. But backsliding comes easy when you spend most of your weeks on the road. Sometimes she'd visit a church if she had to stay out of town over a weekend, and when she made it home, if she had the time, she'd attend a nondenominational church across the river from her condo.

Last month, in fact, she distributed food at the church's food pantry. Adam thought it was terrific she helped with the community, and he encouraged her to do as much as her schedule allowed. Once, he even popped over to help her flip pancakes at the church's breakfast for the homeless.

Maybe Adam would come to church with her when she got back in town in two weeks. Leaning next to him in a pew would sure beat sitting there all alone. In a quick prayer, she asked God to work on Adam's heart, along with a rundown of her other current needs.

The dryer signaled the end of its cycle. She traipsed down the hall to retrieve the load of whites and spied her sketchbook on a side table. Years ago, when she'd bought her first one, the drawings and calligraphy served as an artistic outlet, but over time, the endeavor had also become entwined with her prayer life.

Feeling an urge to review her old sketchbooks, she knelt on the plush bedroom carpet and pulled a clear plastic storage container from the bowels of the closet. She flipped through one book after another, her eyes widening. Without a doubt, the evidence in her hands proved one thing: her

FALLING APART, FALLING FOR YOU

spiritual walk had not been the upward trajectory she'd presumed. *Just look at those prayers. So superficial. So self-centered.* Over and over, she'd done little but ask God to do her bidding. She winced in shame as she slid onto her knees, bent her head to the floor, and sobbed. *God forgive me. Fill me with your Holy Spirit. Guide me. I surrender everything to you. Don't let me take back what I've surrendered to you now.*

She stood up straight and tall, a new energy surging within. *Lord, what is your plan for my next job?* No specific answer came to mind, yet she felt a peacefulness she hadn't felt in a very long time. She slid the container of sketchbooks back into the closet, this time leaving them accessible in front.

Her head clear, she turned her thoughts to Phoenix. She needed to call Barbara Marlander before catching the plane. Barbara and her husband Burt were sure to make their fundraiser a posh event, and Suzanne loved posh. She danced around the condo in search of her cellphone. Not on the nightstand. Not on the coffee table. Not in her purse. *There it is.* It sat in full view on the kitchen countertop where she'd left it to charge. She smacked herself on the side of her head.

The moment her fingers touched the phone, a call came in—Adam.

"Hello, *mon coeur*," Suzanne answered with a breathy voice. "My heart" was her pet name for him.

"How's my little cabbage doing today?" Adam snickered.

"Fine—and how about you?" She plopped on the sofa and slunk sideways onto an oversized throw pillow.

"Just got home. Happy to report, Tom's going to pull through."

"That's a relief."

"Not sure about his marriage, though. Spent a lot of time talking with his wife Shirley—more than with Tom, in fact."

"You let him go?"

"Uh-huh. That was part of what I discussed with Shirley. The bank's sexual harassment policy is zero tolerance.

Everybody who works here knows it. If it'd been something minor, like telling an offensive joke, he would've gotten a slap on the wrist or, at his level, maybe been denied a bonus."

"But he went way over the line—you had no choice but to fire him."

"Uh-huh." Adam's voice went low.

"He's the bank's chief marketing officer—this'll make the newspaper, won't it?"

"Yeah." Adam sighed.

"Could be ugly."

"A PR mess, for sure—but I think I can tamp it down."

"How?"

"Tom agreed we could announce he's in the hospital and needs to step down from his job, implying he's leaving for health-related reasons. I'll call the business reporters myself. I want to make sure the message is conveyed correctly."

"Tom's lucky to have you handle this. You're so smooth."

Adam didn't acknowledge the compliment, just continued with his plan. "I'll take on his responsibilities until I can find a replacement."

And so busy. "Look, Adam, I'm sorry to bring this up now—I know you're swamped—but I have some bad news." She tensed her whole body, all the way down to her perfectly manicured toes.

"Okay—what is it?" Adam spoke in measured tones, as if fearful of another blow.

"The airline's not renewing my contract."

"Really?" His voice registered surprise. "Sorry to hear that. You had a good thing going with them. What are you going to do?"

"Not a clue. I wanted to talk with you about it last night, but of course, that didn't happen."

"It might be best not to do anything right away. Take some time to think about what you'd like to do next. We can talk when you're back home in two weeks."

FALLING APART, FALLING FOR YOU

"Thanks." She took a deep breath. Taking time to think sounded like a great idea. And he wanted to talk when she came back home. She felt better already.

"What time's your flight?"

"Two-ish. I'm all packed and need to leave within the hour." Suzanne rose from the sofa as their conversation wound down.

"Okay. Too late to do anything today. By the way, thanks for being so understanding yesterday. I'm sorry you had to put up with all that. We'll do something special when you get home."

"Remember, we have another fundraiser coming up at the Marlanders. I'll RSVP for us."

"Okay. Anything else on the agenda?"

Suzanne's eyes spotted her blue leather Bible. "I wonder if you would like to go to church with me when I get back?"

"I'll call. We can talk about it later." Adam could be smooth. He could also be so darned evasive.

"All right. Hope it goes well with the reporters."

"Thanks. Pack your suntan lotion, *mon chou*."

Suzanne checked the clock. Still enough time to call Barbara. It was at one of the Marlanders' many parties that she'd met Adam. She'd always love Barbara for playing matchmaker that night. At the seafood buffet, Suzanne was stabbing a piece of lobster when she happened to look up and saw Adam staring at her across the black linen tablecloth. Thin but well built, with a chiseled face, and standing as if he were posing for a Brooks Brothers photo shoot.

"You look like someone I'd like to meet." Adam pasted an impish grin on his face, and she fell for his line like a naïve teenager. Later, he admitted Barbara had emphasized Suzanne liked men who were bold. Otherwise, he said, he never would've used a line like that. But it had worked, and they were still dating several months later.

She poked Barbara's name on her cell's favorites' list.

"Suzie-Q, how are you?" Barbara laughed as she used her silly nickname for Suzanne.

"Hi, Babs." Suzanne still sometimes called Barbara by the name she'd given her back when they were "stews" at the airline. "I'm good. Leaving soon for two weeks in Phoenix. You?"

"Busy as always, but good. Are you calling to RSVP? I hope you and Adam can come. You two are such a fun couple."

"Aw, thanks. We'll be there, barring any unforeseen complications like a delayed flight home or ...." Suzanne stopped herself before she mentioned anything about Adam. Barbara had a way of digging for juicy gossip. And spreading it.

"Everything okay with Adam?" Her antennae were up.

"Oh, yes. I just hung up with him, in fact. He's busy too."

"Well, I hope he's never too busy for you. He's a gem, but he is so intense about his career. Sometimes I wonder if that's the reason he and Pauline got divorced. Or maybe it's because they never had any children."

Suzanne didn't take the bait. "Gotta catch my plane. See you in two weeks."

CHAPTER 5

Rachel

The hazy skies darkened to slate gray and dumped an April shower on Port Mariette, pummeling Rachel's yard with big bouncy drops of rain. Cinders sat motionless at the back door, staring outside as if he'd never seen a downpour before.

She'd already cleared the last remnants of the breakfast she'd made for her boys and their families. With the house empty, she didn't know what to do with herself. It was way too soon to clean out Stan's clothing. She could still smell him in their bedroom closet and on their sheets. Nope, she wouldn't be doing his laundry anytime soon. With it raining, she couldn't even cut the grass or let Cinders out back. Hamstrung, she'd do what she did anytime she felt anxious or upset—she cooked.

"Let's make a lasagna, Cinders." Rachel boiled some noodles then layered them with cheese, sausage, tomato sauce, and spices. "Smells great, doesn't it, buddy?"

Cinders sniffed, seeming to understand.

After the casserole had cooled, she cut it into ten squares and wrapped them in foil. When Stan and the boys were all here, the whole thing would've been gone in a single meal. Now, she'd store most of it in the freezer.

She turned on the TV. On one of the religious channels, an overly enthusiastic preacher proclaimed God makes all things happen for good. *How can Stan's death be good?*

Her sons, in a manner of speaking, were all gone too—three of the four had married and established themselves in places far away from southwestern Pennsylvania. When she and Stan encouraged their boys to explore going to college in other states, how could they have anticipated they'd end up marrying girls who lived in states she and Stan had never even visited?

She regretted more, though, that she'd spoiled their youngest son, Brian. Knowing she couldn't bear any more children, she'd doted on him from the moment he left her womb. He wore hand-me-downs and played with used toys, yet she and Stan made up for it with extra love and attention.

And then their baby went off to college in California.

She and Stan never questioned Brian's need for extra money. Living in California cost more than other states, they rationalized. Only when they got the visit from the police did they learn where the money had gone.

Death by drugs—an unfathomable, shameful thing to happen.

Rachel sighed. Of all her boys, Brian had been their most challenging to raise. All those rosaries, all those Masses, all those Hail Marys. Surely, they weren't all for naught. She blew her nose as the preacher emphasized other parts of the Romans 8:28 verse—"all things work together for good to those who love God, to those who are the called according to his purpose." For sure, Rachel loved God, and she'd always believed that her purpose was to serve God by serving others. Who would she serve now?

A text from Bernadette buzzed—*Could I stop by with some pastries?* At least from outward appearances, Bernadette seemed to have managed well after her husband Dick, barely sixty, had unexpectedly passed a few years back. A visit from Bernie might be helpful right about now.

Rachel rose in slow motion, an ache drilling through her right hipbone in reaction to the wet weather. She waddled into the kitchen and set out two mismatched mugs and a box of teabags.

Soon, she heard Bernadette marching up the creaky porch steps. The woman was a doer, always on a mission, whether making pastries, giving someone a ride, or explaining how to get rid of the groundhog burrowed beneath your porch. Invariably helpful, sometimes funny, never nosy. A cousin who knows your family history but behaves more like a trusted friend. Just the kind of person Rachel needed right now.

Rachel opened the front door as Bernadette reached the top step.

"Oh!" Bernadette caught her breath. "You look much better than I thought you would."

"Gee, how bad didja think I'd look?" Rachel responded with one hand on the edge of the door and the other on her hip.

Her cousin tittered and stepped inside. Turning serious, she shook her head back and forth as she looked into Rachel's eyes, as if to say this sorrowful situation shouldn't be happening. She reached out her arms and bear-hugged Rachel until the tears came, patting her back like she was an oversized baby. "That's good, let it out. Crying is healing."

When the tears subsided, Bernadette took her cousin by the shoulders. "You'll get through this. You will. Give it time." She cocked her head. "Do I smell your sausage lasagna?"

Rachel let out a laugh. "Good sniffer, Bernie! Wanna piece?" She microwaved a square of lasagna and set the plate on a faded pink placemat, then chose a chocolate croissant for herself. They settled in at the old wooden kitchen table.

Bernadette swallowed her first mouthful. "Mm. Your lasagna's outta this world." She leaned toward Rachel and touched her hand. "Look, Rach, I know this feels like you've joined a club you never wanted to be part of—the club of widows. There are plenty of us in this little town—Ann, Penny, Brenda, Caroline, and others. You may think you're alone, but you aren't. God's always there, and so are we."

Rachel's eyes misted. "I feel so lost, so adrift."

Bernadette nodded but said nothing.

The silence encouraged Rachel to speak her heart. Soon, pent-up words came tumbling out, the depth of emotion surprising even her. Many tissues later, she announced she'd take a baby step. "I'm going to tell Herbie I'll help with our high school reunion. Reliving some of the good ol' days will be fun, and it might give me a new perspective on my life too."

First thing the next morning, Rachel called Herbie, who asked her to track down missing classmates. Theirs had been a small class, not even a hundred graduates. He emailed her a list of everyone's names, some with email addresses or phone numbers and others left blank. Three names mattered most to Rachel—Suzanne Schwartz, Marla Galani, and Tony Mastriano.

She tracked down Suzanne's number by calling her mother, Mrs. Schwartz, still listed in the St. Cyprian's church directory.

According to her, Suzanne still lived in Pittsburgh and traveled for her job with an airline. "She's in Phoenix for two weeks. Give her a call around seven any evening. I'm sure she'd love to hear from you."

Suzanne's life sounded far more exciting than hers. After all these years, and having taken such different paths, how could they possibly renew their friendship? Rachel shrugged and called the number at 7:00 p.m. sharp. After the second ring, Suzanne's still-familiar lilting voice said hello.

"Suzanne! Hi. It's Rachel Symanski—Rachel Baran."

"Omigosh, it's great to hear your voice." A pause. "You must be calling about the reunion."

"I am. Can you believe it's been forty years? Your mom said you live up in Pittsburgh."

"That's right. I have a condo on top of Mount Washington. It has a great view of downtown Pittsburgh."

"Stan and I had dinner on Mt. Washington for our twenty-fifth anniversary. What a gorgeous location. And it's still pretty close to your mom in Port Mariette." Her voice dropped. "My mom moved to Florida after my dad died a few years ago. It's hard without her being around."

"I'm sorry to hear that. And I'm sorry I fell out of touch with you—and Marla too."

"Well, flying all over the place probably made it hard for you to keep in contact. Anyway, you always said you wanted to leave town and travel the world. I guess you've been living your dream."

Suzanne chuckled. "I don't know about that, but I do love travel. In fact, when I was working as a stewardess in my twenties, I married a pilot—but we're divorced now." She let out a sigh. "We had one daughter, Jill. She and her husband live in New Jersey."

"And you're working for the airlines still, right?"

"Uh-huh. I was a flight attendant for a long time, and then I became a contract trainer for the same airline—which means I bounce around the country a lot. So that's me—now, tell me about you."

Rachel updated Suzanne on Stan and her sons, then asked to change the subject. "I'm sure there are happier things to talk about, and I could use some cheering up."

"Sure. I understand." Suzanne said it softly. "Have you tracked down Marla yet?"

"Our 'Plus one'?" Rachel giggled. "I'm working on it. It looks like she's living in either New York or Florida and owns some fancy fitness centers in both places.

"Her parents were loaded, weren't they? Maybe they set her up in business," Suzanne mused.

"Such a sad soul, living here with her aunt, stuck in that huge house on the edge of town." Rachel doodled on her reunion list, drawing hearts and stars by those she remembered most fondly. "I don't think she ever felt like she fit in with our class."

"Small wonder. New York City and Port Mariette aren't just miles apart—they're worlds apart. In hindsight, I don't even understand how you and I managed to get along with her."

"Oh, she fascinated me! So mysterious, so worldly." Rachel tittered. "Sort of the opposite of me."

"And so much drama. Her parents were going through a divorce, weren't they?" Suzanne sounded uncertain. "My memory's fading but I think that's right."

"Yes, I remember that." Rachel put a mammoth star next to Marla's name.

"On a funnier note," Suzanne said, "another thing I remember about Marla is that Sister Beatrice used to get on her case because of her—what did she call it?"

"'Potty mouth.'" Rachel laughed at the memory. "Marla sure talked dirty, didn't she?"

"She talked real fast too. Must have been the Manhattan in her."

"My gosh, high school seems like a lifetime ago."

"Remember Tony? How he broke my heart when he took Mary Frances to the prom?" Suzanne let out a quick sigh, as if the memory came from last week rather than forty years ago.

"That *was* sad. But at least you were prom queen." Rachel silently recalled her own disappointment over Tony that night.

"Small consolation. If you remember, I ended up going to the prom with 'Boring Bill,' my chemistry partner. He thought I liked him because I treated him so nice, but I stunk in that class and needed his help for a passing grade."

"Yeah, I remember that. Chemistry was tough. But you did well in English and art."

FALLING APART, FALLING FOR YOU

"And you, in home ec and bookkeeping. Everyone's different."

"True." Rachel nodded. "Hey, don't you want to hear about Tony?"

Suzanne gasped. "He's dead, isn't he? I saw his name in an obituary when I looked him up this morning."

"Aw, no—his wife Veronica died, not Tony."

"Oh—that's good. I mean—well, you know what I mean."

"So, you were looking Tony up on the internet this morning, eh? I did some digging, too, and it seems he owns a restaurant called Signore's in Pittsburgh."

"How about that. Good for him! Have you called him about the reunion yet?"

Rachel giggled again, sounding just like she did in high school. "No, not yet."

"When you call him, tell him I said hello. And after you connect with Marla, maybe the three of us can get together on a video call."

"Sure. I'll be in touch." Rachel would arrange a video call. But she didn't feel good about it. She'd gained a lot of weight over the years and had a suspicion Suzanne and Marla hadn't.

She called Tony next. Her hands clammed up and her throat constricted as she called Signore's. Like Suzanne, Rachel had memories of Tony, but they were her private memories. On top of that, what would Stan think if he knew she was calling her high school crush, just days after he went to his grave? What a wicked woman she was.

"Signore's," said a young female voice, in a listless tone.

"Hi, is Tony there?"

"Yeah. Hold on." She dumped the phone down with a thud.

"Hello?" Tony's voice sounded deeper than she remembered.

She threw on a smile. "Tony, this is Rachel Symanski from your high school days—Rachel Baran now."

"Rachel! What a nice surprise. What's up?"

"St. Cyp's is having a fortieth reunion in July. I'm helping Herbie track down our classmates. I just talked with Suzanne. She said to tell you hi."

"That's nice. How's she doin'?"

"We didn't talk long. I have her number, if you wanna call her."

He paused before speaking. "I think I'll wait for the reunion. We had a big, uh, miscommunication, I guess you could say, near the end of senior year."

"Yeah, I remember. You had a sudden change of plans for the prom. I never knew you liked Mary Frances."

"It wasn't that. Suzanne and I had argued about something stupid. I can't even remember why. I thought it was over with her, so I asked Mary Frances instead."

Rachel's heart hurt even at the memory. Why had he asked Mary Frances instead of her? She thought they had a connection that could have ignited. But he'd chosen that snob Mary Frances instead. Even now, it still burned her up.

"Maybe you and Suzanne can talk about it at the reunion." Rachel hoped she sounded gracious but feared she might say something she'd regret, so she switched gears. "Let me have your email address, and I'll send you details."

"Sure, but first, what have you been doing all these years? Still tossing a baton?" He chuckled. "And remember that mission trip to Guatemala? You and I had a lot of fun together on that. Remember?"

"Oh yeah, sure." Rachel would never forget how she and Tony had clicked on that trip. She felt like they both knew it at the time, but once they returned home, they pretended nothing special had taken place between them. Maybe he remembered it the same way she did after all—but if so, why hadn't he asked her to the prom?

She shifted their conversation to his business. "I've always harbored a desire to have my own restaurant."

FALLING APART, FALLING FOR YOU

Tony laughed. "Here's the best advice I can ever give you on that—don't do it."

"Why do you say that?"

"It's a crazy business. The cooks act like divas, when all they're making is chicken parm, and the servers throw away silverware because they're too lazy to put it in the dishwashing pile when they scrape food off the plates.

"Between the employees and the food vendors, no wonder I've lost most of my hair."

Such a pity. Back in high school Tony's thick black hair was legendary.

"I love to cook. Here in Port Mariette, my sausage lasagna is as famous as your hair used to be in high school."

"Then it must be *magnifico.*" He let out a hearty guffaw, sounding just like he did in high school. The guy always knew how to enjoy himself.

"It is." Rachel twisted a lock of her hair with her fingers. "I feed armies with my sausage lasagna. Or at least I used to ...." She went on to tell Tony about her losses.

Maybe he was doing it out of sympathy, but Tony suggested she get certified to prepare food in her own home. He even offered to sell her sausage lasagna as a weekly special.

Stunned by what she learned in their conversation—about the prom, about Tony's restaurant, and most of all, that he also remembered the times they shared at the orphanage, she wished they'd stayed friends after high school.

She took down Tony's email address and ended the call. Cinders, splayed out on the braided rug beneath her feet, looked up expectantly. "Well, buddy, I think I've taken enough steps for one day." She patted the top of his bony head. "Wonder what tomorrow will bring."

CHAPTER 6

Marla

"Bangs or Botox,' that's what my hair stylist told me my choices were once I turned fifty. I've had bangs ever since." Marla lifted the long bangs angled across her forehead and leaned into her computer screen to show Suzanne and Rachel what she'd look like without them. Even on a video call, Marla obviously looked better with the bangs. "I will not do Botox. I'll have bangs till the day I die."

Marla hadn't meant to say the word "die" so soon after Rachel had talked about the deaths of her husband and son. Thank goodness she seemed not to have noticed.

"I think the bangs make you look young. Maybe I should give them a try." Rachel's shoulder-length hair, parted on the side and beginning to gray, hung as lifeless as fur on a poorly groomed Pekingese.

Suzanne tugged her bangs. "I'm keeping my fringe forever. But as long as we're talking beauty secrets, Marla, how do you keep your skin so flawless? I've invested plenty in facial creams and I think my skin looks pretty good, but you, Marla—you don't have a single wrinkle."

"Thanks, but the lighting in this room is kind to my wrinkles. I've got a few too." Marla pointed at her neck as she leaned toward her computer screen. "See what I mean?"

"Your neck looks a thousand times better than mine," Rachel pointed to her double chin.

"We all have imperfections." Marla said it firmly, as if settling the matter. "How about I demonstrate a few of the facial exercises we used at my fitness centers?"

"That would be great!" Suzanne's face lit up.

Marla stretched her face and neck this way and that, while explaining the purpose of each exercise. "This one looks strange," Marla said as she tilted her head backward and jutted her jaw toward her nose, "but it gets great results under the chin. And this one's my favorite." With her forefingers and thumbs, Marla stretched apart the skin above and below her eyes, then squeezed them shut. "This prevents droopiness around the eyes."

Suzanne and Rachel took copious notes.

As they were writing, Marla noticed how little Suzanne had changed—and how much Rachel had. Funny, Marla's life had been so much harder than Rachel's, at least until recently.

Suzanne put down her pen and confessed why she was so interested in looking young. "Last week, the airline told me they're not renewing my contract. I think it's because they think I'm too old. On top of that, I've been dating an amazing man named Adam—but he's moving at a snail's pace. After all my years of being divorced, he's the first man who's really appealed to me. He seems to be interested in me, too, but something's holding him back." She twisted a few times on her kitchen stool. "It makes me wonder … maybe I'm not attractive enough for him at my age."

"He's lucky to have you." Rachel wagged a finger at Suzanne in the screen.

"Don't ask me what to do about Adam." Marla laughed. "I'd steer you wrong. As for finding a new job, I don't know what the market's like for your skills, but you look terrific. Your hairstyle and makeup are current and well suited for your oval face. It sounds like you have some great experience. I should think you'd land a job with little trouble."

"Thanks for the vote of confidence." Suzanne smiled.

Marla hoped to encourage Rachel too so, without singling her out, she continued talking about health and beauty tips. "In the years I've run women's fitness centers, I've learned that when we're going through a valley, it's good to spend extra time on ourselves—a new haircut, a trip to a day spa, a different exercise regimen, even a good book can be helpful."

"All sounds good to me." Rachel let out a giggle.

How could a fifty-seven-year-old woman look so old but still sound so young? Marla squinted as she examined Rachel in the screen.

"I agree," echoed Suzanne. "Thanks for the pep talk. But let's talk about you, Marla. The three of us were together for such a short period of time, but our senior year was a pivotal one, and we went through a lot together. I'd like to know how things turned out for you."

After all the troubles both women had just recounted, how could Marla tell them she'd just sold her business for millions of dollars—and her biggest problem was figuring out how to spend it? That's why she'd tried to skip chattering about herself and talk girl talk instead, like she'd always done with her Gemstone Gym clients. None of them cared about Marla herself. She ran in some self-centered circles and was accustomed to that kind of behavior. But now, forty years after last seeing Suzanne and Rachel, these two seemed to have a genuine interest in her life.

"C'mon, Marla, tell us everything. I'll bet you've had an adventurous life." Rachel leaned forward in her chair.

Marla's mind raced through her past, as she attempted to pick out the parts that were acceptable to share.

"Well, you probably remember, my parents were big in property development in New York and Florida. They were always so busy. It took its toll on their marriage. They were going through a divorce when I came to live with Aunt Adele my senior year."

"I always loved your aunt—but talk about culture shock! It must have been so hard for you to come here," Rachel said. "But you never complained. How come?"

"I was so depressed that whole year. If you two hadn't decided to be friends with me, I don't know how I would have coped." Marla looked down at her perfectly manicured hands spread across her thighs. "Frankly, I was afraid if I complained about anything, you might drop me."

Suzanne jumped in. "I figured it must have been tough on you, but I had no idea it was that bad. I'm sorry I didn't know. We could have talked." She took a deep breath. "My parents almost got divorced a few times while I was in high school. My mother was a saint, but my dad? Hardly ever home, and when he was, I wished he wasn't. But you know how things were back then, no one—at least not anyone from St. Cyprian's—got divorced. That's why I never talked about it with either of you." In a soft voice, she added, "I wish you and I had talked about our parents, Marla. It might have been easier for both of us."

"We were all young and stupid. What did we know when we were in high school?" Marla let out a laugh. She wanted to lighten the mood. All this talk about deaths, divorces, and now missed opportunities made her wish she hadn't agreed to the call.

"That's right. We were all idiots." Suzanne laughed too, but kept the spotlight on Marla. "So, tell us, what happened to you after graduation?"

"I went straight back to Manhattan and tried living with each of my parents over the summer. They were divorced by then but still arguing. I couldn't take it. Who cares who gets the clock on the mantel? In the fall, I went to college to become a nurse, of all things. I think I wanted to be in a profession where people cared for one another." She squirmed. "Except for my aunt, you see, I hadn't experienced a lot of love or attention. Anyway, I ended up being a horrible nurse. I got a job in a long-term care facility." Her voiced dropped low. "One night, I gave a man the wrong medicine." She winced. "He died."

"Oh my gosh!" Rachel and Suzanne chimed in unison.

"I lost my job, of course, and I could never again work as a nurse. My parents were adjusting to their separate lives and didn't want to hear about my troubles. I had some friends who worked in entertainment. They helped me get some gigs; it helped me escape. I did a little singing, some theater, a few commercials. Once I even did a dog food commercial." Marla shook her head at the memory.

"Nothing wrong with that. Cinders loves to watch dog food commercials on the TV. He sits in front of it and whines when he sees a dog eating anything. He's like me, always hungry. Right, Cinders?" Rachel pulled the dog in front of the screen.

"Well, dog food commercial aside, it became clear my future would not include acting. I worked in a pizza shop at the same time to make ends meet. The owner developed health problems and asked me to run the business for him. In time, we expanded to five locations. Profits skyrocketed as I learned how to manage and grow a business. Lorenzo wanted to retire and sell me the business, but I wanted to do something new. That's when I opened my first location of Gemstones Gym."

"How did you get the idea for it?" Suzanne asked.

"I've always been interested in health and fitness—"

Rachel cut her short. "You loved gym class."

"I did." Marla smiled, touched that Rachel would remember such a tiny fact about her. "When we graduated, Aunt Adele gave me an emerald pendant with a tiny cross etched on it, and that sparked the idea for creating something unique in the fitness business. Over the years, I expanded into Florida. My mom's still in Manhattan and my dad has remarried. He lives in Greece."

"What a story, Marla. Even condensed, it's an amazing life," Suzanne said.

"You put us all to shame." Rachel added.

"I do have a confession to make." Marla suddenly spoke with a tentativeness she'd not displayed beforehand.

Suzanne spoke up, filling the sudden silence. "We love you no matter what."

Marla's eyes darted around the screen, as if searching for the right words. After a long pause, she spoke. "Everyone in Port Mariette always assumed I was Italian. I do have olive skin and my hair was almost black back then, and 'Galani' does sound like an Italian name. But I'm only half Italian—my dad is one hundred percent Greek."

"Ha. You had me fooled." Suzanne pointed a finger at Marla's face in the computer screen. "I thought you had something serious to say. But you're right, we all did think you were one hundred percent Italian."

"Maybe you shoulda been an actress after all." Rachel giggled, then shifted the conversation back to the reunion. "So, the reunion will be the weekend of the Fourth of July. Any chance both of you can come to town a little sooner? It would be great to have time together, just the three of us."

"Let's look at our calendars and talk about it again next week. I can't wait to see you both." Marla clicked off her screen and gave a sigh of relief.

That was close. In a fit of nostalgia, she'd nearly spilled the whole story of her pregnancy to Suzanne and Rachel. Thank goodness she came up with that ridiculous comment about being half Greek. Even though it was true, it fell far short of a major confession. What a relief both women seemed to accept it.

CHAPTER 7

Suzanne

Suzanne prayed the airline mechanics wouldn't arrive while she was still on her knees in the hotel hallway. It wouldn't do to start her "Sexual Harassment & Sensitivity" seminar like that. She snatched the last of the handouts that had fallen on the floor, rose in triumph, and brushed the front of her skirt.

A soothing male voice spoke from behind her. "Excuse me, miss."

Although still hourglass-shaped, Suzanne was far from being a "miss." She appreciated the man's sensitivity. Might even find a way to fold it into her content for today's seminar.

Suzanne arched an eyebrow and turned to see a well-built man about her age, sporting a gray-specked beard and wearing a navy suit with a striped tie. A faint scent of cologne wafted from him.

Definitely not an airline mechanic.

"Forgive me if this is inappropriate, especially considering the topic you'll be speaking on." He leaned closer to whisper, "But your zipper appears to be down."

Suzanne clutched the back of her skirt. Sure enough, the zipper was all the way down. Her white blouse even poked out, like a tiny white surrender flag. She bit her lower lip and winced as she yanked the zipper up. Forcing a half-smile, she studied the man, noting his neat shock of dark hair and crisp white shirt.

"Oh! Thank you. I'd much rather be told my zipper's down by a handsome stranger than to have thirty people snickering behind my back." She winced again. Did she just call him handsome? No matter. He hadn't noticed. He'd been looking at her ring-less left hand.

"My name's Rob Jackson, and I'm guessing from the seminar sign, you're Suzanne Fleming?" He nodded toward the sign, but his eyes never left hers.

"That's right."

"Well, uh, Miss Fleming, I'm wondering—are you stuck in Phoenix for a few nights like I am?" He cocked his head to the side and shuffled his feet.

The hint of vulnerability touched Suzanne. "Yes, I'm here until Friday."

Rob's eyes lit up. "Great. Me too." He flashed a bright smile and leaned an inch closer. "If you happen to be available tonight, I'd like to invite you to dinner at that steakhouse down the street. Hotel meals can get boring, and somehow I don't think you like boring."

A few airline mechanics meandering toward the registration table distracted Suzanne with their loud voices, but Rob soldiered on. "I'd love to talk with you now, but I'm due in the ballroom down the hall." He reached into his suit jacket pocket. "Here's my card." He placed it into Suzanne's palm with a steady hand and a little extra eye contact. "Think it over. Let me know what you decide."

Suzanne glanced down at the business card, then raised her eyes to absorb the man. As he smiled at her, the skin around his mouth and eyes crinkled into well-defined lines. She couldn't help but smile back. "I'll let you know."

He strode down the hall toward the ballroom. Suzanne stared until he disappeared behind the double doors. *Well, that's an unexpected start to my day.*

FALLING APART, FALLING FOR YOU

Working on the road for most of her career, she'd often been asked out by men who knew she'd be in town for a stretch, from hotel managers to bored businessmen. In most cases, she declined. But something about this Rob seemed different. She studied his business card for clues.

Back home in Pittsburgh, even though she'd been dating Adam only a few months, their relationship looked promising. No matter what, she wouldn't put that at risk. The older she got, the more she realized that love, by itself, wasn't enough. Adam Pederson was a polished executive in solid financial shape, an impeccable dresser, and as far as she could tell, in great health. In Suzanne's eyes, A-d-a-m spelled "secure future."

But this Rob Jackson had a point. She *was* easily bored, and she'd been holed up in Phoenix for nine days, with five to go. Maybe she'd pray about whether or not to have dinner with him tonight.

Another group of airline mechanics, guffawing their way into the room, interrupted Suzanne's rumination. Today, she'd do her usual two sessions, this one from 9 a.m. till noon, and another from 1-4 p.m. In the evening, she usually swam in the hotel's pool or walked a few miles on a treadmill. But as for tonight? Still not sure.

At her lunch break, after a quick prayer and some mental sparring, Suzanne agreed to have dinner with Rob. *It's only a dinner, for crying out loud.* Besides, something about Adam didn't quite add up, and she couldn't seem to put her finger on it. Going out with another man could give her clarity.

She wrapped up her half-eaten turkey sandwich and pressed it into a tight foil ball. She cocked her wrist and shot the ball into the waste can across the room. Tonight, she'd dine at a steakhouse with a stranger named Rob Jackson. She felt more excited than she thought she ought to be.

The aroma of grilled steaks drifted into Suzanne's rental car the moment she cracked the door open and stepped out. Steamy heat radiated from beneath her shoes; tiptoeing prevented her kitten heels from sinking into the asphalt. She squinted as she looked around for Rob and spotted him standing outside the restaurant door, brilliant sunshine lighting up his hot pink golf shirt. Only a man with a tan and a healthy dose of masculinity could dare to wear that color.

Coming up behind him, Suzanne noticed Rob glancing at his watch. She took a breath and spoke in a soft voice. "Did you think I'd stand you up?" Suzanne prided herself on always being on time, but this evening, she'd been delayed a few minutes trying to find keys to the rental car.

He turned and grinned, displaying a wide row of almost perfectly shaped, pure white teeth. "I'm glad you decided to come." He waved his hand toward the entrance.

She smiled in return, hoping he'd notice her dimple. "How could I say no after you rescued me from being humiliated in front of thirty airline mechanics?"

"Just call me Superman." Rob laughed, then pulled open the massive carved oak door. The muscles on his forearm tightened as he held it open. A surprising shiver of electricity zinged right through Suzanne's entire body.

Once they entered, a stout man in a black vest greeted them. "Table for two?" He led them to a corner table with padded leather chairs. The softly lit steakhouse, with its black tablecloths and vases of red roses, seemed designed to encourage cozy conversation.

Rob rolled out a chair for Suzanne, giving her the window view, and sat next to her.

She fluttered her thick eyelashes a tiny bit. "So, your business card says you're a psychologist."

"That's right. I've also authored a few books. That's why they invited me to give the keynote speech this morning. It's a conference for psychologists." He slid his menu to the side as he looked at Suzanne. "People often have the surprising notion that if you can write, you should also be able to deliver a speech."

"Can you?" Suzanne opened her eyes wider.

"I'll never win an Oscar, let's put it that way." Rob smirked.

"But to do a keynote, you must be pretty good." She smoothed the cloth napkin on her lap.

"Well, the more I do it, the easier it gets." He placed his tanned arms onto the table and leaned toward her. "Maybe you've heard Jerry Seinfeld's joke about how people are more afraid of public speaking than death, meaning that most people would rather be in the casket than giving the eulogy."

She chuckled. "That's so true. Then why do you do it?"

"I like to stretch myself." He imitated pulling something apart with his hands. "Plus," he laughed, "my agent says I have to do it to sell my books. In all seriousness, I can handle the speeches, but I'm lousy at fielding bizarre questions. I imagine you do that a lot."

"Every day." Suzanne nodded. "This morning, in fact, one of the mechanics noticed you were asking me out on a date. In front of the whole class, he asked if that qualified as harassment." She tilted her head flirtatiously and toyed with her dangling earring. "I said I didn't feel harassed—just flattered."

"Glad you felt that way." Rob winked.

Suzanne held his gaze for a moment then opened her heavy leatherette menu.

Rob followed suit, then they both reached for their reading glasses.

"I don't really need them," Suzanne coyly said.

"Yes, you do." Rob chuckled. "So do I." He studied the wine list. "Mind if I order us a bottle of merlot? I live near wine country in California, and I've been learning to appreciate wine."

"Please. I love merlot with a steak."

The waiter introduced himself and took their order. Rob leaned back, putting his hands on the armrests. "No rush on the meal. We're here to relax."

"Yes, sir." The waiter nodded and disappeared, soon returning with the wine.

Rob reached for his glass, swirled the wine, then put the glass down. With elbows on the table, he folded his hands together. "You might be wondering why I asked you out this morning. After all, it was somewhat sudden." He gave her a sheepish grin.

"A little." Suzanne chuckled.

"I apologize for the abruptness. When I saw you on the floor picking up those papers, I have to admit I was staring."

Suzanne raised an eyebrow.

"When I noticed your zipper, I remembered how my dad would tell my mother if she'd forgotten to zip up or if a label on her blouse was sticking out."

Suzanne nodded. When she was young, her dad had sometimes done the same thing with her mother.

"You caught my eye when you were kneeling on the carpet, but when you stood up and turned around, I—I, well, I felt even more attracted to you. I figured, hey, I'm stuck in a hotel for a few nights, why not ask the lady out?"

"Well, I'm glad you were so brave, Mr. Superman." His honesty and directness touched her. Adam tended to dance.

Rob took a sip of wine then moved to a new subject. "You enjoy your work?" He looked her in the eye as he asked.

"Being a contract trainer for the largest US airline is an oxymoron. I call it 'an adventurous routine.'"

"Something surprising happens every day?"

"Yes, and I love surprises—at least the good ones." *Like this one tonight.* "But tell me more about you."

"I have two children, Kevin and Emily. Neither one is married, so no grandchildren yet. Who knows, maybe never." He shrugged, a sad look on his face. His voice softened. "I'm divorced."

Suzanne smoothed her linen napkin and waited for him to go on.

"My ex-wife, Meg, became an alcoholic after a tragic car accident."

"How sad." She searched his eyes and sensed his pain.

Rob held her gaze for a moment and continued. "Before all that, she was a wonderful wife. I took my marriage vows to heart, but everyone has a breaking point." Rob lowered his voice. "Later on, a doctor diagnosed Meg with dementia. She now lives in a memory care unit."

"I'm sorry to hear that. Must be so hard."

He nodded, then averted his eyes a moment before looking at Suzanne again. "By the way, I noticed you were wearing a cross necklace this morning—along with a few other things." He teased. "Sorry. I'm going off topic."

"Perfectly acceptable." She loved it when a man knew how to use words to make her feel appreciated.

"So, is it safe to assume you're Christian?"

Suzanne nodded. "I am." She felt a strange need to connect with this man. In a soft voice, she confessed, "I'm divorced too." She had divorced Mike more than twenty years ago, yet the memory still stung, even now.

Rob's soft brown eyes were gentle and understanding, so she continued. "My husband worked as a pilot, and I was a flight attendant, part of his crew. When I got pregnant, I took a job training new flight attendants at our headquarters in Pittsburgh. I suspected Mike cheated on me, but I was busy with my own priorities and turned a blind eye."

Suzanne rolled her eyes and shook her head. "I have a tendency to stick my head in the sand."

"A slight flaw, no need to set up an appointment at my office." They laughed and held eye contact for a second.

"Anyway, one day, during a break in one of my training sessions, I happened to be in a stall in the ladies' room.

Two flight attendants came in after me. They didn't realize anyone was there, and one of them said, 'How can she stay married to that philandering jerk? Doesn't she know that Mike got Pam Hays pregnant?'"

"That must have been quite the shock."

"I'll say. I threw up in the toilet! Then I washed my face, rinsed out my mouth, and marched back into the classroom to finish the session. When Mike got home a couple days later, I had already boxed up his belongings."

Suzanne ran her fingertip along the edge of her water glass as she recalled that awful day: Her stomach heaving the moment Mike pulled into the garage. Switching off the radio as it played a Whitney Houston love song. Reviewing the script she thought she'd memorized but now seemed to be written in a foreign language. Quivering all over. Eyes unleashing tears of hurt and anger. *Why wasn't she good enough for Mike? Would she ever be good enough for anyone?*

She blinked and focused her eyes on Rob. They stared at one another in mutual understanding, then he broke the silence. "It's good to talk. Helps us heal. I've seen it time and time again in the people I work with." He gazed into Suzanne's eyes. "The pain of a divorce has a peculiar way of uniting the initiated, doesn't it?"

"It does." She replied in a whisper, relieved that the server had arrived with their meals. She'd blurted out far more than she had intended.

"Everything looks great." Rob nodded at the server. "Thank you." He turned his attention back to Suzanne. "Would you mind if I said a blessing?"

"Please." Adam had never prayed a blessing at any of their meals.

"Heavenly Father, thank you for your abundance, your provision, your love, your mercy and compassion. Bless this meal and our conversation, in Jesus's name."

"Amen." They said it in unison.

FALLING APART, FALLING FOR YOU

Rob cut into his T-bone. "Now, where were we?" He held up his fork, a chunk of juicy meat dangling from it. "Oh, right. Divorce. But now, we've got to change to a less depressing subject. What do you do in your spare time?"

"I'm at hotels all week, so I exercise a lot—pool, treadmill, weights. I mix it up. Sometimes I do calligraphy and pen and ink drawings too."

"Do you sell them? Or are they for your eyes only?"

"They're my conversations with God. I write a prayer and create a pen and ink drawing to go with it." Suzanne had her current sketchbook in her purse, so she pulled it out and flipped through a few sketches, taking care not to show the one of Adam. She stopped at a drawing of her daughter. "Jill's married. She and Drew live in New Jersey."

"She's lovely. Looks like you." He looked up and smiled at Suzanne. "And these pictures are beautiful too." He flipped through a few more pages. "So's the calligraphy." He returned the sketchbook to her. "You're quite the artist."

Suzanne slid it back in her purse. "Thank you. This is the first time in years I've shown my artwork to anyone. In fact, no one else has ever seen this sketchbook."

She inhaled a deep, slow breath to remind herself to *stop talking*. She was telling this man from California, a man she'd never see again, all about the most personal parts of herself. Suzanne clamped her teeth on her tongue to prevent herself from saying another word.

"I'm honored to be the first person who's ever seen your sketchbook." Rob held eye contact with her.

She smiled but kept her tongue in check.

Rob sliced off another bite of steak. "That reminds me, I did a 'first' today too."

"What did you do?"

"Right before my speech, a Winston Churchill quote popped into my mind: 'A good speech should be like a woman's skirt—long enough to cover the subject, but short enough to create interest.' I used it as my opening line, hoping that no one in the audience would consider it insensitive."

"Bet you got some chuckles."

"I did. But do you think it might have come across as insensitive?"

"No, not in that context." She smiled. Most men wouldn't bother to ask.

"Because I was thinking of you as I said it." He winked. "I would like to think I'm a sensitive guy."

She smiled in response to the banter, but Rob lived in California and Adam didn't. To head off further flirtations, she told him a few details about Adam.

"I see." He looked away for a moment, then returned to Suzanne, "But right now, you're not engaged to him or anything like that, right?"

"I'm not."

Rob leaned back in his chair and splayed his hands on the armrests. "Ever thrown an ax?"

"An *ax*?"

"Tomorrow evening, the conference is hosting a Wild West Night. What do you say we make the most of our time together here in Phoenix?"

Suzanne hesitated a moment. "Will there be guns?"

Rob took Suzanne's hand and squeezed it. "Not to worry, only cap guns."

CHAPTER 8

RACHEL

"Mind if I join you?" Frank called to Rachel as she and Cinders paraded past his front porch. The old mutt halted and sniffed a cluster of dandelions growing out of one of the sidewalk's many cracks.

Ever since Frank's wife had passed on, Rachel couldn't recall seeing her neighbor step on his sidewalk, except to retrieve the mail or get into his pick-up truck. *He probably wants to talk about the service station again.*

She waved for him to join her. "Sure. Cinders isn't much of a conversationalist."

"Nice day today, isn't it? A little overcast for the first of May, but nice." A grin spreading across his face, Frank descended the creaky porch steps, right leg first then left leg onto the same step. Good thing there were only three steps. Otherwise Cinders might have gotten impatient and pulled on his new leash.

"Yeah, I love overcast days. Bright sunshine bothers my eyes. People like me with blue eyes are often more sensitive to light. They call it photophobia."

"Wendy used to say the same thing. I think it was because she had dry eye syndrome."

"She did. I remember." Maybe Wendy was the one who had told her the blue-eye theory. "I miss her. I'm sure you do too."

"You bet I do. How are you coping these days?" Frank raised his bushy eyebrows.

"It's lonely, but I'm doing all right. I'm trying to get back in shape for my fortieth reunion. It's a little more than two months away."

Frank looked her over and smiled. "I think you look fine just the way you are."

"Thanks, Frank." She appreciated his compliment, a touching contrast to Stan's crumbs. She stole a sideways glance at her neighbor. Quite the paunch and three years older. Still, she remembered him when he was younger—thinner, stronger, carried himself with confidence.

The road began to rise to a slope. Frank's breathing became labored, so Rachel slowed her pace until the sidewalk leveled off.

"Do you play canasta?" He asked in a tentative voice when his breathing returned to normal.

"Stan and I used to play. He's so competitive—I mean, he *was* so competitive—that if he'd lost the hand bad, he'd throw the cards down and refuse to count up his score." Rachel giggled and shook her head. "I'd always say, 'That's okay, hon, I still won.'"

Frank's voice rose to a higher pitch. "Maybe you'd like to play sometime?"

"Maybe sometime." Rachel didn't want to rule out the possibility. One day down the road she might have a dark day and need a friendly game of cards to lift her spirits. But for now, she changed the subject. "I thought you might be wanting to talk about the service station again."

"Well, since you brought it up ...."

"I've been thinking about it, but I'm not going to do anything right away. I've got Lou Gestler running the place weekdays, and a few high school kids handle evenings and weekends. For now, at least, it'll be a gas station only, with none of the servicing like Stan used to do."

"That makes sense. Right now, you should take your time with everything."

FALLING APART, FALLING FOR YOU

Like this walk. They'd been going at the pace of a toddler taking first steps. "I'm going to pop in to see Bernadette while I'm up this way. I'll see you later, Frank." She cut to the right and turned onto the walkway leading to her cousin's house.

Rachel marched up the creaky wooden steps, with Cinders leading the way, his tail wagging in anticipation. Bernadette always had a treat for visitors. Even dogs knew it.

The doorbell hadn't worked since Dick was alive, so Rachel knocked. Bernadette pulled the door's lacy curtain to one side, then stood behind the door as she creaked it partway open.

"C'mon in, Rachel. You, too, Cinders." Bernadette grinned. "Pardon my appearance." She pointed with outstretched hands to her faded flower-print housedress. "You're looking at one of the advantages of being a widow. I get to wear whatever I want, whenever I want. Welcome to my world."

Rachel stared at her cousin's dress. *That will never be my world.*

"Everything okay?" Bernadette asked.

"Oh. Yeah. I'm just trying to escape my walk with porch-sitter Frank."

"Porch-sitter Frank was *walking* with you?" Bernadette opened her eyes and mouth as wide as they could go.

"He caught me as I walked by and asked if he could come along. What could I say? I thought he wanted to talk about the service station again, but he asked if I wanted to play cards."

Bernadette laughed. "Frank's a good guy. I'm sure he's lonesome and figures you are too." They entered the kitchen and sat on wooden chairs worn smooth over the years. "Wanna pastry?" She opened a box of mixed Danish.

"No!" Rachel said it with more force than she'd intended. "I mean, no thanks. I'm trying to lose weight."

"A cup of tea then?"

"Thanks, but I'll pass."

"So, what's your plan?"

"My plan?"

"For losing weight. Are you going to join a gym or go on one of those diet plans they advertise on TV? Some kind of support system, y'know?"

"I just decided it this morning, Bernie. Walking the dog and turning down your pastry is as far as I've gotten."

"I'll help you. I won't tempt you with my pastries." Bernadette closed the box and toted it across the kitchen, hiding it in a tall kitchen cabinet. She pulled a bone-shaped treat from a cardboard box and tossed it onto the floor next to Cinders, where he lay spread out on the checkered linoleum. He snapped to attention and chomped up his treat.

"Maybe I'll ask Suzanne and Marla to help too. Remember them? They were my best friends in high school. We've been talking lately. They're coming to town for our fortieth reunion in July."

"I remember them. Marla was the one who moved here for her senior year, wasn't she?"

"Uh-huh."

"A pistol, that one. Anyway, reunions are a great motivation. I like your idea of asking for support from your old high school friends too. You'll make a lot of progress in just a few weeks."

Rachel glanced at her cousin's worn housedress one more time. Energized, she rose to leave.

"I think I'll head up the street to my sister's."

"I'm glad you two are getting close. I know she's a lot older than you, but you need each other to lean on."

"Yeah, our age difference seemed huge when I was a kid. Now, it doesn't matter so much."

The cousins meandered to the door and pecked each other on the cheek as Bernadette pulled the door open.

FALLING APART, FALLING FOR YOU

With Cinders tugging at his leash, Rachel poked up the steep hill, catching sight of her sister Terrie pulling out of her driveway and headed in their direction. Rachel stepped in the middle of the street and flagged her down.

"What's up with you, Sis?" Terrie rolled down her window and cast Rachel a quizzical look. "I've never seen you walking Cinders anywhere, much less up this mountain."

"I'm on a fitness kick."

"Good for you." Terrie put a hand on the steering wheel. "Hey, I can't talk right now. I have to pick up a prescription for Bud."

"Is he okay?" Rachel leaned toward her sister in concern.

"Same." She shrugged. "I forgot to pick up something up the other day and he's all out. I gotta run. Let's talk later, okay?"

"Sure. Whenever."

Bud was battling cancer, and Rachel felt pretty sure her sister would be the town's next widow. For a little while longer, Rachel would have to fight the desire to share her own emotions with Terrie.

Rachel ambled down the hill, waved to Frank who had already returned to the rocking chair on his porch, and bounded up the steps to her front door.

After a salad and some canned tuna fish, she texted Suzanne and Marla, asking if they could do another video call sometime. Marla never responded, but Suzanne said she'd be free Monday evening.

Suzanne controlled the beginning of their conversation, going on about her grueling trip to San Francisco. "I got stuck on a four-hour delay in Charlotte last night." She heaved a sigh. "Thunderstorms. We finally got on the plane, and then they announced we had mechanical difficulties, so we had to wait until they fixed that. Instead of landing at midnight, I arrived around 5 a.m. Lucky I did some catnapping on the plane."

"You poor baby," Rachel said in earnest. "I don't know how you manage all that traveling on top of the work you do once you land."

"Well, I won't be doing it much longer. Maybe that's a good thing. Next time you and Marla and I are together on a call, I'd like to talk about what kind of job I should look for."

"I think you could do anything you set your mind on. Maybe you could make a list of things you enjoy doing. That would give us a starting point."

"Great idea. Then we can brainstorm. Wait a minute, let me find something to write on. I've got to make a note to myself, otherwise I'll forget."

Once the scratching of Suzanne's pencil stopped, Rachel said, "I loved seeing you both on our video call. I can't get over how good you and Marla look. I think you're both the same weight you were in high school."

"Trust me, that's not the case for me." Suzanne was telling the truth. "I've gone up a least one clothing size."

"I have to admit, I was feeling jealous of you two. Then I thought, maybe this is the perfect time for me to get back in shape. My whole world's in a state of flux, so why not change my bad habits while everything's in an upheaval? My cousin Bernadette—you remember her, she graduated a couple years before us—she said I should join a support group. I thought maybe you and Marla could be my support group?"

"I'll be part of your support group for fitness if you'll be mine for my job search. And for dealing with the men in my life."

Suzanne laughed, but Rachel remembered that half-hearted laugh. Suzanne was serious.

FALLING APART, FALLING FOR YOU

"Like Tony?" Rachel sidestepped the issue and teased her instead.

"Very cute. I'll admit I'm interested in seeing Tony again, but only to clear the air with him."

"Okay, I believe you."

"You have to remember, I've got some issues with men. My dad wasn't the best father, and Tony knocked me on my butt right before the prom. Mike turned out to be a cheater." She sighed. "Sometimes I think half the reason why I travel so much for work is to escape having a relationship."

"I thought your relationship with Adam was pretty tight."

"Not as tight as I'd like. We met about five months ago—right before Christmas—but we only see each another when I'm home on weekends."

"Maybe you'll have time for Adam when your contract ends."

"I hope he'll have time for *me*. He's a bank executive, very high up, and is always so busy. Meanwhile, I'm here in San Francisco right now—" Suzanne giggled like a teen. "—and I have a date with a guy named Rob this weekend. Can you believe it? I met him in Phoenix last month—never dreamed I'd see him again."

Rachel jerked her chin back. "Oh!" She paused to process her thought. "So, I guess you and Adam don't have—what do you call it—a committed relationship?"

"No, we've never even discussed that. Sometimes I wish we would, but I'm also afraid of being disappointed by another man." She lowered her voice. "I've learned to avoid conversations about commitment. But ever since Jill got married, I've been feeling maybe it's time for me to settle down. Heck, even my mother said that to me the other day."

"Moms know best." Rachel smirked.

"So true. And who knows what Adam's thinking about our future—I think he has hang-ups of his own. Sometimes he's so into me, and other times, he's aloof. I can't figure him out. At first, I thought going out with Rob could help me get perspective on Adam, but now, it seems I'm unnecessarily complicating my life." She snorted. "Maybe I'm a little nuts for seeing Rob again, but we had such a great time together last month in Phoenix, and we've been keeping in touch these past few weeks. He's a terrific guy. Too bad he lives in California."

"Sounds to me like you're having fun." Rachel tried to be supportive.

"You're right. I am." She paused, then spoke with a soft tone. "Do you think you'll ever date someone?"

Rachel quivered at the thought. "I can't even begin to think about dating right now." Her mind darted to Tony. "But maybe someday, who knows? Stranger things have happened."

"It'll be good for you to talk with the guys at the reunion. Having conversations with men is different from talking with your girlfriends. Maybe someday you'll have a male companion. Nothing wrong with that. Anyway, let's talk about what you need from your support group. What are you thinking?"

"That I'm disgusted with myself. I've been gaining weight since I stopped twirling batons in high school."

"When I was a new stewardess, I worked with my friend Barbara. The airline had stringent rules on our weight and would fire us if we went over the limit. We obsessed over it. One morning after weighing herself, Barbara realized that she'd gained a pound a year since graduating from high school. She said, 'At this rate, I'll be obese in thirty-two years and three months.' We both laughed, but I never forgot that message."

"My doctor says I'm obese." Rachel couldn't believe she'd said the word.

"Well, my point is, the extra weight creeps up on us over time, and I think it makes sense to take it off that way too. Unless you want to start jogging." Suzanne chuckled.

FALLING APART, FALLING FOR YOU

"It'll never happen. I like what Joan Rivers said, 'the first time I see a jogger smile, I'll consider it.'"

Suzanne chuckled. "Funny lady."

"My mom loved her. I think I told you my mom's living in Florida now. She moved to one of those 55-plus communities after my dad died. She loves it there. She goes to yoga classes and swims every day. She's still recovering from surgery right now, but overall, even at age ninety-two, she's never been healthier and happier in her whole life."

"Sounds wonderful. Maybe I should move to one of those communities and just live off my savings."

"Now stop it. We're years away from that. In fact, the other day, my mother said I should try to look at this next part of my life as a gift from God instead of a tragedy. I look at how well my mom is doing now. I want to make the rest of my life happy and healthy too." She lifted her chin. "My dad always said to anyone who wanted to lose weight, 'Skip a meal.' I thought maybe I'd try to skip lunch every day."

"If you have the discipline to do that, great. I'd find it hard to make it through a day without lunch. I did read somewhere that if you want to lose weight, you should never wear pants that have a stretchy waistband. It makes it too easy to put on weight without realizing it."

Rachel tugged on the elastic waist of her brown polyester pants. "Is that so?"

Suzanne yawned. "I'm beat. How about we talk again soon?"

"Sounds good." Rachel ended the call and made her way upstairs. She pulled off her brown pants and squeezed into a pair of jeans. She tugged at the zipper and got it all the way up, but she had to leave the rivet at the top unbuttoned so she'd be able to sit.

In her nightstand drawer, she found an unused notebook. Pen in hand, she stared at her navel in the dresser mirror and knew what she'd write as her first fitness goal.

CHAPTER 9

Marla

Marla slipped on a new designer dress, royal blue with a bejeweled diagonal stripe that drew attention to her figure and alluded to her current fame. Earlier in the week, she'd gone on a shopping spree, snagging a couple outfits for a few thousand dollars. Marla had her "look"—classic with some pizzazz—and was always particular about her wardrobe.

Todd rapped at the door, then used his key to enter Marla's condo. She stood ready to greet him, frozen in a dramatic model's pose. He extended his arms as he walked toward her. "Hoo-ee! Look at you, babe!" He twirled her around to get a full look. "It's going to be a good night."

Todd looped his arm around Marla's waist and led her to the limo waiting downstairs. Tonight, they'd make the rounds at an exclusive club and two parties. News of Marla's business deal had made them a popular couple. The chauffeur opened the door, and they slid onto the black leather seat.

With the privacy window shut, Marla questioned Todd about the driver. "He's a little scruffy, isn't he?" Todd's chauffeurs were always well groomed, but this one looked like he needed a shave and a shampoo.

"Eddie? Aw, you know how hard it is to find good drivers in this city. He does look kinda rough, though. I thought

I'd try him out myself tonight, see how he does." Todd shrugged. "If he works out, I'll have somebody work with him on his appearance."

Many hours later, and having had a little too much to drink, they plopped into the limo's back seat. Marla wasn't sure if the smell of marijuana came from Todd or Eddie. She clicked a seatbelt into place, then rested against Todd's shoulder and shut her eyes.

Pain shot through Marla's left side. The glare of what seemed like a hundred headlights shone overhead. She blinked a few times and a man dressed in white came into view, leaning over her.

"What's going on?" Marla mumbled.

The doctor spoke in a slow, clear voice. "You were in an auto accident. You're in the ER. We're trying to determine the extent of your injuries."

"How about Todd?" The details of the night were coming back to her.

"He's in surgery right now. Banged up, but he'll be okay."

"The driver?" Marla couldn't remember his name.

The doctor seemed to ignore her. Maybe he couldn't hear her above the other voices in the room. And then an infusion of medicine kicked in, sending Marla far away from the pain.

"I got bad news. Eddie is dead." Todd mumbled the words with little expression.

The nurse who had wheeled Todd into Marla's room crossed her arms. "He insisted on coming here to tell you himself."

FALLING APART, FALLING FOR YOU

Todd looked like he'd nod off mid-sentence.

Marla widened her eyes. "How'd this happen?"

Todd stared at the marbled ceiling tiles above his head. "Eddie had been smoking something, the cops said. Must've been going close to sixty on a side street, didn't see someone pulling out of a parking space." Todd dropped his chin and looked down at his wrinkled hospital gown. "Cops said he had a history of speeding tickets." He kept his eyes averted. "And drugs."

Todd winced in pain as he turned his face toward Marla. "My HR person must've forgotten to do a background check on him. I'm sorry, Marla."

The nurse spoke to Todd in a loud voice, as if pain caused deafness. "I need to get you back to your room now."

She addressed Marla in the same loud voice. "He's just a few rooms down the hall. You can talk again tomorrow."

As the nurse wheeled Todd away, a doctor slipped past them into the room.

"I've got some good news to report. We were concerned you had internal injuries. But the tests turned up negative, except for badly bruised ribs and a lot of cuts and bumps. You'll be in considerable pain for a few weeks, but after that, you should be fine. Lucky you were wearing a seat belt."

Then the doctor turned somber. "The testing, however, showed you recently suffered a TIA—a mini stroke. That's a serious matter, and we want to keep you here a while to see what that's all about."

Marla shut her eyes and threw a hand over her mouth. A mini stroke! Just like her mother's first one. Realizing she'd been spared from both a car accident and a mini stroke, tears broke through Marla's closed eyelids "Thank you, God," she whispered. It was the first time she'd talked to God since leaving St. Cyprian's.

She shivered. Was she cold, afraid—or shocked she was still alive? And for what purpose did God save her?

Adorned by neither make-up nor jewelry, Marla lay shrouded in a rumpled hospital bedsheet, staring at the repeated patterns of the acoustical tile ceiling. Her thoughts alternated between the pain in her upper body to the millions she'd recently parked in her bank account.

Clutching a dizzying assortment of get-well balloons, Deanna bounced into the hospital room, her black twisted hair bobbing on her shoulders. "Wow! You look good, girl. I sure hope you feel as good as you look."

"Knock off the happy talk, Deanna. My ribs are killing me, I hurt all over, I'm bored to tears, and by the way, did I tell you I had a mini-stroke?"

"A mini-stroke? Nah-uh!" Concern washed over Deanna's face. "You poor baby. You gonna be all right?"

"Yeah, provided I lower my blood pressure. They also said to limit alcohol to one drink a day and to stop using recreational drugs." Marla pursed her lips. "These doctors are such killjoys."

"They're just doing their job." Deanna spoke in a soft, soothing voice as she tied the balloons to the handle of a cabinet.

"My mother had a couple mini-strokes before having a big one." Marla blew a breath from taut lips. "They say there's often a hereditary tendency."

Deanna's big brown eyes looked upward.

Marla shook her head. "Oh, I know what you're thinking, Saint Deanna. You're thinking this is going to turn out to be a good thing for me, that I'll change my ways and be a good little girl from now on. Well, let me tell you, I'm not." Marla knew she could rail at Deanna, and she'd forgive her. She always did.

"Look, Marla." Deanna curled her sepia-toned hands on the side rail of the bed, her eyes boring into Marla's. "Life's different now. You've been going through big changes—selling your business, the limo accident, and now, learning you've had a mini stroke. You can rant at me all you want, but you're a smart cookie. You know you've gotta to make some changes—if you want to stick around to spend your millions, that is."

Marla started to fold her arms across her chest to show Deanna what she thought of her sermon, but it proved too painful. Instead, she raised her chin and harrumphed. "I know, I know." She peered out the window and stared at the gray sky and the pathetic view below it. Not a single shade of green in sight, just asphalt, metal sheeting, and rusty pipes. "I feel so ... so lost." Not wanting her sudden tears to overflow, she kept her head turned toward the window, waiting for her eyes to absorb them.

Deanna scraped a plastic-covered chair across the linoleum floor, situating it next to the bedrail. She sat down with a crunch, then placed her hand on top of Marla's as she prayed aloud for what seemed like a very long time and a lot louder than the nuns used to pray. But Marla didn't pull back her hand.

Deanna concluded her prayer with an emphatic "Amen."

I wish I could pray like Deanna. Her prayers are so heartfelt, so comforting.

A petite young woman in a sleeveless dress burst into the room without knocking. Her bouncy hair froze as she stopped short and planted herself several feet away from Marla and Deanna.

"Ms. Galani, I'm sorry for interrupting. I'm Kaylee Storm, Todd's HR manager."

Marla's body tensed. *Look at her, she's barely twenty and shaking like a scared puppy. What's a child like this doing handling Todd's HR matters?*

"What do you want? Cut to the chase. I'm in no mood for small talk." Marla jutted her chin toward the young woman.

Kaylee stood ramrod straight. She took a deep breath then spoke in a tone so firm it caught Marla by surprise. "Todd lied to you about Eddie."

"What are you talking about?" Marla demanded.

"Todd never told me he hired Eddie as a chauffeur. I never had any paperwork on him. I never interviewed him. Never saw the guy. I don't even know his last name."

"Then where did he come from?" Marla barked.

"He knew one of Todd's buddies. We were short on drivers that night, so Todd told Eddie he could take care of his new hire paperwork on Monday."

"Are you serious?" Marla jerked her head, wanting the explanation to be false.

Kaylee nodded, unblinking. "I just learned the details a minute ago, when I talked with Todd. I wanted to tell you myself. He promised he'd tell you the whole story." She looked down at her shoes. "But to be honest, I'm not sure I can trust him."

Over the months they'd dated, Marla had heard enough lies and distortions from "Spinmeister Todd," as she sometimes called him, to know this young woman was telling the truth. Until now, the facts hadn't mattered all that much. They'd been too busy having fun.

"Thank you for telling me, Kaylee." Marla turned her head to the overcast skies, signaling the end of the conversation.

"I hope you're better soon, Ms. Galani." Kaylee acknowledged Deanna with a nod bordering on a curtsy and skittered out of the room.

Marla snorted as she attempted to run her fingers through her thick tangled hair. "Well, that sure throws a bucket of ice water on my relationship with Todd, wouldn't you say?"

FALLING APART, FALLING FOR YOU

It took a while, but Marla managed to dress herself in the outfit she'd asked Deanna to bring for her—designer pants, spiked heels, and a striped cashmere sweater, accented by some of her distinctive gem jewelry. Few patients looked this fabulous while awaiting their hospital discharge papers. Marla always liked to be an exception.

How Marla felt, however, was a different matter. Gingerly, she moved down the hall toward Todd's room. Not wanting to jar her ribs, she slid more than stepped, her heels registering a light clicking on the polished linoleum.

She pushed open the door to his room. "Wake up, Todd!" She blurted, rousing him from his slumber. He blinked a few times, then waved with a motion of his fingers.

"Good news, they're discharging me later this morning. When are they going to let you out of this miserable place?"

"Me? I dunno. Nobody tells you nothin' here."

"I think my apartment key must have fallen out of my purse during the accident. Where's the key you use?"

"It should be in my pants pocket. Over there." Todd lifted a forefinger toward a narrow white cabinet.

Marla reached in and snatched the key. She tucked it into her bra and headed toward the door.

"Where you goin'?"

"Like I said, Todd, I'm getting discharged. I'm going home." Her voice sounded like ice in a deep freezer.

"Aren't you going to stay a while and keep me company, Babe?"

She crept closer and bored into his eyes. "I know the truth about Eddie." She thrust a finger at his nose. "Don't you ever call me again."

She took a step to leave, then glared at him one more time over her shoulder. "And by the way, Spinmeister Todd, you look like crap."

Marla had been so busy with the sale of her business, and then the accident, that she hadn't been able to have a lengthy phone conversation with her father in days. His living seven time zones away in Greece added another degree of difficulty to their communication. Today, though, they'd managed to connect, and she told him about the accident.

"I have a question for you," said her father. His voice sounded weak, but he could still banter with his daughter. "When those doctors were looking for internal damage, did they find an extra organ that generates success?" He chuckled.

"Very funny, Dad. But thank you for the compliment."

"I framed that article about you in the *Wall Street Journal*."

"Which one? The original one, or the one about the sale of the business?"

"The second one. I can't find the original one. This place is a mess. Ida refuses to use a housekeeper. She says they steal everything."

"How's Ida doing these days?"

"Her mind's declining. And my body's declining. Together, we've got one good person." He snorted.

"Aging is so cruel." Marla said it with tenderness.

"Yes, my dear, it is. But it wouldn't be so bad if I weren't dealing with cancer. It's like a game of whack-a-mole. Every time the doctors think they've gotten rid of it in one body part, it pops up in another. The doctor said it won't be much longer. Weeks, maybe a few months."

"Oh, Dad, I am so sorry." This time, Marla made no attempt to hold back her tears.

"Don't be sorry. I have that blessed assurance of knowing that when I leave this earth, I'll go to heaven. I can't wait to get there, and I hope I'll see you there someday too."

Marla had to shake her head at the difference in her father. He'd been the one pushing for her to have an abortion, and now he never missed an opportunity to preach to her. Too bad he'd never met Deanna. They would've gotten along famously.

"Father Kouris and I have talked about the funeral. He'll know what to do."

"Okay, Dad."

"Ida won't be able to live alone once I'm gone. I've made arrangements for her to live in a nice facility, like the one your mother's in. How's she doing, by the way?"

Marla blew her nose so she could talk. "The same. Still isn't talking. I have no idea if she even recognizes me."

"That's too bad. I'm glad you're able to visit her. Next time you go, please tell her I'm sorry for all the mistakes I made. Believe me, I made plenty of them. I'd do it in person but this old body of mine can't manage a trip like that. I'm so tired and weak these days." His high-pitched voice creaked as he spoke.

"Of course I'll do that, Daddy."

"I do have one piece of good news, though."

"What's that?"

"The doctors gave me one concession. They said I could make one last short trip, as long as I traveled with my nurse."

He fell silent for a moment, then spoke with a strength and determination she hadn't heard from him in a long while. "Marla, I want to go one last time to my favorite city in the world. Can you meet me in Paris? I have some papers I want to give you in person."

CHAPTER 10

Suzanne

Suzanne checked herself in a full-length mirror, front and back, noting with a smile that her zipper was closed. She said a quick prayer before picking up her purse and room key, then caught an elevator to the hotel lobby.

Rob was waiting at the elevator bank. As soon as she spotted him, she felt that same zing of electricity. *Mercy.*

He wrapped her in an embrace, and in the process bumped one of her earrings off. It disappeared on the marble floor as another elevator door opened and several people scurried past.

"Don't worry, I'll find it." Rob's eyes scoured the floor. He spotted the earring, but the backing remained hidden in the marble's camouflage.

"Mind if we run up to my room so I can put on another pair?"

They caught an elevator and strolled to her room, but Rob stopped at her doorway. "I'll just stay out here."

"Don't be ridiculous. C'mon in. I'll only be a minute."

In front of the mirror, she brushed her hair aside to remove the other earring. Rob came up behind her; she took in a breath. If he kissed her again like he did last month in Phoenix, this might be trouble.

He laced his arms around her waist then peered over her shoulder, looking into the mirror. "It's wonderful to see you again, Suzanne." He nudged her hair and placed a tender kiss on her neck.

How did he know that was her weak spot? She let out a small inadvertent moan.

He turned Suzanne around toward him. Their eyes connected, signaling an unexpected and strong longing.

She pulled back, almost imperceptibly.

"We'd better get out of this room now, right?" Rob raised an eyebrow.

Suzanne nodded, then changed her mind before they reached the door. "Wait—I do have one piece of news that I'd rather tell you about in private, as long as we're here. I could've told you when we were in Phoenix, but frankly, I never imagined we'd have the chance to see one another again."

"Is that so?" He teased as he lifted her hand and kissed her fingertips. "What's your news?"

"Nothing good, I'm afraid. My contract with the airline isn't going to be renewed. My sessions will end in three weeks, on June 12." She searched Rob's eyes to gauge his reaction.

"That's sure a surprise. I know you like surprises, but only the good kind." His face gave nothing away.

"Yeah, it's a lousy surprise. I'm pretty upset about it." She took a step away from him.

"You can't do training for another airline, or another industry?"

"Maybe, but I'm pretty sure they'll all think I'm too old for a job like this."

"So, you think it's age-related—even though you have the energy of a thirty-year-old?" He reached for her and put his arms around her waist again.

She rested her head on his chest and nuzzled under his chin. "I can't prove anything, but I've heard similar stories over the past few years. It's demanding work. You're on your feet all day and you have to pay attention to every word you say. On top of that, the travel is exhausting." Tears welled in her eyes. "Once you're branded as too old, no one wants to touch you."

"How can I help?" Rob stepped back and put his hands on her shoulders.

"This has knocked my self-confidence for a loop. It would help if you just listen to me when I need to talk about it." She dabbed the tears rimming her mascaraed eyes.

"I can do that." Rob studied her eyes as he held her shoulders.

"Thanks." Suzanne looked down at the thin, floral carpeting.

Rob lifted her chin with his forefinger. "What's the matter—more bad news?"

"I'm afraid, yes. It looks like this will be my last trip to the West Coast. I'll be conducting the remaining programs in Pittsburgh."

"Well, things may look bleak right now, but you know how life is—nothing ever stays the same. We can talk about it over dinner." He gave her a hug. "This weekend, how about we do what we did in Phoenix—let's make the most of our time together."

She wrapped her arms around his waist and rested her head on his chest once again. It felt so right.

He squeezed her with one arm and combed his fingers through her hair with his free hand. "It'll all work out."

They linked hands and made their way to Rob's car.

"We have a dinner reservation right down the road." After opening the passenger door for Suzanne, he popped into the driver's side and looked at her, a smile on his face. To her surprise, he chuckled.

She pouted her lips to feign being slighted. "What are you laughing about? I'm still thinking about being out of work next month."

"Sorry. Maybe I'm out of line, but I've been wondering how I'd feel when I saw you again. In case you're curious, it's the same as in Phoenix." He paused. "Actually, since we've been keeping in touch the past month or so, it's even better."

Suzanne loved how Rob said whatever was on his mind, and always in such a sweet way. And his cellphone didn't ring to interrupt them with a crisis. "I know what you mean. I feel the same."

Rob winked at her and started the car. Their phone calls and texts these past few weeks had kept the momentum going, allowing them to pick up where they'd left off in Phoenix. Unlike Phoenix, however, the weather in San Francisco felt chilly and damp.

"Mind if we turn on the heat?" Suzanne rubbed her hands over her arms.

Rob pressed a few buttons and the warmth flowed from the vents.

She crossed her legs and leaned toward Rob. "I had a stunning realization this morning."

"Really?" He widened his eyes. "About *us*?"

"Nope. About myself."

"Oh." His eyes drooped, making him look deflated. "What did you realize?"

"I made a list of names of people I know that I should contact for networking. For my job search, you know. It was a surprisingly short list. I realized that during these years of traveling, I've neglected my old friends, and haven't added many new ones."

"How do you feel about that?" He crinkled his forehead.

"You just put on your psychologist hat, didn't you?" She laughed.

"Sorry. Was it that obvious?" He lifted his shoulders. "But how *do* you feel about it?"

"It makes me sad. Even so, I'm glad I realized it. Once I stop traveling, I'm going to reconnect with old friends and make some new ones too."

In minutes, they arrived at the restaurant, a Tudor cottage, charming and cozy, decorated with dried flowers, wicker baskets, and local memorabilia. The hostess seated them in a nook, at a small round table with a lacy tablecloth and a delicate crystal chandelier hanging above.

Suzanne glanced at the lacy paper menu. "Everything looks scrumptious. It's hard to choose." Eventually, she decided on a seafood salad.

"You asked me to suggest some things you could do in your next job." Rob unfurled his napkin and slapped it on his lap. "I have some ideas for you. Have you ever visited the Monterey Bay area?"

Suzanne nodded. "Once, a few years back. It's a fabulous place."

"My house is in Carmel Highlands, on the Monterey Peninsula. You'd love living in the Monterey Bay area—not only because of the beauty of the place, but also because it's a very artistic community. You could get a job working at an art gallery, or have your own calligraphy business, or sell your artwork at one of the shops in town."

"You're suggesting I relocate?" Suzanne furrowed her brow.

"Well, you haven't been living in Pittsburgh all that much, when you consider the traveling you've been doing."

"I don't want to rule out relocation entirely, but my mom's still in southwestern Pennsylvania, and Jill and Drew live in Jersey."

He tapped a finger on the table a few times. "Here's another thought. My pastor has a casita you could live in for a few months. It would give you a chance to get a taste of living in the Monterey Bay area."

"What's a casita?" Suzanne scrunched her nose.

"A guesthouse. I do some favors for Paul. I'm sure he'd allow you to stay there a while for free."

"That's quite an offer. Thank you so much." Suzanne poked at her food, not sure what to say next.

"I know you've got to think it over. How about we tour San Francisco tomorrow, then on Sunday, we can explore the Monterey Peninsula."

Early next morning, Rob picked Suzanne up at her hotel. Clearly, he'd planned their day in advance—their agenda was packed. They watched people practicing tai chi in Chinatown, drove over the Golden Gate Bridge, walked the labyrinth at Grace Cathedral, toured Alcatraz, and hopped on a cable car.

"You're a fabulous tour guide," Suzanne said with a flutter of her eyelashes.

Rob smirked. "When I first moved to the area and was building my practice, I supplemented my income doing tours." He smiled. "Just so you know, Suzanne, you're not the only person who enjoys traveling."

"I wondered how you knew exactly where to go every moment of the day." She gave him a gentle punch in the arm for keeping his tour guide experience a secret.

"Would you like to go to church with me tomorrow?" Rob asked.

Suzanne had never had a "church date" before, but she readily agreed.

Rob picked her up early the next morning. They breezed southward down Highway 1, got off in Carmel, and drove a few more miles on local roads. Rob pointed out his house on a cliff high above them. "We'll stop there later today, if you'd like."

They pulled into an empty church parking lot. Suzanne peered around. "Are we too early?"

Rob turned off the ignition. "I have a few things to do before the service." He ran his hand through his hair. "I'm ... I'm actually filling in for the pastor today."

"Casita, tour guide, back-up pastor—got any more surprises for me this weekend?" Unsmiling, she darted a glance at him.

FALLING APART, FALLING FOR YOU

"I'm sorry I didn't tell you last night. I thought you might not come if you knew I'd be preaching. Can you forgive me?"

Suzanne looked out the car window, digesting Rob's latest surprise.

"Look, if it's too much for you, you can sit in the pastor's office instead. It's too late to take you back now."

She remained silent, still looking out the window.

"Suzanne, I'd like you to know this part of my life. My church is very important to me. Today is the only time I can share it with you, since you don't think you'll be back here again, and it happened to be the week Paul's on vacation. Can you understand why I sprang it on you?"

Moved by his plea, Suzanne softened. "I'd like to hear you preach, Rob. Let's go." She squeezed his hand.

As they walked inside, Rob explained that his educational background enabled him to fill in for the pastor on various matters such as preaching. "It's a nondenominational church, and our rules on how to do things are a lot more flexible than in mainline churches."

"Yes, I don't think having you as a pastor would fly in my old Catholic church back in Port Mariette."

The sanctuary looked ethereal, with bright light streaming from the windows. Curved rows of cushioned pews directed all eyes toward an enormous silver cross hanging at the front.

Rob waved his hand across the sanctuary. "Sit anywhere you want. Just don't make any funny faces at me while I'm preaching." His face remained serious as he threw her a wink.

She chose a seat near a side aisle and did her best to engage in the service, but her emotions had already sped into overdrive. *What worship song did they just sing?* She couldn't remember. Soon it was time for the sermon. Rob spoke eloquently and intelligently about suffering, and how it's what we do with it that changes our lives for the better. Her admiration for him grew.

Afterward, they drove to Rob's house and relaxed on his patio overlooking the Pacific.

"It's breathtaking." Suzanne said it five times if she said it once.

"If you think I'm a good tour guide of San Francisco, watch me here on my home turf."

They drove down the coast all the way to Bixby Bridge, came back north to stroll along Ocean Avenue in Carmel-by-the-Sea, then snapped photos at the Lone Cypress in Pebble Beach.

Miles later, Rob swung into a parking lot. "This is a funky new restaurant here in Pacific Grove. What do you think?"

Suzanne's eyes scoured the multi-colored frame building. "Looks like fun."

"Good." He glanced at her sideways. "I already made us a dinner reservation."

They crunched through the gravel parking lot, holding hands more for stability than romance. People jammed the foyer waiting for open tables.

The hostess led them to the back of a long dining room, to a small wooden table with two armless chairs, supported by uneven legs. The fireplace, blazing at the front of the room, did nothing to warm them. Close to a shiver, Suzanne pulled her sweater tight around her chest.

Rob leaned toward Suzanne and whispered, "A bottle of champagne could rescue this situation."

Suzanne let out a laugh that turned the heads of the people at the next table.

The champagne warmed Suzanne up and also loosened her tongue. She told Rob stories about her family, like how her mother, a very feminine woman, didn't care for their family name, Schwartz. "To offset it, she gave all three daughters very feminine first names."

"You're feminine, like your mother."

Suzanne smiled at the compliment.

FALLING APART, FALLING FOR YOU

"How many sisters do you have? I thought you said you only had a younger sister."

"That's Andrea. She's the one who still lives in Port Mariette. She's got a lot of issues, as they say, including three kids who drive her batty." Suzanne lowered her voice so the people at the next table couldn't hear. "I had an older sister named Juliet. She died on her eleventh birthday." Suzanne teared up. "We still celebrate it every year."

Rob reached for her hand and held it tenderly for a moment before speaking. "One day, you'll see her again."

"Yes. That's true." She took a deep breath. "That's enough about me. Can we talk about your family now?" Selfish enough in her prayer life, she didn't want to be self-centered in her conversation with Rob too.

"I need to talk with you first—." Rob cleared his throat, his expression serious. "About us."

Although she had a forkful of crabmeat halfway to her mouth, she set it back on her plate and gave Rob her full attention.

"I want to be upfront with you, Suzanne. When I met you in that hotel in Phoenix, I never dreamed we'd start a relationship. Sure, I felt attracted to you physically. You reminded me of a mermaid without fins, did I ever tell you that? Shapely and tantalizing, with beautiful shiny hair." He chuckled.

"No, you didn't. I guess you are Superman and I'll be Ariel." She smiled as she imagined it.

"After that first evening, though, I realized I wanted more from you than a single date. I could be wrong, but it seems to me you have some doubts about Adam. And now that the airline isn't renewing your contract, I'm thinking this could be an opportunity for us to spend time together, to see where this could lead."

Suzanne opened her mouth to speak, but Rob raised his hand. "But like I said, I want to be upfront with you. My ex-wife is a complication."

"In what way?" Her voice trembled.

"I told you she'd had an accident, but I didn't give you the details. Before she left to pick up her sister Ellie that day, Meg and I'd had an argument. When she was driving with Ellie later on, she was still upset and crying. That's why she went through the red light. And that's why I carry guilt about Ellie's death and about Meg's spiral into alcoholism."

"Oh my." Suzanne's fingers flew to her lips. "Such a shame."

"Two years ago, when they diagnosed Meg with dementia, I ended up having to make the arrangements for her to live in a memory care unit. She alienated our kids a long time ago, and I'm the only one who visits her now."

"You visit your ex-wife?" Suzanne's brow registered concern.

"Yes. Once a week. Sometimes more." Rob didn't move a muscle.

"Does she still know who you are?"

"She used to recognize me, but not anymore." He took Suzanne's fingers into his hand. "Look, I know this is a lot to take in. I'm sorry for telling you now and ruining our evening." He glanced at the people sitting at the next table.

They swiveled their heads away from Rob and Suzanne and resumed eating as if they hadn't been listening.

Rob grimaced. "Like they say, truth's stranger than fiction. That's why people love to hear about other people's lives."

He looked deep into Suzanne's eyes. "If what I need to do for Meg is a deal breaker for us, I understand. I wanted to get it out in the open tonight before you go back home." He put his elbows on the table. "Life's all about choices, and our choices determine our destiny. Years ago, I made the choice to marry Meg. I made the choice to have that argument with her. And I'll continue to face the consequences until the end."

FALLING APART, FALLING FOR YOU

Suzanne placed her palms over her eyes to block Rob out while she processed her thoughts and emotions.

"What's the matter? What are you thinking? Do you want to leave?" Rob asked. Their half-eaten food had turned cold anyway.

Suzanne nodded.

He handed the waiter some bills, practically tossing them at him. "Keep the change."

They squeezed their way out of the restaurant.

In the car, Rob said, "Suzanne, talk to me. What's going on in your mind?"

She sat still, looking straight ahead, unsure of what to say.

Rob tossed his arm over the steering wheel. "It looks like I have two strikes against me—Meg and California. But the game isn't over, at least not in my mind."

She crossed her arms and looked toward the horizon. "I'm pretty sure you think I'm overreacting. Maybe I am. But you have to understand, I have a painful history with the men in my life. I'm not going to allow myself to get hurt again."

"I understand, but look, Suzanne, here's how I feel." He took his arm from the steering wheel and faced her. "In my life, I've proven myself in all ways. I have a good life, but there's a certain emptiness. I'm looking for human closeness. I'd like to be with a woman I love deeply and can spend the rest of my life with. I'd like to marry again and do it right."

"Good grief, you sound like you're getting ready to propose!" Suzanne's eyes widened as she sputtered out the words.

"No, no." Rob shook his head. "It's way too early for that. What I am proposing, though, is that we continue our relationship. I've been honest with you about who I am, and I think you've done the same. We have a lot in common, and I think this could develop into something lasting, if we put in the effort. What do you think?"

She gave him a tender look. "I appreciate how you're able to express yourself. You say what's on your mind and in your heart."

"It goes with the territory when you're a psychologist." He chuckled. "Having a failed marriage and some maturity tends to teach a guy—if he's paying any attention at all."

Suzanne looked down at her lap and fussed with her flowing skirt. After a moment, she looked over at Rob. "You've hit me with a lot of surprises this weekend—filling in for your pastor, lining up a casita for me to live in, thinking that I could pick up and move to California—and, most of all, the situation with your ex-wife. Spiritually, you're miles ahead of me. Physically, we live miles apart, and neither of us can relocate. Emotionally? I don't even know where your heart is—it sounds like it's still with Meg."

Rob looked away, as if he knew what was coming.

"You've been honest with me, Rob, so let me be honest with you. It's all too much for me. This is just not going to work."

CHAPTER 11

Rachel

Soft morning light filtered through the dusty eyelet curtains, decorating Rachel's kitchen table with tiny white dots. For a time, the only sound was the tick-tock of the clock above the sink.

Rachel and her sister sat across from one another, elbows on the table and a cup of coffee in front of each of them. Terrie was dressed in her usual faded stretch pants and polyester top, with Rachel in her dark navy jeans. She leaned back a smidge so she could tolerate the waistband's closed rivet.

"I don't know which is worse—a total surprise like Stan's or knowing it could happen at any moment." Rachel lifted her cup and blew on the steamy coffee before taking a sip.

"Stan had just turned sixty-two," Terrie said in a deep voice born from years of smoking. She'd quit a while back, but her body had failed to receive the message. She still crooked her fingers as if she held a cigarette. "Bud has eight years on him, and even seventy seems so young. Maybe that's because I'm seventy too." She chuckled. "Thank goodness I have my daughter to lean on. How hard it must be for you, with your boys scattered."

"I'm okay." Rachel meant it. "Everyone's been supportive, especially my old high school friends. It's like going back in time, talking with Suzanne and Marla. And with the reunion coming up next month, I've been talking with lots of other people from our class too." She leaned toward Terrie. "I've learned I'm not the only one who's widowed. My old high school friend Tony Mastriano said he recently lost his wife."

Terrie rubbed her finger along the rim of her cup before speaking, her eyes downcast. "I've lost touch with a lot of my old friends."

Rachel reached across the table for her sister's hand. "I may be your younger sister—"

"My *much* younger sister." Terrie gave a weak smile.

"—but I'll always be your friend too." *When did it happen, that they'd become close? Some time before Stan's death or only after he died?*

Terrie's eyes brimmed with tears. "Thanks, Sis. You're a sweetie pie. I don't know how you manage so well."

"I have to admit, it can be hard—driving myself to church, watching TV alone, eating meals by myself. Stan and I had routines for how we did everything, and now my life's all out of sync."

Her eyes drifted to her dog. "Thank goodness for Cinders. I talk to him a lot. He's a good listener, aren't you, buddy?"

The dog clip-clopped to the screen door and whimpered.

In a whisk, Rachel opened it. "Out ya go, big fella." She let it slam shut, then crossed her arms and leaned the small of her back against the kitchen counter. "Money's a little tight now that Stan's gone, but I'll be okay." She raised an eyebrow. "You and Bud have taken care of things like that, right?" Money could be such a delicate topic, but sisters ought to be able to discuss it.

"Yeah. I can make do with the surviving spouse benefits from his mill pension."

Rachel stepped to the table and slid onto her chair. "Thank goodness for the steel mill. And the coal mines. Some people looked down on those union jobs, but they kept this town going strong for years."

"Mm-hmm. That's right."

"Once that new highway is finished, I suspect we'll get a lot more people coming through the town, and that will perk things up a bit."

"Well, they may stop here to buy your gasoline or grab a bite to eat at the pizza shop or even have a meal at Dom's, but I don't think they'll do much for the funeral parlor or the insurance agents."

"True." Rachel nodded. "Hey, did I tell you I'm getting certified by the State to do food preparation in my home? Then I can sell meals to restaurants."

"Really? What are you going to make?" Terrie's eyes lit up.

"Pasta and pierogies."

"Your specialties." Terrie tipped her head sideways. "But how would you even get started selling them?"

"Tony owns a restaurant up in Pittsburgh—you remember him from St. Cyp's, don't you? The one whose wife passed away? I had a huge crush on him in high school." Rachel giggled. "But he was dating Suzanne back then. Anyway, when I connected with him for the reunion, that's when we got talking about pasta and pierogies."

"Wasn't Tony the one who broke Suzanne's heart?"

"Yep. That's the one. You have a great memory."

"The way you went on about it, who could've forgotten? You woulda thought he was *your* boyfriend. Anyway, glad my brain's still in working order." She tapped the side of her head.

"I don't want to make any pasta or pierogies for a while, though. I'm trying to lose weight before the reunion. I'm walking a lot to get fit."

"Well, Mrs. Fitness, I heard they're starting a yoga class at the rec center across the river."

Rachel let out a chuckle. "Would you like to try it with me? Marla told me it's easier to exercise if you do it with someone."

"I'd like to, but I need to stick close to home right now. Besides, I don't know if I could do something like that. How on earth could my lungs produce a deep yoga breath? Can you even imagine this body getting up from a yoga mat? It's a challenge just getting up from my chair." She cackled, and then the coughing began, so she stopped talking and sipped some coffee.

"Well, maybe we can take walks together sometime. Did I tell you Frank came out of his house again this morning when I walked by with Cinders? It can't be a coincidence."

Terrie snorted. "He must be watching for you from behind those dusty old Venetian blinds."

Rachel drummed her fingers on the table. "I'll fool him. From now on, I'll sneak out the back door and walk through the alley so he won't see me."

"Now, now. Be nice." Terrie chuckled as she pushed herself up from the chair. "I'd better get going."

"Could you drop me off on Main Street? I have some errands to run, and that'll force me to walk home."

"Sure."

Rachel stood up. "Could you let Cinders back in while I grab a few things?" She sped up the steps to her bedroom, packed her wallet and a bottle of water in a cross-body purse, then slid on a brand-new sun visor and her most comfortable tennis shoes. Finally, she clipped a step counter on her waistband. While making a pit stop in the bathroom, she hollered downstairs, "I think I'm going to regret having that cup of coffee."

She bounced down the steps, then they took off in Terrie's SUV.

"Drop me off on the far end of the street, if you don't mind," Rachel said as they neared the center of town.

"If you need a bathroom, I'm sure they'd let you use the one at the bakery."

"Not to worry. I have an 'in' with the people at the gas station."

FALLING APART, FALLING FOR YOU

"Oh, right." Terrie smacked the side of her head.

"Thanks for the ride." Rachel popped a kiss on her sister's cheek and slid out of the vehicle. "Tell Bud I said hi."

First, she stopped at the bank to get some cash. With its pitched mansard roof, the bank was her favorite among all the commercial buildings on Main Street, even more so now that it had been renovated. The rotunda's stained-glass dome always made her feel like she should be praying instead of doing her banking.

One of the tellers, Lynn, waved Rachel over to her window. "Good to see you. Heard you're helping organize our reunion."

"You coming?" Rachel signed the back of her check and slid it toward Lynn.

"I dunno." She twirled her pen. "I'm afraid I won't remember people."

"We'll all be wearing nametags. The names will be huge and easy to read."

"That's good."

"And remember, those of us who still live in town see one another a lot—after all, that's why it took us forty years to bother having a reunion. So don't worry, you'll know plenty of people right off the bat. The ones who moved away are the ones who might feel nervous. They won't know anyone."

Lynn brightened as she opened her cash drawer. "Twenties okay?"

"Yep."

Lynn counted out the bills then tittered. "See you at the reunion."

Rachel headed toward the Dairy Mart, but first she had to get herself past the pizza shop and bakery. Passing the pizza shop? A snap. The scent of pizza wafted in the air, but at ten in the morning, the place was closed.

After an empty storefront, the bakery came next. Testing herself, she stepped inside. The bell on the door jingled to announce her arrival, and an old floorboard creaked a welcome. A paddle fan whirring above mixed the smells of sugar, chocolate, and cinnamon in the air. She inhaled, her eyes half-closed. *Coming in here may have been a mistake.*

Both of Bernadette's granddaughters stood at the front counter, blank looks on their dewy faces.

"Hi, girls. Smells incredible in here. Is Bernadette in the back baking?"

"She left a few minutes ago," one of them said.

"Tell her I'm sorry I missed her. And sorry, but I'm not buying anything today. I'm trying to lose weight before my reunion."

The girls giggled. They weighed about a hundred pounds apiece. What did they know about dieting?

Rachel walked out, pleased with her resolve. She passed a few empty storefronts then dropped into the Dairy Mart to pick up chicken breasts and romaine lettuce.

Herbie Herbinger stepped into the checkout line behind her.

"Hi, Rachel. Only six weeks till the reunion! How's it going with the list?" A busy businessman, he got right to the point. He'd do well with Marla in New York.

"I think I've reached everyone who is reachable," Rachel replied.

"How many of us are dead so far?" Herbie joked.

"I didn't count, but there's a handful." Rachel's lips formed a flat line.

He winced. "Sorry, Rachel. I shouldn't have joked about that."

"It's okay, Herbie. By the way, I think Suzanne will do the nametags and handle the registration table."

"That's good. I've already talked with the country club about the menu, and I've got a few people lined up to do decorations. Mac set up an account at the bank for depositing the checks, and Donny Blue's going to be our D.J. Can you think of anything else we need to do?"

FALLING APART, FALLING FOR YOU

"Sounds to me like we're all set."

"Thanks for helping out, Rachel. You got stuck with the toughest job of all."

"I didn't mind." *I like to serve others.* Rachel smiled as she waved goodbye.

She passed the barbershop next. A shorthaired mutt rested on the sidewalk, his leash attached to a hitching post for dogs. The town had installed two posts last month, one on each side of the street—an improvement so rare it made the first page of the *Port Mariette Gazette*. Next time, she'd bring Cinders along.

At the end of the commercial part of Main Street, she stopped in the gas station, catching Lou Gestler by surprise. Lou was a gentle soul, and Rachel considered it a stroke of good fortune after losing Stan when Lou said he could work full-time Monday through Friday. Having worked there on weekends for many years, Lou knew the business well.

"I didn't see you pull in." Lou's eyes darted around to see where she'd parked.

"Just walking by. Thought I'd stop in. Any problems?"

"Nope. All quiet here."

A customer came through the door to pay for her gas, so Rachel opened the drawer to pick up yesterday's paperwork. She waved goodbye to Lou and began the hike back home.

A few people driving by beeped hello, and she waved.

Ted and Sandy Roczinski stopped their SUV in the middle of the street. Sandy rolled down her window and hollered, "Did your car break down?"

"Nope, car's fine. Just decided to enjoy the beautiful weather." Rachel's chin rose as she thanked them for asking.

Her pace slowed as she continued walking, but eventually she made it to her house. She poked her way up the uneven porch steps, then Cinders greeted her with a toothy pant and danced around her as she set the grocery bag on the kitchen counter. "Calm down, let me catch my breath. I'll get you something in a minute."

After feeding Cinders, she made yet another chicken and romaine salad and situated herself at the table. Her step counter read two thousand, one hundred seventy-seven steps. She made the sign of the cross and said grace, just as her cellphone rang. "Hello, Pete."

"Hi, Mom."

"You sound stuffed up. Got a cold?"

Of the four boys, Pete resembled his father the most, both in personality and physique. Even his voice sounded like Stan's, deep and comforting. She shouldn't favor one child over the other, but how could she not love her firstborn the best, especially now that her baby Brian was gone?

Once Pete moved to Denver, he called every weekend—and since Stan's passing, he called her a couple times a week, even though he worked at a big accounting firm crunching numbers all day long. Rachel couldn't understand why he'd picked a desk job over something more physical. He'd always enjoyed working at the service station with Stan. At least it seemed that way to her.

"I did have a cold, but it's almost gone. I gave it to Marianne." He let out a fake laugh.

"I hate getting colds. The older I get, the harder it is to get rid of them. They just seem to hang on and on."

"I know. Hey, when I was at the house, I noticed some things that need to be taken care of. Not just that old grandfather clock, but big things like the front steps and the porch. Someone could fall on those old wooden steps. The porch needs to be painted before the wood rots. Lots of other small stuff, too, like loose doorknobs and dripping faucets."

"I know, your father always ran out of gas when it came to fixing up the house. Get it? He ran out of gas!"

FALLING APART, FALLING FOR YOU

"Yeah, Mom, I get it." He gave a weak chuckle. "Anyway, I thought I'd come spend a week or so with you to take care of those things."

"Petie, that's so sweet of you. But, my goodness, you'll be using up your vacation time. Won't Marianne be upset?"

"We've already talked about it. It's okay. She's always so busy at work and this will give her some peace and quiet. We all need that sometimes."

"When would you be able to break away? Maybe sometime this summer?" Rachel's head was spinning from all the conversations today.

"How about Sunday?"

CHAPTER 12

MARLA

"Sorry I couldn't join our video calls for a while. I've been busy with some unexpected matters." Marla sat up straight, careful not to apply pressure on her still-sore ribs.

"With the sale of the business?" Suzanne asked from her computer screen.

"I wish. No, I was in a bad accident in one of Todd's limos."

"Oh my gosh!" Rachel's eyes widened.

Suzanne leaned forward to examine Marla on the screen. "You look as good as ever. What happened?"

Marla explained the details, along with Todd's lie. "I sure won't be seeing him again."

"My goodness, what you have gone through." Suzanne shook her head as she reached for her bottle of water.

"On the brighter side, I squeezed in a short trip to Paris to see my dad. He wanted someplace beautiful to review his will with me. The Ritz at Place Vendome. Quite the setting."

"Wow. If you lived in Port Mariette, your life would be the headline story every day." Rachel giggled.

"How's your *Greek father* doing?" Suzanne winked.

"He's ninety-one years old, poor fellow, and sad to say, not so great. Cancer. But we had a memorable time together."

"Aw, I'm so sorry to hear he's not doing well," Suzanne said. "But Paris! I'm jealous."

Rachel tipped her head to the side. "Sorry about your dad. I lost mine to lung cancer a long time ago. It's hard." She righted her head and leaned in. "I hope you'll still be able to come to the reunion, though. I know you're busy, and compared to what you're used to, our reunion might be boring, but everyone's so curious to see you again. Especially me."

So, I'm still a curiosity. "Not to worry, I'll be there. I'm looking forward to a walk down memory lane. In fact, I'm driving to Port Mariette sometime next month."

"You'll be in town in June?" Suzanne asked.

"Mm-hmm. I have to see what's happening with Aunt Adele. Her health is failing, and I'm not sure how well she's managing on her own. I'll stay with her a few weeks to assess her condition. I'll have plenty of time to see both of you too."

"Great! My last day of training is June 12, and until then, all my work is here in Pittsburgh. I can come down to Port Mariette anytime. Then the three of us can get together in person."

"This is going to be a blast." Rachel grinned.

"Have you finalized the reunion list yet?" Suzanne asked, looking at Rachel on her screen.

Rachel picked up her notepad and showed them her marked-up list. "I've talked with almost everyone. Of course, a few people have already died, which is a scary thought at our age. There were two I couldn't find—Marion Meehan and Karen D'Amico. And Dave Wallace said he can't make it, which is too bad because now the barbershop quartet can't perform. Everyone else should be there."

"Remember, I'll be happy to do the registration table." Suzanne pointed her forefinger upward. "I'm an ace at that, number one at nametags."

FALLING APART, FALLING FOR YOU

Rachel thanked Suzanne for volunteering, then clapped her fingertips a few times. "Oh my gosh. This will be incredible. Three best friends together after forty years. I'll bet I can get a picture of us in the *Port Mariette Gazette*."

Gee whiz, just like getting my photo in the Wall Street Journal.

Before driving to Port Mariette, Marla had a few details to tie up with her lawyer. She'd arranged to meet Warren for lunch at his favorite restaurant, one of those steak and potato places oozing with masculinity. She'd pick up the tab too. With important matters to discuss, she'd stacked the deck to make sure he'd be in a receptive mood.

Already waiting at a booth when she arrived at twelve on the dot, Warren looked up and gave a tight wave of his hand. He tapped something on his cellphone. *He started his time clock, and I haven't even sat down yet.* Even though Warren had made a bundle of money from her over the years, in particular during the sale of her business, he always made sure to bill every red cent. Sometimes it irritated her. But most of the time, she admired his business savvy.

Marla had often turned to Warren for advice, not just on legal matters. The man was street-smart, well educated, and articulate. Good-looking too, with a body kept in shape courtesy of the gym at his own law firm.

They'd had a fling before she hired him, but that fell apart when she learned he didn't like mixing business with pleasure, and besides, he was married to his profession. So overall, she benefited when they stopped dating and he became her lawyer.

She clicked her heels along the restaurant's polished wood floor, turning many male heads along the way. Slinking like a willowy model, she could have been one even now. Men whispered as she passed by. Many of their wives had been her clients at Gemstones, and they wouldn't be happy to know about their husbands' wandering eyes.

Warren stood to greet her. "Great to see you, Marla. Glad you're still with us on this earth."

Marla smirked. She'd always appreciated Warren's dark sense of humor. *If I'd left this earth, would I have ended up in heaven—or hell?* Her dad and Deanna both seemed to know where they'd go, but about herself, she wasn't sure. She slipped onto the cushioned leather bench.

He already knew all about the accident, of course, and based on some of the comments she overheard while walking to the table, it seemed most everyone in the city knew. "Thanks, Warren. It's good to still be alive. You know how it is, only the good die young."

"Ha, that's what I love about you, Marla. Nothing ever takes you down."

"We'll see about that." She looked around in search of a server, then turned her attention back to Warren. "I've got a few things on my plate I want to bounce off you."

"Okay. Before we start, want a drink?"

"Sure. I'm allowed to have one a day now."

"Just one? How come?" He raised a graying eyebrow.

"I had a TIA—a mini-stroke."

"Really? Tough break. Sorry to hear that." He paused, but she gave no reaction, so he filled the void. "I know a lot of people who've had them, and afterward, they never had another problem."

"That's my hope. And that's why I'm behaving myself—except for the one drink a day."

Warren tipped his head in the direction of the oncoming server. "Name your poison."

Marla chuckled. "Give me a glass of your best sauvignon blanc."

"One for me too."

The waiter nodded and slipped away.

FALLING APART, FALLING FOR YOU

"So, what's on your mind, Marla?"

She first brought up some loose ends regarding the sale of her business, and Warren made a note to handle the matters. Next, she told him about her dad's failing health. "The will he gave me in Paris said I'd inherit his villa in Porto Heli—along with a boatload of money."

"Sorry about your dad's health, Marla. Never easy to lose a parent. Porto Heli—that's on the Greek Riviera, isn't it?"

"Yes. His place is one of those whitewashed villas overlooking the Aegean Sea. That water is crystal clear, no exaggeration." She showed him a few photos on her cellphone. "Check out the swimming pool."

"Wow, what a place. Let me know if you'll be needing a butler."

She set her phone back on the table. "My dad bought it years ago. I didn't go there often, though. Couldn't stand my dad's second wife, Ida. Besides, I was always working."

"I hear you." He nodded a few times then took a sip of his drink.

Marla leaned forward, elbows on the table and hands folded. "I think I might need a referral from you. I'm going to be dealing with the legalities of intricate and large inheritances—here in the US and abroad. I don't believe you handle those kinds of matters, do you?"

"Not typically, but occasionally, yes."

"I hope my situation is one you can handle. You know I trust you. At least on legal matters." She winked.

Warren chuckled. He pushed his wine glass aside, all business now.

"Here's the situation." Marla let out a deep breath. "Soon, I'll own that villa in Greece. My mother's near the end of her life too. When she dies, I'll inherit property and money from her as well. I'll be inheriting my aunt's house with some acreage in southwestern Pennsylvania. A lot of fracking has been going on in that area, meaning potential legal issues about oil and gas rights."

"Quite a laundry list." He drummed his fingers on the table. "Normally, I'd refer someone with those needs to someone else, but I'd like to handle that for you. Over the years, you've entrusted me with all your legal issues, and I'd be happy to remain your lawyer for these personal matters."

As long as I pay my bill on time. "Good. That's a relief—with all these changes in my life, that's one less I'll have to worry about."

"I appreciate your trust in me." He looked her in the eye. "I'm sorry about your parents. I know it's sad to be losing them, but they're leaving you quite the financial legacy." Warren cocked his head. "You sure don't seem excited about it though."

Marla took a tiny sip of her wine, wanting to make it last. She put the glass down then tapped the side a few times with a ruby-red fingernail. She looked up at Warren, her chin held high. She wished for just a moment he were her husband, not her long-time lawyer. Life—and now, the possibility of death—could be exhausting. An understanding husband would come in handy right about now. But she hardly had time to deal with her life as it stood, much less consider getting involved with someone—even someone as appealing as Warren.

She blinked a few times, then focused her eyes on Warren. "I ... I ... I ..."

"Yes?" Warren looked at her, confused.

After taking one deep and long breath, she blurted it out. "I have a daughter. I want to find her. I need your help."

"I see." He showed no emotion, just waited for Marla to continue.

She appreciated his control. It helped her keep her emotions in check. "I've found a few women on adoption registries who *could* be her, but without more information,

FALLING APART, FALLING FOR YOU

I can't be sure. I don't want to go poking around in the town where I delivered her. My aunt still lives near the hospital, and I don't want to stir anything up for her. Plus, I'm going back there soon for my high school reunion. I don't want any awkward moments."

"I understand." He continued to sit there, still and stone-faced.

She leaned forward. "I'm sure you can figure out a way to find her through legal channels. No matter who she is or where she lives, I want to meet her. She's my sole heir." Marla lowered her voice. "Look, you may know people who've never had a stroke after a TIA, but my mother's not one of them, so my odds don't look so good. I want to meet my daughter and have a relationship with her while I can." Her voice caught just a bit. "I want to know the person who will someday, in all likelihood, inherit everything I own."

"You have no other relatives at all? I mean, except for your aunt, who I assume will predecease you."

"None."

"No nonprofits you'd want to write into your will?"

"None meaningful enough to me."

"A church?"

"C'mon, Warren. You know me better than that." She waved his question away.

He chuckled. "I was thinking your near miss with death might have caused a conversion."

Marla smirked. "You sound like my dad." She turned serious again. "Fact is, my daughter is my only hope."

Warren flipped to a fresh sheet of paper. "I'll need some information. What's the name of the hospital?"

"Mercy Hospital. It's in Dunham City, Pennsylvania. That's next to the town where I went to high school."

He picked up his pen and began writing.

"Where did you go to high school?"

"St. Cyprian's Academy in Port Mariette." She articulated each syllable.

"O-kayyy ...." Warren raised his eyebrows as he wrote down the school's name.

"It wasn't as bad as it sounds. I do have a few good memories of my senior year there." Marla looked up at the ceiling and smiled. "A guy I liked at St. Cyp's gave me a compliment I've always remembered. He said, 'You're a classy gal.' Not much of a compliment, mind you, but it stuck with me. Funny how someone can say the simplest thing to you, and it affects the course of your life."

"Ah yes, the power of the tongue." He tapped his lips a few times with his pen.

"I had two best friends there—Suzanne and Rachel. They were my lifelines, and I loved them for it. But I was so jealous of them. They were beautiful, popular, and adored by the boys. They represented everything I wasn't." She looked away.

"I find it hard to believe you weren't beautiful back then." A note of tenderness surfaced in Warren's voice.

"That was a tough year." She shrugged. "I didn't do much to make myself appealing."

"We all have our strange high school memories—broken hearts, missed opportunities, stupid behavior." Warren waved her concern away with a flick of his hand.

"Some more than most."

He asked for a few more details about the baby's birth, then leaned toward her, his inquiry complete. Tenting his arms in front of his chest, he looked straight into her eyes. "Thank you for trusting me with this important matter, Marla. I will find her for you."

"I'm grateful I can always count on you."

He reached across the table, and for the first time in years, touched her hand in a way that was not a handshake.

Was it the money motivating him, or could his concern be genuine? No matter. She'd tell him to keep his hands off her *after* he'd found her daughter. Right now, she had too much on her plate to even think about anything else.

CHAPTER 13

Suzanne

On a warm June afternoon in a crowded Pittsburgh hotel conference room, Suzanne welcomed thirty airline employees to her last training program. She'd done this Sexual Harassment & Sensitivity seminar for a year now and found that in this hypersensitive, zero-tolerance world, those working in blue-collar jobs—older men in particular—often struggled the most with her topic. On the plus side, they were willing to ask questions, which kept the class animated and informative.

Right off the bat, a middle-aged man named Nick asked why he'd gotten in trouble for asking a coworker—someone he'd worked with for years—if her leopard-skinned purse matched her panties and bra.

Next time we talk, I have to tell Rob this one. That's another thing they had in common—appreciating the complexities of human nature. No wonder she'd picked up the phone and called Rob a few days after saying goodbye to him in California. Just couldn't get the man totally out of her mind.

She waited for the laughter to die down, then responded with a canned response, one she'd given dozens of times. "Commenting on a woman's attire, especially when it seems to imply anything of a sexual nature, can be considered out of line, insensitive, or rude. Even if you know the coworker well, or you've both joked around many times before, today might be the day the person draws a line and claims something you've said or done is offensive."

Her eyes scanning the audience, she drove the point home. "We all know where behavior like that can lead. It's not worth taking the chance." She looked directly at Nick. "So, what do you think about those odds? Want to bet on a situation like that?"

He shook his head with a knowing laugh. "Lousy odds. Not worth the chance."

Suzanne smiled, satisfied he understood. She had a way of persuading an audience to agree with her. She made a mental note of it. A trait like that could come in handy on job interviews.

At four o'clock, the attendees filed out of the room, unaware she'd never again teach a class for them or their employer.

She thought she might cry, but instead, a surprising wave of relief washed over her.

Freedom. It felt so good.

Even with the Friday rush hour, Suzanne pulled into her parking garage in less than an hour. She changed clothes and plopped on the sofa with a glass of Chablis. Now that her days as a road warrior were behind her, she'd have time to relax like this. Unaccustomed to such a feeling, she tapped her toes a few times. *What to do next?* She picked up her phone and called her daughter.

Jill barked a hello. Suzanne's heart sank, and at once she wished she hadn't made the call. As their conversation went on, she wished even more she hadn't raised the topic of Jill having a baby. *Why did she bring it up again, especially when Jill sounded so irritated?* When it came to her daughter, though, Suzanne had a bad habit of saying precisely what she shouldn't.

"You can be so controlling, Mother." Jill always called her "Mom" unless she was in *a mood*. Then, she'd icily transform "Mom" into "Mother."

Yet, like a dog that wants its bone regardless of the cost, Suzanne forged ahead with her train of thought.

"I know I can sometimes be pushy, but please understand, I only want what's best for you. You're my daughter. I love you. The years slip by so fast, and they go faster the older you get."

Suzanne finished her glass of wine and poured another. "Look how fast my years of being on the road went by. It's a blip on the radar. I just don't want you to have any regrets."

"I wish you'd stop interfering with our decisions. You always think you know what's best for me and Drew. Why don't you worry about your own life instead?"

"What's wrong with *my* life?"

"You're out of work, for one thing. You divorced my father who cheated on you, and you've never been able to recover from it. You're dating a man who gives no evidence of his intentions to marry you. Need I continue?"

Suzanne couldn't absorb the blows. In shock, she hung up.

She ran the conversation over and over in her mind. *Maybe my life is a mess*. She couldn't decide which of Jill's comments hurt her the most. And ... could Jill be right about Adam? Was her burgeoning desire to settle down clouding her perception of him, or could Jill be overreacting for reasons of her own?

"I wish we didn't have to go tonight." Adam blew air through his pursed lips as he drove through the heavy rain.

The windshield began to fog, so Suzanne reached to adjust the air conditioning. "I'll get it." He waved her hand away and adjusted it himself. "This is the second fundraiser they've had in two months. Enough's enough."

"I thought you liked the Marlanders." Suzanne pulled back her hand as she turned to scrutinize Adam's body language.

"Burt's a good guy, and I can take Barbara in small doses. I guess I'm not in the mood for another Saturday night fundraiser."

Did he just roll his eyes? Adam always seemed to live for these social events. He was making no sense. She adjusted her clothing so it wouldn't wrinkle under the seatbelt. In anticipation of a special evening, she'd worn one of her favorite outfits, a form-fitting dress with shining rhinestones scattered across the front. It made her look youthful and cheery. Adam usually commented on her attire, but tonight? Not a word.

Rob would've noticed.

In a fit of kindness—or maybe desperation—she offered Adam an escape. "We can always beg off, say one of us isn't feeling well."

"No, I've got to keep up appearances—show up and smile. Part of my job."

"Have you always felt this way?" Suzanne squinted in confusion.

"No." He shifted gears with relish and gunned it. "Just since I had to fire Tom."

"You're under a lot of stress. You're doing his job as well as yours and interviewing for his replacement." She said it in a slow and even voice, as if she needed to soothe a psychiatric patient threatening to fall off the couch.

"That's true, but it's more than that. What Tom and his family went through was so unfair. Yes, he'd made a mistake, but with the way the bank treated him, you would've thought he'd bought a rifle and shot a couple

FALLING APART, FALLING FOR YOU

tellers." His voice rose. "The crime didn't fit the punishment, at least in my book. But I'm the one who had to carry out the sentence."

"And you can't rinse the bad taste out of your mouth?"

He stared straight ahead. "It's souring my feelings about a lot of things."

A lot of things? Suzanne froze. This conversation wasn't sounding promising.

Adam turned into the Marlanders' horseshoe driveway, and the discussion came to a halt.

The valet whisked Suzanne's door open. She leaped out, hoping a change of venues would improve Adam's mood.

It didn't.

Inside, Adam put his happy face back on and served as a delightful representative of his bank, but Suzanne sensed the difference. He reacted well to anyone who approached him, but otherwise made no effort to engage. They hadn't even left the driveway when he blurted, "I am so glad that's over." He turned to her, his face serious. "Thanks for putting up with me tonight."

Suzanne reached over and patted his hand. *There, there.* She prayed he'd return to his old self. Perhaps a change of subject would help.

"I've taken a few more steps in my job search." Their prior conversations about it had dead ended, so this time, she forced herself to say it in a chipper tone.

"Oh. Good." His interest seemed underwhelming.

"I've come up with a list of things I do well, and I'm looking up the keywords on job boards."

"Finding anything?"

"Other than Walmart greeter, not yet."

"You'd be a great Walmart greeter." Adam laughed in earnest for the first time that night.

"You think?" She leaned toward him with a grin, encouraging their banter to continue.

"You have good observational skills, so you'd catch all the shoplifters. You love to talk with strangers, and there are lots of strange people who wander into Walmart. And even at your age, you're still able to stand all day."

Offended but unwilling to further explore Adam's moods, she turned away and puffed out a sigh. "I'm whipped. That last week of training did me in. How about dropping me off?"

"Look, Suzanne. I know I've been annoying tonight. I'm sorry. It's got nothing to do with you. Maybe we can do something tomorrow. I promise to be in a better state of mind."

"Want to go to church with me?" *May as well go for it.*

The side of his mouth twitched. "Nah. I'll pass. How about a trip to the aviary in the afternoon? Maybe you can feed the penguins again. You really enjoyed that last time."

"Sounds terrific. Two o'clock?"

"Perfect. See you tomorrow, *mon chou*." He leaned to his right and pressed her cheek with a quick kiss.

Suzanne let herself out of the car. She trudged along the walkway to her condo, rode an elevator to the eleventh floor, unlocked the door, dropped her purse to the floor, and threw herself onto the couch, feeling exhausted mentally more than physically. Try as she might, she couldn't figure the man out. But she wouldn't give up easily.

In the past, Suzanne would not have gone up for prayer. But today, at the end of the Sunday service, she flew down the aisle and planted herself in front of a middle-aged man-and-woman prayer team.

"And what do you need prayer for today, precious one?" The man asked as gently as she imagined Jesus would.

Suzanne, choking up, reached in her pocket for a tissue. "All of a sudden, my life's in an uproar."

FALLING APART, FALLING FOR YOU

"How so?" Concern washed over the face of the woman to his left.

"My daughter and I had a nasty exchange on the phone the other night. I'm out of work with no prospects in sight." Suzanne wiped her nose but let the tears fall. "And the man I thought was falling in love with me is behaving strangely." She wiped her nose again.

As she talked, the man and woman murmured a few soothing mm-hmms. They laid their hands on Suzanne's shoulders and prayed aloud for her.

Sobs, uncontrollable ones, heaved from deep in her chest, making it difficult for her to hear the words. When they finished praying, Suzanne wiped her nose again and thanked them.

She plodded over to an empty pew to continue praying alone. Others around her talked, laughed, or prayed. The noisy hum comforted her. Then someone turned up the lights, signaling the need to vacate for the next service. Even though she still had no answers, she figured they'd come in time. After all, she'd prayed.

A few hours later, Suzanne peered out her living room window and spotted Adam's red coupe in the distance, zipping along the winding street leading to her building. She glanced in a mirror to adjust a tendril of hair, checked the zipper on her white slacks, and unbuttoned an extra button at the top of her red linen blouse. Satisfied, she grabbed her clutch and caught an elevator to the ground floor.

Already waiting outside, Adam leaned on his car door, arms folded. As soon as he saw her coming out of the elevator, he stepped forward to open the condo door for her.

"You are such a gentleman." Suzanne teased.

He planted a kiss on her right cheek, then held her by the shoulders and kissed her on the left. "Love that perfume." He took a second inhale of her.

She pretended to fan herself and laughed, deep and sexy.

"Aren't we in a good mood today." She lifted her chin high as she dropped herself into the low bucket seat.

"Yes, I am." Adam circled the car and hopped into his side. "I promised you I would be." He grinned.

"Any particular reason?" Suzanne raised an eyebrow. *Maybe today will be a good time to discuss our future.*

"Oh, I just had a great conversation with someone in New York. Business, you know." Adam started the car and shifted into drive.

"On a Sunday?" She looked down and adjusted a ring on her right hand.

Adam kept a hand on the gearshift and glanced at her. "Yeah. Something's brewing, and I want to stay on top of it."

"Another big problem like Tom?"

"No, not a problem, just something looming on the horizon." A ray of sun lit up his clean-shaven face as he turned to her. "Have you found any job openings you like?"

"Not yet. I finally posted a résumé. It's not my best effort, but if I'm lucky, someone will call me and save me the headache of pounding the pavement."

"If you're interested, I could probably get you a job in our Training and Professional Development department."

"Really?" She sat in silence as she considered the offer.

"Well, what do you think?" He shifted gears and glanced over at her.

"You're such a sweetheart." She rested her hand on his and squeezed it in appreciation. "I'm sure you could pull strings and get me a job at your bank, but I don't think that would look so good for you. And if people got wind of my connection to you, it would hurt my credibility."

FALLING APART, FALLING FOR YOU

"Your choice." He steered left.

"But thanks." She gave his hand another squeeze. "Thoughtful of you to offer."

"Keep in mind, too, we're going to that key customer event next week. It ought to be a good networking opportunity for you."

"Could you get me a list of everyone who'll be there? Then we can strategize about who would be best to talk with."

"Sure. I'll forward it to you."

A long line of people wound around the side of the aviary. Adam threw his hands up from the wheel. "Forget the aviary. Must be some kind of special event going on there today. How about we take a walk in West Park instead?"

She shrugged. "Sure. Doesn't matter to me."

Adam parked a couple blocks farther down the road. He opened Suzanne's door and she linked her arm in his. They wound their way along the asphalt paths of the old city park.

"I love all the mature trees in this park." Suzanne looked up and waved her arm high toward the canopy shading them from the bright sun.

"When I was in sixth grade, I collected leaves for a science project. I've loved leaves ever since. And tree bark too. Look at that beautiful, speckled sycamore." Suzanne pointed to one on her left. "Nature's camouflage tree, that's what I always call them."

He took hold of Suzanne's arm. "Let's cross the street and walk along the Lake Elizabeth Bridge."

They reached the crest of the small bridge and leaned on the warm cement railing.

Suzanne fluttered her fingers on it. "I'm not sure what kind of job I should aim for." *I'm being as evasive as the camouflage of a sycamore tree.*

"What do you mean?" Adam's chin pulled back. "I thought you wanted to do training, like you've done all your career."

"Probably. But I don't know if I should travel. I thought maybe you'd want me to find a job where I'd stay local."

He looked out over the lake beneath them. "It's not up to me to say. It's your career, Suzanne, and it's your decision. I would never try to tell you what you should or shouldn't do."

"But I'd like to know—"

A disheveled young man approached them. "Got a few bucks to spare, mister?"

Adam dismissed him with a shake of his head, and the man shuffled on. Adam leaned over the railing and stared in the dirty water below. "A place like this always looks better from afar, doesn't it? Let's go see if the aviary has cleared out."

The line still snaked around the building. Adam shrugged. "I don't think this is our day for bird watching, do you?"

"It's okay. We can go back to my place and have a glass of wine, maybe watch some golf on TV, if you'd like."

"Tempting. But I think I'm going to do some follow-up on that call I had earlier today."

He dropped her off. She stood at the curb and stared as his sports car pulled away. *What is going on with him?*

CHAPTER 14

RACHEL

Rachel kept to the speed limit and stayed in the slow lane all the way to Pittsburgh International Airport. *Stan should be driving. He always did the highway driving.* She took a few deep breaths to prevent herself from crying, then plastered a fake smile on her face. It made her feel ridiculous, but someone had told her that you can't cry when you're grinning. She held the pose for a minute. *My gosh, it works!*

Near the airport, the signs popped up fast—departing flights, arriving flights, rental cars. She kept moving, thankful the speed limit signs now read fifteen miles per hour. If only the other drivers would obey. Signs for parking options came up next. Short-term parking, long-term parking, extended parking, VIP parking, Gold Key parking, and cellphone parking. *Who wants to park a cellphone?*

At the last possible second, she careened into the short-term lot. She found an open spot, planted her parking ticket inside her wallet, and scurried toward the terminal. She located a ladies' room just in time.

Signs directed her to a jam-packed area where she could wait for Pete. Thank goodness he agreed to delay his trip until June. She'd needed some time alone after Stan's passing. But now, she looked forward to having Pete around.

She picked an open spot in the front of the crowd so she'd have a clear view of arriving passengers. The man to her left reeked of cigarette smoke, somewhat offset by the heavy perfume of the woman on her right. To distract herself from the odors, she read her step counter. Nine hundred twenty-two steps. The closed rivet on her jeans hadn't given her a stomachache during the long drive here.

"Hi, Mom."

Rachel looked up, having neglected to notice a stream of travelers disembarking the tram.

"Pete!" She wrapped him in a bear hug. Sudden tears slipped down her cheeks. She wiped them with her sleeve.

She'd just seen Pete a couple months ago, but he looked somehow different to her now—a little weary, with a few gray hairs popping out at the temple. "How was your flight?"

"Good. Direct flight, but hard on the legs in the window seat." Pete massaged his thigh.

"Let's get you home." Rachel squeezed his arm.

Pete took the escalator to retrieve his luggage as Rachel went for the car. She found him waiting in the passenger pick-up lane. As he loaded his suitcases in the trunk, she skirted around the front of the car and flopped onto the passenger seat. With a sigh of relief, she handed Pete the keys.

He chuckled and took the wheel of the Chevy. "How long did it take you to get to the airport?"

"More than an hour. But once they finish that highway, it'll be a lot quicker."

He glanced over at her. "You're looking good, Mom."

"Thanks, Petie. That's sweet of you. I've been walking a lot."

"Good for you."

Rachel examined her son's profile as he drove. He looked so much like Stan, just a younger version. *Would Pete suffer a heart attack at an early age too?* She turned off the radio. "You keeping on top of your health?"

FALLING APART, FALLING FOR YOU

"I try." He gave a one-shoulder shrug. "But it's hard to find time to exercise. I work long hours, and by the time I get home, all I want to do is have a beer and chill out."

"Maybe doing some physical work around the old house will be good for you." She crossed her legs. *When was the last time she'd been able to do that?* "And you know how much I appreciate it." Feeling safe in the passenger seat, she relaxed the rest of the trip.

"Doesn't the drive home always seem shorter?" She asked rhetorically as Pete pulled onto the red-dog stone driveway.

As he opened his door, he looked down. "I've never seen a driveway made of this stuff anywhere outside this area. Wonder why."

"I don't think you'll see much red-dog now, no matter where you go. They made it from the burned-up waste at the coal mines. On windy days, the smell carried all the way up here from Lyondale."

She scrunched her nose. "Phew-ee, it stank—everywhere except high up on Hilltop where the rich people lived. Remember that awful smell?"

"I do remember, now that you mention it." He pulled two huge black suitcases from the trunk.

Rachel poked him in the arm. "You didn't need to bring your whole wardrobe, Pete. I have a washing machine."

"It looks like this will be our last video call before you two get to town. Can you believe it? The reunion's only three weeks away." Rachel beamed, as if she were head of the welcoming party for arriving dignitaries. "You'll get to meet my oldest son, Pete. He's visiting from Denver."

"How nice," Suzanne said. "My daughter hasn't come to Pittsburgh in a long time." She sighed as she played with a lock of hair. "We had words on the phone the other day. I think Jill hates me."

"I'm sure she doesn't hate you." Marla rolled her eyes. "You'll patch it up. I've heard parents say their grown children are harder to deal with than when they were kids. But I can't prove it. I never—I never raised a child."

"My son, Pete, bless his heart, says he can tell I'm losing weight already. My clothes do fit better. But I'm not sure what I'll wear to the reunion. I was thinking of wearing this dress." She reached beside her and held up a bright floral dress. "What do you think?"

"Hmm. A bit loud, perhaps. What's that fabric?" Suzanne asked.

Marla scrunched up her nose. "You're *not* wearing that dress, Rachel. When I get there, I'll take you shopping. We'll go up to Pittsburgh."

"How fun," Suzanne said. "I'll show you the best places to shop here. How about we also get a facial, maybe a massage?"

"I've never had a massage." Rachel spoke with a note of tentativeness.

"No worries. We can skip the massage." Marla waved it away with her hand. "How about we go to a hair salon instead? My treat for everyone."

Rachel clasped her hands and bounced a few inches in her chair. "I've never done anything like this in my life. I can't wait." She turned serious and leaned toward her screen. "I appreciate you've offered to pay, Marla. So generous of you. To be honest, lately I've become a little concerned about my financial situation. Now that Stan's gone, the gas station isn't doing as well as I'd expected."

Marla crooked her head. "Why not?"

"At first, I thought it was because no one is doing any servicing—inspections, tires, that sort of thing. We're only pumping gas and selling typical convenience store items now. But the numbers aren't adding up." Rachel scrunched her face.

FALLING APART, FALLING FOR YOU

"I don't know anything about gas stations," Marla said, "but if the numbers aren't adding up, I suspect some funny business is going on with whoever's working there now."

"Oh, I don't think so. Lou Gestler's running it weekdays. He used to work evenings and weekends but offered to switch to daylight when Stan died. I have two high school boys from St. Cyp's for evenings and weekends. They're good kids. I know their families."

Marla raised an eyebrow. "Have you checked your security cameras?"

"Security cameras?" Rachel snorted. "We don't have any of those."

"Ask Pete to buy some. Do you think he'd be able to install them himself?"

Rachel shrugged. "I guess. He's very smart. He works with computers all the time."

"Good. Ask him to install the cameras some night after the place has closed."

Rachel pulled on her terrycloth robe and hurried downstairs barefoot. *Who needs an alarm clock with Pete in the house?* The sun peeked from the horizon as Pete clanked around in the kitchen making a pot of coffee.

In a flash, she sliced some sausage into a pan and turned on the gas.

"Sure smells good, Mom, but I think I'll have some cereal."

"You feeling sick?"

"No. Just trying to eat healthy, at least as much as I can. I figure eating well counteracts sitting on my butt all day." He pulled a box of cereal out of a cabinet and read the nutrition label. "Fourteen grams of sugar. Oh well, at least it won't clog my heart like sausage."

"Right." Rachel turned off the burner and whisked a quart of milk out of the refrigerator.

Pete filled a bowl with cereal and poured milk over it. "I think I'll work on the porch steps today."

A while later, when the banging had stopped, Rachel opened the front door to check his progress.

He'd already removed all five of the wooden steps. Pete wiped his hands on his jeans to clean off the dirt. "These steps were an accident waiting to happen." He tipped his head toward the house next door. "Mr. Sowak said I can borrow his pickup to bring home some lumber and paint. Do you need anything else while I'm over in Dunham City?"

Rachel hollered over to Frank, sitting in the usual spot on his front porch. "You're a good neighbor, Frank. Thanks."

"Glad to help out." Frank waved a hand and continued rocking.

"I'll give you my credit card." Rachel motioned for Pete to follow her inside. She repeated the conversation she'd had with Marla. "She seemed pretty sure we'd discover someone stealing."

"Could be. It'd be easy for someone working there to say unexpected loss is due to expired inventory being thrown out. Shoplifting's another possibility. I'll pick up some security cameras. We'll figure it out."

Cloud cover blocked any possibility of illumination from the heavens when Pete and Rachel pulled into the gas station near midnight, but the streetlights dotting Main Street provided some welcome pockets of light.

Pete parked behind the gas station so anyone passing by wouldn't be suspicious. They entered through the back door.

FALLING APART, FALLING FOR YOU

Rachel held up a large flashlight as Pete hung the cameras. He was working on the second one when someone pulled up in an SUV.

"Rats! It's the police." Rachel said it as if they'd been caught in the middle of a heist.

A uniformed police officer shone a flashlight at them as he stepped toward the entrance.

Pete squinted as he made his way to the front door. "It's Sergeant Dan," he whispered.

"Hi, Dan." Rachel smiled as she unlocked the plate glass door for him.

"Whatcha up to here, Rachel? Pete? Didn't expect to see you here so late." Dan spoke in a neutral voice as he shined his flashlight all around the inside of the building.

Rachel explained, and the police officer nodded.

"Makes sense. I'll get off your property right away so I don't stir up any questions. Let me know if you need help apprehending the culprit."

"We will for sure, Sarge. Thanks for keeping an eye on the place." Rachel closed the door behind him. She turned, pressed herself against the door, and laughed. "My heart is racing! I felt like we were getting caught committing a crime."

Pete chuckled. "It reminded me of the time I got caught throwing eggs at the Middleton school bus when their football team creamed us."

"What? You never told me about that."

Pete winked at her. "Dad and I knew how to keep secrets."

Rachel drizzled some red sauce onto the vegetable lasagna, then slid the casserole into the hot oven. She turned to look at Pete, still leaning into his computer screen. He'd been at it for hours, gathering information from the cameras.

After jotting a note on his tablet, Pete flicked his ballpoint pen. "You ready to watch this?"

Rachel stepped over to the table and sighed. "May as well get it over with."

He fast-forwarded to a scene of Lou Gestler at work. "Here he is, going to the men's room." Pete skipped ahead on the camera feed. "Here he is twenty minutes later, going to the men's room again."

Pete continued showing the same kind of scene until Rachel interrupted. "So, he goes to the bathroom a lot. That's not a crime."

"Right. But look at what happened when he went into the bathroom."

"There aren't any cameras in the restrooms. What are you talking about?"

"It seems some kids have realized Lou uses the facilities a lot, and they capitalize on the opportunity to shoplift. Let me show you what I mean."

"That's the Anderson boy—Brandon ... Brendon ... no, it's *Braydon*." Rachel wagged her finger at the boy on the screen. She pointed to another boy. "And that's little Donny Moore—if his mother only knew!"

"Well, there are a few more shots of these two shoplifting. We can talk more about that later. Here's what you *really* need to see. Pete played with the keyboard for a moment then turned the computer screen so Rachel could see it. "This is the high school boy who worked last night."

"That's Ethan." She stretched her neck toward the screen and squinted. "What's he doing with those customers?"

"I hate to say it, but I think he's dealing drugs."

Rachel's mouth fell wide open. "In *my* gas station?"

"It looks that way. We'll have to take this computer over to Sergeant Dan. He'll figure it out."

FALLING APART, FALLING FOR YOU

"I don't want to get involved in this!" Rachel threw her hands up in the air. "This is stuff your father could deal with, but I can't." She stormed out of the room, alternating between crying and saying words she was sure Pete had never before heard from his mother.

A while later, she returned, jaw set and hands on hips. "We'll take care of this, and then I'm going to sell that gas station. Nothing like this would've happened if your father were alive. I can't deal with these kinds of issues alone. I'm a bookkeeper, not a police officer, and I hate managing employees—most of all when there are ugly problems like this."

Pete picked up the laptop and put his arm around his mother. "Let's go to the police station and see what Sarge has to say. You can decide about the business later."

She complained all the way there.

CHAPTER 15

MARLA

Marla turned onto Aunt Adele's driveway, hands tight on the wheel of her white BMW coupe, as she began her ascent of the long, winding red-dog trail. A tall stand of hemlocks loomed ahead on the right. Once she passed them, the old Victorian mansion would be in view.

After the last hemlock, she put the car in park. Reflection didn't come naturally for her, but here in this driveway, she chose to absorb every detail of her experience. Steeled for this unrepeatable moment, she looked up at the house. In spite of all her mental preparation, she hadn't anticipated the flood of emotion that struck her like a hard slap. She had to force herself to breathe.

Painful memories leaped to her mind—the party back home that led to her banishment to this remote house, the isolation she endured at St. Cyprian's Academy, the void in her heart that could have been filled by keeping her baby. Her baby. She hoped her daughter's life had turned out well. *Maybe God took care of her. I sure didn't.*

Her eyes focused on the details of her aunt's home. The creamy white paint had faded to a dingy gray. The windows were caked with dust, and several appeared cracked. The once-dainty shrubs surrounding the house now threatened to conceal the entire first floor.

This home where her mother had grown up, and where Aunt Adele still lived, had once been a showcase, more spectacular than the mansions on Millionaire's Row. Its setting distinguished it most of all—high atop a hill, overlooking both the town and the river, surrounded by fifty acres of woods, meadows, and rolling hills. A jewel of a house.

No more.

"Marlee! Marlee!" Aunt Adele waved to her from the wraparound porch. All these years, she'd never called her anything but Marla.

She waved back and clambered up the curved stone steps to the porch. "Aunt Adele, it's so good to see you!"

As they hugged, Marla petted her aunt's thin white hair, pasted to her scalp. It had once been thick, a lustrous black mane.

Aunt Adele wept, tears draining into the wrinkles around her eyes and mouth, as Marla patted her thin, bony back. *Is she eating right?*

The tears finally spent, Aunt Adele led Marla into the home. "Please excuse the mess." She fluttered her hand back and forth. "I've been having such a time keeping up with the cleaning."

Marla did a quick intake. Toast left on a plate. Stacks of *Port Mariette Gazettes*. A thick coating of dust on the antique furniture. When she lived there her senior year, she used to say if she stood still long enough, Aunt Adele would dust her.

"The place looks lovely," Marla said. "It just needs a little TLC."

They entered the high-ceilinged kitchen. Aunt Adele shuffled toward the teapot then turned toward Marla. "Would you be a dear and make some tea, Marlee?"

Certain she'd heard her say "Marlee" this time, Marla furrowed her brow. "Is that a new nickname you've created for me?"

FALLING APART, FALLING FOR YOU

"Nickname? No, that's your name, dear."

"My name's Marla. Not Marlee." She was filled with a rush of guilt for not keeping in better touch.

"Oh, right. Marla is your name. I remember now. You have to understand, I'm 88 years old ... or is it 89? Anyway, things get a bit muddled at my age."

Marla heated some water and made the tea. Sitting at the cozy round table in the turret, she clinked the china teacup back on its saucer. "Tell me, Aunt Adele, what's life like for you these days? How do you spend your time?"

Her aunt looked out the window for a moment, as if searching for an answer. "I do a little of this, and a little of that."

"Such as?"

"Oh, that's a difficult question. Let me think about it for a moment."

"Okay. While you're thinking, I'll take my suitcases upstairs to my old room. No need for you to get up. Maybe I'll take a look around upstairs, too, if you don't mind."

"Go right ahead, dear." She drew the teacup to her lips.

Three floors and a basement to cover. Thank goodness she'd worn flats. On the second floor, she entered the room she'd occupied during her year of penance. It looked just as she'd left it—antique white furniture, a cotton-candy colored bedspread, and teen magazines still stacked on the dresser. She picked one up— Daryl Hall and John Oates on the cover—and flipped through a few pages. She blew out a loud breath, a combination of a sigh, a laugh, and a cry.

Humming "Private Eyes," she sauntered down the hall toward her aunt's bedroom. The closer she got, the stronger the smell became. Urine? Decaying food? Lack of bathing? *Probably a combination.* She peered into the room. Rumpled bedding, laundry overflowing in a plastic basket, and a dusty display of ceramic knickknacks, Victorian dolls, and Smurfs on the dresser. She backed out of the room and took the steps to the upper floor. Empty, as it had been forty years ago, except for a collection of cobwebs and dead bugs.

She returned to the kitchen and found Aunt Adele staring into her empty teacup.

"Oh! Marlee, when did you get here?"

Marla thought for a moment before responding. "I just got here, Aunt Adele. Let me look in the refrigerator to see what we'll need from the store." She poked her head inside. Salad dressings, condiments, limp carrots, expired milk, moldy Swiss cheese, yogurt, and butter. "When's the last time you went grocery shopping?"

"Oh, I don't know. Sometimes one of the ladies from St. Cyp's takes me to church, then we pick up some food after Mass."

Judging by the expiration dates, last trip was probably in May. Marla tucked her clutch under her arm. "I'm going to run to the store. I'll be back soon."

Guilt washed over her as she drove. Should have visited her, or at least called more often.

Marla pushed a squeaky grocery cart up and down the Dairy Mart aisles, tossing into it anything she thought might appeal to her aunt—especially anything that didn't have an upcoming expiration date. By the time she arrived at the checkout lane, groceries sprouted from both sides of the cart.

The man in line ahead of her turned. Staring at the overflowing cart, he jerked his head. "Feeding an army, eh?"

He was a tall man, perhaps in his early sixties, fit and tan, with light gray hair that wanted to stick out like straw rather than lay according to the shape of his head.

Marla explained she was buying for her aunt.

He looked her over. "You don't live here, do you?"

"How could you tell?" Reaching in her Hermes handbag, she pulled out a red ostrich leather wallet.

He shook his head and chuckled. "You stand out in this town like a swan in a coal mine."

FALLING APART, FALLING FOR YOU

"That's a compliment?"

"Of course." He grinned. "Who's your aunt?"

"Adele Napoli."

"Sweet old lady. Haven't seen her in a while. Tell her Mitch said hi."

The cashier had finished bagging the man's order. He paid with cash, and she gave him his change.

He tipped his head to Marla. "Welcome to Port Mariette." He turned and strode out the door.

The cashier, a rotund middle-aged woman wearing a flowered apron with ruffled edges, nodded hello to Marla, then rang up her items.

Marla watched the man named Mitch lope across the street. He hopped into a green pickup truck with a logo on the door. She squinted but couldn't make it out.

"That'll be ninety-one dollars and eighty-two cents, ma'am."

Marla handed her a credit card.

The woman read the name on it before swiping it. She looked up at Marla and smiled before handing it back to her.

Marla grabbed the bags to leave. As she neared the door, a balding, bespectacled man entered. His eyes opened wide. "Is that you, Marla?"

"Yes. I'm Marla." She stared at his pale lunar face for clues but didn't recognize him.

"Herbie Herbinger. You're in town for the reunion?"

"Oh, Herbie. How nice to see you! Yes, I came early to spend time with my Aunt Adele."

"You know, I read about you in the *Wall Street Journal*. A pretty amazing story. Your husband must be proud of you."

"Are you asking if I'm married, Herbie?" She tipped her head to one side.

He spread his hands out to the side. "I've been divorced for a dozen years, Marla. Look at you—can you blame me?"

"A leopard never changes its spots." She laughed as she shifted the bags of groceries around with her fingers.

"Let me help you with those bags." He reached for a few without waiting for a response. "Want to sit on a bench? There's one right outside. We can catch up for a minute."

"Why not?" She had some questions she'd like to ask him. They sat down on a wrought iron bench in front of the antique shop.

"How's the old town looking to you after all these years?" Herbie grinned as he waved his arm from one end of the street to the other.

"Truthfully?" Marla arched an eyebrow.

Herbie jerked his double chin back. "Well, sure."

She decided to be kind. "Let me put it this way. It could use some attention."

Herbie frowned and looked down at the sidewalk. "Since the coal mines closed and the steel mill cut back operations, things have changed. Most of the young people moved away over the years, and those of us who remain are just trying to keep things going."

"I see."

Herbie brightened. "I'm expecting the town will pick up again when they finish the new highway by the end of the year." He pointed to the left. "They're expecting to put an exit about a half a mile from the gas station. Plenty of people will need a place to stop for gas or a meal, and I think that place will be Port Mariette."

"Could well be." She tapped a forefinger on her lips. "I guess time will tell."

"Your aunt must be glad you're spending some time with her. How's she doing?

Marla told him about Aunt Adele's mental slide. "She can't continue to live alone in that house. She needs someone around to help her with meals, bathing, and keeping her mind active."

"There's a nice place near here where our old folks go— Sunset Hills. It's one of those 'continuum of care' facilities. They decide what level of care a person needs, and the

FALLING APART, FALLING FOR YOU

payment is based on that. My mother used to live there. She loved it. They even have an indoor pool. Many of the older people around here have pension plans from either the coal mines or the steel industry, so they can afford a nice place."

"I'll check it out. Thanks for the idea."

"Your aunt's house looks like it might need some help too."

"It does." Marla nodded.

"If you want to fix it up, you might want to talk with Mitch Mitchell. He's a contractor, lived here all his life. He can handle any kind of construction or renovation. Earlier this year, he renovated the bank." He pointed up the street.

"It looks marvelous. Maybe I'll look him up."

"Or if you want to sell it, Mary Frances from our class is the only real estate agent in Port Mariette. She's right across the street." He jutted his chin in the direction of her office.

"You're a wealth of information, Herbie. I appreciate it." She uncrossed her legs, preparing to leave.

Herbie cleared his throat. "I ... I know you're busy with your aunt, but I'd like to take you to dinner sometime while you're here. You're quite the celebrity, and it would be an honor to be with you even for an evening."

Marla smiled at Herbie's simple request. "You've been so helpful to me already, Herbie. Sure, it'd be nice to have dinner with you sometime. Here's my number." She handed him her business card as she stood. "I've got to get this food back to my aunt's."

On the drive back, Marla's phone rang. It was Rachel. "Heard you're in town."

The dust brought forth new allergies in Marla. She sneezed herself awake around dawn, padded down to the kitchen to get a cup of tea, then made her way back upstairs to shower.

"Good morning, Marla," Aunt Adele chirped from her bedroom. "Did you sleep well?"

"Like a baby."

"Come in and talk with me."

Marla took a deep breath and stepped into the room.

Aunt Adele patted the bed for Marla to join her. "What would my favorite niece like to do today?"

Marla smiled. It had been years since she'd heard that term of endearment from her aunt. "How about we take a drive around town? I'd love a tour."

Aunt Adele clasped her hands to her chest. "Oh my goodness, I would *love* to do that!"

They were in Marla's car within the hour. "Let's start at Hilltop Drive. Millionaire's Row is my favorite street."

As they approached the first mansion, Aunt Adele pointed to the right. "Stop there."

Marla pulled over as Aunt Adele launched into tour guide mode.

"This mansion is now a funeral home, but the Bixby family built it. Harry Bixby was president of the steel mill and an elder at First Presbyterian Church." She pursed her lips. "He tried to keep it quiet that a man had been killed in the hot mill. The story got out, of course, and they fired Mr. Bixby."

She pointed to a mansion across the street. "The owner of the coal mine built that one. In those days, people didn't finish their basements, but his had a bar stocked with booze and a wine cellar, along with an upholstered sofa. Some say it rolled open into a bed." She winked at Marla.

Marla chuckled. "Your memory is amazing."

"Some days it is. Some days it isn't." Aunt Adele bit her lips. She looked at Marla with pleading eyes. "It's hard living alone. I know I'm doing better just having you here for a day. Would you like to move in with me again?"

FALLING APART, FALLING FOR YOU

Marla took her aunt's hand in hers. "I'd love to, but I can't. I'll be here for a month or so, then I have to go back to New York." She softly squeezed her aunt's hand. "I'm sure living alone can be hard."

"It is." Aunt Adele nodded.

"Maybe you'd like to live with some other people who can make life easier for you?"

Her aunt stiffened and pulled her hand away.

The silence continued. Marla let the matter go. "Tell me about this one up here on the left, the Queen Anne. I love all those gables and dormers."

Her aunt lit up again. "The founder of the bank owned that one. He had three daughters, and they all became nuns. People say the girls saw an apparition of the Blessed Virgin and that's why they all joined a convent. I don't know if that was true, but I'd always hoped so."

"It would be nice if it were, wouldn't it?"

"Yes, indeed." Aunt Adele pointed again. "This one on the right, with the cupola and slate roof—it was a safe house in the Underground Railroad, but no one knew until Mrs. Forrest died. She left behind a notebook describing how she and her husband provided for the slaves. Once they left here, they'd make their way to Ashtabula, Ohio, then cross Lake Erie into Canada."

They continued along, with Aunt Adele recounting stories at each mansion.

Marla parked in front of the last one. "Some of these houses are in great shape. Wonder who lives in them now."

She looked at Marla. "I'm glad you never got divorced."

"Well, to get divorced, you have to be married." Marla chuckled.

"Marriage—pff! It's not all it's cracked up to be. I've had a wonderful life as a single woman. I think St. Paul had the right idea when he said it's better to remain single if you can."

They dipped down to Hickory Road, the mansions now high on the hill behind them.

"I heard there's a place near here called Sunset Hills." Marla tried to sound casual. "Ever heard of it?"

"Oh yes, that's where all the old folks go." She let out a titter, then folded her hands in her lap and stared at them. "It's time for me to go there, isn't it, Marla? That's what the women from St. Cyp's have been telling me."

Marla pulled the car to the curb and stopped. She leaned over and caressed her aunt's face. "Yes, my favorite aunt. It's time."

CHAPTER 16

Suzanne

*"I love you.
 I'm sorry.
 Can you forgive me?"*

After agonizing for a few days, Suzanne wrote these words in elaborate calligraphy at the bottom of a drawing of herself and her daughter. Their arms were wrapped around one another's waists and their heads touched, temple to temple. The pose, although far from the reality of their current relationship, did represent Suzanne's hope for them. *Does Jill have the same hope?*

Suzanne slid the artwork into a silver frame, then bubble-wrapped it with three layers. The bundle reminded her of when she used to swaddle Jill as a baby. *You can say anything to a baby, and they love you. Adult children, everything you say is suspect.*

She placed the gift in a sturdy cardboard box and filled the extra space with packing peanuts. After a prayer that the message inside would be well received, Suzanne vowed she'd never again ask Jill about having a baby.

But could her behavior really be as bad as Jill had said? She called her mother to find out. "Hi, Mom. Got a minute?"

"Sure. Let me turn off the burner. I'm frying a little bacon and I don't want to burn it." She clunked the phone down. "Okay. What's on your mind?"

"I have a question for you, Mom, and I'd appreciate a direct answer." Her mother had a way of dancing around issues, like Adam did. "Am I controlling?"

"Controlling?"

"Yes, as in 'manipulative'?"

"Hmm. Maybe a little, dear."

Oh boy. There it was—her mother's confirmation. To her, "a little" meant "a lot." She probably had a whole pound of bacon in that pan right now.

"Why do you ask?" Without waiting for an answer, she continued in a hushed voice. "Oh, no. Did something happen with Adam?"

"Not Adam—Jill. She told me I'm controlling. She got upset because I asked her if she and Drew would ever find time to have a baby." Suzanne bit her lip and rolled her eyes. "I've obviously asked her that before."

There was a pause, her mother breathing. "Is that the only time she's told you you're controlling?"

"No. She's told me before." Suzanne tensed her facial muscles.

Her mother stayed silent, so Suzanne answered the question herself. "I guess I need to be less controlling, huh?"

"We all have room for improvement."

"But how do I *do* that? I mean, how does a controlling person become ... less controlling?"

"An expression just came to my mind. 'Go let ...'—no that's not it—'Let God' ... hmm."

"It's okay Mom, I'll figure it out."

"I've got it! 'Let go, let God,' Yes. 'Let go and let God.' Maybe God is speaking to you, sweetie. Give it some thought."

"That's good, Mom." Suzanne scrunched her lips. "I will. Thanks."

"You're welcome."

"I'm going to work on my finely honed procrastination skills now. I've got to get cracking on my job search. Love you, Mom."

FALLING APART, FALLING FOR YOU

"Love you too, Suzie. Bye."

Suzanne opened her laptop and read the résumé she'd written last week. *What a pathetic effort.* She vowed she wouldn't get up until she had refined it and posted it on some job boards.

She picked up a lined tablet from the kitchen island and reviewed the list of traits and capabilities she'd written down earlier.

Experienced trainer
Good communicator
Artistic
Persuasive, fun, can talk to a stone
Independent, reliable, trustworthy
Flexible, love change and surprises

Surprises. Rob was always full of surprises. Maybe not such a bad thing. But then again, he had more bad ones than good ones. Like being anchored in California. Near his ex-wife. It would never work.

She trained her thoughts back to her job search but made no progress. She called Marla for ideas. She'd always been the smartest one of the three.

"Marla, it's Suzanne. Are you busy with your aunt, or do you have time to talk?"

"She's napping. What's up?"

"Can I brainstorm with you for a minute? I've made up a list of my traits and skills for this job search, but my mind's a jumble."

"Sure. Read me the list."

Suzanne ticked off what she'd written.

"Sounds to me like you're a natural at sales. People who can sell are always in demand."

"I never even thought about selling something."

"You could sell either a product or a service, but since you've spent most of your career in training, selling a service like training programs would be right up your alley. If you still want to deliver seminars, there are companies that send trainers across the country. They repeat the same program over and over but to people from all walks of life. Or if you don't want to travel, you could deliver training at one location—like a large employer's corporate headquarters."

Marla took a breath then continued her barrage of ideas. "Or, since you're so artistic, maybe you'd want to sell art products, or work in an art gallery, or be a fundraiser for an art museum. You could give demonstrations of how to use products, do voiceovers for commercials, or start a calligraphy business."

"Gosh, Marla, in five seconds you've come up with more ideas than I have in two weeks. Thanks a million."

"Any time."

Suzanne twirled her pen. She realized she had, once again, been thinking only about herself. She switched the conversation to Marla. "So, do you have any stories for the *Port Mariette Gazette*?"

"Nothing newsworthy going on here—I'm just getting to know my aunt again."

"I'm sure she's thrilled to have you home for a while."

"She is, but it's jarring to see how much she's aged."

"I can imagine. Forty years is a long time to be away. I can't wait to see you and Rachel in person. It kind of makes me giddy, like I'm in high school again."

"Let's leave those giggles for Rachel. She was always queen of giggles in our little group."

"That she was. When the three of us get together, I'll stay overnight at my mom's if we're going to be out late. I don't want to drive in the dark all the way back to Pittsburgh."

"In Manhattan, I never drive. I had to ship my car from Florida so I could drive it here from New York. Anyway, maybe we can talk Rachel into being our tour guide."

Tour guide. Would Rob enjoy a tour of Port Mariette? Of Pittsburgh?

FALLING APART, FALLING FOR YOU

"Rachel's so accommodating, I don't think she'd mind squiring us around town." Suzanne put down her pen. "Thanks again for your ideas. You'd be a great career counselor."

"You're most welcome. See you soon."

"This is going to be wild," Suzanne said. "At least by Port Mariette standards."

The next morning, Suzanne's inbox brimmed with messages. Most of them turned out to be spam, but one email appeared promising.

The message came from a large, well-known insurance company. The sender, a woman named Lily Frantz, wrote that Suzanne appeared to be well qualified for one of their open positions. The woman closed her email with a request—"Please call as soon as possible to discuss the opportunity."

Suzanne threw her arms high in the air. "Yes!"

She rushed to the bathroom to shower. She applied her makeup with care, then combed her closet for the perfect outfit. She chose a royal blue sweater, accenting it with a classic gold chain necklace and gold ball earrings. After all, this phone call with Lily might well turn into a video interview.

She took a few slow, deep breaths to calm herself, put a smile on her face, and dialed the number.

A robot answered.

Suzanne plugged in the extension Lily Frantz had provided in her email.

Lily popped on the line after the first ring.

Suzanne introduced herself. "I'm calling to follow up on the email you sent me about a job opening."

In a chirpy voice, Lily thanked Suzanne for calling. She chattered about the company's reputation, its exciting plans for the future, and the array of products and services in the company's portfolio.

This went on for about ten minutes. *She must be serious about me.*

Next, she ticked off the skills Suzanne seemed to possess. "Based on your résumé, I imagine you're persuasive, that you have great verbal communication skills, a professional demeanor, and you're people-oriented. Do you agree?"

"Oh, yes." Suzanne stood and walked around the kitchen island to burn off some of her growing excitement.

With breathy confidence, Lily said, "Great! We think you'd be an ideal insurance agent."

Oof. Suzanne's face fell so low, it felt like it reached her chest.

"You *are* interested, aren't you?" Lily asked in her chirpy voice.

"Thank you, but no. I wouldn't be interested in selling insurance. Do you happen to have any openings in your training department?"

She knew the answer before Lily even replied. The call ended a moment later. Lily no doubt had other people to hoodwink with her email.

In a funk, she pulled out her sketchbook and flipped through the pages of drawings—the river, the city, trees, flowers, and the people in her life. She noticed a drawing of Rob she'd started but not finished. She'd captured most of his facial features, but none of his personality. Perhaps she should remove his page from the sketchbook. After all, in their last conversation, they'd agreed to be "just friends."

She flipped to a blank page. She gripped an ink pen and stared at the page, not knowing what to write or draw. Jill, Adam, and her job search were pushing her to the end of her tether.

FALLING APART, FALLING FOR YOU

Tears welled up in her eyes. Sobs of frustration built to a crescendo of wails. She let it all out. That peace she'd felt weeks ago, the peace she'd felt when she'd surrendered her life to the Lord—where did it go? *I've taken everything back again.*

"Lord, forgive me for taking my life back." She prayed aloud. "I surrender again. I surrender everything—my life, my job, my relationship with my daughter, my relationship with Adam, my 'whatever this is' with Rob."

She jotted down the prayer she'd just said aloud. She didn't want to repeat her mistake of taking her life back and hoped a written prayer would serve as a reminder the next time she backslid. She left the sketchbook open on her nightstand to allow the ink to dry and went to the kitchen, where she spotted the box containing the drawing she'd done for Jill. It practically screamed "procrastinator" at her.

She made a beeline to the post office. On the way back, she popped into the grocery for yogurt and gave Dorothy a jar of arthritis cream, then she stopped at one of the observation decks. Her eyes zeroed in on the baseball stadium across the river.

Good batters don't hit every pitch—maybe a third of the time at best. Yet they never stop trying to improve. All these years, I've been like a coach who has trained everyone else to be better. But I failed to improve myself.

She made a mental list of the negative traits she'd work on. Seeing no one around, she spoke out loud to the vast expanse above her. "I used to be a selfish, controlling, procrastinating, backslidden Christian.

"But no more."

CHAPTER 17

RACHEL

Sergeant Dan chicken-scratched another note on his lined legal pad as he peered into Pete's computer. He swiveled his chair around to the coffeepot on the credenza behind him and refilled his mug, then looked over his shoulder at Rachel and Pete. "Coffee?"

"No, thanks," said Pete.

Rachel shook her head and pursed her lips. *Let's get this over with.*

The sergeant poured a generous amount of half-and-half. He took his time stirring, then tapped the spoon on the lip. One-two-three. Mug in hand, he turned around to face Rachel and Pete on the other side of the gray metal desk.

Rachel fidgeted in an old cracked-leather armchair. She kept her hands in her lap, not wanting to touch anything, and pressed a cuticle back with her thumbnail.

Pete sat next to her in a dirty cloth chair, stiff as an ironing board.

Rachel looked up. "Well, what do you think, Sarge?"

"Looking at these tapes, I think your son would make a good detective." He smiled as he leaned back in his chair and rested his hands across his ample stomach.

"Yes, but what can we do about what showed up here?" Rachel jabbed her finger toward the computer screen.

"It depends. You have to make some decisions about what you're willing to do." Sergeant Dan reached for his mug and took a gulp.

"Like what?" Pete asked.

"You'll need to talk to Lou Gestler about why he's going to the can every twenty minutes. Maybe it's boredom. Maybe it's a medical issue. Who knows? But you can't have your only employee leaving the place unattended like that. It's an invitation to punks like Braydon Anderson and Donny Moore. They spot an opportunity, and then, *car-pay dee-um.*" He waved his hands around, raking in some imaginary merchandise.

"Okay, I'll talk with Lou, but what about Braydon and Donny?" Rachel crossed her arms with a sigh.

"How much money are we talking about here, Rachel? How much has been lost?"

"It's difficult to say because it's more of a hunch than hard numbers. When Stan ran the place, I knew what to expect every week. But since I switched from being a service station to a gas station, I haven't had enough history to know for sure."

Sergeant Dan leaned over his desk, his hands tented in front of him. "Can you give me a guesstimate?"

Rachel scrunched up her nose and shrugged. "Maybe ten dollars a week at first, but now, more like twenty-five?" Her voice went up at the end.

"So, we're talking small potatoes."

"Small to you, but it's out of *my* pocket. Besides, I don't like the trend."

"I don't think you want to take something like this to the magistrate."

Pete leaned forward. "What would you suggest?"

"Might be better if I call the parents. Bring them and their kids in. Give the boys a good talking to." He took a gulp. "I find in these petty theft cases, sometimes it's best to catch 'em when they're young, scare the—the crap out

FALLING APART, FALLING FOR YOU

of them. They're more prone to get back on the straight and narrow."

Rachel brightened. "I like that idea. It sounds reasonable, and I won't have to appear in court. That would give me the creeps."

Pete piped up. "Okay, that sounds like a good solution to the first situation, but what about the other problem—Ethan doing drug deals?"

"Now that's a little trickier." The sergeant leaned back in his chair as far as it would allow.

"How so?" Rachel feared he might land on the floor. She nibbled on her bottom lip.

"We've suspected for a while that Ethan was dealing drugs, but this is the first hard evidence we've come across. With his parents so well known in the community, we didn't want to move prematurely. Getting this evidence on tape is a big breakthrough."

Sergeant Dan looked at Pete. "Brilliant of you to install security cameras, by the way."

"Not my idea, but thanks."

"A friend of mine from New York City suggested it," said Rachel. "She's a successful businesswoman. She knew the cameras would help solve the mystery." Rachel broke eye contact with the sergeant and looked down at her lap. "We don't want anything to do with drugs in our gas station."

Pete crossed his arms. "My brother Brian died of an overdose. This is a hard topic for our family."

"I remember. Very sad." Sergeant Dan tapped his pen on the desk. "Does Ethan work the same schedule every week?"

"Yes. Tuesday and Friday evenings," said Rachel.

"According to the date stamp, it looks like this happens around the same time in the evening. If that's the case, we can catch him in the act the next time he works. We'll take him down right there. We'll call you when it's all over. Then neither of you will have to be involved."

"I like your plan." Rachel said, a smile in her voice.

"Good." Sergeant Dan nodded once and put his pen down. He pointed at Rachel. "So, you'll talk with Lou about his bathroom problem, right?"

"Right."

"We'll be ready for Ethan on Tuesday evening, and I'll take care of the petty thieves and their parents within the week." He clapped his palms together. "We're good to go, then. Keep in touch."

A grin formed across the sergeant's face. "Now don't you leave town, Rachel. You're not out of the woods on this just yet." He winked at her.

Rachel's eyes widened for a second, and then a smile washed across her face as she realized he was joking. "I'll be here." She shook his hand. "Thanks, Dan. I appreciate your help."

Pete nodded his thanks then guided Rachel by her elbow to the exit. Outside, he said, "I'll bet you're glad that's over."

"I hope it is." She slipped her arm around Pete's.

Rachel flitted around in her kitchen, putting last-minute details on the lunch she'd prepared for Suzanne and Marla. Even though they'd talked many times on video calls, seeing one another in person here in Port Mariette, in her own home, would be far more meaningful.

She'd come up with two recipes for their Sunday afternoon meal. For "Greek" Marla, she'd made spanakopita. For Suzanne, who'd spent so much time flying, Rachel had made a dish called Airplane Chicken Breast. Part of the chicken wing remained attached to the boneless breast, so it would resemble a plane's fuselage and one of its wings. Rachel hoped Suzanne was already familiar with the dish,

FALLING APART, FALLING FOR YOU

because what was baking in her oven didn't much resemble anything Boeing made.

The two dishes didn't complement one another, but Rachel hoped her friends would appreciate her efforts to please them. She'd never prepared either before today, and if one didn't turn out well, she figured they could just eat the other one. And if both failed to please, they'd fall back on a dozen of Bernadette's cookies.

Pete poked his head in the front door, paintbrush straight up in his hand. "One of your girlfriends just parked across the street. Be sure not to touch the railing. It's still wet."

Rachel wiped her hands on a plaid dishtowel as she rushed out the front door waving it. "Suzanne!" She hollered. "I can't believe you're here." Rachel held a hand to her chest as she scurried across the street to greet her.

Before Suzanne could utter a word, Marla beeped and pulled up behind Suzanne's car.

"Group hug!" Rachel shouted as the three squeezed together in the middle of the street, laughing and crying with joy.

"Don't you love happy tears?" Suzanne pulled tissues from her purse and passed them around.

They made their way across the street and wobbled up the steps with their arms draped around one another.

"Don't touch the railing—it's wet." Pete called out as Marla reached to steady the threesome.

"These are my dear friends, Suzanne and Marla." Rachel extended a hand toward Pete, beaming. "This is my oldest son, Pete."

"Nice to meet you, ladies." He opened the door for them.

They ambled into the house, and Rachel provided a quick tour. "This is the living room, there's the dining room, and the kitchen's over there. Bathroom's at the top of the steps." She pointed up the stairs.

"So homey, so cozy." Suzanne repeated the words throughout the tour.

"What are you making in the kitchen?" Marla took a step in that direction and sniffed, her face posed like a detective's.

"It's a surprise." Rachel clasped her hands. "Go have a seat while I check on it."

"Wait. First, let's pop this baby open." Marla pulled a bottle of champagne from her bag.

Rachel giggled. "Let me turn down the oven." She returned in a moment holding three beer glasses. She shrugged. "I don't have any wine glasses."

"Beer glasses work for me! Bring them over here." Marla poured the champagne like an experienced barmaid, ensuring the glasses were full but not overflowing. "So, what happened with your theft problem at the gas station?"

"You were so right about those cameras. I can't thank you enough."

Marla passed out the glasses of champagne.

Rachel lifted her glass high. "Shall we do a toast?"

Suzanne lifted hers. "To our renewed friendship. May it continue forever."

They clinked their glasses and grinned at one another as if all forty years had been erased.

"Okay, now tell us about the gas station, Rachel." Suzanne leaned forward.

"It was like being on a TV show. The police sergeant. The evidence. The criminals being caught." She provided some details. "Best of all, I didn't have to testify in court."

"How about the guy who spent all the time in the loo? What was he doing in there?" Marla laughed and leaned forward in the rocking chair, awaiting Rachel's answer.

Rachel squirmed.

Suzanne's eyes opened wide. "Reading dirty magazines?"

"Oh, no. Nothing like that. The only thing he confessed was that he'd started taking a medicine that makes him need the bathroom a lot. It was just a little awkward to have a conversation with him about it."

FALLING APART, FALLING FOR YOU

"Bor-ing!" Marla laughed. "I expected something far more sinister from the guy. You know how it is. It's always the quiet ones who have something up their sleeve." She turned toward Suzanne. "How's your Adam doing these days? And your job search?"

"Not making headway on either front." Suzanne rolled her eyes and sighed. "I don't want to ruin my happy mood by talking about either one right now." She tipped her head toward the front door and asked Rachel, "How's it going with your son being back home for a while?"

"Kind of a mixed bag. He's fixing this place up and I do appreciate it. I didn't realize how bad things had gotten. When you live in a place for so many years, you just don't notice. And that mess at the gas station—I don't know how I would have handled it without Pete. It was like he was filling in for my Stan." She wiped her eyes with her fingers. "But of course, it's a change to have Pete here. He likes to get up early and believe me, when Pete's awake, so's the whole neighborhood." She giggled. "I have to plan our meals and make the things he likes to eat. He told me he wants to go vegan." She slapped her hand onto her knee and laughed. "Imagine that." She looked at Marla. "Look at you—I'll bet you eat healthy all the time." She took another sip of champagne. "And how's your aunt doing? She must be in her late eighties by now, I imagine."

"She's either eighty-eight or eighty-nine. She can't remember. In fact, there are a lot of things she can't remember."

"That doesn't sound good." Suzanne took a sip and set her glass on the coffee table.

Rachel crossed her legs. "They say Sunset Hills is a nice place."

"Funny you'd mention it. We've already visited there. At first, she had her doubts, but when she saw that indoor swimming pool, she squealed like a kid. She told me there used to be an outdoor pool here in Port Mariette, and when she

155

was young, she spent her summers there. I guess she feels like she can relive her youth. Anyway, she's excited about moving in there soon." Marla finished the last of her champagne. "Now I need to figure out what to do with her house."

"Has Mary Frances called you yet?" Rachel tittered.

"Herbie mentioned her to me the other day. I'm going to talk with a contractor first. He's coming over Tuesday."

"Mitch Mitchell?" Rachel asked.

"Mm-hmm. Herbie said he's the only one in this area who could renovate it."

"That's right." Rachel nodded. "I hate to say it, but if you put a lot of money into that house, I'm not sure anyone around here could afford to buy it."

"Actually, I'm thinking of getting a zoning change and turning it into commercial property."

"What kind of business?" Suzanne asked.

"Not sure yet. I've been brainstorming with my dad. You remember my parents were in property development. My dad agrees with Herbie that once the new highway is finished, this town could be revitalized—provided we have an exit straight into the town and there are enough reasons for people to stop here."

"Your mind never stops working, does it?" Rachel said in awe, as she set her empty glass on the end table. Tipsy from drinking so fast, she stared at Marla, trying to determine which of her features had caused her to turn into such a striking beauty. Each feature, examined by itself, was pleasant, but none seemed remarkable. Her classic nose—Greek, of course—along with her large dark eyes, nearly flawless skin, her wide mouth and full lips—everything came together to form a perfect face.

Still staring at Marla, Rachel blurted, "Are we going to get a facial when we go to Pittsburgh on Saturday?"

"Of course." Marla nodded.

Suzanne took her last sip. "I've already made our reservations."

CHAPTER 18

MARLA

"I've got a surprise for you, Aunt Adele." Marla traipsed into the living room, two shopping bags in tow. Her aunt was sprawled across a gold crushed-velvet loveseat, watching a TV game show.

"A surprise?" She sat up straight.

"Come upstairs and I'll show you."

Aunt Adele took to the steps, holding fast to the carved banister with her bony hands. Marla followed close behind.

When they reached her aunt's bedroom, Marla upended both bags, flinging six bathing suits of assorted colors and patterns onto the chenille bedspread.

"I only need *one* bathing suit." Aunt Adele held a few fingertips to her thin lips.

"Wouldn't you like to have at least two? Then, one will always be dry."

"Good thinking." She stared at the display of colorful swimwear. "Two will be fine. Remember, I lived through the Depression."

"I understand." Marla nodded. "Would you like to try them on?"

"Can't wait." Aunt Adele laughed, then waved Marla out of the room.

"If you'd like a second opinion, give me a shout. I'll be down the hall."

Several minutes later Aunt Adele called to Marla. "How does this one look?"

Marla scooted back to see.

Aunt Adele was giggling like a teenager as she twirled around in her bare feet.

Marla looked her over, front and back. "I like it. It's very flattering and the orange flowers look good on you. Most people can't wear orange, but you can."

"I agree." Aunt Adele examined herself in the full-length mirror. "I'm not going to bother trying on the others. It's so darned hard to get in and out of these things."

"Which one do you like second-best?" Marla pointed to the choices on the bed.

Aunt Adele adjusted a loose strap as she examined her options. "The polka dot one."

"Okay. I'll return the others."

Aunt Adele collapsed on the bed, still in her bathing suit. "I'm exhausted. Maybe I'll take my nap dressed like this."

"You can do anything you want. You've earned the right." She patted her aunt on the top of her head and tucked the bedspread over her. "I'll load up the car with a few things you said you want to take to Sunset Hills. Maybe we can have dinner there too. It would be nice to ease into the place."

"Sounds delightful." Aunt Adele yawned while closing her eyes.

Marla scooped up the bathing suits and stashed them in the bags. Her cellphone rang from her bedroom—Warren's ringtone. *My daughter!* She dashed to locate the phone.

"Hello, Warren!"

"You sound breathless, Marla. What are you up to?"

"Nothing. Have you found my daughter?" Excited, she spoke in a loud voice, with her hand pressing on her chest.

"I'm sorry. Not yet. I'm just calling with an update. Whoever arranged for the adoption covered their tracks well. You know how it is, sometimes the family who adopts doesn't want the birth mother to come calling."

Marla clenched her fists and paced the hallway, floorboards squeaking as she walked. "So, are you saying there's no hope—or that you need more time?"

"A bit of both. It's harder than I expected. I have a few more avenues to try, and I'll need time for that."

"Okay." She stopped pacing and sighed. "Keep me informed."

"You coming back home anytime soon? Maybe we could go out to dinner sometime."

"I don't know. I've got so much going on, I can't think straight." She ran her fingers through her thick hair.

"That's okay. I get it. Just asking."

"I've got to run." She ended the call.

Aunt Adele called to Marla. "Can you come in here?"

"I'll be right there." Marla popped into the bathroom to soothe her warm face with a cool, wet washcloth, then joined her aunt.

Aunt Adele sat up, still in her bathing suit. "Sit here next to me." She patted the bed. "Certain parts of my body may be weak, but my ears are as good as ever. Now tell me, are you trying to find the baby you gave up for adoption?"

"I am." Marla's voice sounded small, her breath shallow.

Aunt Adele's eyes twinkled. "I know a few things about that."

"You do? I thought the church handled everything." Marla's lips parted in surprise.

"They did." She shivered. "I have to use the bathroom. Give me a minute, then I'll tell you what I know." She shuffled down the hall in her orange-flowered bathing suit and creaked the bathroom door shut.

A moment later, Marla heard a dull thunk. "Are you all right?" She called out as she darted down the hall and flung the bathroom door open. Her aunt was splayed out on the tile floor, motionless, blood flowing from her forehead.

Marla dropped to her knees. She searched for her aunt's pulse while dialing a number on her cellphone with the other hand.

"911, what's your emergency?"

The ER doctor whipped the feathery curtain open and eased himself sideways next to Aunt Adele's bed, pushing aside the wires attached to her. He looked her over, glanced at the readings on the machines, then addressed Marla. "She seems comfortable now. So far, we know she's got a concussion and a broken pelvis. The pelvis ought to heal fine in time, but we're not sure how that concussion's going to affect her." He glanced up at a beeping machine, then pressed a few buttons to silence it.

"She seems confused." Marla leaned over her aunt and brushed some hair from her forehead. "More confused than she's been."

"It's a concern. A neurologist is going to do some testing. We're getting a bed ready for her right now."

Aunt Adele opened her eyes and tried to raise her head from the pillow. "Where am I? I want to go home."

The doctor spoke, needlessly loud. "You're at Mercy Hospital. We want you to stay here for a while. It wouldn't be safe for you to go home yet."

Marla folded her arms. "I'd like to transfer her to a hospital in Pittsburgh."

"We can arrange that, if she wants." He looked down at his patient. "What do you want to do, Adele?"

"I don't want to go to Pittsburgh. I want to go home."

"I have her medical power of attorney right here." Marla reached for her bag.

"That's fine, but she said she doesn't want to go to Pittsburgh, at least not right now. We have to honor her wishes as long as she's capable of making her own decisions."

FALLING APART, FALLING FOR YOU

"I get it." Marla scrunched her lips and put her bag down.

The doctor patted his patient's hand. "Let's see how you're doing tomorrow."

Marla peeked through a dusty lace curtain and spotted Mitch Mitchell's hunter green pickup truck crunching its way up Aunt Adele's driveway.

Mitch parked and jumped out, clipboard in hand. He scanned the house as he strode toward the front door.

Marla stepped onto the porch. "Long time no see." She flashed a smile.

"You again." He replied with a grin.

They shook hands. Accustomed to firm handshakes, she gave him one of her best.

He lifted an eyebrow as he let go of her hand. "How's your aunt doing today?"

Marla tilted her head toward him. She liked the style of this man, comfortable in his own skin. They'd work well together. "Much better, thanks. They'll be releasing her soon to go into rehab. She gave me quite a scare."

"I can imagine." He stuck some fingers into his front jeans pocket, leaving the thumb sticking out. "And after that, she's moving to Sunset Hills?"

"Yes."

"Is she okay with that?"

"She's happy she'll be living among some of her friends, and she's 'over the moon,' as she says, about the swimming pool."

"Sounds like she'll adjust well. Tough getting old. 'Course some people think sixty-four's old. They tell me it's time to retire. Baloney. In the Bible, no one ever retired, and I never will either." He chuckled.

She looked him over. No, he did not look sixty-four and he had more energy than any retired man she knew. He'd definitely be able to take on Aunt Adele's house.

Mitch rubbed his chin. "So, you're thinking of getting this property rezoned commercial?"

"Right."

His eyes roamed over the house. "What did you have in mind?"

"I've got some ideas, but I'd like to hear your opinion." She turned a palm up toward him. "What do you think would go over well in this town?"

He put a weathered hand on his hip. "Maybe a B&B. Or a retreat house. There are a lot of church-going people in this area. In fact, my Assembly of God church might be interested in a retreat house. We've been talking about having one for years."

"I've been thinking about turning it into a spa *and* a retreat center." She tucked a lock of hair behind her ear, exposing a ruby stud. "The land would provide a place to do all sorts of retreat-type activities—meditate, pray, hike, paint nature scenes—you name it. The spa itself would be in the house. People could get a massage, a facial, a mud bath—"

"A *mud* bath? Why would someone want to lay in a tubful of mud?"

Marla laughed. "It's a special kind of clay that cleanses your skin. You just wash it off."

"I would hope so." He shook his head. "Have you talked with Penny or anyone on council about rezoning?"

"Penny?"

"Penny Frampton, the mayor." He placed his arms akimbo. "She's not real keen on change."

"I haven't talked with any officials yet. I wanted to get some rough numbers from you first." She tipped her head up. "You ready to tour the house?"

"Sure. Let's start outside." They circled the exterior as Mitch scratched some notes. "Some new windows and a fresh coat of paint ought to do it on the outside. Landscaping, too, but you'd have to hire a landscaper for that."

"I understand. Let's see what you think of the inside." She stepped toward the front door.

Mitch held the edge of the door to let Marla enter before him. He stepped into the living room and whistled. "Look at that woodwork. That fireplace. Those stained-glass windows in the turret. What a beauty this house is."

"I'm glad you feel that way. I have a hard time seeing past the dust and odors."

"That's superficial stuff. I'm looking at the bones of the home. So far, it's looking surprisingly healthy."

After Mitch finished examining the rest of the interior, they sat at the round table in the turret. "I know what this house looked like in its glory days, and I'd be happy to restore it to its original condition."

"I have no doubt." Marla smoothed a pucker in the needlepoint tablecloth.

"Port Mariette's a small town, but it has a big history. I consider it my mission to save as many of our homes as I can." He leaned back and wrapped his fingers around the arms of the chair. "A lot of folks let things go until it's too late to fix them, but this structure appears to be sound. Paint, windows, a good cleaning out, and refinishing the floors—some rewiring too—that'll do it."

"Okay, good."

Mitch folded his arms. "Even so, I think you know that fixing this place up—for whatever purpose you decide—is going to cost a bundle."

She looked him in the eye. "Look, Mitch ... you're a straight-shooter, so let me be up front with you. Aunt Adele has signed the house and property over to me, and I can afford to make the renovations."

Marla glanced around at the rooms within view. "I lived here only one year, but it was a pivotal time in my life. This house holds some of my most significant memories. I want to preserve it."

"I get it." He nodded. "We all have those parts of our history that hold special meaning. For you, it's this house. For me, it's the whole dang town." He chuckled as he scratched his head.

Marla knew many New Yorkers who devoted themselves to whatever made them rich or famous, or both. But seeing an ordinary fellow in tiny Port Mariette so zealous about the town's preservation? Admirable. "I respect your tenacity and passion, Mitch, to say nothing of your obvious expertise. When could you get me a rough estimate of a full restoration?"

"Rough? A day or two."

"In the meantime, I'm going to get Herbie's opinion about whether a day spa could succeed in this town."

"Herbie? Ha. He's in my golf foursome. He cheats. I wouldn't trust his opinion." Mitch chuckled, breaking into a grin that accented the lines of his rugged face. He crossed a foot over the opposite knee and cupped his hands behind his head. "Herbie told me he's taking you to dinner, to Dom's, that Italian place that overlooks the river."

"Ah, yes, news travels fast in Port Mariette." Marla smirked. "Don't read anything into it. I just want to discuss commercial property development with him."

"Right." He chuckled again. "Anyway, Herbie's a good guy. We like to poke at each other is all. He actually has a thing for Penny, but it's 'unrequited love.'" He laughed as he said the words.

"Boys will be boys." Marla shook her head and laughed. Funny how this man could be a serious businessman one minute, then joke around like a kid the next.

His face turned serious again. "Do you golf?"

"Not much. Sometimes in Florida, but only for business."

"I'd like you to see the course over at Starlight Country Club. Herbie and I've been trying to talk Penny into taking better care of it."

FALLING APART, FALLING FOR YOU

"Penny owns Starlight Country Club?" Marla raised her eyebrows.

He rolled his eyes. "Yep. Her husband died a while ago, so she runs it now. She's a stubborn mule. Maybe if you talked with her, woman to woman, you'd get somewhere. A nice golf course would be an asset to this town, no matter what you end up doing with this house." Mitch uncrossed his legs. "When can you play?"

"Nice SUV." Marla slid her hand over the black leather seat of Herbie's slate gray Ford Explorer.

"Four-wheel drive comes in handy on snowy days."

"It looks like it just came off the lot." Marla raised an eyebrow. "Did it?"

He smiled sheepishly. "I had it detailed yesterday. I work out of my car a lot and it gets pretty messy in here."

He shifted into drive, and they cruised along a few streets with running commentary from Herbie. Eventually, he pulled into a parking lot next to a nearly windowless red brick restaurant, Italian and American flags fluttering on its flagpole.

The portly owner greeted them with arms wide open. "Mister Herbinger!" He grinned as he accentuated each syllable of Herbie's name in a loud voice, probably to overcome a soprano's aria on the sound system.

Marla blinked from the heavy scent of garlic and onion.

"Hey, Dom. Good to see you." He slapped Dom on the arm. Herbie raised a hand toward Marla. "This is Marla Galani. She's visiting from New York City."

Dom flashed his eyes wide for a millisecond, then tipped his head. "An honor to have you here tonight." He escorted them to a cozy corner booth and extended a hand toward it with flourish. "Our best table." He snapped his fingers, and a server hustled over with menus. "Enjoy your meal." He gave Marla a slight bow and a long stare.

Marla unfolded the paper napkin and smoothed it on her lap. "Mitch told me you two golf together." Herbie was wearing a golf shirt, the bright colors suiting his big personality.

"Yeah, he cheats." Herbie deadpanned.

"Funny, he said the same thing about you."

"Inside joke. Mitch and I clown around about cheating at golf, but believe me, he's a straight arrow." Herbie lifted his glass of water, preparing to take a sip. "What did he tell you about your aunt's house?"

"Other than it will cost a lot of money, not much yet. I'm waiting to hear from him with an estimate." She looked at the menu, front and back. "Don't they have a wine list here?"

"I think your choices are red and white." He chuckled. "I recommend the red. I think it's Chianti."

"Red it is." She shrugged. "I'm thinking of converting the house into a spa and retreat center."

Herbie listened attentively to the details but didn't comment. He motioned to the server and asked for two glasses of red.

"Your thoughts?" Marla tipped her head to the side.

"The truth?" He raised his eyebrows.

"Nothing but."

The server appeared with their wine and flipped open her notepad. Marla ordered osso buco and Herbie, the spaghetti.

"I think you have a great idea," Herbie said, "but, even with the new highway, I don't know if you'll be able to draw enough people to make it work. What else is there in this town?" He held up both hands and looked all around. "Nothing! Even if you could arrange for your clients to golf at the country club, that course is in bad shape."

"So I've heard."

FALLING APART, FALLING FOR YOU

"I've tried to talk Penny into improving it, but I can't get anywhere with her." He chuckled. "Heck, I can't even get her to go out to dinner with me."

The server arrived with their food, steaming hot.

"I've got some ideas to run by you." Marla took a bite of osso buco and wished she'd ordered the spaghetti.

CHAPTER 19

Suzanne

The note from the florist read: "Mon petit chou, forgive me for being a moody jerk."

Suzanne rolled her eyes. She flicked the card onto the kitchen island and plodded down the hall to the spare bedroom closet to retrieve a huge crystal vase. She lugged it to the kitchen, and one by one, plunked the long-stemmed red roses into it.

Thirty-six.

The scent overwhelmed her. *Sort of like Adam*. Why did he exert such power over her? Was it his executive position at the bank? His wealth? His influence? Good looks? Personality? Intelligence? Stability? Maybe all those things combined. After all, he packed a desirable mix, especially at this stage of life. Finally, after all these years of being alone, she felt a tug to settle down, and Adam had seemed so right—so what was going wrong?

Maybe he wasn't enamored with her after all. Or maybe his divorce made him wary of commitment. Maybe Pauline had done a number on him—financially or emotionally—and he still hadn't recovered. Hopefully soon, they'd have a deep and honest conversation.

Now, though, Adam's note was spot on. Lately, he *had* been a jerk. Take tonight's key customer event for example.

He'd claimed it'd be a great networking opportunity for her. But yesterday she'd scrutinized the guest list, and every single person owned a business in Ohio. She lived in Pennsylvania! Did he think she wanted to relocate? Did he *want* her to relocate?

She let out a groan and walked to her closet, where she donned a red silk blouse in acknowledgment of the roses. Back in the kitchen, she rubbed a few petals behind her ears and on her wrists. Adam would notice.

He texted her he'd arrived early—no traffic on a Tuesday evening—so she grabbed her silver clutch and slipped out the door. As she stepped off the elevator, he reached for her. He slid his hands from her shoulders to her elbows, pulled her close again and inhaled. "Mm. You got the roses." His eyes twinkled.

"Yes, thank you. They're beautiful." She looked into his sparkling eyes, hoping for greater understanding of this complex man. She'd often heard that men were simpler creatures than women—all they wanted was sex or a sandwich. Adam? Not so easily pegged.

Inside the car, she waited for him to comment on the key customers. After all, he'd said he'd prep her for who she should meet. Almost there, Adam was still prattling on about how he wished he hadn't bought some new drapes for his condo.

Suzanne interrupted him. "Before we arrive, could we talk about the names on the key customer list?"

"Oh, sure."

"Did you happen to notice every single one of them is from Ohio?"

"I thought you could focus on the ones from the eastern part of the state, like Cleveland and Akron. Even Columbus is only about three hours from Pittsburgh. Besides, lots of people work remotely these days."

"I hear you, but I'm still confused. Do you want me to move away? Travel for work again? Or doesn't it matter to you?" She fussed with her bangle bracelet. Her voice dropped, sounding sad, sweet, and serious at the same time. "Ever since I've been back home, you've been giving me the impression you're not thrilled to have me here full-time." She crossed her legs and tilted her head as she placed a hand on his thigh. "Tell me the truth, are you trying to give me a message?"

He covered her hand with his. "Suzanne, you can be a little ex-as-per-at-ing." He said it with a smile, but with the way he elongated the word, his smile seemed as fake as her sweetness a moment ago. "You're reading too much into everything. People who live in Ohio know a lot of people in Pittsburgh, and vice versa. Why don't you stop trying to control every detail and see what comes out of your conversations?"

"Oh." She took a moment to process his comment. *Controlling, again!* "I'm sorry. I see your point." She flicked a speck off her sleeve, relieved by his answer, even though not fully persuaded. "I've been so stressed over being out of work that I think I'm reverting to the worst parts of my personality."

"Don't worry, I understand. I've been doing some reverting myself the past few weeks." He rolled his eyes as they pulled up to the valet. "Remember to talk with our president, Mark Lawton. He knows everyone."

One thing became clear to Suzanne at last night's key customer event—not a single executive in Ohio had any interest in hiring her as a corporate trainer, onsite or remote. It shouldn't have come as a surprise. Over the years, training had become a commodity, and her level of expertise cost too much to garner interest.

Standing in the kitchen, she filled a tall glass with ice, added some sweetener, and poured a cup of tea onto the cubes. The familiar sound of ice clicking against the spoon comforted her. As she contemplated her current challenges, she stirred faster and faster. *How could life suddenly become so confusing?*

She owed Rachel a call to thank her for the lunch. She plopped down on the sofa, scrunched a throw pillow behind her back, and settled in for some talk therapy.

Rachel answered, a TV playing in the background. "Hi, Suzanne, I was just thinking about you—Pete finished the last of that airplane chicken for breakfast this morning." Rachel clanked some dishes. "What's new?"

"Not much. I'm calling to thank you again for that wonderful lunch. The chicken was delicious, and it's been years since I laughed so much."

"Amazing how one bottle of champagne, even split among three women, could have such a potent effect." Rachel giggled.

"Leave it to Marla to have a bottle of chilled champagne in her purse." In school, Suzanne was the one who claimed to love surprises, but Marla had always been the one to pull them off.

"I ran into her this morning at the Dairy Mart." Rachel's voice sounded suddenly serious. "Her aunt fell in the bathroom on Monday, hit her head on the sink."

"Oh no!" Suzanne's fingers flew to her lips. "How is she?"

"She has a concussion and a broken pelvis, but it looks like she'll be okay."

"Poor thing." Suzanne sat up and took a sip of iced tea.

"Marla said she was going to golf with the contractor who's going to renovate Aunt Adele's house—Mitch Mitchell. Maybe you remember the name. Marla claimed Mitch invited her for a round of golf 'for business purposes,' but she seemed a little too happy about it, if you know what I mean." Rachel clucked.

"She's got a lot on her plate right now. Maybe she needs some diversion. What do you know about him?" Even after

FALLING APART, FALLING FOR YOU

all these years, Suzanne still felt somewhat protective of Marla. The woman came across as omnipotent, but when it came to men, Marla had vulnerabilities just as Suzanne did, and it bonded them.

"His great-grandparents were one of the founding families of Port Mariette. He has two brothers, and they're self-employed too. They might be too independent for their own good, though. Both brothers are divorced, like Mitch. I think Mitch's marriage lasted only a few years."

"Sounds like they'd have a few things in common, especially because they're both entrepreneurial."

"True. Not too many women in this town have good business minds—for sure, not me."

"Aw, Rach, don't put yourself down." Of the three, Rachel had always been the one who supported others, not the leader or the decision-maker. "I think you're doing fine with the gas station, especially in light of all the problems you've had to deal with."

"Thanks, Suzanne. It's a struggle, but I'll survive. How about you? I know you didn't want to talk about anything the other day, but I'm concerned about you."

"To tell you the truth, I'm struggling—with my job search, with Adam, with my daughter." Suzanne's voice quaked. She gave Rachel a quick summary of her woes.

"Oh, my. I can only imagine. You've got so much going on."

Suzanne closed her eyes to hold back the tears. "I remember in high school, when I got upset about anything, you could always make me laugh or help me put things into perspective. Those were minor problems compared to what I'm dealing with now. I'm a bit out of control."

"Well, you always did like to be in control." Rachel chuckled. "Let me tell you a story from high school. Maybe you'll get a laugh out of it. Remember when you went ballistic because you got a B in French?"

"I remember that. I was sure my test scores were good enough for an A, and I needed that A in French to offset the D I got in Algebra."

"You made Mr. Marseigne review every single test score with you, and when he realized he'd made a mistake, you practically did a victory lap around his desk."

Suzanne snickered at the memory then turned serious. "That reminds me—remember what Sister Philomena always said? 'When things are out of control, go to the One who is always in control.'"

Rachel turned serious. "Of course, I remember. She said it a zillion times. So let me ask you, have you been praying?"

"You sound like my mother." Suzanne's eyes widened. "The other day, she told me to 'Let go and let God.' I'm going to take what you said as a confirmation." Suzanne stood and put a hand on her hip. "My church has a service tonight. I think God's telling me to go to it."

Suzanne had never attended church on a Wednesday evening. The crowd was small but intense in worship, with arms waving as people sang with passion.

The lyrics of each song seemed intended for Suzanne alone. Tears streamed down her cheeks as she prayed the words more than she sang them.

An assistant pastor rose to speak, one she'd never heard before. She plucked a pen from her purse, her heart and mind prepared to learn.

The preacher spoke in a soft voice but with passion in his eyes and words. "God sometimes tests us in order to show us what's in our hearts." He described the religious practices of the Pharisees, then cautioned the congregation. "If we look at our behavior as the litmus test for how we're doing spiritually and we forget about the importance of

FALLING APART, FALLING FOR YOU

examining our motives or the root of our actions, we're like baby Christians who can only drink milk."

The message intrigued Suzanne, but as she reflected on it while driving home, she knew she'd grasped just the surface. *I'm like the baby Christian he talked about.*

Rob was the one person who could help her make sense out of the sermon. Since they'd decided to be "just friends," calling him to have a serious discussion might be awkward, but her desire to learn warranted it. She didn't want to be that baby Christian anymore. As soon as she locked her condo door, she dialed her phone.

Rob answered on the first ring. "Hey, Suzanne, how are you?"

Hearing his welcoming voice unsettled her even more. She choked up. "Not so good."

"What's the matter?" He sounded concerned.

Suzanne pulled out a kitchen stool and sat on it, her elbows resting on the island. "I went to church tonight, and the sermon kind of spoke to me, but I know there was more to it than what I took away from it. I'm hoping you can help me piece things together." She paused to find the words. "I ... I feel like God had a message for me, but I'm not grasping it."

"Tell me what you recall about the sermon." The gentleness in Rob's voice calmed her.

She told him the key points she'd written down.

Rob paused.

She could hear him whispering a short prayer.

Then he spoke. "Anytime a sermon, a song—or anything, for that matter—speaks to us with conviction, we should ask God to help us understand. That sermon must have spoken to you. Have you had some quiet time with the Lord yet?"

She looked to the ceiling for an answer. "I thought about the sermon driving home."

"Did you get any insight?"

"Honestly? No. The only thing that came to my mind was—and this will sound strange, but—a fig tree, like the one Jesus cursed."

"Interesting. Let me ask you a question. Are you producing fruit?"

"I'm not sure if I know what you mean. Remember, I was raised Catholic, and sometimes other denominations say things in a way that's hard for me to understand."

"Sorry. I should have been clearer. By 'producing fruit,' I mean your outward actions that reveal the condition of your inner self—your heart."

Suzanne's chin jutted high. "I've been working on that. Just the other day I prayed about not being so controlling or selfish."

"And that's good to pray about our sinful behaviors, to ask for forgiveness and to be changed."

"I'm trying hard." Suzanne sounded earnest.

"Trying is good. But you know what's better?"

Suzanne couldn't imagine what could be better than striving for an A in behavior.

"Maybe you also want to focus on your relationship with God, and just receive his love. Sometimes we're so focused on pleasing God with how we perform that we think if we do everything right, God will bless us. He does honor us when we avoid sin, but more than anything, God wants us to be in a relationship with him."

The line went silent for many seconds.

"I think I get it." Suzanne nodded her head with conviction. "I've been trying to be a perfect mother, a perfect woman, a perfect job candidate. But I'm good enough just because—I heard this expression a while ago in an Anglican church—I'm a 'daughter of the King.'"

She paused to write a note before continuing. "Thank you, Rob. I knew you'd be able to explain it to me."

"Anytime."

"I've been blubbering on about myself. Forgive me. How are *you* doing?"

FALLING APART, FALLING FOR YOU

"I'm good. I've got a speech coming up in Chicago, and I'll be able to visit my daughter now that she's settled into her new job there. Becoming a manager has been a challenge, but she seems to be adjusting. And Meg—she's been sick—her cold's still lingering, and on top of that, she has a UTI now. Nothing serious, just annoyances I'm sure she doesn't need."

"I hope she's better soon."

The line went quiet for a moment.

"Are you there, Rob?"

"Hey, I have to run. Someone's waiting for me."

CHAPTER 20

Rachel

Waiting for Marla to pick her up, Rachel assessed herself in the full-length mirror of the coat closet. *Is this the right outfit for their girls' day out?* The dressy slacks she normally reserved for church and a lacy long-sleeved top seemed right to her, but she had a gnawing feeling she'd look woefully out of place.

Exactly how *should* one dress for a day that would include a facial, mani-pedi, hair appointment, lunch, and dress shopping? She stared at her reflection and shrugged as Marla toot-tooted outside.

"Pete, are you up there?" Rachel called from the foot of the stairway.

"On the phone with Marianne." His muffled voice came from behind the bedroom door.

"Marla's here. Just wanted to let you know I'm leaving." *When I return, I'll be a new woman.*

She hopped in the car and gave Marla a quick hug. "Thanks for driving. It's such a relief not having to drive to downtown Pittsburgh." She glanced at Marla's outfit—yoga pants and a cotton top. Rachel allowed her body to relax in the leather bucket seat.

"I've set the GPS." Marla lifted her chin toward the dashboard. "You won't have to worry about giving me directions."

"Let's see—you're driving, you've set the GPS, and you're paying for the entire day." Rachel shook her head in disbelief. "I don't know how to thank you."

"I'm glad to do it." Marla gave Rachel's knee a quick pat. "Consider it a thank-you for everything you've done for me. Not just now, but in high school too."

"Oh, I don't think I've done that much for you."

"Sometimes we don't realize how much our words and behavior impact others." Marla took her eyes off the road for a second to glance at Rachel. "You were so kind to me in high school, and now, you're making me feel welcome here a second time. I owe you more than you think."

"Well, I'm glad I've been helpful." Rachel adjusted her seat belt. "Being back in Port Mariette again must be weird for you."

Marla laughed. "'Surreal' is the word that keeps coming to my mind."

"I'll bet. How's your aunt doing?"

"Still in rehab but progressing well."

"Tell her I'll say a rosary for her."

"I'm sure she'll appreciate that."

Before long, they pulled into a parking garage. Just as they arrived, another car backed out of a space. Marla slipped into it.

Rachel clapped her hands. "Oh, goodie! You know what this means, Marla—"

"No, I don't."

"A good parking spot—especially on a busy Saturday—is an omen for a good shopping day!"

"I'll go with that." Marla boosted herself out of the driver's seat.

They dashed to the dress shop where Suzanne waited inside, flicking through dresses on the rack. She grinned at them like a schoolgirl playing hooky.

They group-hugged then chattered about the wide selection of beautiful dresses.

FALLING APART, FALLING FOR YOU

"How will I ever choose?" Rachel held her fingers up to her lips then giggled. "Toto, I have a feeling we're not in Walmart anymore."

"How about this one?" Suzanne held up a dress with a dark red skirt and a red-and-gold striped top.

"Looks like our school colors." Rachel touched the fabric. Her eyes opened wide as she saw the price tag. Her hand flew to her chest. "Oh my gosh."

Marla finger-slapped Rachel's other hand, knocking the price tag away. "Stop that. You aren't allowed to look at the tags." She eyeballed the dress. "That one's a possibility."

Suzanne passed the dress to Rachel, who folded it over her arm and caressed its silky fabric.

"Here's one with ruching on it." Marla held the hanger high.

"Ruching?" Rachel's brow furrowed.

Marla pointed to the dress's midsection. "Ruching is like wardrobe magic. The folds of the fabric make the dress cling to your figure, but at the same time, they camouflage any imperfections."

Suzanne patted her tummy and looked at Rachel. "Ruching—and shapeware—are two of a mature woman's best wardrobe secrets."

Rachel stared at Suzanne. "Shapeware?" She tilted her head.

"It's like a girdle for the twenty-twenties." Suzanne smoothed her hands over her hips. "More comfortable, and it doesn't have all the bumps of an old-fashioned girdle."

"Ruching and shapewear—are they only for fat women?" Rachel felt singled out. She shifted the dress draped over her arm so it shielded her midsection from scrutiny.

Marla looked Rachel over, top to bottom. "First of all, you're not fat. Second, every woman's figure benefits from helpers like ruching and shapewear." She inclined her head toward Rachel. "Only the unlucky ones don't know about it." She shoved the dress with the ruching into Rachel's arms. "Gold is a great color on you. Try this one on for sure."

"Thanks. I feel better now." Rachel's smile returned. She relaxed her hold on the dress and jutted her chin high. "I'm eating better since Pete's been staying with me." She sucked in her stomach.

"Good for you." Suzanne patted Rachel on the shoulder. "Let's find some more dresses for you to try on."

Like mice in a labyrinth searching for cheese, the three raced through the dress racks and came up with fourteen possibilities.

Rachel tried them all on, one after another, without complaint or objection. As soon as she put on a rosy-pink, ruched dress, she opened the curtain so the other two could see.

"Ooh la la!" Marla waved her fingers at Rachel in the mirror.

"That bateau neckline is perfect on you." With delicate fingers, Suzanne adjusted the fabric on Rachel's shoulders to hide a bra strap. "You'll have to remember to pin this."

At the register, Marla paid for the dress, shapewear, and a pair of heels.

"Thank you." Rachel choked up. "So generous of you." She hugged Marla.

"My pleasure." Marla said. "Now let's get something to eat."

The three traipsed across the street for lunch at the trendy boutique hotel where Suzanne had made reservations. "Glad I'm not wearing heels." Suzanne pointed to a sandaled foot. "These cobblestones are a killer."

Inside the restaurant, Rachel's eyes widened as she took in the glittering chandeliers, fresh flowers, and crisp white linen tablecloths.

"Nice choice, Suzanne." Marla nodded her head in approval.

Suzanne sniffed the air. "I wonder what they're grilling. Smells delicious. Maybe lamb."

The three slid into a curved booth, Rachel enveloped between her two dear friends.

FALLING APART, FALLING FOR YOU

Marla flicked a crumb off the leather bench. "I had dinner with Herbie the other night."

The other two looked up from their menus.

"And?" Suzanne arched an eyebrow.

"We talked about how the town might change once the new highway is finished."

"You and Herbie were pretty good friends in school, weren't you? Both of you were—are—so smart. Co-valedictorians." Rachel looked up at Marla with admiration.

Marla cocked her head. "How do you remember this stuff?"

"It's all in our yearbook. I've been looking at mine since the day Herbie emailed me about the reunion." Rachel averted her eyes. "That was the day of Stan's funeral." She flattened her napkin on her lap. "Thinking about our senior year and planning for the reunion has been a wonderful distraction for me." She scanned her menu again and noted the prices. "I think I'll have ... a salad."

"No looking at the prices, Rachel." Marla snatched the menu from Rachel's hands and laughed. "Chicken piccata, lamb chops, or broiled cod?"

"Broiled cod is perfect." Rachel tittered. "Can I have a side salad too?"

"I can smell those lamb chops from here. That's what I'm going to have." Suzanne closed her menu.

"I'll do the cod too." Marla put her menu down just as the bow-tied waitress arrived to take their orders.

With an elbow on the table, Rachel parked a fist under her chin and squinted at Marla. "I've never been to New York City. What's it like?"

"I always say it's like a kaleidoscope. All kinds of people, frantically busy doing anything you can imagine. You can eat at a nice place like this or grab a pie at a pizza joint. Go to an opera or get loaded at a bar. It's restless and crowded, yet somehow lonely. And it's dirty." She choked out a laugh. "People say there are five times more rats than people."

"Ew." Suzanne scrunched up her nose.

"What do people talk about? I don't imagine New Yorkers talk about church bingos or the price of gasoline." Rachel giggled.

Marla smirked. "Right, we never talk about church bingos. We don't talk about religion at all, for that matter. You can talk about weird sex, designer shoes, or what you did during the pandemic, but heaven help you if you want to talk about God or your faith. Definitely a conversation stopper."

"What a shame." Suzanne tapped a polished nail on the side of her water glass. "I like to talk about my faith. It helps me understand things better. Rob and I have talked about it a lot."

"You and *Rob*?" Rachel's eyebrows raised high.

"Yes, Rob. We still talk a lot, even though I haven't seen him since early May, when I was in California. I wish I had faith like that man." Suzanne's eyes went glassy for a moment. "When I was young, my faith was more of a habit than a belief. I went to church, but I really didn't understand what it was all about. I recited prayers I'd memorized. Lots of times I didn't even know what I was saying. So, with such a weak foundation, falling away came easy."

She paused, as if wondering if she should stop this vein of conversation. With both Rachel and Marla staring wide-eyed, she continued. "So many times, my life seemed empty, without purpose. When I realized how broken—and how sinful—I am, I guess you could say I became a searcher. When I traveled for work, sometimes I'd find a church near the hotel. It didn't matter what the denomination was—I was searching for a relationship with God, but I didn't know where to look."

"Did you find what you were searching for?" Marla asked, with a tilt of her head.

"It took time, but yes. I wish I could say I had a lightning bolt moment like some people experience, but for me, it's been a gradual unfolding. I've spent hours reading the Bible, praying, listening to sermons. At some point, I realized I had to put my life into God's hands instead of trying to control it myself." Suzanne smoothed the tablecloth in front of her. "To be honest, it's still a battle." She chuckled. "Being in control is my preferred state."

Marla spoke in a soft voice. "Since I sold my business, I've been thinking about connecting with God. I've seen how people's faith affects them. How it changes them." She looked at Rachel, then Suzanne. "You've both changed. I see it." She fiddled with her napkin then continued. "I see it in Mitch, and in Deanna who used to work for me. My Aunt Adele too. She's always at peace no matter what happens."

"Have you been to church at St. Cyp's since you've been back?" Rachel raised her eyes expectantly.

"Not yet. I thought I'd take my aunt there once she's out of rehab. And Mitch invited me to go to his Assembly of God church."

Rachel opened her mouth, and Marla held up a hand. "Don't read anything into it. We're just talking business possibilities."

"How nice to go to church with a man, even if he's not someone you're dating. Sitting alone in a pew is so lonely." Suzanne sighed.

"Tell me about it." Rachel rolled her eyes.

"Adam's never gone to church with me." Suzanne folded her hands in her lap. "He likes opera, and I like church. Sounds like maybe we have a bit of a disconnect, doesn't it?"

The waitress interrupted their conversation, serving the meals from a round tray.

As soon as the plates touched the table, Suzanne said, "Mind if I say a blessing?"

The other two assented, so Suzanne bowed her head. "Lord, thank you for all the blessings of our lives, and in particular today, for our friendships with each other—and most of all, with you. We ask your blessing on this food and on those who prepared and served it."

"That's beautiful how you pray from your heart." Rachel took a bite of her cod. "Yummy. I think the blessing made it taste even better." She set her fork down and squirmed before speaking. "I've gotten a manicure for my boys' weddings, but I've never had my toes painted. And I've never had a facial either."

"Don't worry, you'll love it." Suzanne sliced into the lamb.

"I'm sure I will. Just unsure of what to expect." Rachel took a sip of water. "Maybe all this fussing is too late for me. Don't they say, 'By sixty, you get the face you deserve'?"

"Coco Chanel said that. I believe she said it was by age fifty—but we're fine with the faces we have." Marla winked. "We just have to do a little maintenance from time to time."

Rachel poked at her cod. "My sister's a lot older than I am. She once told me, 'Wait till you get older, you'll become invisible.' I think she was right. Sometimes I'll be in the middle of a group of people, and it seems like no one's talking to me or even looking at me. I wonder if it'll get worse as I get older."

Suzanne piped up. "I know what you mean. It used to be when I was on the road, I'd turn heads when I walked into a room. But the last few years—wait, now that I think of it, I did turn a head earlier this year! I was kneeling on the floor of a hotel in Phoenix when Rob practically tripped over me, staring at my skirt's wide-open zipper." She laughed at the memory.

Rachel's mouth dropped open. "Is that how you two met?"

"Mm-hmm. He's such a great guy. Too bad he lives in California." Suzanne smiled as she looked away. "When we were together in San Francisco, he told me he finds it sexy the way I walk into a room, strong and fit and confident."

Rachel rested her chin on her fist again. "Don't you love it when a man says things like that? My Stan was a good man, but words were not his strength. One time he gave me an anniversary card with a handwritten note inside. I was thrilled—until I read it. He wrote something like, 'you're so good at taking care of me' and 'you keep our house nice and clean.'" She laughed as she shook her head at the memory.

"I'm sure Stan was a good husband." Suzanne said softly.

Rachel nodded and looked down at her plate.

"Here's how I look at it now." Marla held her fork high. "We have a different kind of beauty at our age. Maturation creates a special beauty both inside and outside. Anyone who sees who we are on the inside sees true beauty."

"I wonder if any of our classmates will see my beauty?" Rachel asked. *Will Tony?*

Marla leaned in. "Believe me, Rachel, after this afternoon, and with that dress on, everyone will notice your outside beauty just as much as your inner beauty."

Rachel blushed like a teen.

"Speaking of beauty, our appointments start soon. We've been talking so much, and we've got to get moving." Suzanne snagged a final bite.

They strode a few blocks to the spa, located in the midst of several tall office buildings. The spa, decked out with dainty coffee tables, dusty pink paint, and vases of fresh flowers, served as a welcome contrast to its stark urban setting.

"I picked this spa because we can be together in the same room for everything. Won't that be fun?" Suzanne grinned.

Marla picked up a flyer listing the spa's services and tucked it in her purse. "This seems like the perfect place."

First, the esthetician worked on their faces, making it challenging to converse, but once they got to the pedicure chairs, their discussion picked up full steam.

"Your old chemistry partner, Bill, will be at the reunion." Rachel teased Suzanne.

"Oh goodie." Suzanne squiggled her toes. "I'm sure he hates me after how I treated him at the prom."

"What did you do that was so awful?" Rachel asked.

"Let's see ... I remember telling him the corsage he bought didn't match my dress. Then, at the prom, I talked with my friends more than with him. I hardly danced with him at all. When he dropped me off, he tried to kiss me on the lips, but I turned so the kiss landed on my cheek." She rolled her eyes and let out a big breath. "I could go on, but you get the idea."

"We all did dumb things in high school." Marla stared ahead. "Forgive yourself. And if you still feel guilty, ask Bill for forgiveness."

"Ladies, have you chosen your colors?" The manicurist pointed to a huge display case.

Marla zeroed in on a hot pink, then turned toward the uniformed woman. "We'll need to touch up before the reunion, so can you add a bottle of each to the bill?"

When Rachel couldn't decide on a color, Marla picked an orangey rose shade for her. "You need something a little darker on your nails so it'll stand out but also coordinate with your dress."

Rachel stared at the bottle. "It's perfect. Like today. The whole day is perfect." Overwhelmed by love for her friends and the experiences of the day, and before the nail polish was applied, she grabbed hold of her friends' hands and squeezed them.

On the way home, Rachel flipped down the sun visor to admire her new look in the mirror. Marla had to make a phone call, which allowed Rachel to sink deep in thought. She did feel like a new woman, like she'd turned the pages to a new chapter in her life. Looking back, she recognized her marriage hadn't been as perfect as she'd always pictured it. There were cracks before their son Brian's overdose ... and before Stan died too. When he wasn't at work at the

FALLING APART, FALLING FOR YOU

service station, he'd be playing sports with the guys or watching them on TV.

She recalled the night a few years ago when the Steelers were getting a beating in their final game of a losing season. Stan sat on the couch grumbling through the final quarter as she went upstairs to find a black silk nightgown she'd come across while rummaging at Goodwill that morning. After slipping it on, she sprayed some perfume on her wrists and brushed her hair into an updo. She sashayed down the steps, then across the living room.

"You're blocking the TV!" he hollered.

She slid onto her seat at the opposite end of the sofa and sighed.

At the commercial break, he glanced over and said, "Aren't you cold in that thing?"

Obviously, his new prescription wasn't working. She went upstairs and changed.

Even still, overall, he'd been a good husband. Rachel smiled wistfully. She had no regrets about her past.

Yet she did wonder what her future held.

CHAPTER 21

MARLA

As the sun rose on a cloudless horizon, Marla opened her car door and stepped onto the cracked asphalt parking lot at Starlight Country Club's golf course. She smoothed the wrinkles from her shorts and sleeveless shirt.

Her clubs were still stored in a Florida closet, but no matter. Mitch had insisted their round today would be more about Marla seeing the course than playing serious golf. She could rent clubs or even use his.

She wound her way up a hill to meet him in the pro shop. The glass-paned wooden door, jammed from too many coats of paint, required a good shove. She pressed hard and it popped open. A tinkling bell announced her arrival.

Mitch was conversing with a birdlike woman in a denim dress, his hands spread out on a glass countertop as he leaned toward her.

He waved Marla over.

"Good to see you, Marla. This is Penny Frampton. Penny owns this place. She's also mayor of Port Mariette." He tipped his head in Penny's direction.

Marla extended her hand as she stared at Penny's nose—pointy, with a tip like the eraser on the end of a pencil.

Penny gave a wan smile as she placed a few limp fingers into Marla's waiting hand. "Sorry, I'm not used to shaking hands. We're pretty informal here in Port Mariette. Where are you from?"

"New York. I'm visiting my aunt while I'm in town for the St. Cyp's reunion."

"Did you grow up here?" Penny's eyes widened.

"In a manner of speaking, yes." Marla smirked.

"What's your aunt's name?"

"Adele Napoli."

Penny tilted her head and squinted her beady eyes. "I don't think I've ever met her."

"She worked at the library." Mitch folded his arms. "You'd recognize her if you saw her. Retired a long time ago." He turned toward Marla. "How's she doing?"

"Okay. She'll be discharged from the hospital today, then she goes to rehab."

Marla glanced at Penny. "Poor thing had a fall. Concussion and cracked pelvis."

"I hope she's better soon." Penny looked Marla up and down, from her collarless shirt to her white fabric tennis shoes. "Looks like you weren't planning to golf during your visit."

"No, I didn't think it'd be on the agenda. I've got heels of all heights in my trunk, but these tennies are the closest I could get to golf shoes."

Penny pointed at Marla's feet. "What size do you wear?"

"Eight."

"C'mon back to my office. I have a pair of shoes you can borrow. Clubs too." Penny led the way. She pulled the door open and held it for Marla. The office was sizeable but chaotic, with golf paraphernalia scattered across the floor and her desk.

Marla looked around for an empty space. "Oh, I'm a leftie, by the way." She found an open spot and stood there waiting as Penny fussed around the room. "So, what's it like being both the mayor and the owner of the country club?"

FALLING APART, FALLING FOR YOU

Penny thrust her hands on her hips. "It's like when I was a kid with three older brothers. They always wanted to tell me what to do. I had to learn how to push back—and that's what I'm still doing today."

"I used to own some gyms for women—wealthy, fussy women." Marla rolled her eyes. "Their biggest gripe was cleanliness. If someone forgot to wipe down a machine after using it, five women came running to complain."

Penny laughed. "Then you can relate to my trials."

"What complaint do you hear most often?" Marla leaned against a filing cabinet.

"Here at the country club or in town?"

"Both, I guess."

"Here at the club, the men complain nonstop about the condition of the golf course. That's what Mitch was doing, in fact, when you came in. The women tend to complain about the facility—the dressing area, the showers, the restaurant." She shook her head. "In town, the complaints vary. Everyone has a pet peeve, whether it's better street lighting, the condition of the roads, dilapidated buildings—I could go on and on. But the bottom line is, everyone wants me to spend money."

"Sounds like you've got a lot on your shoulders. Do you ever have time for some fun?"

"What's that?" Penny smirked.

"Why don't we plan a foursome—you, me, Mitch, and Herbie? How about tomorrow?"

Penny cocked her head. "I don't know." She bumbled around among the piles and located a pair of size eight shoes, a set of left-handed clubs, and a glove. She thrust a hand on her hip. "Sure. A golf outing might be fun. Let's do it."

Marla hoisted the bag of clubs onto her shoulder and gripped the shoes with a hand. "Thanks, Penny. I owe you."

"That's a dangerous thing to tell a mayor." Penny laughed, and the two made their way back into the pro shop.

"Mitch, this woman has persuaded me to join you and Herbie in a round of golf tomorrow." Penny jabbed her finger Marla's way.

Mitch arched an eyebrow. "That'll be quite the foursome. Who's going to inform Herbie?"

"You, silly." Penny poked him in the arm.

"It'll be fun." Marla smiled. "Thanks for the loan, Penny."

"Keep everything until you're ready to leave town. I have plenty of extras." She patted the bag on Marla's shoulder.

Mitch and Marla exited the pro shop and headed for the first tee.

"How did you do that?" Mitch's voice registered surprise. "I mean, Herbie's been trying for a year to get together with Penny, and you arranged it in less than ten minutes." He glanced her way as they bumped along the cart path.

"I'm skilled in quickly developing useful but highly superficial relationships."

"I'd say so."

"Let's hope I can be as convincing when I talk with her about the condition of her golf course."

"Ha. I see." Mitch took his foot off the accelerator and the cart stopped. "Which tee box do you prefer to use?"

"The 'ladies,' of course." Marla slipped a glove on.

"You're a lefty?"

Marla grinned.

"Hoo-boy, watch out."

Mitch teed off from the pro tee box and drove the ball about two hundred fifty yards, straight down the middle.

"How about that." Marla lifted a club and stretched it over her head. "My turn." They hopped back into the cart and pulled up to the ladies' tee.

Marla took a few practice swings. Relieved her ribs had healed so well, she took her stance to tee off. She sneezed. "Sorry. I must be allergic to the grass or the pollen here." She pressed her forefinger against the tip of her nose.

FALLING APART, FALLING FOR YOU

"I sneeze when I'm at Aunt Adele's too. The dust." She sneezed again.

"I think this round of golf might take us a while." Mitch chuckled. "I have a towel if you need it."

"Thanks, I've got something." She pulled a tissue from her shorts pocket and blew her nose.

She readied her driver then lifted the club high above her left shoulder. The club came down smooth and fast.

She whiffed it.

Laughing so hard she had to hold her belly, she looked over at Mitch leaning against the golf cart with his arms crossed, stifling laughter himself.

"Can I try again?"

He rolled his eyes. "You'll fit right in with cheatin' Herbie."

Marla repeated her swing. This time, she connected. The ball soared high in the air and plopped onto the fairway about a hundred yards away.

"That's more like it." Mitch jumped behind the wheel.

Marla dropped the driver back in the bag and scooted onto the seat beside him. The bumpy path caused her to bounce into his shoulders a few times. It felt good. It felt normal.

"Do you think you're a normal person, Mitch?"

"Is there such a thing as normal?"

Marla gave him a little punch in the shoulder. "You know what I mean."

"The way I look at it, everybody's normal till you get to know them. So no, I'm not normal, and neither are you."

Marla pouted her lips. "How am I not normal?"

"Never married, for one thing. No kids, right?"

She looked down at her hands in her lap. "Yes, that appears to be true."

"You lived most of your life in New York City, but spent your senior year in Port Mariette, living with your aunt. Somewhat un-normal, wouldn't you say?"

"Agreed." She giggled, sounding like Rachel.

"And you're the only person I know who has been featured not once, but twice, in the *Wall Street Journal*."

She swiveled her head toward him. "How did you know that?"

"Herbie, who else?"

"Okay, so I'm not normal." She folded her arms. "But neither are you."

"Previously established, but how so?" He tilted his head toward her.

"You've been a single man most of your life—even though I'm sure you've had plenty of chances with women here in this town."

He snorted.

"You've owned a thriving business, yet you never left town for greater opportunities."

"By choice."

"And I'll bet your first name really isn't Mitch."

He chuckled. "You're right about that."

"Well, what is it?"

He looked at her over his sunglasses. "Ezra."

Marla had to put her hand over her mouth so she wouldn't laugh out loud.

"My great-grandfather's first name was Ezra. So, it's an honor to have that name, but let's face it, the name doesn't belong in this century. I was five when I asked my parents to start calling me Mitch."

"Smart kid." She smiled at him.

"You're smart too. Don't they say if you can make it in New York, you can make it anywhere?"

"And it's true. New York is a tough town. But you know what I find hardest about being successful?"

"What?"

"Having someone around who's happy for you."

FALLING APART, FALLING FOR YOU

"How's my sweet aunt doing today?" Marla interrupted the nurse typing on a computer outside Aunt Adele's hospital room.

The nurse glanced up but continued to type. "She had a bad dream last night and seemed somewhat confused when she woke up, but she's fine now. I'm working on her discharge papers right now."

Marla slipped into her aunt's room. Aunt Adele's arms were finally free of all wires and tubes as she napped in peace. When Marla arranged herself on the chair next to the bed, the crackling of the plastic seat awoke her aunt. Marla stood back up and took hold of her aunt's veiny hand. "How do you feel today?"

She opened her eyes and gave Marla a weak smile. "Pretty good. I want to go home." She closed her eyes again.

"Soon. You have to go to rehab for a while." She patted her aunt's hand.

She sighed. "I had a dream last night." She opened her eyes and furrowed her brow. "I dreamed I forgot to tell you something, and then you were gone. I woke up sad, because I thought you'd really left."

"It's still June. I'll be here a while longer, don't you worry."

"I realized why I dreamed that. We never finished talking about your daughter."

"I know. I didn't want to bother you about it until you felt better." Marla continued to massage her aunt's delicate hand.

"I remember some things that happened years ago like they happened yesterday. Things that happened yesterday—well, that's a different story." She shook her head, her eyes sad.

"It was springtime. April, maybe May. Your mother called me in a panic, said you were pregnant, due in August.

Right away, I suggested you come live with me. It was a simple solution, and for me, a lifesaver." She looked out the window a moment. "You see, the man I was in love with had moved away. He had ended our relationship without so much as a warning. I was devastated."

"I had no idea. I am so sorry." Back then, she'd been too focused on her own troubles to notice anyone else's pain.

Aunt Adele turned her head to Marla and smiled. "And then you came to live with me. You were a gift from God. And you still are." She reached for Marla's hand and drew it to her lips, giving it a tender kiss.

"Before you arrived, I talked with our pastor. He promised me the church would take care of everything. He didn't tell me any details. Not my business. I imagine the only others who knew about your baby were some people here at the hospital and maybe the church secretary."

A nurse rapped at the door then stepped into the room, her shoes squeaking as she crossed the linoleum floor. When she saw Marla looking at them, she winked and said, "So people can hear me coming." She turned to Aunt Adele. "I just need to take your blood pressure." She pumped and read the numbers aloud. "Pressure's fine."

Once the squeaking retreated down the hall, Aunt Adele continued her story. "After you graduated and moved back home, the years went by, and I tried not to think about your baby. Then one day, the first-graders at St. Cyp's came to the library. One little girl reminded me so much of you as a child, I thought my mind was playing tricks on me. That night I got my photographs out of the closet and found some of you around that age. That little girl at the library, I knew without a doubt, was your baby."

Marla reached behind herself for the arm of the chair and eased her body down.

Aunt Adele's voice dropped to a whisper. "I learned through friends at church the little girl was the daughter of Denny and Theresa O'Donnell. They'd been living up in Pittsburgh since they married but had recently moved back to Port Mariette so their daughter could attend St. Cyprian's Academy."

"So, the parents grew up here in Port Mariette?"

"Yes. Theresa's mother was the church's secretary."

"I see. That's the connection." Marla nodded in understanding. Her eyes opened wide. "Do you remember my daughter's name?"

"Grace. Grace O'Donnell."

Tears formed in Marla's eyes and then trailed down her cheeks. "Do you know if she still lives here? Is she married? Does she have any children?"

Aunt Adele raised a hand to stop the questions. "I don't know. I used to see her in church sometimes at the ten o'clock Mass, but anytime I go to church now, my lady friends take me to an early Mass."

"Grace O'Donnell. Grace O'Donnell." Marla said the name with awe. She stood and leaned over to hug her aunt. "Thank you for telling me."

Squeaky shoes neared the room.

"Sounds like your discharge papers might be ready." Marla headed to the tiny closet to retrieve Aunt Adele's belongings.

Right after she'd gotten her aunt settled at the rehab facility, Marla keyed "Grace O'Donnell" and "Port Mariette" into her cellphone. She held her breath after hitting the enter button. The results showed Grace lived at 214 Poplar Drive. She keyed in "Dennis O'Donnell," and after that, "Theresa O'Donnell." Same address.

Marla's hands shook as she shoved her cellphone back into her purse. She forced herself to take deep breaths.

In—one, two, three, four.

Out—one, two, three, four.

She put her car in gear and drove straight to Poplar Drive. She spotted the house on the right side of the road and parked on the opposite side, one house away, to give herself a good sightline to Grace's house. She turned off the engine. Silence. Her nerves jangled. She wished she had a drink. She sat a while longer. Conversations she'd had with others about God flitted in and out of her mind. Would God allow her to meet her daughter, even after all the mistakes she'd made over the years? *Please, God.*

Her stomach churned. She rooted through her purse, found an antacid, and popped it in her mouth. She chewed it while thinking through various scenarios. How should she start a conversation? Would Grace even talk with her? If her daughter wanted to develop a relationship, how would they do that, with Grace living here in Port Mariette and Marla returning to Manhattan?

Trying to anticipate an emotional event like this would be sheer folly, she concluded. She switched her tactics and once again asked God for help. At last, calm came over her.

An hour later, no one had come in or out of the house, and she'd have to find a bathroom soon.

As far as she could recall, the church was the closest public place, so she headed there. Finding the ladies' room unlocked, she let out a "Thank you, God." On her way upstairs, she smelled incense emanating from the sanctuary. It drew her inside.

The place was empty, with the lighting low, inviting, and comforting. She meandered to the front of the long church, looking left and right at the stained-glass windows that she'd studied out of boredom during twelfth grade—St. Paul, St. Peter, St. John, and of course, St. Cyprian. *Why were the saints never smiling?* She'd always wondered about that. Shouldn't they have been happy?

At the front of the church, she felt a strange comfort in looking at the painted statue of the Blessed Virgin. She lighted one of the few candles not already burning, then lowered herself onto the red velvet kneeler. Memories of her senior year flooded her mind. Such a difficult time of her life. She hadn't realized it then, but this church had always been a comfort. She surely knew it now.

Shuffling footsteps in the distance grew louder.

Marla turned to the back of the church where an elderly woman in drab clothing closed one of the doors. A nun, perhaps?

Marla stood up, startling the woman.

"Oh! I didn't know anyone was in here." The woman raised a hand to her heart. "I'm leaving now. Five o'clock. Locking up for the day."

"I was just leaving too." Marla smiled at the woman as she exited. Eager to resume her wait, she returned to Poplar Drive.

CHAPTER 22

Suzanne

Who was the "someone" waiting for Rob? Suzanne fussed with a few unruly strands of hair as she stewed about Rob's need to end their recent phone conversation. *Probably a patient, but it could have been a date.*

She needed to put Rob out of her mind. Why had doing so become harder lately? She'd be leaving in an hour for an interview. *I need to focus.*

This time, the job was a legitimate possibility—a training position in a large manufacturing firm with plants throughout the tri-state area. She'd drive to their locations to conduct training in the company's conference rooms. Driving sure beat running through airports, but she had doubts about spending a lot of overnights in the remote towns where they had plants.

Sitting on a stool in front of her dresser mirror, Suzanne responded out loud to some sample interview questions she'd printed from the internet.

"Sure, I've had some people in my workshops who didn't want to be there. Sometimes I joke around with them, other times I stand near them while I'm talking, and other times I call on them to answer an easy question to get them engaged. I've learned to sense which method will work best in a given situation."

She sifted through her walk-in closet for something suitable to wear, weighing the pros and cons of each outfit, same as she always did when choosing what to wear on a date with Adam. Today was muggy, but she'd be interviewing in an air-conditioned office. For a manufacturing business, it'd be best not to show up overdressed. Above all, though, she had to look young. After working her way through the entire closet, she opted for a belted, short-sleeved cotton dress. Simple yet professional—and youthful.

She packed a tablet, some pens, and an extra copy of her résumé into one section of her briefcase, then dumped the contents of her purse into the other side. She'd read somewhere she shouldn't fumble with multiple items in the reception room.

She glanced at Adam's roses on the kitchen island and plucked a few petals but shoved them down the garbage disposal when she remembered she'd also read one should never wear anything scented on an interview.

At last, she felt prepared. She caught an elevator to the underground garage and situated herself in her car, taking care not to wrinkle her dress.

A sixth sense told her she'd forgotten something. She took a few breaths and recalled everything she needed for the interview—address, cellphone, job posting, résumé, references, tablet, pens, briefcase, keys, reading glasses. Convinced she'd remembered everything, she touched the start button, then winced as she realized she'd overlooked the most important thing of all—prayer.

She closed her eyes and asked for God's will, not hers, to be done in the interview.

The process took only an hour. The woman who interviewed her looked younger than Jill. She asked a lot

FALLING APART, FALLING FOR YOU

of challenging questions, like what kind of software did she use for her training, and how did she handle it when she felt unsafe delivering training programs in hotels. Suzanne answered the best she could. That's all she could do. She let it go.

Home by noon, Suzanne went straight to her bedroom to peel off her dress and step out of her heels. She pulled on a pair of cropped yoga leggings and an oversized shirt, then slipped on her favorite flip-flops.

Having skipped breakfast because she'd read somewhere that people interview better without a full stomach, she searched the refrigerator in the hope of making a sandwich but found herself short on ingredients. She'd have to make a grocery run. The moment she picked up her purse, her phone rang—Jill's ringtone. *She must have gotten the package.*

"Hi, Mom. Are you busy?"

"Not at all, honey. How are you?"

"I'm good. I'm actually downstairs in your foyer. Can you buzz me through the main door?"

"You're *here*?" Suzanne's excited grin disappeared as she put her hand to the nape of her neck. Jill had never shown up unannounced since moving to New Jersey. "Are you all right?"

"Yeah, I'm fine."

Suzanne pressed the button on her wall. "I'm buzzing you in right now." She opened the door of her condo and waited.

The silver doors separated, and Jill emerged. Suzanne stretched out her arms to welcome her. As if she were still a little girl, Jill melted into her mother's arms. Still hugging, they shuffled into the condo. Suzanne kicked the door closed with her foot, not wanting to break contact with Jill.

"Let's sit down." Suzanne tugged Jill toward to the sofa, where they sat down side by side.

"I got your drawing." Jill leaned against her mother's shoulder.

"That's good." Suzanne's fingers combed through Jill's long brown hair.

Jill sat up straight and looked into her mother's eyes. "I'm so sorry. I didn't realize how bad I made you feel. Drew and I had been having problems, and I took it out on you."

Children of all ages do that to their parents. Suzanne's mouth started to open but she managed to close it before a syllable came out. She waited for Jill to continue.

"We *do* want to have a family, but with our work schedules, we knew it wouldn't be right. We argue about it sometimes. Couldn't find a solution. I mean, what's the point of having babies if you have to put them in childcare to be raised by some stranger?"

Suzanne felt vindicated. For so many years, she'd felt guilty about having her mother watch Jill after school until Suzanne got home from work. Jill always complained that Grandma was boring. But at least Grandma was family. Maybe Suzanne hadn't been the worst single mother on the planet after all.

Jill tucked a long strand of hair behind her ear, catching it on a hoop earring. "And Drew, well, you know he comes from a family of eight kids. His parents have nagged him about having a baby since we got back from our honeymoon. So anytime you mentioned anything about a baby, it triggered something in me. I overreacted. I'm sorry."

"Honey, it's okay. I shouldn't have butted into your business. I appreciate that you came here to tell me you're sorry. You didn't need to drive all the way here, but that's incredibly sweet of you."

Jill looked at Suzanne with a wide grin, then picked up one of her mother's hands and squeezed it. "Mom, I'm pregnant."

Suzanne sucked in some air as she tried to think of what to say. "Oh, my goodness!" There. That was a safe, neutral-but-happy statement.

Jill's smiling eyes filled with tears. "I want to quit working in a few months, but we need two incomes."

FALLING APART, FALLING FOR YOU

Suzanne reached to hug her daughter again, but then had to let go to get tissues for both of them as they cried and laughed. It was hard to tell the difference in the emotions—they both involved tears.

Suzanne's mind raced as she considered the implications of what she'd just learned. She had questions and she had ideas. But she'd learned to be careful about what she said, at least to Jill, so she asked a safe question. "When are you due?"

"I don't even know yet. My period was late, so yesterday, I took a home pregnancy test."

"What do you think you'll do about your job?" Suzanne felt it was a good line.

"Well, Drew's in the car downstairs. I wanted to talk with you first before he came up. How about we get him up here and we can put our heads together?"

Jill texted Drew and he showed up fast, sunglasses tucked in the neck of his T-shirt and keys dangling from a finger.

"What fabulous news, Drew." Suzanne hugged him, then motioned for him to sit with Jill on the couch. Suzanne sat opposite them in the upholstered chair and savored the moment of joy.

"You two must be thirsty." She patted her hands on her knees. "How about some iced tea?"

They nodded, so she popped into the kitchen to pour three glasses, serving them on a silver tray Jill had given her one Christmas. Suzanne sat down and clamped her teeth on her tongue, releasing it only to sip her drink. She would not drive this conversation.

Drew leaned forward, his hairy kneecaps sticking up above the coffee table between them. "The pregnancy's a surprise, but we're thrilled about it. The problem is that it's so expensive where we live. We need to make some kind of change."

Suzanne nodded, encouraging him to continue.

He glanced at Jill. "We've been thinking it would be good for us to move to Pittsburgh."

"Oh my gosh!" Suzanne had never dreamed that would be a possibility. Jill and Drew loved living on the East Coast.

"The cost of living in Pittsburgh is lower, and it's a nice place to raise a family. Good schools, safe neighborhoods, easy commutes, that sort of thing. It shouldn't be too difficult to find a new job here." Drew took a gulp of iced tea and set it on a coaster. "I thought maybe Adam could help me get hired at his bank or give me some networking contacts."

"I could help too. I'm getting pretty skilled at conducting a job search."

"Right." He pursed his lips to dismiss her.

Suzanne had always disliked Drew's attitude. Was he dismissive to all women or just her? She glanced at Jill, who seemed oblivious to Drew's behavior. Suzanne let his comment slide. She had her hands full with Adam and didn't need to take on Drew too.

"Anyway," Drew continued, "it would be a lot simpler to look for a job while living here. Our lease is up in a few months and the timing would be perfect for us to quit our jobs and move here."

Suzanne nodded, not knowing what else to do.

Drew turned his head toward Jill, cueing her to speak.

Jill flipped her hand palm up. "It would've been perfect if you still had your job because we could have asked to stay here for a couple months while you were on the road. The three of us would've overlapped maybe a few weekends. But until you start a new job, we'd drive you crazy if we all lived together in a two-bedroom condo."

Suzanne leaned forward. "I had an interview this morning that seemed to go well. Even if it doesn't pan out, I'm sure I'll land something pretty soon."

Drew glanced around the condo, as if to imagine how three people could live there together. He stood up and strolled behind the sofa to the picture window overlooking downtown. "This is a nice condo. Great location, a stone's throw to town. Easy access to any part of the city."

Suzanne looked at Jill. Her face looked so hopeful.

"How about I call Adam and see if he can help you land a job?" No one stopped her, so Suzanne reached for her phone and touched Adam's number.

"*Mon chou*! How'd the interview go?"

"Oh, that. Fine. I'm actually calling about something more important. Do you have a minute?"

"I've got ten."

She filled him in on the situation and explained that Drew had a degree in finance and accounting, along with an MBA.

"Let me talk with him."

Suzanne handed the phone to Drew, her eyebrows raised and a hopeful smile on her face. Drew strode to the kitchen island, sat on a stool, and reached for a notepad and pen. "Hello, Adam."

Suzanne had never heard Drew speak in a business context, and his commanding tone surprised her. She plopped onto the sofa next to Jill and held her hand. "Let's say a prayer."

Jill shrugged, so Suzanne whispered, "Lord God, we pray for a job in Pittsburgh for Drew—one with a good salary and a bright future, so Jill can be at home with their baby. We ask this in Jesus's name. Amen."

CHAPTER 23

RACHEL

"Fireplug ahead on the right, Cinders!" Rachel called out as they walked home from the Dairy Mart, her mood still bright from fitting into a pair of jeans one size smaller than what she'd been wearing the last couple years.

As they turned onto her street, Rachel could see Frank sitting on his porch a few houses away. What would she say if he asked about a game of canasta? Or the gas station?

The high school boy she'd hired to replace Ethan, who'd been arrested for dealing drugs, hadn't shown up for work yesterday. The other boy didn't answer when she called, so Pete had volunteered to relieve Lou Gestler.

Nope, she wouldn't tell Frank what had been going on at the gas station.

He already had his eye on her. She waved.

He returned the gesture and stood, waiting for her. "Got a minute to relax?" He called as soon as she came within hearing distance.

"Sure thing." She was sweating from the heat. Rocking a few minutes on a breezy porch had its appeal.

Cinders clicked up the wooden steps and waddled toward Frank to sniff his tennis shoes.

"Sit, Cinders." Rachel sat, too, on the rocking chair next to Frank's, as she set her bag of groceries on a dusty white plastic table.

"Car break down?" Frank rocked as he spoke.

"No, just trying to get some exercise." She leaned down to pet Cinders on the head.

"If your car ever breaks down, I'll be glad to give you a lift."

"Thanks, Frank. You're a good neighbor." He really was a dear, and she was thankful for his kindness and even his attention. She never felt invisible when Frank was around.

"Pete's been mighty busy at your place. He must have the whole house renovated by now, attic to basement." He laughed.

"It's been wonderful having him home, but he'll be leaving soon."

"I saw him at the gas station last night. Somebody call off sick?"

Lousy at keeping secrets, Rachel let out a sigh. "The new hire didn't show up last night. Pete offered to fill in."

"He's a handy guy, that Pete. Just like his dad."

In no mood to talk about Stan, she changed the subject. "How are *you* doing these days?"

"Good. The warm weather's easier on my arthritis." He smiled as he rocked. "Guess what, my boys bought me a dreadmill for my birthday."

"A dreadmill? What's that?"

Frank chortled. "A treadmill. Get it?"

"Oh. Have you been using it?"

"Every day."

"Good for you."

"Can't you tell?" He patted his belly.

She looked him over. "I can't tell when you're sitting, but you do look healthier in your face, now that you ask." She rocked a few times. "How are your boys doing?"

"They're all fine. Joey said to tell you 'hi.'" He chuckled. "He wanted to know if you're still angry at him for busting up your picture window."

FALLING APART, FALLING FOR YOU

Rachel still remembered the day Frank's sons were playing baseball in the street. She'd hollered out the front door to be careful where they hit that stupid ball. It wasn't five minutes later when Joey's line drive smashed into their living room window. That was replaceable, but a delicate porcelain figurine she'd gotten from her grandmother didn't survive. Rachel still kept the broken-off head in her dresser drawer.

"Tell Joey I'll never forget." That boy was a troublemaker, a constant worry he'd be a bad influence on her own sons. Rachel stood. "I guess I'd better get these groceries into the refrigerator. Nice talking with you, Frank. C'mon, Cinders." She moved down the steps before Frank could register an objection.

"Okay. Nice talking with you. Stop by anytime."

She waved goodbye over her shoulder and sighed with relief when she got inside her house. As she arranged the groceries in the pantry, she glanced down at Cinders. "I didn't buy a single item that needed refrigeration. I'll have to remember that next time I go to confession."

"You talking to yourself, Mom?" Pete bounded into the kitchen. He tossed the *Port Mariette Gazette* onto the kitchen table. Must have been reading it in the bathroom upstairs, just like Stan used to do.

"World still turning?" Rachel wiped off the countertop with a soapy dishrag.

"It is—in spite of all efforts to stop it." Pete sat and rested his arm on the back of the chair.

"How'd things go at the gas station last night?" She rinsed out the dishrag and squeezed the water out.

"Fine. Lou had to teach me how to use the new point-of-sale system before he went home, but it was simple. Working there seemed like going back in time—except for Dad not being there." He looked down and tapped his heel a few times.

"There was a guy checking out that empty lot on the corner, across the street from the gas station. After a while, he drove over to buy some gas. He came inside, walked up and down our aisles, looked everything over, but didn't buy anything except ten dollars' worth of gas. When he pulled out cash to pay, I figured he might want to be anonymous. I pretended I was an employee—a talkative one."

"That must have been a struggle for you." Rachel smiled, knowing Pete took after his dad.

"I've learned to fake it." He crossed his foot over a knee. "Anyway, I think he was checking out that property as a potential location."

"For what?"

"Not sure. Maybe for one of the big gas companies."

Rachel's heart sank. She picked up a striped dishtowel and dried off her hands as she sat down next to Pete. "You think? What did he say?"

"First, he made some small talk about what a quiet little town Port Mariette is. He said it was his first time passing through."

"Uh-huh."

"I said something like, 'It's going to get a lot busier here once they finish that highway.' He pretended he didn't know about it. Then he asked if there were other gas stations around here. I laughed and told him he didn't have to worry about running out of gas—there's one in every little town in this area."

Rachel furrowed her brow. "No matter how much traffic comes through from that new highway, there won't be enough to support two gas stations in Port Mariette."

"I agree."

"I guess there's nothing we can do to stop them, though." Rachel folded her arms. "Is there?"

"You could talk with whoever's in charge of commercial zoning here in Port Mariette. They might know if someone's interested in that property."

"Maybe I should call Mary Frances too. She only sells residential real estate, but that woman always has her ear

FALLING APART, FALLING FOR YOU

to the ground." Rachel reached for her phone but laid it back down. "I'm gonna go upstairs to say a rosary first."

Rosary beads now back in the nightstand drawer, right next to the porcelain head, Rachel picked up her phone to place a couple calls. Finding no one available, she went down to the kitchen and put together a salad for lunch.

She'd just taken her first bite when Pete burst through the back door, startling her. She put down her fork. "You look so hot. Let me get you a lemonade." She went to the refrigerator, got out the plastic pitcher, and poured a tall glass for him.

He used the bottom of his T-shirt to wipe sweat from his head and neck. Grass clippings clung to the legs of his jeans.

"It was muggy even when I took Cinders for a walk this morning." She plopped back down at the table. "Thanks for cutting the grass. I can do it myself, but I sure appreciate it." Rachel ate another forkful of salad and slit open a piece of mail. "I placed a call to the zoning officer. They said he's out today. I left a voicemail for Mary Frances too."

Pete leaned against the kitchen counter and took a gulp of lemonade. "Okay."

Rachel pulled a piece of paper from the envelope and shook her head. "Thirty-nine dollars for water. When it rains, I should go outside and collect it in buckets for free." She slit open another envelope. "Pennsylvania Department of Agriculture. Oh my. This must be about my application to sell homemade food."

Her eyes caught the first sentence of each paragraph. She stopped at the final paragraph and sighed.

"What does it say?"

"I can't do it."

"How come?"

"I have a dog, for one thing. It says you can't sell food that's made when there's a dog on the premises." She glanced at Cinders spread out on the linoleum floor, sleeping with limbs splayed like a flattened frog on the roadside. "Oh yeah, he's a threat to food preparation." She turned back to the table. "And the food can't be anything that needs to be temperature-controlled. That nixes my sausage lasagna." She crossed her arms and bit her lower lip.

"Bummer." Pete walked over and patted her shoulder.

"You're not kidding." Rachel put the letter down and stabbed a cherry tomato with a fork. "Oh well, at least I tried." She chewed then swallowed. "I'll have to let Tony know. He seemed excited about putting my pasta dishes on his menu." She picked up the newspaper and skimmed the headlines. "What's new with Marianne? She must be missing you by now."

"She's been busy."

"She's always busy, isn't she?"

"Yeah." Pete pulled out a chair and sat down. He took another gulp of lemonade and set the glass down hard. "I have to tell you something, Mom." His body seemed tensed, with his jaw set.

"What's wrong?" The newspaper dropped from her hand.

"I'm ... We're, uh, getting a divorce."

The shock took a moment to register. "What?"

"Marianne and I are getting divorced."

"Why?" Rachel's face scrunched up as if she expected someone to land a blow on it.

"Lots of reasons." He patted the table with his outstretched fingers. "But the last straw was when we had some friends over for dinner." Pete put his elbows on the table and tented his hands in front of his face.

"Marianne and Amanda were in the kitchen, and I overheard them yapping about how they were getting old, and their bodies were changing. Marianne said, 'I can't wait for the day when I don't have to take birth control pills anymore.' Just then, she looked up and saw me. By the look on her face, she knew I'd heard."

Rachel held her hand to her mouth, holding herself back from saying anything. Or from saying the wrong thing.

Pete let out a loud breath and continued. "The thing is, we tried to have a baby all this time. When she didn't get pregnant, we both went to doctors to get checked out. They tested us and didn't find any reason we couldn't conceive." Pete's face writhed as he fought back the tears. "She was lying to me all that time, Mom. She never got checked out with her doctor. She just didn't want to have a baby. Her career was more important to her than a family."

"Oh, Pete, I am so sorry." Rachel put a hand on his knee. She didn't want to invade his space. He looked so fragile. All those nagging questions she'd had in her mind about Marianne, about why they'd never had a baby—they were all answered in that instant.

"I'm going to try to get our marriage annulled. I think we have the grounds to do it. Marianne doesn't care one way or the other, but it matters to me."

Rachel spoke in a soft voice, hoping to lessen his pain. "Your dad and I always wondered why you two never had any children. We never asked because it wasn't our business. But we always felt bad. I wish your dad were here for you today."

"Marianne never wanted me to talk about it with anyone. She told me the situation caused her too much pain and she didn't want anyone to know about what she called 'our struggle.' What a load of crap." Pete's lip curled.

"Now I see why you wanted to escape for a while."

"I did want to fix the house up for you—but I'll admit, the timing couldn't have been more perfect." He looked up and gave Rachel a crooked smile.

"So, what are you going to do now?" she asked.

"Not sure yet."

The next morning, Rachel awoke to the sound of Pete moving about on the creaky floors in the bedroom next to hers. In the next instant, she remembered he'd be going back to Denver soon—and that he was getting a divorce. She closed her eyes, wishing it was a nightmare she could wake up from.

Before going downstairs, she forced herself to do her new morning routine—exercises in bed. She'd found that doing yoga stretches, leg lifts, and a thirty-second plank while still semi-conscious seemed easier, and it prepared her mind and body for the day.

Exercises accomplished, she donned a cotton robe and stepped downstairs.

Pete sat at the kitchen table eating shredded wheat. "I have an idea I want to run by you." He put down his spoon.

"Okay." Rachel yawned. No point in saying "good morning" today anyway.

"It seems to me, the only way we can make sure a competing gas station doesn't move in across the street is to make your gas station so appealing that customers will choose it over any other place." He made a fist. "Squeeze out the competition, y'know what I mean?"

Rachel filled a pot with water and turned on the burner. "That makes sense, but I have no idea how I could ever do that." She set a tea bag on a saucer and carried it to the table, sitting down to face the window.

"There's a lot of unused space at the gas station, now that Dad isn't there servicing vehicles. With a little money and some elbow grease, we could add a commercial kitchen and turn those bays into a convenience store that serves take-out food—like your pasta and pierogies, and some baked goods from your cousin's bakery, and maybe someone could make sandwiches and wraps too. You already have coffee and soft drinks and packaged snacks, along with cigarettes and newspapers. This would expand your range to include just about everything." He stopped speaking and looked at her. "Your water's boiling."

Rachel jumped up to turn off the gurgling pot and poured the water into her cup. "It sounds like a great plan, Pete, and I appreciate you came up with the idea. I'd love to have a place like that as a commercial kitchen, but I don't have the ability to run a big operation. I'm already in over my head with the gas station alone."

"I understand." He looked her straight in the eye. "I'd like to run it for you."

"Oh!" Rachel jerked her teabag out of the cup, missing the saucer.

"I'd be there most days, and Lou could be there when I'm not. If we needed more help, there's always high school kids. Or maybe Bernadette's granddaughters would want to work there part-time."

He stood, waving his arms as he talked. "I can envision how I'd fix the exterior up, making it look like a gas station from the Fifties. Paint it white, add red stripes around the top, create a sign that looks old-fashioned." He put his hands on the table and leaned toward Rachel, his voice rising. "There are lots of junkers in this town. We could paint a couple of them real fancy and park them on the lot as an attention getter. Old pickups are always a big draw for guys."

"Some of us girls like them too." Rachel smiled to see Pete so excited.

"The gas station is the first business people will see when they exit the new highway. I think everyone who gets off would have to stop, even if just out of curiosity. Maybe it'd become a selfies spot."

"I love your idea. I think it could work." Rachel took a sip of tea and looked at her son over the rim of her cup. "Where would you live?"

"Maybe here for a while, if that's okay with you, until the place is up and running. I haven't thought that part through yet." He sat back down and put his elbows on the table.

"There sure is a lot to think about."

"I know." He leaned forward. "If you like the overall idea, we can work out the details."

"Okay. I do like it. What a great mind you've got, a real head for business. You remind me of Marla." She touched his hand. "Let me ponder this for a while."

Rachel cleaned up the kitchen then marched up the wooden stairwell to her bedroom. On the top step, her cellphone rang—Mary Frances.

Rachel put on her sweetest voice. "Thanks for calling me back so fast."

"Sure. Were you calling about the reunion?"

"You're still coming, aren't you?" Rachel tried to sound like she cared.

"Wouldn't miss it for the world. If you need any help, I'll be happy to lend a hand. Maybe at the registration table?"

There she goes again, looking for a way to interrogate people about their real estate plans. "Thanks, but Suzanne's already volunteered to handle registration. Of course, if she needs help, you could jump in."

Rachel went on to tell Mary Frances about the stranger at the gas station.

"Hmm." Mary Frances paused. "I don't know anything about that lot across from your business, but you probably heard the highway project has had tremendous cost overruns. The State's going to announce it has to eliminate some of the exits to save money."

"Tell me you're kidding."

"I wish. There's a chance Port Mariette could lose its exit. People are saying it's due to our decreasing population. At least that's the rumor going around."

"That would be awful."

"Wouldn't surprise me if Penny and the council are pushing to have our exit eliminated. Most of them don't support change for this town in any way. That's all I know right now, but I'll keep you posted."

"Thanks for the information, Mary Frances. I'll see you at the reunion." Rachel ended the call, then tapped Marla's number.

CHAPTER 24

Marla

Having had no luck yesterday, Marla once again sat at attention behind the steering wheel of her car, positioned in the same parking space. A light breeze, scented by nearby roses and hydrangeas, blew through the car's open windows and tickled her nose. She sneezed once, then a second time.

She rifled through her purse for a tissue and her cellphone. As she blew her nose with one hand, she held the phone above the dashboard with her other hand to check emails. Through it all, she kept 214 Poplar Drive in view.

An email from Warren popped up. "Still working on it."

Gotta stop his clock. She fired off a text, letting him know she'd already located her daughter. Well, at least her house.

He texted back. "Good. Hope all went well. Call me when you get home."

A moment later, children's happy voices sounded nearby.

"Stay on the sidewalk." A woman's voice, both stern and loving, came from somewhere behind Marla's car.

Years ago, that woman could have been her. Should have been her. Right now, Marla would give up every dollar in her bank account to go back in time.

The little girls strolled by, followed by their mother. As she passed, she looked directly at Marla, a grin on her glowing face.

Marla's lips twitched in acknowledgment.

Could she make up for the lost years? What if Grace wouldn't allow her into her life even now? What if she hated her for abandoning her? Marla shuddered.

Another woman's voice emanated from a distance. "I'm going, Mom." The screen door at 214 Poplar swung open. A dark-haired woman in a black tank top and pink yoga pants emerged, the door banging shut behind her as she bounded down the steps. She hesitated a moment to glance across the road at Marla, then strode toward the blue SUV at the end of the driveway.

Marla couldn't catch a good look at the face, yet she knew by the way the woman moved and the shape of her figure—this had to be her daughter. Her heart pounding, Marla burst out of her car and clutched its roof.

The woman backed out of the driveway and headed in Marla's direction. She slowed to a creep and stared, her eyes wide and eyebrows raised, questioning Marla.

Frozen in shock, Marla leaned over the roof of her car, only able to eke out a crooked smile.

The driver slipped into a parking spot across the street. *It has to be Grace!*

The woman crossed over the asphalt street, her posture erect, eyes dancing with excitement.

"Grace?" Marla choked up. *What do I say?* Her legs felt weak. She held onto the car door.

The woman's eyes widened as she neared Marla. "Yes, I'm Grace." She took another step closer, then stopped a few feet away, a grin spreading across her face. "I believe we've met."

Marla could do no more than nod and smile. She blinked back tears so she could examine her daughter. No one could dispute their resemblance. Grace had the same Greek nose, the same dark eyes, the same fit figure. Her long hair, dark like Marla's used to be, flowed well beyond her shoulders.

In a strong voice, sounding so much like Marla, Grace continued. "I always hoped you'd find me."

Overjoyed by Grace's words, Marla stretched out her arms and managed a step toward her daughter.

"Not here." Grace tipped her head toward her house. "We need to meet someplace else, where no one will see us. Maybe somewhere in Lyondale."

Marla finally found her voice. "Of course. I understand. Where?" Marla paused. An idea lit up her eyes. "Wait a minute. Do you know where Crescent Lane is?"

"Sure."

"My aunt lives at the very end of the street, up a long driveway."

"Miss Adele, the librarian, is your aunt?"

"Yes. She's not home right now. We could meet there, if you'd like."

"Perfect. I'll see you there." Grace took a step toward her vehicle then turned around. "I did want to find you, you know. My grandmother and parents wouldn't tell me anything, though."

"I'm sure they had their reasons." Marla's eyes misted. "Lots to talk about."

Grace hopped back into her SUV and sped down the hill.

Marla kept her distance, not wanting to call attention to the two of them. Her BMW with Florida plates already drew enough scrutiny around here.

As soon as they arrived, they leaped out of their vehicles and rushed toward one another, embracing long and hard.

Marla patted her daughter's thick hair and inhaled her scent. Clean, fresh, a hint of flowers. Every nerve in Marla's body felt alive as she absorbed the details of her daughter—her face, physique, words, body language. She'd never experienced such stirring feelings—an unexpected wash of pride, a sense of ownership, an overwhelming joy in seeing the baby who came from her body but was now fully grown. Marla desperately wanted to know everything about her.

Grace's body shook with emotion. "I—I don't even know your name!" Grace sobbed in Marla's arms.

"It's Marla. Marla Galani."

Grace collected herself before speaking. "Marla Galani. Such a beautiful name."

Marla stepped back while still holding Grace's fingertips, marveling at the woman her baby had become. *This is what it feels like to be a mother.* She put her arm through her daughter's. "How about we go inside."

They swayed up the steps.

"Please, Grace, sit anywhere. Make yourself comfortable." Marla waved her hand across the living room. She wanted to ask questions, talk about the past forty years, and get to know this woman perched on the crushed velvet loveseat, but she held back. *Let Grace talk.* Marla leaned toward her from the rocking chair.

Grace's brow furrowed. "Look, before we begin, I have to tell you—no one can know we've met."

Marla cocked her head.

"It would be too hard on my parents. My dad has cancer and is near the end." Grace's face scrunched up and tears welled in her eyes. "On top of that, my mother has emphysema. She's not doing so well herself."

Marla covered her mouth with her hand for a moment, then spoke softly, "I'm sorry to hear that. I had no idea."

"I can't burden them with my birth mother showing up right now." She crossed her legs and held onto her knee, like Marla did when she was tense. "In this town everybody knows everybody's business. My parents and grandparents knew an adopted baby would be the subject of great curiosity. They didn't want a shadow over me the rest of my life, with people questioning me about my birth

FALLING APART, FALLING FOR YOU

parents and that sort of thing. They went to great lengths to keep my adoption a secret."

"I understand." Marla nodded, encouraging Grace to continue.

"No one except my parents and grandmother knows I was adopted." She paused and looked down at the worn Oriental rug. "Even I didn't learn about it until I was fourteen."

"Oh, my." Marla wanted to ask questions but her daughter's forthright way of talking was just like her own. She'd get the details soon enough.

"I wasn't real happy when they told me I was adopted, but I understood why they'd kept it a secret." She shrugged. "Anyway, my mom and dad lived up in Pittsburgh before I came along. When they learned they could adopt me, my grandmother concocted a story that my parents had to move across the country for a special assignment my dad had gotten for his job." She chuckled. "He worked as an auditor, so the idea sounded peculiar but not *too* unbelievable.

"So, one day when the assignment *supposedly* ended and they moved back to Pittsburgh, my mom had *supposedly* already delivered me somewhere in California. They told everyone they'd kept it a secret because there were complications with the pregnancy, and they didn't know how things would turn out."

"And then, when you were school age, you moved to Port Mariette?"

"Yes." Grace nodded. "No one suspected a thing."

"That's amazing." Marla pressed two fingers to her lips.

"It *is* hard to believe, especially since I look nothing like either of my parents." Grace tipped her head to the side. "I look just like you, don't I?" She broke into a wide smile, and they both laughed at her sudden realization. "No wonder I always had an idea of what you looked like—it was like looking in a mirror!" Grace shook her head, and her lips turned up in amusement.

"Anyway, my dad told everyone I was the spitting image of his Italian grandmother. He'd open his wallet and pull out a grainy black and white photo of an old woman from Catania. Anytime I misbehaved, Dad would say, 'She's erupting, just like Mount Etna.' He had everyone, including me, convinced I was the reincarnation of his nonna."

"A creative idea." Marla chuckled as she rocked.

"Even my aunt and uncle fell for it. They're both a lot younger than my mom. You know how it is when you're young—you're into your own life, blissful in your ignorance of what's going on around you. They never questioned a thing."

"What a story." Marla folded her hands in her lap, unsure of what to say. After a moment of silence, she asked, "How did the pastor at St. Cyp's choose your parents?"

"Grandma." Grace smiled. "She was the church secretary. She told the pastor her daughter and son-in-law were unable to conceive, and since my parents have always been practicing Roman Catholics, he agreed." She tilted her head. "They've been wonderful, loving parents. I thought you'd want to know that."

"Yes, thank you. That's comforting to hear. I'd love to meet them, but maybe now's not the best time." Marla fussed with a piece of lint on her slacks and looked up. "I live in New York City. I'm here for a visit, taking care of family matters like this house." She waved a hand toward the rooms then stared at her daughter's features again. She wanted to touch her, hold her. But she held back, letting Grace do whatever felt right to her. "For now, I'm thrilled to have found you, and I'd love to get to know you."

"Me, too. I want to know about you—and my birth dad too." She tapped her hands on her knees. "Well, where do we begin?" Grace laughed and Marla noticed even their teeth were similar. Large front teeth, uncovered by a big wide smile.

"How about if we begin at the beginning?"

FALLING APART, FALLING FOR YOU

Grace nodded, wide-eyed.

"I was sixteen, living with my parents in New York City ...."

"I found Grace!" With a hand over her heart, Marla loped into her aunt's room at the rehab facility. In the evening light, the place looked even drearier than when she'd brought her aunt there. With the loud TV bolted high on the dull green wall, and the pervasive scents of urine and cleaning products, Aunt Adele's room reminded Marla of her short-lived career as a cardiac nurse at a nursing home. She had to get her aunt out of here.

"You found her! I want to hear all about it." Aunt Adele listed to the left in a large chair, held in place with blankets stuffed on both sides. "But first, can you help me get back into that bed? Then you can sit in this blasted chair. And turn off that confounded TV. The overhead lights too. They shine right into my eyes when I'm in bed."

Marla flicked off the lights and the TV, then slipped her hands under her aunt's arms and guided her out of the chair onto the bed. Marla plumped the pillow and tucked a sheet around her aunt. "Comfy?"

"As comfortable as a woman my age with a broken pelvis can be." She sighed and flopped her arms down on either side of her. "Now tell me about Grace."

"You were right. She does look like me. Even sounds like me." Marla spread her hand like a fan over her breastbone.

Aunt Adele's rheumy eyes twinkled.

"She's very smart. She said she noticed my car sitting across the street from her house and when she caught a glance at me, she knew right away who I was."

"How about that! Is she a savvy businesswoman like you?"

"She's the manager of a department store in a mall about twenty minutes away. She took the job when her dad got diagnosed with cancer so she could move back home and still be close to work."

"He's lucky to have such a good daughter."

Marla cringed to hear her aunt refer to Grace as someone else's daughter. Now that Marla had met her, she considered herself a parent for the first time.

"Is she married?" Aunt Adele's eyes opened wide.

"No, she's not." A hint of sadness crept into Marla's voice. "I think she might be like you and me—a bit unlucky when it comes to matters of the heart. But she loves kids, does volunteer work with them. I suspect she's a bit lonesome and the kids help fill the void."

Marla plopped onto the chair beside the bed. "She has a creative side too. She makes jewelry out of tiny pieces of river rock."

"What an interesting woman." Aunt Adele blinked a few times. "How are her parents doing?"

"Not well." Marla sighed. "Her father has cancer. In fact, he's close to dying. And her mother has emphysema. Grace doesn't want me to meet them." Marla winced. "She thinks it would be too upsetting for them to meet me right now."

"That's too bad." Aunt Adele pressed her lips together.

"It's a huge disappointment." Marla shifted in the chair. "I didn't want to tell her I feel like a ticking time bomb myself—or that she'd be my sole heir. It would be too much to pile on her right now."

"What do you mean, you're a ticking time bomb?" Aunt Adele's eyes registered alarm.

"Oh. I shouldn't have mentioned that. I don't want to worry you too." Marla crossed her legs and rubbed her knee. "When I was in the hospital after that car accident, they ran a lot of tests. They discovered I'd had a mini-stroke."

"Oh dear. Your mother had her first one in her early sixties, as I recall." Aunt Adele's brow furrowed in its well-

FALLING APART, FALLING FOR YOU

worn lines. She lifted her head off the pillow. "Are you following your doctor's orders?"

"Yes, I am. No more than one alcoholic drink a day and taking my meds."

"Good girl. You can live a long and healthy life if you take care of yourself. I'm sure you know that your mother, shall we say, misbehaved. And look at where she is now, poor thing." Aunt Adele shook her head.

"She loved her Manhattans and gourmet dining. No one could convince her to change her ways." Marla scrunched her lips.

"I tried to influence her." Aunt Adele wagged a finger. "But we all make our own choices, and we all face our own consequences."

"So true. Anyway, I'd dearly love to meet Grace's parents and thank them for all they've done before it's too late." Marla uncrossed her legs and leaned toward her aunt. "I'd like them to know I'll support Grace any way I can, financially or otherwise. Even though that might be a comfort to them, I guess they'd be concerned their secret would get out."

"Maybe you could write them a letter." Aunt Adele waved an imaginary pen, then put her hand down. "Of course, as long as you're here, it would be better if you could meet them in person." She stifled a yawn.

"Who knows how soon—or how often—I'll be back here." Marla lifted a hand, palm up. "It would be a shame if I missed the chance to meet either one of them."

Aunt Adele perked up. "Did you happen to mention me to Grace?"

"Oh yes. We met at your house, in fact. She loves the place. We even took a walk along the main path. She remembers you from the library. One time you paid her library fine on an overdue book because she didn't have any money."

"She remembered that! How sweet." Aunt Adele's mouth stretched into a long yawn. "Forgive me. I'm tired, and this is a lot to take in. I want to hear more, but I need a nap. Before you leave, could you write down Grace's phone number?"

"Sure. But why?"

"One of the few advantages of being ancient is that people will do your bidding. It's time for someone to pay me back with interest."

Marla stood outside Mitch's golf cart, hands on her hips, pleased that Penny had kept her commitment to golf with her and Herbie and Mitch, but finding it hard to stay focused on the group's conversation. Her emotional meeting with Grace yesterday kept coming to mind, and her heart raced just thinking about it. *Focus, Marla.*

She snapped to attention and called ahead to Penny, sitting in a cart with Herbie. "Keep your eye on him. I've heard he cheats."

Herbie called out over his shoulder. "At least I hit the ball when I swing." He laughed and stomped on the accelerator. He and Penny bumped along toward the first tee.

"Now, don't you ruin our little outing with acrimonious talk." Mitch laughed as he lowered his sunglasses onto the bridge of his nose. "You didn't know people in Port Mariette could use such a big word, did you?"

Marla slid into the cart and leaned back on the seat. A genuine smile washed across her face. Smiling—she'd been doing a lot of that lately. Reuniting with Suzanne and Rachel was giving her a new perspective on life. Meeting Grace? A life-altering experience. Spending time with Aunt Adele touched her heart. Herbie and Mitch energized her with their conversations about the town, as well as with their friendly banter. Penny, she wasn't sure about that woman yet, but today she hoped to learn more.

FALLING APART, FALLING FOR YOU

Both carts pulled up to the first tee. Herbie bounced out, swinging his driver as he approached the tee.

Marla whispered in Mitch's ear. "Big words, no matter where they're spoken, are not a sign of intelligence. Believe me, there are plenty of dumb people in New York City who use big words."

"Is that so? I never would've guessed." Mitch chuckled as Herbie teed off.

"Sometimes I think I'm one of the dumb ones."

Mitch stepped out to get his driver, then poked his head back in the cart, his hand on the roof. "We'll discuss that later." He marched to the tee box and smacked the ball straight down the fairway, so far ahead Marla couldn't see where it landed.

"Wow." Her eyes open wide, she looked at Mitch as he sauntered back to the cart. "How often did you say you golf?"

"As often as I can." He dropped the driver into the bag. "I held back yesterday. Didn't want to intimidate you." A smirk on his face, he slid into the driver's seat. He rested his forearm on the steering wheel. "Golf's a great sport. It lets me engage in a little competition while having fun with the guys."

Marla crossed her legs. "One of the things I like about golf is that you have all sorts of conversations with the people you play with. You get to know one another at a deeper level."

"For guys, the course is safe terrain for talking. We cover all kinds of ground."

"Like what?"

"Oh, how to deal with a health problem, or tell a dumb joke, or have a deep discussion about your hopes and dreams." He laughed, but his face looked serious. As they moved along the course, their conversation covered everything from Marla's mini-stroke to Mitch's church.

Marla rolled a golf ball back and forth in her palms. "I'd love to continue our conversation, but I need some one-on-one time with Penny. How about I switch carts with Herbie for a while?"

"Understood." He glanced down the fairway. "Hey, Herbie, let's play musical carts. Get your clubs and c'mon back here."

Herbie saluted and got out of his cart. He pulled off his clubs and put them on Mitch's cart. Before sitting down, he hollered, "Cover your ears, Penny. In high school, Marla knew more swear words than the boys."

"Herbie's right." Marla chuckled as she strapped her clubs onto the cart. "The nuns were always on me for my potty mouth, as they called it." She shook her head at the memory. "I behaved like such a jerk in high school. To tell you the truth, if they'd had a contest for 'Least Popular Girl' I'd have won, hands down." She hopped in the passenger side.

Penny's eyes widened. "I never would've guessed." Driving them to the ladies' tee, she turned a few times to look Marla over.

Marla plucked a tee from the dash. "In fact, Herbie was the only guy in our senior class who ever said anything nice to me."

"Really? What did he say?"

"He told me I was a 'classy gal.' I don't know why he said it, or if it was true, but those were pivotal words for me. Made me feel like someone noticed me, that I had some worth."

"Aw, that's so touching." Penny's voice softened as she spoke.

"I know Herbie likes to joke around." Marla rolled the tee between her finger and thumb. "He's a funny guy, and people love that about him. But there's a lot more to him. Not only is he smart, but he's an astute businessman, even a bit of a visionary when it comes to this town."

FALLING APART, FALLING FOR YOU

"You don't have to sell me on Herbie. I like him." Her voice dropped lower. "I know he wants to date me, but at my age, it's hard to even think about doing that."

"At your age? That's ridiculous!"

"Is it?" Penny sighed as she pressed the parking brake with her golf shoe. "Sometimes I wonder if he's interested in me because I'm the mayor or because I own the country club." She glanced sideways, like maybe she'd said too much.

"I don't think that's why."

"He's been consumed about the growth he envisions for this town." She folded her arms.

"How so?"

Penny tensed her lips and emphasized each syllable. "He just has."

"Well, there will be a lot of opportunity here, once they complete that highway exit." Marla crossed one leg over the other.

"I like things the way they are. More traffic and strangers will cost this town plenty. Can you imagine what those big rigs will do to our roads? And how about the congestion on Main Street? No thanks! We'd have to create more parking spaces and widen some of the roads. Our crime rate would shoot up. I want no part of it, and I have no intention of spending money the town doesn't have. As long as I'm mayor and the council members stay the same, nothing's going to change."

Marla forced herself to speak slowly, softly. "Do you think it's possible the benefits might outweigh the potential negatives?"

Penny replied through tensed lips. "Not. A. Chance."

Hmm. Marla might have underestimated this woman. In an effort to come up with something—anything—to change Penny's immovable stance, Marla ran multiple scenarios through her mind, then tried each angle on Penny, hoping for a punch that would knock some sense into the woman.

But Marla was no match for Penny's mulish ways. All attempts proved fruitless.

Finally, Penny uncrossed her arms and glared at Marla. "Look, when you suggested we do this foursome, I was happy to agree. Now that my husband's gone, I get lonesome, and I thought this would be fun." She looked down at her left hand and played with her wedding ring. "I could use some fun."

"I'm sure it's hard to lose someone you loved so much." Marla tried to sound genuine.

Penny straightened her back. "But let me be clear—Port Mariette is fine the way it is. Herbie, with all his ambitions and ideas, won't change that"—she jabbed her finger at Marla—"and for sure, you're not going to come to *my* town and tell *me* how to do *my* job as mayor." She jerked her chin up and leaped out of the cart.

CHAPTER 25

SUZANNE

Suzanne scanned the tables at Dom's. Even though the place was jammed with noisy diners, the opera music still grabbed her attention. *Bolero* from *Carmen*. She chuckled. *What are the odds?*

"Reservation?" The tattooed young woman at the podium asked with a wan smile.

"Six o'clock, for three. Fleming." Suzanne followed her a few yards to a round table.

As the hostess removed the fourth place setting, Suzanne poked in her purse for her reading glasses, smiling as she remembered Rob's comment about them on their dinner date in Phoenix. "Do you have a separate wine list?" She looked up at the hostess. "This just says 'red wine' or 'white wine.'"

"The red's Chianti and the white's a chardonnay."

"O-kay. Thanks." Suzanne twitched her lips.

Rachel and Marla's laughter announced their arrival. Suzanne waved them over and stood for their group hug. "Keep laughing, ladies. The wine list is limited to Chianti and a chardonnay."

Marla chuckled. "I know. Herbie told me to get the red when we were here."

"Wish they had beer." Rachel put a hand on her hip.

"Sorry, Rachel. Just red and white wine." Marla patted her on the shoulder.

The three plopped onto the cushioned chairs in unison as a waitress with short spiky hair swung by to take their drink orders.

"How about a bottle of Chianti?" Marla looked at Suzanne and Rachel, who both gave her a "why not?" look.

In an instant, the spikey-haired girl returned with the bottle and poured three glasses. "This is on Dom." She jutted her chin toward the owner as she poured.

Dom leaned over the bar, smiling at Marla, giving her a wave.

The three women lifted their glasses and mouthed their thank-yous across the room.

"I guess you made an impression the other day, Marla." Suzanne chuckled. "So, how's your aunt faring?"

"Still in rehab. She's doing okay, but that fall set her back." Marla took a sip of the Chianti.

"Such a sweet woman." Suzanne shook her head.

"What's new with your job search?" Marla smoothed the paper napkin on her lap.

"I had an interview on Monday. It went well, but I don't think I'd want the job anyway. Now that I know the details, it sounds kind of boring." She leaned forward, her hands on the edge of the table. "I do have big news, though—Jill's pregnant!" Suzanne's eyes lit up and her smile went wide.

Rachel stiffened. "How wonderful."

"I take it you and Jill have patched things up?" Marla raised an eyebrow.

"Oh yes. She and Drew drove here all the way from New Jersey to tell me about her pregnancy. Before she told me about the baby, she apologized for her behavior." Suzanne watched for Rachel's reaction.

Rachel sat stone-faced, one hand toying with her fork.

Suzanne placed a hand atop Rachel's. "How you doin', kiddo?"

FALLING APART, FALLING FOR YOU

Tears welled in Rachel's eyes. She covered her face with her hands, then swiped the tears with her sleeve. "Pete's getting a divorce."

Suzanne wrapped an arm around Rachel. "Oh my. I'm sorry."

"It's the first divorce in our family. I'm so ashamed."

"What do you have to be ashamed of? You didn't do anything." Marla's face contorted in confusion.

"You're from New York, not Port Mariette. Here, it's a shameful thing to get a divorce. I've never recovered from the shame of Brian's drug overdose, and now this." She sniffed as she plucked a tissue from her purse.

Suzanne tilted her head. "Let's face it—no matter what our denomination, we Christians all have our secrets and shames." She shifted in her chair. "As long as we're being honest, Jill and Drew never go to church. They're 'too busy for meaningless rituals.'" Suzanne made air quotes with her fingers. "Anyway, I admire you for being honest about your life, Rach. Truth sets us free."

Marla crossed her legs, the split in her skirt exposing a sliver of toned thigh. "You're stronger than you think, Rachel. Look at what you've gone through. Not only are you still standing, but you're doing well. You're taking good care of yourself, making plans for renovating your business, and doing it all right after losing your husband. You should be proud, not ashamed."

"We admire you." Suzanne hugged Rachel with one arm.

Rachel rubbed her nose with the tissue and stuffed it in her handbag. "Thank you both. I feel better." She laughed. "Not great, but better."

Marla reached into her purse and pulled out two small black velvet boxes. She checked a note on the bottom of each box and handed one to Suzanne and the other to Rachel. "I think these will work well with your reunion dresses."

Rachel stared wide-eyed at the pendant in her box. "This must've cost a fortune."

"That's rose quartz." Marla pointed at the gem. "It'll look perfect with your new dress."

"What a breathtaking necklace!" Suzanne lifted her delicate chain of small rubies and held it high with both hands. "I don't know how to thank you."

"Me neither." Rachel teared up again. "This is the most beautiful piece of jewelry I've ever owned."

Suzanne handed Rachel another tissue. "Happy tears—that's what we like to see."

"Gee, Marla, we never know what's going to come out of that purse of yours." Rachel hoisted her glass of wine. "Here's to Marla's purse ... and renewed friendships."

They laughed and clinked their glasses.

Suzanne reached over to the empty chair, picked up two wrapped rectangular boxes, and gave one to each of the others. "Rachel, remember how you showed me what I'd written in your yearbook?"

"'May this circle of friends never be broken.'" Rachel grinned. "You wrote it in Marla's too."

Suzanne nodded. "We may have taken a forty-year hiatus, but we're together now."

"Let's keep it that way!" Rachel chimed in.

Marla opened her gift first. "Aw.... You wrote it in calligraphy, with an ink drawing of our high school graduation pictures. How beautiful." She looked up at Suzanne. "Such a thoughtful gift."

"I love it!" Rachel held it with outstretched hands. "Thanks so much. I'll hang it in the living room for everyone to see." She leaned over to pick up two plastic bags from the floor. "My gift's not anywhere near as great as either of yours, but I hope you'll like some homemade pierogies." She grinned as she handed the bags to Suzanne and Marla. "They're frozen so they're sure to make it home okay."

FALLING APART, FALLING FOR YOU

"I've never had pierogies in my entire life." Marla pulled the package from the bag. "I can't wait to try them."

"I'll share mine with my mom while I'm in town," said Suzanne. "She'll be thrilled she won't have to cook for a change. Thanks, Rachel. Very thoughtful of you."

The waitress reappeared at their table, raising her pen and readying her order pad. "Ladies?"

"The other night, Herbie said his spaghetti was delicious. I wouldn't recommend the osso buco, though." Marla put her menu down. "I'll have spaghetti, please."

"He was right about the red wine, so I'll go with the spaghetti too." Suzanne handed her menu to the server.

"Ditto." Rachel giggled.

"Maybe you can't trust men on everything, but when it comes to food, they're pretty reliable." Suzanne chortled as the server turned and headed toward the kitchen.

"Speaking of 'reliable' ..." Rachel smoothed a wrinkle in the paper placemat and looked at Suzanne. "I heard it from a reliable source—Mary Frances—that Penny Frampton is scheming to change the plans for our town's exit."

Marla nodded. "I asked her about it when we golfed yesterday. She said she has no intentions of allowing Port Mariette to change. But if we don't get that exit, this town will shrink to nothing in no time."

"My mother was right!" Suzanne bumped her fist on the table.

"Mothers are always right." Rachel nodded with a serious look on her face, then leaned toward Suzanne. "So, what did your mom say?"

"A couple years ago, when Penny became mayor, my mother said to me, 'There's the final nail in Port Mariette's coffin—first the closing of the coal mine, then the cutbacks at the steel mill, and now Sally's daughter will run us all the way into the ground.' I asked her what on earth she meant. She said, 'Penny's just like her mother. When she was young, everyone called her mom "Same Dress Sally"'—she wore the same dress over and over."

"Maybe her family was poor." Rachel cast a sympathetic glance at Suzanne.

"I think so." Suzanne tapped her fingers on the table a few times. "My mom said Penny's dad worked in the mill, but even though they had as much money as anyone else in the town, he gambled. That's an expensive habit. Penny's mom probably felt poor all her life, and Penny learned to be tight with money too."

"That could be, but maybe Sally wore the same dress because she hated change." Rachel said.

"Maybe she *feared* change more than *hated* it." Marla took a sip of wine and hoisted it with a smile toward Dom, looking her way from the bar. "Lots of people fear change. They don't like to lose control."

"Are we talking about Penny or me now?" Suzanne chuckled. "No matter. What you said could be true, Marla. We're really just guessing about Penny." Suzanne lowered her voice. "Here's another thing to consider: My mom said Penny's husband was involved in state politics. Maybe Penny still has contacts in Harrisburg. She might have political reasons for squelching our exit."

Rachel squinted her eyes. "Well, whatever the reason, we have to persuade her to allow the exit to be built. My gas station depends on that exit and so does your spa, Marla."

"My sister, Andrea, said she wants to open an art consignment shop, and our mother wants to sell crocheted items there." A smile washed over Suzanne's face. "I'd love to sell some of my artwork at Andrea's too."

"Really?" Marla's eyes registered surprise.

"Even when I get a job, I can still do something artistic on the side."

"Well, then," Marla said, "seems we all have a vested interest in making sure the exit is constructed."

FALLING APART, FALLING FOR YOU

Suzanne nodded. "How about we think about it overnight and meet again tomorrow to come up with a plan. Noon at the pizza shop?"

CHAPTER 26

Rachel

Rachel snapped her seatbelt into place and crossed her legs. "Thanks for driving, Pete. I hate driving to the airport, most of all in weather like this." Rain slashed onto the windshield in heavy sheets. Even on triple speed, the wipers couldn't keep up.

Rachel poked at her cell phone screen. "According to the radar, this downpour should ease up soon. And—good news for you—it looks clear all the way to Denver."

"Great. I got an aisle seat this time, so it ought to be a decent flight."

Rachel crossed her legs with ease and gave herself a mental pat on the back. She'd eaten only half of her spaghetti dinner last night at Dom's, and earlier this morning, just a yogurt.

Her phone rang. She chirped a cheery but fake hello to Mary Frances.

"Are you driving in this awful weather?" Mary Frances yapped. "I can hear your windshield wipers. You shouldn't be driving while you're talking on the phone."

"Don't worry, Pete's driving." Rachel rolled her eyes. "What's up?"

"I just overheard a couple council members—Fred and Marvin—talking in the bakery about that empty lot across the street from your gas station." Mary Frances lowered her voice. "I pretended to be indecisive about the cookies so I could listen to their conversation."

"How clever." Rachel could imagine Mary Frances hemming and hawing over the wide selection and hoped Bernadette wasn't the one behind the counter. For sure, her blood pressure would've gone up.

"It turns out the man who looked at that lot owns a couple tire stores up in Pittsburgh. He wants to expand to a location near a busy gas station that doesn't sell tires. The lot across the street from you would've been perfect, but when he got wind that plans for our exit could change, he lost interest."

Rachel turned toward Pete and answered loud enough for him to hear over the windshield wipers. "What a relief another gas station won't be moving onto that lot."

"You may be relieved," said Mary Frances, "but Fred is steaming—he owns that empty lot."

"I didn't know that. He must be furious. What did Marvin have to say?"

"He couldn't get a word in edgewise. But from his body language, I'd say he agreed with Fred's point of view."

"Thanks for the info, Mary Frances. I don't want to distract Pete from his driving, so I'll let you go. See you Saturday."

"Wait! Will you need me to help at the registration table?"

"Suzanne will be sure to let you know if she needs anything. See you Saturday." Rachel hung up and repeated the full conversation to Pete.

"Always good to know someone who's skilled at dredging up gossip." He chuckled.

"Suzanne and Marla and I are meeting today to talk about strategies to make sure Port Mariette gets its highway exit. Got any ideas?"

FALLING APART, FALLING FOR YOU

Pete rubbed the stubble on his chin. "I don't know, maybe arrange a town meeting or get something written in the *Port Mariette Gazette*. You've got to convince a lot of people to be involved in order to overcome Penny Frampton. She's a force. When I see Marianne, I'll ask her for some pointers." He chuckled. "A sneak like her would know how Penny's mind works."

"Now, Pete ..."

"I know, I know. Not a very nice thing to say about the woman I'm still married to."

"Or anyone, for that matter."

Pete looked over at Rachel. "I'll pray for Marianne instead, how's that? And I'll pray about Penny and the highway too."

"But do let me know if Marianne has any ideas, okay?" Rachel tilted her head.

Pete laughed. "Will do."

"I'm glad you'll be moving back to Port Mariette, even though I don't like the reason for it."

"Me too."

"I get lonesome sometimes."

"I'll get back as soon as I can."

"You're a wonderful son, Petie."

"And you're a wonderful mom." Pete pulled under the overhang in the passenger drop-off area. He grabbed his carry-on bag from the back seat as Rachel got out of the passenger side.

"Thanks for everything." He hugged her. "I'll call you when I land."

"Okay. Love you, Petie."

She slid into the driver's seat, gripped the wheel, and said a prayer. As the car emerged from under the overhang, rain pelted it once again. With every muscle tensed, she clicked on the turn signal and merged onto the highway, hugging the right lane as cars sped by on her left. Soon the downpour lessened into a rainfall, then to a drizzle. She sang along with the radio as she passed a slow-moving truck. By the time she pulled onto her street, everything looked dry.

Frank, trimming the hedge in front of his porch, waved his clippers at her as she got out of her car. *He looks a little trimmer himself.*

"Hi, Frank. It looks like you've been putting your *dreadmill* to good use." Rachel looked him up and down.

"You're my inspiration." He winked at her.

"Exercising does get easier once you establish a habit, doesn't it?" Rachel shut the car door. "I'll be taking a walk with Cinders after lunch, if the rain holds off. Join us?"

"Sounds good."

Rachel bounded to the front door where Cinders greeted her with a panting grin.

"Hey, big fella, just you and me again." She patted his head. "Maybe that's not so bad after all."

She tossed the car keys into her purse and hung it on a hook near the front door. "You hungry, too, Cinders?" She leaned down to scratch behind his ears, then went to the kitchen to get him some kibble. "Mm. This stuff looks good to me, Cinders. Even smells pretty decent. I guess I really am hungry."

Her thoughts drifted to Pete. Although his divorce would be the first in their family, plenty of others at St. Cyp's had experienced a divorce or two. She shouldn't have been so surprised by Pete's announcement, but still, she was devastated. For years, she'd said the country was sliding down a slippery slope. Now, her own family was in the lineup.

She sighed. With a few minutes to kill before meeting Suzanne and Marla for lunch, she spread the *Port Mariette Gazette* across the kitchen table. Before she could read the headline, her phone lit up—Sandy Roczinski calling. A pang of guilt struck Rachel. Since Stan's passing, she'd lost interest in going to bingo, even though she and Sandy

FALLING APART, FALLING FOR YOU

usually laughed their way through the game, telling stories of what their husbands and kids had done the past week.

"How you doin', Sandy?" Rachel hoped her friend wasn't calling about bingo.

"I'm good. But Ted—" She heaved a loud sigh. "He's not doing so well. He had to schedule spinal fusion surgery."

"Oh my! That's too bad. I thought he'd been doing better."

"For a while, yes. But lately the pain's gotten worse. Doc said this is Ted's last option."

"Oh my. How long will recovery take?"

"He can go back to work on a modified schedule after a couple weeks. Here's the problem, though—we've already scheduled our vacation to Poland in August. It's a nine-day tour, mainly in Warsaw and Krakow, but also some side trips to places like Czestochowa. Ted's not going to be able to handle a trip like that."

"What a pity. You've been looking forward to that for so long." Rachel looked out the kitchen window and scowled at the darkening skies. She'd be leaving soon and would surely get soaked.

"Yeah, Ted didn't care too much, but I want to go back to the 'old country.' Seems like a rite of passage for so many of us at this time of life."

"I remember when my aunt and uncle went back there for a visit. They had a fabulous time, even visited some of our relatives near Konin. Ever since I was a little girl, I've always dreamed of going." Rachel's eyes drifted to the clock. "So, what are you and Ted going to do—cancel the trip?" She stepped to the guest closet and located an old golf umbrella.

"No, it's already paid in full. I'm determined to go, but here's the thing ... I need a travel partner. I wondered if you'd be willing to go with me. We've already paid for the trip, so you'd only have to pay for your flights, which would be about a thousand dollars."

"A trip to Poland?" Rachel's heart leaped. She wasn't ready for bingo—how could she tackle Poland? "But—but I don't even have a passport."

"It's easy. I'll help you get one." Sandy chuckled. "So, do you want to go with me?"

Rachel held her hand over her heart. A trip to Europe would be a big stretch, but why not? "*Tak*! Yes! I'd love to go with you!"

CHAPTER 27

Marla

Marla shook off the rain like a wet sheepdog as she hurried into the foyer at Sunset Hills. The last time she'd been caught in a beating rain like this was more than a dozen years ago when she'd flown to St. John's for a last-minute getaway with a man named Rick—or was it Rich? A hurricane had unexpectedly shifted its path, causing them to huddle in a Red Cross shelter for a day. No physical harm to either of them, but their relationship didn't survive.

A few doors from the foyer, Aunt Adele's well-lit quarters gushed with cheeriness, a snub to the gloom outside.

Her aunt, looking peaceful in her recliner, glanced up and grinned as Marla entered. Only a day after moving into Sunset Hills, the old woman looked as perky as the bright floral curtains.

"I've been making a list of things I'd like you to bring here." Aunt Adele handed Marla a lined sheet of paper with two long columns. "The first column lists the furniture, and the second is items to hang on the walls."

"You've been a busy lady." Marla scanned the extensive list, squinting to read her aunt's scribbles and wondering how she'd be able to transport everything in a BMW coupe. Maybe Rachel's son Pete could help when he returned from Denver. Or Mitch with his pickup truck. "I'll get everything here as soon as I can."

"Take your time, dear. I know you'll be busy with Grace's parents tomorrow and then your reunion on Saturday." She folded the afghan on her lap. "I'm not going anywhere—except to the swimming pool." Aunt Adele pulled her long cotton robe open a few inches to show Marla her polka-dot swimsuit.

"You crack me up." Marla shook her head. "Before you go for your swim, can we talk about what to do with your house?"

Aunt Adele waved a dismissive hand. "Do what you want with it. It's yours now."

"What would you think if I turned it into a day spa?"

Aunt Adele's eyes lit up. "Sounds like lots of people would have the chance to enjoy it. I like that." She arched an eyebrow. "Who would run it?"

"I thought I'd talk with Grace about it."

Aunt Adele nodded thoughtfully.

"Thanks again for persuading Grace to arrange a meeting with her parents. I don't know how you did it."

"Oh, I'm a crafty old lady who knows how to call in a favor." Aunt Adele winked.

"Speaking of crafty ... I'm meeting my girlfriends for lunch at the pizza shop. We're trying to figure out how to make sure Port Mariette gets its highway exit. Rumor has it Penny's trying to prevent it."

Aunt Adele wagged her finger. "Be as shrewd as a snake around that Penny. She could well be like her mother. Sally lost her real estate license because of her shady dealings."

"Thanks for the tip—got any others?" Marla wished she'd relied on her aunt's wisdom more often. Maybe she could have avoided some pain and suffering over the years.

"I have every confidence you'll figure out a way to resolve the highway issue. But keep in mind, no one likes to be humiliated like Sally was, in front of the whole town."

Aunt Adele reached for the bars of her walker and boosted herself up. "Now, go have lunch with your lady friends while I catch a swim."

FALLING APART, FALLING FOR YOU

Marla arrived early at the pizza shop. She chose a table next to the window and slid her dripping umbrella underneath her seat. Drumming her fingers on the vinyl tablecloth, she imagined what might happen in tomorrow's meeting with Grace's parents. Personal wealth, impending death, and the truth about a secret adoption were not commonplace topics. Might be best to let Grace and her parents do most of the talking.

Soon, Rachel thrust the door open, shaking both her head and her golf umbrella, derailing Marla's train of thoughts. "I looked at the radar when I dropped Pete off at the airport. It said it'd be dry all afternoon." She leaned over to hug Marla. "Technology." She rolled her eyes. "Drives me nuts." Rachel stared at the table as her hand touched the edge. "This is where Stan and I used to sit." She pointed to the chair next to Marla. "He'd sit there, and I'd sit here." She slid a chair back and sat down reverentially.

A moment later, Suzanne burst in. "I hope I'm not late. I had a long conversation with my mom about the consignment shop." She took a seat between her friends.

"A valid excuse." Marla unfurled the paper napkin wrapped around the fork and knife. "I arrived early, and Rachel beat you by a minute. How about we order, then get down to business?"

Rachel called to a server. "Hannah, can you get us a large veggie pizza? And three waters with lemon?"

Suzanne leaned forward, her eyes bright with excitement. "My mom showed me a trunkful of crocheted items she's made over the years—everything from christening gowns to doilies."

"Doilies? I love 'em. I'll be her first customer." Rachel's hands flew up in excitement.

"I'm excited about selling my artwork there too." Suzanne talked fast, a smile wide across her face. "It's always been my dream to do more artistic work, but flying all over the country made it impossible to do anything beyond pen and ink drawings and calligraphy."

"No wonder you're excited. You're an amazing artist, and doing this will help you stay connected with your family down here in Port Mariette too." Marla pictured herself with her own new 'family.' Would they stay connected like Suzanne did with hers? Would they even get connected in the first place?

"Who knows, maybe I'll move down here for a few months. I could live with my mom and let Jill and Drew live in my condo until they find their own place."

"We could be walking buddies!" Rachel clapped her hands together.

Hannah soon appeared with the pizza, the peppers and onion still sizzling.

"Looks great and smells even better." Rachel grinned at Hannah.

"Let's say a blessing." Suzanne prayed over the meal, then Rachel began serving the slices.

"I think there'll be others who want to open businesses here—provided we get that exit." Rachel served herself a slice. "Maybe that tire store owner will decide to open a location after all. And, of course, Pete and I will renovate and expand the gas station." She wiped tomato sauce from her finger with a paper napkin. "I talked with Tony yesterday. He said he'd love to sell Signore's to his son and open a small restaurant here in town." She chuckled. "I told him it couldn't be Italian. People here are too loyal to Dom's—not because of his food, but because everyone loves Dom."

Suzanne cocked her head. "You were talking with Tony?"

"Yeah, I had to let him know the State won't let me prepare food in my home. Too many rules."

"Sorry to hear that, Rach. I know you were looking forward to doing that." Suzanne cast her a sympathetic look.

FALLING APART, FALLING FOR YOU

"Maybe you'll think of a way around it." Marla lifted her plastic cup of ice water and took a sip. "Herbie's got plenty of ideas for the storefronts he owns, and Mitch thinks the houses on Millionaire's Row could be a tourist attraction. Someone could drive a renovated school bus through the town on tours. Maybe visit the closed coal mines or whatever's left of the steel operations."

"You know how to think big, Marla. I'll give you that." Suzanne twirled her pen. "But what we really need to discuss is how to make sure Penny doesn't prevent the town's exit from being constructed. How about we do some brainstorming?"

An hour later, they'd worked through a barrage of ideas, filling several pages on Suzanne's notepad. She slid the notes into her bag. "This is a nice start, but we need to get other people involved. Good thing we'll be acting fast." She pulled out a throat lozenge. "My throat's so dry. I must have talked too much."

"You did have a lot of great ideas." Marla jotted a few notes on her napkin. "I'll make time for a few more conversations."

"And I'll draw some mock-ups." Suzanne took a sip of water. "How much longer do you think you'll be in Port Mariette, Marla?"

"Hard to tell. I'd like to be around for the renovation of my aunt's home and for at least some of the town's renovation. But everything depends on that exit."

"If you convert your house to a day spa, who will manage it?" Rachel asked.

"Not sure yet." Marla toyed with a piece of pizza crust then dropped it back on the plate as she looked up at Rachel through her long lashes. "Look, before we leave here today, I've got to tell you something, and you're not going to like it."

Rachel's face suddenly turned splotchy. "What?"

Marla took a deep breath. "You know when I moved to Port Mariette, my parents were going through a divorce.

Such a terrible time for me. I hated moving here. I hated St. Cyprian's Academy and being the new girl. And it seemed everyone hated me, even both of you, until our senior year mission trip."

"It must have been so hard for you." Suzanne touched Marla's arm.

Marla squeezed her hands into fists and sandwiched them between her knees. "You two were popular, the guys all liked you, you had good families, even the nuns liked you. Every aspect of your perfect lives reminded me of how imperfect I—and my whole life—was." She bounced her heels on the gritty floor and stared at her fists. "I was jealous. I wanted what both of you had."

Marla paused, still uncertain of what she wanted to say. "You might remember, our three lockers were close to one another in the hallway. Tony used to hang around yours, Suzanne, waiting for you."

Suzanne nodded. "I remember."

"Rachel, your locker was right next to mine, and every day, guys showed up there to talk with you."

Rachel nodded too.

"They were all in love with you, Rachel, and they all ignored me—except one day, a few weeks after I started at St. Cyp's, Herbie struck up a conversation with me while he was waiting for you. He said, 'You're a classy gal.' That little compliment may not sound like much, but at that time in my life, my self-esteem was even lower than the Port Mariette coal mines."

"Aw, you poor thing." Rachel cast a sympathetic look at Marla.

"Don't feel sorry for me. I was a jerk. You happened to come to your locker right as Herbie said it." Marla's eyes blinked at the memory. "You burst out laughing."

"Really? I don't remember that at all. I'm sorry if I did."

"Well, believe me, you did laugh. It cut me to the core, and I'm ashamed to tell you, I took revenge."

FALLING APART, FALLING FOR YOU

"What did you do? I don't remember anything happening." Rachel's face contorted in confusion.

"You were such a nice girl in school—your nickname was 'Never Say No Rachel.' Always so accommodating."

"Right." Rachel's voice quaked.

"Well, the first time I heard that, I thought people meant you never said no to the boys, that you were ... easy." Marla winced.

"Oh no! You were the one who passed that note!" Rachel spat the words. "How could you have done such an awful thing?" She looked around to make sure no one could hear, and she whispered in anguish, "I was a virgin, for crying out loud. Do you have any idea how humiliating that was? Back then, being called easy was the worst thing that could happen to a Catholic girl. What if Stan had heard about it? He wouldn't have married me!" She grabbed her umbrella and handbag as she got out of her chair.

Marla stood, pleading. "I'm so sorry, Rachel. Please forgive me."

Rachel tossed a ten-dollar bill on the table and stormed out the door before the Marla could squeeze in another word.

"Maybe I shouldn't have told her." Marla slunk back into her chair.

"Why did you, then?"

"I'm trying to clean up my past. I hope she can forgive me."

"Give her a day or two to cool off." Suzanne waved a hand, as if pushing the problem away. "She's got a lot on her mind. It's only a couple months since Stan died."

"But the reunion is the day after tomorrow. I hope this doesn't ruin it for her."

"I've been down this road with the queen of grudges more than once. Who knows if she'll be able to let it go." Suzanne looked into Marla's eyes. "I knew you struggled at St. Cyp's, but I had no idea how bad it must have been for you. I'm sorry I wasn't more supportive."

"Thanks for saying that. Funny how, as we age, some of our early memories are the most vivid. And a lot of times, the most painful too." She shrugged. "I guess that's how we learn. If we're paying attention, that is."

"Right." Suzanne nodded.

"Looking back," said Marla, "it seems most of what I learned in school didn't come from any teacher."

"I made mistakes too." Suzanne shook her head. "Remember that mess I made with Tony, arguing with him about something stupid before he asked me—or would've asked me—to the prom? I could have repaired that relationship, but my pride held me back from apologizing, so he took revenge by asking Mary Frances instead. What a terrible way to end my senior year." She looked out the window again. The rain had slowed to a drizzle; sunlight glistened on the wet sidewalk. "Come to think of it, if Rachel was the queen of grudges, Tony could've been the king. He loved to hold onto things too."

"Well then," Marla said, "I guess it all worked out fine. And with Tony owning a restaurant, if you'd gotten married, you'd probably look like the side of a house by now." She stretched her hands out as far as they could go. They both laughed, then turned silent, lost in their thoughts.

A few seconds later, Suzanne let out a loud sigh. "Adam may be a late arrival, and he may not be perfect, but he's a good partner for me at this stage of life. I hope we'll get married one of these days." She scrunched up the paper napkin on her lap and dropped it onto her empty plate.

Marla pushed back her chair as they prepared to leave. "If that's what's best for you, that's my hope too."

CHAPTER 28

Suzanne

Once she got home from the pizza shop, Suzanne perched herself on her kitchen stool and stirred a sticky gob of honey into some hot green tea. She'd never believed rainy weather brought about colds, but here she sat, two days before the reunion, with a scratchy throat. She would *not* allow herself to get sick.

She took small sips from the turquoise china teacup Jill had given her on her fiftieth birthday. Decorated with the names of God in fancy gold handwriting, the cup had a way of lifting her spirits—which she sure needed after that awkward experience with Marla and Rachel.

Oh, those high school memories—some good, some not. With both elbows on the kitchen island, she sank into her fists. *What would Tony be like at the reunion? Would they feel any of that old chemistry?*

The other day, she'd read about a man and a woman who'd dated when they were only sixteen. Things got out of hand, and their parents forbade them from seeing one another again. The young couple complied, eventually marrying others. But in their sixties, when they both became widowed, they reunited on Facebook and got married.

Those stories always resonated with Suzanne. Yes, Adam's a great guy and just about perfect for her at this stage of life. But still. No woman ever forgets her first love. She sipped her tea while imagining various scenarios of her and Tony at the reunion—their eyes locking, a knowing smile, laughing as they recounted precious memories. *Grow up, Suzanne. You've got your hands full with Adam.*

Her phone dinged, knocking her back to reality. Rachel. Nuh-uh. No way would she get caught in the uncomfortable space between Marla's secret and Rachel's grudge. That call can go right into voicemail. They're both big girls—let them work it out on their own.

Seconds later, the phone rang again. This time, the caller ID said it was the hiring manager at the manufacturing firm. Suzanne's heart pounded. Right now, she couldn't bear to talk with a potential employer. That call can go into voicemail too.

The message appeared and she tapped it open. *We're pleased to extend an offer ... We'll email you the offer letter by tomorrow ... Let us know your decision by Monday.*

What a relief she hadn't taken the call. No thrill in an offer twenty percent less than you used to make. But then again, at the moment, she had no other options on the table. Who could help her decide what to do?

If she called Jill, she'd encourage her to accept the offer so the condo would be available. Her mother, on the other hand, would want her to turn it down, since the job required travel. Their votes would cancel each other out, so what was the point? Talking with Rachel or Marla, at least until they patched things up, was out of the question.

She texted Adam. *Got a job offer.* He was still in New York, but she hoped to catch him between meetings.

No reply.

Rob. He's the perfect one to help me decide. She dialed his number and sighed as her call went into voicemail. At the beep, she left a message. "Hi, Rob. I got a job offer. Can you get back to me when you have a minute?"

FALLING APART, FALLING FOR YOU

She squinted with concentration. Who else might help her decide? Aha! Barbara Marlander. Suzanne had worked with her many years, and she knew Adam well, too—putting her in a position to offer solid advice. Suzanne called Barbara and told her about the job offer.

"Congratulations!" Barbara nearly sang it.

"I'm not sure if I should accept it." Suzanne took a sip of tea. "I need to talk it through first."

"Hmm." Barbara perked up. "How about if you and Adam come over here for dinner tomorrow night? The four of us can talk about it then. By the end of the evening, you'll know what to do, then you'll be able to enjoy your reunion on Saturday."

"That's a terrific idea." Suzanne sighed with relief, as if the correct course of action had already become evident.

"You're sure Burt won't mind?" Burt was one of Adam's key customers. Suzanne didn't want to intrude on the man's schedule, especially without clearing it first with Adam.

"Positive. Burt complained this morning that we have nothing at all planned for Friday. You know how he loves to socialize."

"Fabulous. I'll bring the wine."

Suzanne ended the conversation, then swiveled off the stool to pull her current sketchbook from her purse. Trying to make sense of her emotions, she dashed off a quick caricature, first a profile of Adam, then one of Rob. For fun, she even added one of how she imagined Tony might look today. After all, you never know what might happen at a reunion.

At the Marlanders', she hoped to discover how Adam truly felt about her. Then, at the reunion the next day, she might even have a pleasant surprise—although she certainly wasn't counting on that.

But what about Rob? He remained the question mark. Why did she even include him in her drawing? She'd tried to forget him. He was firmly entrenched in his California life, and Meg still occupied at least a part of his heart.

Yet every time she and Rob talked or texted, she felt closer to him. She'd never felt such a strong physical attraction to any man, and spiritually, Rob had it all over Adam.

She shook her head. How could she be struggling over men at this stage of her life? It was embarrassing.

On the same page, she wrote in calligraphy: "I surrender all. Thy will be done." She laid the book open on a kitchen counter to let the ink dry when her phone rang.

Adam.

She took it as a sign. With a jerk of her arm, she bent across the island to reach the phone. Her elbow bumped the teacup, sending it crashing to the floor. Shards of china littered her kitchen, the names of God no longer legible. She bit her lip to stop herself from swearing.

She accepted the call, and before she could say hello, Adam's voice boomed. "Congratulations, Suzanne!"

She let out an exasperated sigh. "Wait, you don't even know the details."

"Tell me. But I've only got a minute. I'm between meetings."

"It's that job for the manufacturing company. I'll have to drive throughout the tri-state area to deliver training at their plants, which I'm not crazy about, and the salary's about twenty percent less than I made in my last job. But no one else is knocking at my door right now, so I'm getting nervous."

"Hmm. Tough decision. What are you going to do?"

"Not sure. I hoped you'd have some advice for me."

"Aw, Suzanne, you know I don't want to tell you how to live your life."

"Maybe we could talk it over tomorrow night. Burt and Barbara invited us over for steaks on the grill at six. Will you be back from New York in time?"

FALLING APART, FALLING FOR YOU

"Sure. I'll be at your place around five. I've got to run now. See you then."

Suzanne shoved the phone in her pocket, then swept up the broken cup. Would she be able to find a replacement before Jill noticed its absence? She made a note to remind herself to search online, then went to her closet to consider what to wear on Friday. Her job, her relationship with Adam, and her entire future might well be decided at the Marlanders', so her outfit had to be a knockout. Hair too, but she'd worry about that later.

She flicked through her wardrobe options. Black and white silk? Classy but too stark. A sexy sundress? Not serious enough. Something lacy? Not Adam's taste.

In the end, she decided on a fun but flirtatious orange ensemble. The bright colors worked well with her skin tone, and orange was Adam's favorite accent color.

Her phone lit up with a call from Jill. Suzanne debated, but let it go into voicemail. Not ready to hear her daughter's opinion just yet. In the voicemail, Jill asked if Adam had any news for Drew. Good thing she hadn't picked up. Adam was busy now, but tomorrow, she could raise the topic.

A few minutes later, the phone rang yet again. *Geez, I feel like a switchboard operator. Do they even have switchboard operators anymore?*

"It's me, Suzanne."

Rob's soothing voice reminded her of the first time she heard him speak to her, back in the spring at that Phoenix hotel. He'd been an unexpected joy in her life ever since. "Hi, Rob."

"Well, should I say congratulations?"

"Ha. Not sure. It's a decent offer, doing training in the tri-state area. I'd be driving instead of flying for a change."

"The enthusiasm in your voice is underwhelming."

"You're right." Suzanne pursed her lips. "I'm not excited about it at all."

"Why not?"

"That's what I'm struggling with. I love to do training, and I love to travel. The pay's lower, but I won't have to stay in hotels all week long—just a night here and there. So, it's actually what I thought I wanted."

"But you don't."

"No."

"Could you be putting your head in the sand again?"

"About what?"

"You tell me."

"What are you driving at?"

"Look, Suzanne. I think you know in your heart why you're unenthusiastic about this job. Like I always tell you, I'm not your therapist. You need to dig deeper to figure it out."

"You're right, you're not my therapist, you're my—you're my—dear friend in California."

"Have you talked with Adam?"

"I'll be talking with him tomorrow." Not wanting to discuss Adam with Rob, she moved to another topic. "By the way, how's your daughter's promotion working out? Does Emily like Chicago?"

"She's doing okay, but moving from Seattle to Chicago is a considerable adjustment. Seattle's a major city, too—but Chicago's a whole other animal. I'm not sure how it's going to work out for her."

"If she struggles, I'll bet she knows a wise man who could give her great advice."

"Thanks." Rob chuckled. "I'm waiting for her to ask." He paused a moment. "Waiting—that's the hard part."

Suzanne nodded. "Tell me about it. How about Meg?"

"She's developed pneumonia now. I spent a few hours over there with her yesterday."

Suzanne winced. "I'm sorry. It must be hard on both of you, for different reasons."

"Yes, it is. Well. Listen, I've got to run."

CHAPTER 29

RACHEL

Finally, around four o'clock, the heavens dried up. Cinders, spread out on a frayed throw rug in front of the living room TV, whimpered in his sleep.

Rachel called to him as she shook his leash, "Let's blow this joint, big fella." Cinders snapped to attention, and she hooked the leash on his collar. She pushed the screen door open, letting it slam behind them.

"Heading out for a walk?" Frank, sweeping his porch, called to her as she hurried toward the sidewalk.

"Yep. Wanna join us?" Rachel wished she hadn't already suggested a walk to him earlier today. She'd been in a far better mood then, before seeing Marla. *Please say no. I have a lot on my mind. I need to think things through—but not with you.* If Suzanne had answered her phone, she could've talked with her, and if Pete were still here, she might have talked with him. But she definitely didn't want to spill anything to Frank.

Frank lumbered down the steps and reached the sidewalk in record time. He touched Rachel's shoulder and pressed her toward the inside of the sidewalk.

Rachel tipped her head. "That's a gentlemanly thing for you to do, Frank, walking next to the curb. I haven't noticed anyone doing that for years." *Certainly not Stan.*

Rachel blinked a few times as the feeling of a man touching her registered in her mind.

"I think it goes back to the days when horses and buggies splashed mud as they passed people walking nearby." Frank waved a hand toward the street. "The man's supposed to protect the lady from harm."

Cinders stopped to sniff a clump of daisies. "C'mon, Cinders. We're here to exercise, not play around." Rachel tugged on the leash.

"You're keeping up with your health kick, aren't you?" Frank raised a brow.

Rachel sighed. "I am."

"You don't sound too excited about it anymore. Something happen?"

Rachel didn't intend to tell Frank her troubles, but she did need to talk with someone. Would it hurt to let her guard down a teensy bit? She chose to raise a topic of mutual interest. "Have you heard anything about the cost overruns on the new highway?"

"Sure. It's in the papers all the time. Nothing new, though. Construction always goes over budget."

"Yeah, but I've heard rumors Penny wants the State to eliminate our exit. She doesn't want the town to change in any way."

"Hoo boy. That's news to me." Frank shook his head. "That Penny ..."

"She—and some of the council members—apparently believe if a lot of vehicles get off at our exit, we'll end up with more crime and a lot of wear and tear on the roads."

"Well, there's always some risk with progress, but this is a no-brainer. Sounds like she's up to her usual shenanigans."

"What do you mean?"

"I was on council with her a couple years back. I told everyone I resigned because of Wendy, but the real reason was that I didn't want to put up with Penny anymore. She's

FALLING APART, FALLING FOR YOU

all about political connections, and she likes to use them to her personal advantage."

"I never knew that."

"And if you're her friend, she'll make sure your fines magically disappear or you get that zoning exemption you need. But if you're not her friend, watch out."

"So, you think the council members are going along with this because they think they have no choice?"

"Most likely." Frank nodded.

"That's helpful information. Thanks." She'd have to pass it along to Suzanne. Rachel looked at Frank with greater appreciation. *What a good neighbor.*

He kicked a rock out of their path. "Hey, your reunion's this weekend, isn't it?"

"Yep." Rachel nodded.

"All ready for it?"

"I was until about noon today." Rachel sighed.

"What happened at noon?"

"One of my best friends from high school told me she'd done something nasty to me in our senior year."

"And you just found out about it now, forty years later?"

"Yeah." Rachel looked away, wincing at the memory. "Marla said she was jealous of me and got even by passing around a note saying I was easy."

Frank chuckled.

"I don't find it funny at all." Rachel glared at Frank as she yanked Cinders's leash, pulling him away from a telephone pole. "Let's keep moving, Cinders."

"Look, I know you graduated a few years after me, but at St. Cyp's, everyone knew everybody else's reputation. If a girl was easy, the boys from every grade were lining up to spend time with her." Frank stopped to look Rachel in the face. "Trust me. No one ever thought that about you."

"I'm relieved to hear you say that." They continued walking. "Even so, I'm still upset with Marla. That note had to make people stop and wonder."

"Let me ask you a question. What awful thing from forty years ago do you remember about Marla? Herbie? Mary Frances? Or any other person you graduated with?"

"I remember Mary Frances finagled a date to the prom with Tony Mastriano, who my other best friend, Suzanne, was in love with."

"Fascinating you'd remember details like somebody else's prom date. It's not like Mary Frances did anything to *you*."

"Well, there's more to the story—*like my gigantic crush on him*—but I don't feel like getting into it." She looked away, pretending to be interested in a neighbor painting his porch.

"Then again, after all these years, you still hold it against Joey for smashing your picture window with a baseball." He winked.

Rachel scowled.

"C'mon, Rachel, how many years ago did that happen? And you're still nursing a grudge against my son?" He sucked in the corner of his cheek.

"It was more than the broken window, Frank. I always worried Joey was too wild, not a good influence on my boys." She thought about telling Frank about the broken ceramic figurine, too, but suspected he'd never understand.

"Let me ask you another question. Do you hold Joey responsible for what happened to Brian?"

Rachel's hand flew to her chest. "Good grief, no!"

"Do you hold Joey responsible for anything that any of your kids did?"

Rachel's head dropped lower as they continued walking. "No, of course not."

They walked in silence, stopping only when Cinders raised a leg over a patch of dandelions.

Frank slid a hand into his pocket. "I was thinking about how your friend Marla said she was jealous, so she did something to you to hurt you. Sometimes people do something they shouldn't do, then they justify it for some reason or another."

Rachel put a hand on her hip. "Are you saying I took out my anger on Marla not because she passed that note but because of some other reason?"

"I don't know. I said people do that *sometimes*. Maybe you did, maybe you didn't. Only you know the answer. Just something for you to think about."

Rachel had always considered herself a model Catholic—church every Sunday and even on holy days, confession once a month, frequent rosaries. Heck, she tried hard to be a good daughter, wife, mother, friend, neighbor, and back in her school days, a good student. She thought she'd covered all her bases. How could Frank turn Marla's sneaky behavior into what amounted to a religion lesson? And why *did* that note bother her so much, anyway? She stopped in her tracks, allowing Cinders to sniff a weed. *Did Tony read that note? Was that why he asked Mary Frances to the prom instead of her?*

After a quick dinner, Rachel poured herself a beer, the first she'd had since Stan's passing. She sat on her side of the sofa and raised the glass of frothy amber liquid high, in the direction of Stan's side. "Here's to you, Hon. Save me a place in heaven."

She downed it in a few minutes then poured herself another.

Frank's comments about her grudges kept playing over and over in her mind. For the first time, she saw the pattern. Mortified by her lack of self-awareness all these years, she took another gulp.

She remembered being terrified her classmates might believe she was easy, or even worse, that her parents or the nuns would hear about it. She'd never dreamed Marla was the one who wrote the note. If she didn't genuinely like Marla, it would have been easy to continue the grudge, but she cared for the woman. In fact, she liked her now even more than she had in high school.

But Frank did have a point. She was jealous of Marla. Look at how her life had turned out, even though she had broken a lot of rules. It really wasn't fair.

A bit sloshed, she picked up her phone and called next door. "Hi, Frank, s'Rachel. You up for some canasta?"

"Deal me in."

Rachel shuffled the cards a few times.

Frank appeared at her door. "I'm glad you called. I was kinda bored watching TV."

"Something to drink?"

He looked at her empty glass. "I'll take a beer if you have it."

Three hands later, Rachel led by more than five hundred points.

"You're a shark, girl! Why didn't you warn me?" He chuckled.

"I've been thinking about what you said to me earlier today."

"Uh-huh."

"I think it all boils down to forgiveness."

Frank took his turn dealing the cards, fifteen each. He turned over the first card of the deck and snapped it onto the table. "An ace! You're too lucky." He looked up. "And have you concluded anything?"

"Not totally. I did realize I have a tendency to hold grudges, to be bitter about things others let go. I know I should let things go too, but it's so unnatural for me." She took her turn and discarded a six.

"Sort of like me always wanting to eat cheeseburgers and pizza. I've done it so long, and I know it's bad for me, but, hey, it's a hard habit to break." Frank snorted.

"Right." She chuckled.

FALLING APART, FALLING FOR YOU

They continued playing, silently, with Rachel's mind processing her thoughts.

"Another thing I've realized is I get so wrapped up in whatever wrong someone has done to me that I'm not always living in the present, enjoying the person or the moment." She put an elbow on the table and sank her head onto her palm. "The past is always hovering there along with the person I'm holding a grudge against."

"So, what are you going to do about it?"

"Not sure. Maybe I'll pray about it."

"Sounds like a great idea."

Rachel's eyes widened as she looked at the cards on the table. "Did you just go out on me?" Her mouth fell open.

"Yep." Frank grinned. "I hope you won't hold it against me."

CHAPTER 30

MARLA

Trying to push yesterday's confrontation with Rachel out of her mind, Marla whisked a few articles of clothing fresh from her aunt's dryer and basked in the fabric's comforting warmth. She'd chosen the most casual outfit she'd packed—beige capris and a sleeveless red top—along with gold hoop earrings, like Grace wore the other day. Plain and simple. Marla hoped it would help her fit in with Grace and her parents.

Grateful the rain had finally stopped, Marla slipped outside to walk off her jitters on the grounds of her aunt's home, now hers.

Grateful. She was grateful for the house, of course, but far more so for her daughter, and that she'd be meeting Theresa and Denny later today.

At Mitch's church a couple weeks ago, the preacher spoke about the power of gratitude. At the time, the message seemed light and fluffy. But today, she understood its power.

Only a few months ago, her future was completely up in the air. But now, she could see a glimpse of the horizon. She'd found Grace and would soon meet her adoptive parents. She was playing a role in the transformation of the town by hiring Mitch to convert Aunt Adele's house into a beautifully appointed day spa, and by lending her marketing expertise to Mitch and Herbie. Mitch and his crew would restore Millionaire's Row to its former glory, while Herbie and others would fill the empty storefronts of Main Street. She'd reconnected with Suzanne and Rachel, and even though the relationship with Rachel was rocky right now, she felt hopeful they'd restore it.

What was missing? Not much, though it would sure be nice to have someone beside her, a man she could share her life with. But who could that be? Warren? He'd be more interested in her money than in her. Herbie? A funny fellow, good company and a good mind, but for her, a blade of grass held more physical attraction. Mitch? Great guy all around, but work and golf consumed his time, leaving no room for a relationship. Men like Todd occasionally spiced up her life, but she'd grown accustomed to being alone, and so Deanna, her former right arm, had ended up being her only consistent sounding board. Right now, while preparing to meet Grace's adoptive parents, she yearned for a pep talk.

Marla strode along a path until reaching a wrought iron bench nestled among tall white pines. She settled herself on the seat as she tapped Deanna's number on her phone. "Hey, Deanna, got a minute?"

"I wondered when I'd hear from you." Deanna chuckled.

"What do you mean?"

"You can't take it when life's boring, Marla. You always have to stir up the pot. I've been waiting to hear what you're up to."

Marla filled her in on Aunt Adele, Suzanne, Rachel, and Penny, as well as the day spa, golfing, her ideas for Main Street, and her concerns about the town's new exit.

"Wow. Even for you, that's an impressive list. What could be left to do now?"

Marla had never shared her past with anyone outside the family except when she asked Warren to help find Grace. Maybe now was the time to get comfortable explaining it.

FALLING APART, FALLING FOR YOU

"I have a daughter—I gave her up for adoption forty years ago." Marla tensed her body, unsure of how Deanna would react.

"Omigosh, Marla! Are you going to try to find her?"

"I already have. Grace lives here in Port Mariette." Marla described the striking resemblance between them. "She even sounds like me."

"How amazing to meet her after all these years." Deanna paused. "So ... she's the reason you spent your senior year there?"

"Mm-hmm. My parents were furious when I got pregnant. My dad wanted me to get an abortion, but my mother had been raised Catholic and wouldn't allow it. They forced me to live with my aunt here in Port Mariette until I had the baby in August. Then, assuming I'd slip and tell someone about why I'd left town, they made me stay here for my senior year."

"So that's how you ended up graduating from St. Cyprian's Academy, a Catholic high school in a coal and steel town in southwestern Pennsylvania." Deanna clicked her tongue. "Wow. What an adjustment that must have been."

"No kidding." Marla chuckled. She lowered her voice. "I'm meeting her adoptive parents in an hour. I'm kind of nervous."

"I can imagine. How about we pray about it." Without waiting for a response, Deanna launched into a heartfelt prayer.

"Thanks, Deanna. I love your prayers." Marla let out a breath. "A couple weeks ago, I went to an Assembly of God church with Mitch. Their prayers reminded me of yours. I never admitted it, but sometimes I've wished I could pray like you ... or have the faith you have."

"It sounds to me like you're starting your journey."

"But I'll never be good like you. You don't know—you just don't know all the things I've done." Marla stammered and had to stop for a moment to collect herself.

"We've all made mistakes. Next time we talk, I'll tell you some of mine, how's that?"

Deanna's soothing voice calmed Marla. "Sounds good, Deanna."

"I'm glad you told me about Grace and your senior year. It all makes sense now."

"Maybe to you." Marla's eyes searched the skies.

"God's plan is not our plan. His ways are higher than ours. Keep watching, you'll see how God has this all mapped out for you."

"I wish I could see the map." Marla eked out a chuckle.

Deanna laughed. "But that would take all the fun out of God's adventures."

As she rang the O'Donnells' doorbell, Marla looked down at the green artificial grass carpeting covering their tiny cement porch. Would she ever fit in Grace's world?

The screen door creaked as Grace pushed it open. "Good to see you again, Marla." Her daughter smiled but didn't move to hug Marla.

"You too." Marla didn't reach out to hug Grace either. Not the place for that today.

Grace moved back to give Marla space to enter. "Come in and meet my parents."

She stepped inside, an uncertain look on her face. Considering Denny's health, today might be the only chance she'd get to talk with him. Theresa, too, for that matter, if the conversation didn't go well.

Theresa rocked herself out of a worn corduroy recliner, her eyes already filled with tears. Denny stayed seated on the sofa, propped into place with several bed pillows, a plaid blanket curved around his thin body.

"Mom, Dad—this is Marla Galani."

FALLING APART, FALLING FOR YOU

Theresa stepped closer, tears streaming down her cheeks, fast, as if someone had turned on a spigot. "I don't know how to thank you, Marla." Theresa embraced her hard. "You've blessed us more than you'll ever know."

Marla patted her as they hugged. *How many times had Theresa hugged Grace?* Jealousy surged in Marla's heart, but she shoved it aside and replaced it with gratitude, as she recalled Grace's comment about her parents being so wonderful.

The ice broken, Theresa insisted Marla sit in the recliner. "It's the most comfortable seat in the house." Marla relented and Theresa scurried to the kitchen.

Denny spoke up, his voice crackly. "I don't talk much these days. But thank you for our daughter. You changed our world. We could never thank you enough."

Theresa reemerged, holding a metal tray crowded with cans of soft drinks. After serving everyone, she plopped on the sofa beside her husband. "Grace told us you live in New York City. That must be very exciting—sort of the opposite of Port Mariette." She chuckled then coughed.

Marla shrugged a shoulder. "To tell you the truth, I've discovered a lot happens in a small town—certainly more than I expected."

Grace, perched on the wooden piano bench, straightened her back. "I think it's because people talk to one another in a small town, so you hear more."

Her daughter's good posture pleased Marla. Slouching aged a woman. "Do you play?" Marla asked, glancing at the piano.

"I do." Grace swirled around and played a few chords.

"I took piano lessons too." Marla said it tentatively, unsure how much she should share right now.

"Grace mentioned you sold your business." Theresa folded her hands. "Are you going to start a new business here in Port Mariette?"

"Frankly, I'm not sure what I'm going to do. For now, I wanted to meet you both, and I hope we can create a relationship that's comfortable for everyone."

"Grace told me she explained to you how—and why—we kept her adoption secret." Theresa held Denny's hand as she talked. "It would've been fodder for the gossip mill, and we didn't want any part of that." She looked sideways at her husband. "We obsessed about keeping it a secret, but now—"

"We don't know if anyone would care." Denny shrugged.

"Everything changes over time." Grace waved a hand.

Theresa nodded. "I called my mom and brother this morning to let them know you'd be coming here today. They live in Florida, otherwise they'd be here." She turned a palm up. "Mom obviously knew about the adoption, but we told my brother all the details. His name's Randy, but we call him Chip."

"Chip off the old block," Grace explained, with a wink to Marla.

"Anyway," Theresa continued, "Chip was shocked, but he gets why we kept it a secret. When you have time, Mom and Chip both want you to give them a call."

"I'd love to talk with them." Marla set her soft drink on the cardboard coaster.

"My sister is the only other one we have to tell." Theresa's eyes lit up. "She lives here in Port Mariette, so we asked her to come over today. Told her we want her to meet someone special."

Grace piped up. "You'll love Aunt Sissy. She's a sweetheart. She'll be here in a few minutes."

"I'd love to meet her too." Marla crossed her legs and turned toward Grace. "Before your aunt arrives, I need to talk with you and your parents about something important. You see—well, there's no other way to say this except straight out. I made a lot of money from selling my business, and I'll inherit even more from my parents and

FALLING APART, FALLING FOR YOU

Aunt Adele." She took a deep breath. "On top of that, I—I have a health condition. It's under control now, but who knows what might happen down the road."

She paused to gauge their reaction. All three sat stiffly, wide-eyed.

Marla grabbed onto her knee. "I have no other close relatives besides you, Grace. I hope it doesn't happen anytime soon, but one day, you'll be my only heir."

Theresa and Denny both stared at Marla, mouths agape, then at one another, then back at Marla.

"We had no idea." Theresa's hand covered her heart.

Grace didn't say a word and remained expressionless—like Marla had behaved the day she sold her business.

Denny cleared his throat. "I'm sorry to hear you have a health condition. Believe me, I know how that feels." He pulled his blanket tighter around him. "I have to tell you, Marla, it's a comfort to hear Grace won't have to struggle financially. Knowing that is a tremendous gift." Denny's body quivered. A single tear ran down his cheek. He wiped it away with his finger and looked up at Marla. "Thank you."

The screen door swung open and a middle-aged woman in jeans bounced into the living room, stopping short. She cocked her head and furrowed her brow. "Marla, what are you doing here?"

"Rachel!" Marla's hand flew to her chest.

Rachel put her hands on her hips. "What's going on here, Terrie?"

Theresa couldn't react except to open her mouth.

Rachel looked at her brother-in-law next. "Bud, what's this all about?"

Grace leaped off the piano bench and hugged her aunt. "Come have a seat, Aunt Sissy. We have something to share with you." With an arm around Rachel, she led her to the piano bench and explained about the adoption.

"So, you kept this a secret from me all these years, Terrie?" Rachel glared at Theresa. "I know we weren't always close, but, crying out loud, we're sisters!" Pain washed over Rachel's face.

"I'm sorry, Sis. We'd kept the secret so long, there didn't seem a right time to tell anyone. We never meant to hurt you."

Rachel's eyes bore into Marla next. "And you! Our entire senior year together, and you never mentioned a word about this. Now, with our reunion tomorrow, you spring *this* on me too? What other surprises do you have to upset my universe?" She shot up from the piano bench and sped to the door.

"Sis, hold on!" Theresa tried to get up from the sofa, but she'd sunk deep into the cushions and couldn't move fast enough.

Denny sneezed and Grace reached for a tissue for him.

"Wait, let's talk—" Marla stood, her arms outstretched.

Rachel turned around at the door, glaring at Marla. "I don't need any explanation. I was ready to forgive you for what you told me yesterday, but now, I see there's a pattern to your behavior. You should be friends with that sneak Penny, not me and Suzanne!" She was out the door before anyone had a chance to say another word.

"I never put two and two together." Grace shook her head. "No wonder she was so shocked."

"Poor Sis. She's an emotional wreck these days. Her husband died of a heart attack a few months ago, her son's getting a divorce, and—oh, you probably already know all about those things."

Marla nodded. There was so much more she wanted to discuss with Grace and her parents, but Rachel had sucked the energy out of everyone, including Marla. She picked up her purse and smoothed her slacks as she stood, ready to leave.

Theresa pushed herself up from the sofa. "Could you come back and visit again, maybe early next week? This has been so emotional for all of us."

FALLING APART, FALLING FOR YOU

They hugged their good-byes, with promises to meet again soon.

Marla pushed the screen door open, stepped onto the fake grass carpeting, and sighed. This time, the secret wasn't her fault, but that hadn't stopped Rachel from holding her accountable.

Marla poked her way home and settled in for the rest of the day. Loud clanking on the side of her house caused her to peek out a cracked window. She spotted Mitch's green pickup and went outside.

"I'm dropping a few things off for my guys. They'll be here Monday. Sorry if I disturbed you."

"Not at all." Marla stepped off the porch. "If you have time, stop in when you're done." Still shaken from the visit at Denny and Theresa's, she was grateful—*there's that word again*—Mitch had chanced to come by. Just hearing his baritone voice made her feel calmer.

A few minutes later, he rapped at the door.

"C'mon in." Marla called from the kitchen. "Would you like coffee, a soft drink, beer, or something stronger?"

"Something tells me you're hoping I'll say 'something stronger' so you can match me." Hands on his hips, he arched an eyebrow, giving Marla a knowing look.

"You're right."

"Whiskey or vodka. Surprise me."

She fluttered a hand. "Make yourself comfortable in the living room." She brought in two vodka tonics and spread herself out on the crushed velvet loveseat. "I just had a bad experience."

"Care to talk about it?" He sat on the rocking chair, calmly sliding back and forth.

The movement relaxed her. She tipped back her glass for a gulp, then set it with a thud on the mahogany coffee table. For close to an hour, she rambled, unloading her past on him. She couldn't help herself. If Deanna had been here, she would've been the sounding board, but she wasn't, so Mitch would have to do. He was a "man of God" as Deanna would say, and Marla did have to admit she felt comfortable spilling her story to him. *This must be what it's like to go to confession at St. Cyp's.* Marla, of course, had never done such a thing.

Through it all, Mitch made no judgmental comments, only encouraging ones.

"So let me ask you, do you consider yourself Catholic?" he asked when she ran out of material.

"No, I'm not Catholic. I don't know what I am. I've always considered myself a believer but not a follower, if that makes sense. But now that I've sold my business, I'm feeling like my life has no purpose. I'm at a crossroads, and I don't know which way to go. It's been making me wonder if God is what's been missing in my life."

"Mm-hmm."

"This morning, I told my friend Deanna I sometimes wish I could pray like her, and that I had the faith she has."

"If a person believes, it shows up in their actions. So maybe your faith isn't as strong as you think."

"Hmm." Marla thought about her recent past with Todd. Conviction pierced her heart. "You're right."

"You can have true faith if you want it. It's a decision. You choose whether or not to believe."

"I know." She nodded. "I've heard that before."

"Look, Marla. You're very talented. Sometimes people who are talented can get sidetracked by using their talents for their own purposes, instead of what God intended them to be used for. When you use them for your own purposes, ambition and pride can set in." He took a final swig of his drink. "I know because I've been there."

Marla's eyebrows shot up. She couldn't imagine Mitch any other way but how he was today.

FALLING APART, FALLING FOR YOU

"God's refining fire burns that out, and one day, you're able to turn everything in your life over to God." He stood. "Sounds to me like God has you right where he wants you."

CHAPTER 31

Suzanne

Friday, at five on the dot, Suzanne buzzed Adam into the downstairs foyer. She'd dressed to impress in her orange capris, strappy sandals with kitten heels, and a silky top sliding down her left shoulder. She'd read somewhere that even as women age, their shoulders remain sexy. She never would have guessed that, but hey, at almost fifty-eight, a girl had to take advantage of every available tool.

With a hand on her hip and shoulders back, she waited at her door, smiling demurely and anticipating a kiss, a hug, and a compliment too.

"Hi, Suzanne." Adam's face intense, he brushed past her and strode to the picture window.

Seriously? She could've been wearing a red string bikini and he wouldn't have noticed.

"What's wrong?" Suzanne tiptoed along the carpet after him.

"I've got news." Adam stretched his hands over his hips as he turned from the window. He glanced her way, but his blue eyes never looked below her chin.

She headed to the sofa, gripping its armrest as she eased herself onto the cushion. Adam chose to sit in the upholstered chair across from her.

Her eyes widened at his seating selection. She clamped her teeth, bracing herself for whatever was to come.

Adam leaned forward, elbows on his knees. He ran a hand through his short, bank-executive hair.

"I got a job offer too." He said it in a monotone.

"Oh my gosh." Both her hands flew to her chest. "How exciting!"

He squared his shoulders. "It's the number two job at a much larger bank."

"That's terrific." If they got married one day, maybe she wouldn't have to work at all.

"The job's in Manhattan."

Suzanne sniffed in a breath. Was this good news or bad news for her? Her voice quavered as she put her hands back on her lap. "And what happens to us?"

"Here's the situation, Suzanne." He stood and paced the room, hands in his pockets. "I've been dying."

"Dying?" She threw a hand to the nape of her neck.

"On the inside." Adam stopped his pacing to clarify. "You see, Pittsburgh's a pretty conservative place, and I've had to toe the line when it comes to my personal life."

"What are you talking about? You have a wonderful social life and live in a beautiful condo in the heart of the cultural district."

"I can't be who I am in a city like Pittsburgh."

She scrunched up her face. "Who are you?"

"I'm gay, Suzanne." He said it with a hint of irritation, as if she should have already known.

"Huh?" Her head jerked back.

"Here in Pittsburgh, I have to hide the fact that I'm gay. It wouldn't be good for my career. But in New York, it's not an issue at all. I can be the real me. No secrets."

"All these months, you've let me believe you were straight?" She leaned forward, spitting out the words. "You played me for a fool." She glared at Adam. "You used me!" She punched a fist onto the sofa cushion.

"Look, Suzanne." He sat down across from her again, his hands laced together between his knees. "I can understand

FALLING APART, FALLING FOR YOU

why you're upset, but I tried not to lead you on—or to make you think we had a future. You were on the road so much that it seemed like an ideal relationship for both of us. You wanted a relationship without strings, and I always treated you well. We had many nice times together—dinners, the symphony, parties, fundraisers."

"People will think I'm an idiot." She dropped her face into her hands. "How humiliating."

"They won't think that. No one else knows I'm gay—except my ex-wife Pauline—and believe me, she's the last person on earth who would tell anyone. Once I move away, sure, some of the bank executives here in Pittsburgh might hear something, but you'll never see them again."

Suzanne caught a glance at the clock on the TV stand. "Oh my gosh. It's twenty after five. The Marlanders are expecting us for dinner in forty minutes."

"I already called Burt to cancel." He slid the back of his hand across his forehead.

"How thoughtful of you." Her voice oozed sarcasm. *Was he sweating?*

"Look, Suzanne, I'm sorry to spring this on you. A recruiter called me out of the blue." He shrugged. "Everything fell into place so fast it surprised even me. I know this is the right opportunity for me, and I'm sure you'll figure out if that job offer is the right one for you too."

Suzanne forced herself to take slow, deep breaths.

"By the way, I lined up an interview for your son-in-law. Someone will call him to set it up." Adam swiped his forehead again.

She wanted to hate him, but now, how could she?

He shifted in the chair. "Don't tell Drew, but it's a sure thing he'll get the job. He'll be making more than he did in Jersey."

Suzanne looked down at her knees, unable to look him in the face. "Thanks. I appreciate your arranging that." She shoved herself up from the sofa, stumbled to the foyer in a daze, and opened the door. "I wish you well in your new life." She sounded mechanical but felt proud of herself for at least getting the right words out of her mouth.

He stood beside her. "I'm sorry, Suzanne. I never intended to hurt you. You really are a wonderful woman." He paused, as if preparing to hug her.

She recoiled.

Adam's lips twitched. He turned away and disappeared down the hall.

Suzanne kicked off her heels and stalked to the kitchen. She poured herself a glass of wine.

How did I miss it? His beautifully appointed condo ... the endless talk about draperies ... his supposed concern about respecting my boundaries. *Good grief. I am an idiot.*

Adam's red roses, now dead, stood at attention in the crystal vase on the kitchen island, looking like thirty-six pick-up sticks with bloody heads. She unfurled a garbage bag and thrust the bouquet into it, unconcerned about the drops of water speckling the wooden plank floor. She tied the bag tight and slammed it across the kitchen.

Adam could explain all he wanted. She still felt like a fool.

And now, after this, what should she do about that job offer? She sighed. Corporate trainers—older ones in particular—apparently weren't in great demand. She opened her computer, hoping for an email from someone interested in her résumé.

Nada. Thank goodness she had till Monday to decide.

She trudged down the hall to retrieve her sketchbook, still open to the page with Adam, Tony, and Rob.

Rob. She tapped his name on her phone and plopped onto the sofa.

"What's up, Suzanne? Have you made a decision already?" He sounded surprised to hear from her.

"No. I'm not calling about the job." She paused, not sure what to say or how to say it. "Adam just left."

FALLING APART, FALLING FOR YOU

"And?"

"He got a job offer at a big bank in New York City."

"Oh." Rob's voice lowered. "Will you be moving?"

"Hardly. He also told me he's gay." She took a gulp of her chardonnay.

"What? That's a shock."

"No kidding. I'm so humiliated. He used me as his foil. He needed a woman on his arm so no one would know his secret."

"And in New York, he feels free to come out?"

"Uh-huh." She sighed. "I guess I can add Adam to the list of men who've disappointed me."

"Knowing you, you'll bounce back just fine." He paused. "But even so, nothing wrong with having a brief pity party, maybe an hour or two."

Suzanne chuckled. "Thanks. I'm doing that right now."

Rob cleared his throat. "Let me ask you a question. Did you have fun going out to all those dinners and social events with Adam?"

"Of course I did. Otherwise, I wouldn't have gone."

"Here's another question. This one's harder. Did you love *Adam*—or did you love the *experiences* you had while dating him?"

Suzanne had to think. She sipped some more wine.

"Could it be that, without realizing it, you may have been using Adam too?"

"Ouch." She winced.

"Did I hit a nerve?" Rob said it in that gentle-but-honest way she loved.

"Yeah." She set the glass on the coffee table.

"I'm sorry for being direct, but sometimes that's the best way to say the hard things."

"I've always appreciated that about you." She tapped her glass with her fingernail.

"Thanks. Maybe now's a good time to tell you something else that's been on my mind."

Suzanne froze. *Is today going to be a one-two punch?* "What is it?"

"Well, this is only a thought, so take it with a chunk of salt. I've been wondering if all your years of being on the road training others might have held back your own personal development."

"What do you mean?" She scrunched her face.

"Well, think about it. Monday through Friday, you didn't have a constant flow of everyday-life issues like you would if you worked a regular job, interacting with people all day long. Instead, you delivered the same training program over and over. You had an arsenal of programmed answers to any questions that arose. And evenings? Most of them you spent alone."

Suzanne's eyes darted around the room as she mentally ran through a typical week on the road. Different cities with different people, but rarely did she have a deep conversation or face an extraordinary situation. "I never thought about it that way. Like, maybe I missed an important slice of life?"

"I don't know. I could be wrong. It's something for you to think about. I mean, Look at your friend in Port Mariette—Rachel, right?

"Right." Suzanne nodded.

"She sounds like a good woman, but you said she can behave like a child at times, holding grudges and overreacting. Maybe one of the reasons is because her life's been rather narrow. As an example, you said she never travels, doesn't even go to Pittsburgh all that often, and that's less than an hour away. She's probably missed out on a lot of other encounters and activities. Exposure to a variety of experiences develops a person into a well-rounded human being."

Suzanne furrowed her brow. "So, are you saying I'm flawed because I didn't work a traditional nine-to-five job?"

"Not at all. I'm merely saying that during the workweek, your interactions were probably superficial, where you stood as the authority figure in a classroom setting. It's just a thought, based on my background and what I noticed when we spent time together."

"What did you notice then?" She touched her lower lip with a fingertip.

"Well, in some ways you're very polished—like at the Wild West Night and the cocktail party in Phoenix. But I felt you overreacted to my 'surprises.' Really, is it such a big deal that I sometimes fill in for my pastor? Shouldn't that be a good thing? And that's just one example."

"Hmm." She sighed. "I see your point."

"No wonder you were perfect for Adam. You fit his needs—a beautiful, intelligent, charming—but safe—companion. And until you found out his motives, he fit your needs too."

Suzanne cringed. "I never looked at it that way. It's true—I did use Adam."

"Look, Suzanne. We all have our own motivated self-interests. To be honest, when I met you in Phoenix, I thought it'd be a fun respite, a serendipitous encounter. It surprised me when my attraction to you grew so fast. Frankly, it caught me off guard, and I'm still wondering what to do about it."

She had to agree. "Such a pity we don't live close to one another."

"And let's be honest—Meg's still in the picture. I know that's hard for you to accept."

"You're right." She blew out a loud sigh. "Well, you've given me lots to ponder. I ... I think I'm going to finish this glass of wine and watch an old movie."

"Okay. But what are you going to do about that job offer?"

"Hmm. I think—I think I'm going to turn it down. Yes. Talking with you helped."

A call beeped on Suzanne's phone. "Thanks for the clarity, Rob. You're a sweetheart for helping me through this. Talk to you later."

She clicked to the next call.

"Barbara—what's up?"

"You tell me. Adam told Burt he had some kind of emergency. I wanted to make sure everything's all right."

"It is—and it isn't. Adam just accepted a job offer."

"Really?"

"It's in Manhattan."

"Oh dear. What now?"

"It's the end for us." Suzanne let out a sigh. "I'm sitting here in my snazzy outfit, having a glass of wine and feeling sorry for myself."

Barbara smacked her lips. "How about this. Meet me at Rivers Casino in an hour. Let's go party, just you and me."

Suzanne would never have chosen a casino as the place to drown her sorrows, but Barbara had a way of making any place fun. What the heck. "Won't Burt mind?"

"Nah. He's gorging on some new business book. He won't even know I'm gone."

An hour later, Suzanne and Barbara wove their way through the dizzying kaleidoscope of slots. Suzanne wanted to cover her ears. And nose. "I thought we were in the non-smoking section."

"We are, but that smell drifts." Barbara waved a long-fingered hand. "You'll get used to it."

"I've never gambled, except for playing a few slots in Vegas." Suzanne confessed with a sheepish look on her face.

"Smart girl. Gambling's for those who've got money to burn. Everyone knows the house always wins." Barbara raised her chin and looked in the distance. "Let's go play the craps table. We'll have some fun there." She led Suzanne to a rectangular table surrounded by several men and women. "I'll place a bet and explain the game as we go."

When they neared the table, Suzanne jerked to a stop and whispered to Barbara. "That's the mayor of Port Mariette." She jutted her head toward a small unsmiling woman with piles of chips stacked high in front of her.

FALLING APART, FALLING FOR YOU

"The mayor of your hometown?"

"Come over here." Suzanne pulled Barbara behind a pillar and explained the highway issue. "It's crucial the town gets its exit. Everybody's been trying to think of a way to make sure the mayor doesn't prevent it, but the fact is, no one knows what's going to happen."

"Hmm." Barbara crossed her arms for a minute, then stuck a hand out. "Give me your cellphone."

Suzanne's eyes tailed Barbara as she mingled through the crowd and discreetly snatched a clip of Penny.

With a smirk on her face, Barbara rejoined Suzanne. "You now have video showing your esteemed mayor in the process of betting—and losing—more than ten thousand dollars at the craps table." Barbara thrust the phone into Suzanne's hand. "Quite the leverage for getting that exit."

Suzanne's jaw dropped as she reviewed the video.

A moment later, Penny placed another bet.

Just looking at her face, Suzanne could tell the mayor had lost again. Suzanne sped to the table as Penny reached to gather her remaining chips. "Excuse me, aren't you the mayor of Port Mariette?" Suzanne asked as if she were an admirer.

"No, I think you're mistaken." Penny avoided eye contact as she scooped up her last chips.

"I'm quite sure. I've seen your photo in the *Port Mariette Gazette*." Suzanne spoke firmly as she moved closer to Penny.

"Again, you are mistaken." Penny said the words in a measured tone.

But Suzanne knew she had, as they say in the movies, *the goods*. "Step over here, ma'am." Suzanne narrowed her eyes and jutted her head to the right. "I have something important to show you." They walked behind a pillar.

Suzanne held up her phone so Penny could watch the video. "I might be tempted to show this to Walt Celinski at the *Port Mariette Gazette*."

Penny glared. "You aren't allowed to videotape in a casino. Why would you do that, anyway?"

"Actually, someone else recorded it. Besides, I could ask you the same thing about the highway exit—why would you do that?" Suzanne gripped the phone as her palm began to sweat. This was a fine line she was treading.

The two stared at one another for several seconds. Suzanne held her stern pose without flinching.

"So, you're one of those exit nuts?" Penny jerked her chin up.

"One of many." Suzanne enunciated each syllable and glared deep into Penny's eyes, feeling suddenly thankful for her years as a trainer, able to conceal her emotions.

Penny breathed loud enough for Suzanne to hear above the din. After what seemed like a dozen breaths, she spoke through taut lips. "I'm sure we can come to some kind of agreement."

Suzanne couldn't wait to fall into bed—but first, she had to call Marla.

"Talk about a turn of events!" Marla whooped.

"I know. She caved in a matter of minutes. Penny will never know it, but I could never have brought myself to show that video to anyone else. Even so, it gives us the leverage we need. How do you think we should capitalize on it?"

Marla ticked off some rapid-fire ideas, and by midnight, they fine-tuned the best one.

"That was invigorating. Makes me wish I hadn't sold my business." Marla chortled.

"Don't worry, something tells me you'll find a way to keep yourself busy." Suzanne yawned. "What a night. I'll finish the artwork tomorrow morning, before the reunion. I guess it's not my business, but have you and Rachel patched things up yet? She left me a voicemail, but I've been too busy to listen to it."

"Not yet, but I've got a little surprise planned for tomorrow. I hope it'll get her laughing, and maybe she'll be able to get over the past."

"A surprise? How fun! I hope it does the trick. Well, I hope we both get a good night's sleep. Big day tomorrow for everyone. G'night."

Despite the time, Suzanne couldn't resist pulling her red dress from the closet, the one she'd worn to *Carmen* with Adam, the one she'd wear tomorrow. She wished she could be wearing it for Rob, but that was only a fantasy.

Maybe Tony'd like it. She rolled her eyes, hung the dress back up, and went to bed.

CHAPTER 32

THE REUNION

Hands on her hips, Rachel took one last look at herself in the coat-closet mirror—front, back, both sides. She ran a hand across the neckline of her silky dress and puffed her new hairdo, then nodded in approval. Shapewear, ruching, and her efforts at a healthy lifestyle had paid off. She hadn't looked this good in years.

"The old girl's still got it, wouldn't you say, Cinders?" Rachel patted him on the head and scooted out the door. Unaccustomed to wearing high heels, she took the front porch steps with care. Pete had done a masterful job replacing the rotting wood, yet in shoes like these, any set of stairs could be tricky.

Giddy with excitement, she grinned and waved to Frank as she neared her car door.

Frank stood at his mailbox, staring. "If I could whistle, this is when I'd do it."

Rachel blushed.

He waved a handful of mail at her as he walked toward his house. "Have fun at the reunion."

"Thanks, Frank." All aglow, Rachel slid onto the worn cloth seat and adjusted herself behind the steering wheel. Still grinning, she inhaled deeply to calm herself, then exhaled as she turned the key.

Nothing but a grinding noise.

She tried again. Same thing.

"Oh no!" Rachel draped an arm over the steering wheel and leaned on it, tears already brimming in her mascaraed eyes.

Seconds later, Frank knocked at her car window. He pulled the door open. "Need a ride?"

"Sure looks that way." The tears welled over and streamed down her cheeks.

"Hey, hey, hey. You'll be fine. I'll get you there."

Frank's gentle demeanor made her cry all the more. She grabbed her purse and stepped out of the car. He patted her on the back and gave her an awkward semi-hug. "C'mon, what's going on? It's just a dead battery."

Rachel sniffled, found a tissue, and blew her nose. "Today of all days, the car decides not to start." She shook her head. "I guess I'm so emotional about this reunion." She pulled out another tissue. "It was the day of Stan's funeral when I learned about it, and in my mind, both events are somehow connected."

"Ah, I know what you mean. So many things remind me of Wendy. I think of her every day, but sometimes the memories are more powerful."

Rachel wiped and sniffed. "And this is our first reunion in forty years. I'm nervous about seeing all my classmates who moved away."

She blew her nose again. "And I still don't know what to do about Marla. I'm afraid seeing her is going to ruin the reunion for me." She wadded up the tissues and slipped them into her purse. "I know I should forgive her, but I don't know how."

He patted her on the back one more time. "Say a prayer. God will lead you."

"You're right. I haven't prayed about it. I'll do that later. When I have some time."

"A prayer doesn't have to take long. Why don't you close your eyes right now and tell God what's on your heart?

FALLING APART, FALLING FOR YOU

It'll help calm you down too. You're shaking." He held onto her shoulders as if his strong hands could absorb her nervousness.

The way Frank talked, it sounded like something Father Obringer at St. Cyp's would say to her if she told him about Marla. So, Rachel closed her eyes and prayed silently. *Dear God, please help me forgive Marla. I can't do it without you. Amen.*

"Thanks, Frank. I feel better. But my face is a mess. Can you wait till I touch up my makeup?"

"I'm not going anywhere." He crossed his arms and leaned against the passenger door.

Rachel gingerly walked on the red-dog driveway to the rear of her Chevy. She unlocked the trunk, revealing boxes overflowing with high school memorabilia. "In the meantime, could I ask you to load these things in your truck?" She cast Frank an appreciative smile.

Twenty minutes later, they arrived at the front entrance of the country club.

Frank put his pickup in park and stuck his hand out to Rachel. "Gimme your car keys—I'll jump it when I get home."

"That's so sweet of you." She placed the keys into his large open hand, surprised she liked the feel of contact with him. Not exciting enough to qualify as a spark, but rather, a comforting feeling.

"I'll leave the keys behind your screen door when I'm done."

"Perfect. Suzanne or someone—*maybe Tony*—will give me a ride home. Thanks for everything, Frank. You're such a good neighbor."

"You go on ahead. I'll unload your boxes and then you can show me where to put everything."

Rachel pranced into the foyer, feeling beautiful, healthy, and ten years younger.

As soon as Suzanne entered the country club, she zeroed in on the empty registration table next to the ballroom door and plunked her box of nametags on it. She'd already alphabetized them and stacked them like soldiers, all the names typed in a forty-eight-point font.

She spotted Rachel inside the ballroom.

"I saved you a seat," Rachel mouthed, pointing to a table near the stage.

Suzanne threw a thumbs-up, then delicately seated herself on a chair of cracked faux-leather, possibly purchased sometime before their graduation. She flipped through the yearbook photos one more time then set the book aside, confident she'd be able to connect names with faces.

Classmates began filing into the foyer. Just as in high school, Nancy Samson, Kim Kryzwicki, Jamie Spagna, and Carol Delano arrived in a pack. Suzanne hoped the rest of the classmates would be as easily recognizable as this foursome. She welcomed them and handed them their nametags along with their meal choices and two drink tickets apiece.

Walt Celinski, owner of the *Port Mariette News*, strode to the table a moment later, camera dangling from his neck.

"Hi, Walt. We're lucky you graduated in our class. Thanks for taking photos tonight." Suzanne smiled as she handed him his nametag.

"My pleasure." Walt tipped his head and pinned on his nametag. "It'll be on the front page tomorrow—unless something shocking happens between now and print time." He chuckled.

"What'll the headline be? *Finally, after forty years?*" Suzanne asked, as Walt shrugged. "I dunno. I just write the stories. My wife writes all the headlines and captions. Rosemarie's far more clever than I am." He stepped away to make room for Mary Frances, attired in a bright

FALLING APART, FALLING FOR YOU

polyester ensemble, strikingly similar to the outfit Marla had forbidden Rachel to wear.

"Hi, Suzanne. I'll be over there if you get overwhelmed." As she picked up her name tag, Mary Frances pointed toward the other side of the ballroom entrance.

"So kind of you." Fake smile. "I'll let you know. Pretty corsage, by the way." A lie. White one.

Mary Frances looked down at the pink carnations straight-pinned to her dress as she moved to her station. "Thanks."

Next, a rotund man with a wide band of white fringe approached the table, grinning, with his hands resting on his stomach. He reminded her of a Franciscan friar who used to speak sometimes at St. Cyp's. One time Marla had made fun of him, causing Suzanne to laugh out loud and Sister Mary Edmund to send them both to detention.

Suzanne scrunched her face. Something about this fellow's dark brown eyes seemed familiar. "Tony?"

"It's me." He beamed. "I wasn't sure you'd recognize me. I've put on a few pounds."

Suzanne maintained her poise, as if addressing an audience. "We've all changed." She shrugged then smiled. "Inside and out." As she handed him his nametag, he brushed his hand against hers. No spark, just a tug of nostalgia.

Tony kept staring, though. "You—you look amazing."

"Oh, thank you." Suzanne glanced to his left and right as other classmates milled about waiting to register.

"Well, maybe we can talk later, when you're done here." Tony swiped a hand across his forehead. "How about I save you a seat?"

"I think Rachel already has a table saved. Why don't you flag her down and find out where it is?"

Smiling broadly, Tony nodded and lumbered into to the ballroom.

A ruggedly handsome man appeared at Suzanne's left side. His eyes twinkling, he grinned. "Recognize me?"

Boring Bill. He'd always been tall, but now he was fit, well dressed, and self-confident. Plus, he had all his hair. "How could I forget you, Bill?" Suzanne fluttered her eyelashes as she waved his nametag with her manicured fingertips.

"You've certainly held up well." Bill's eyes ran all over Suzanne.

"Thanks, Bill. You look pretty terrific yourself."

He leaned toward her. "How about I buy you a drink when you're off duty?"

"Sounds wonderful." She tilted her head. "Rachel's saving a table. Why don't you join us?"

"I'll snag a seat next to you." He winked at her and strode toward the ballroom.

"Sure, Tony. I'll save this chair between me and Suzanne for you." Rachel tipped a chair onto its front legs and leaned it against the round table. He'd gained a few pounds since graduating, but, hey, so had she. Those dark eyes still drew her in. "So, what's—"

Herbie appeared out of nowhere. "Rachel, would you mind showing Donnie Blue where to set up his sound system?" He snuck a peek at Tony's nametag, then slapped him on the arm. "Hey, Tony, great to see you. Let's catch up. I'll meet you at the bar in a few minutes." Herbie took off to the other side of the ballroom to say something to a bow-tied waiter.

Tony rested a hand on one of the chairs as his eyes darted from Rachel's head to her toes and all parts in between. "I'm glad we'll have a chance to catch up."

"Me too." She fiddled with the ruching on her dress.

"You're busy right now. We can catch up later." He gave her arm a pat. "I'm going to have a beer with Herbie. Can I get you something?"

FALLING APART, FALLING FOR YOU

"Already got it." She jutted her chin toward her beer on the table.

"Okay. I'll be back." He headed toward the bar, and Rachel took the steps to the stage, her heart beating faster than normal. And not because of the steps.

"Hi, Donnie. Glad you'll be entertaining us tonight." She showed him where to place his equipment, then slid her hands on her hips as she looked over the growing crowd. To her relief, Marla hadn't shown up—at least not yet.

"Let me know if you need anything else, Donnie." Rachel turned and walked back to the steps. As she moved to take the first one, her heel caught on the uneven edge of the old wooden stage. She bounded down all three steps, twisting her left foot as she tumbled to the floor. "Aack!"

Classmates came running.

"Are you all right?"

"Can you stand?"

Rachel's cheeks warmed in embarrassment. She hoped she wouldn't cry from the pain—especially since she hadn't brought any makeup with her.

Suzanne ran over, hollering, "Is anyone here a doctor? A nurse? An EMT?" No one responded. She leaned over and touched Rachel's shoulder. "Don't try to get up. I'll be right back."

She returned in a flash, along with Marla. That woman knew how to make an entrance, with her long strides, sleeveless white linen dress, and display of emerald jewelry.

Rachel tensed just seeing her.

"Don't move, Rachel." Marla dropped herself to the dusty floor, twisted off Rachel's shoe and pressed around her ankle. "Tell me when it hurts."

"Now!" Rachel yelped as the pain shot up her leg.

Marla pressed and jiggled the ankle for a while. "Nothing's broken." She looked up. "Mary Frances, ask a waiter to get us a small bag of ice, a towel, and some rubber bands. Herbie and Tony, can you help Rachel get onto a chair?"

Like seasoned paramedics, they tucked Rachel's arms around their shoulders and boosted her onto a nearby chair.

"You comfortable?" Tony bent down and looked into her eyes.

"Yes, except for extreme embarrassment, I'm fine. Thank you." Rachel smiled wanly.

Mary Frances hurried back, gripping the first aid items. "Here you go!"

As Marla secured the towel and ice to Rachel's ankle, a memory clicked in Rachel's mind. "You were a nurse."

Marla gave her a quick wink. "Don't worry, I won't kill you."

Suzanne leaned over and picked up Rachel's shoe. "I'm sorry to tell you, Rach, this shoe's ruined. The heel's almost off." She held it lower so Rachel could see.

"You could walk barefoot all night." Tony chuckled. "Have to be careful if you dance with me, though."

Rachel plucked the shoe from Suzanne's hand and sighed.

"Any chance you wear a size eight?" Marla tipped her head to the side.

"Seven and a half." Rachel sighed again.

"Close enough." Marla disappeared for a few minutes, reappearing with a pair of leather shoes with a short-stacked heel. "I keep a lot of things in my handbag, but even more in my trunk."

Rachel's mouth dropped open. "They're gorgeous." She examined them more closely. "I should be able to walk in them."

The crowd of classmates had dissipated by now, leaving only four of them at the scene of the accident.

"I think Marla's got this under control." Tony smiled sheepishly at Suzanne. "Wanna go on the veranda and talk about what happened at the prom?"

FALLING APART, FALLING FOR YOU

"Sure." With a smile, Suzanne tucked her hand in his bent arm. They sauntered away, leaving Rachel alone with her nurse.

"Let me put those shoes on for you." Marla knelt before Rachel once again.

Tears welled in Rachel's eyes as she blubbered.

Marla looked up at her, wide-eyed. "Are you in a lot of pain?"

"No. Yes. I mean—I can't believe what you're doing, especially considering what a jerk I've been." She put her hand over her heart. "You fed me, you clothed me, you tried to make amends for the past. Heck, it seems we're even related."

She gazed at the shoes Marla had placed on her feet, then looked into Marla's eyes. "Now you're my nurse and my shoemaker." The tears overflowed. "How unthankful and unforgiving I've been." With eyes downcast, she spoke from her heart. "I don't deserve any of this from you."

Marla placed her hand on Rachel's knee. "If we all got what we deserved, Rachel, we'd either be in jail or hell."

Rachel whispered, "Can you forgive me?"

The rubber chicken dinner was the least of Suzanne's worries. Being sandwiched between Tony and Bill—could it get any more awkward? Tony showed himself to be the same wonderful guy inside, but try as she might, she couldn't get past his outside. The old attraction no longer existed, the flame had gone out. On the bright side, they'd put the prom episode to rest. Even managed to have a good laugh over it.

Boring Bill, on the other hand, had turned into Handsome, Attentive, Smart, and Successful Bill. Despite not wearing a wedding ring, however, she learned he was thoroughly married—for the fourth time. *Maybe he thinks I'm easy.* She shook her head, feeling foolish once again.

After the main course, Herbie stepped on stage to make announcements. "Sorry it took us forty years to round you all up." His eyes scanned the room and he grinned. "We wanted to make sure everyone had enough time to become successful." He threw a few familiar jabs at his old buddies, got some guffaws, and concluded his remarks. "Enjoy your dessert. Entertainment will resume shortly."

Soon, Willie Nelson appeared stage left, guitar in hand and fake braids dangling from a cowboy hat. It was Herbie doing one of his impersonations.

The place roared in approval.

People at the sports bar across the hall must have heard the commotion. About a dozen folks wandered into the back of the ballroom to watch. Mitch and his brothers, all dressed in bright golf attire, stood there laughing, along with Penny, her arms crossed, and several others.

Willie sang a few bars, then said, "Y'know, folks, it's mighty lonely up here. It'd sure be nice if I had some female company, if you know what I mean." He thrust a hand on his hip and got a laugh from the crowd.

From stage right, Dolly Parton sashayed over, hair in a huge bouffant, wearing a tight, fringed, very short white dress, the V-neck baring what appeared to be two balloons.

The hooting and hollering began in earnest.

"Who *is* that?" Rachel scrunched her forehead in wonder.

"*You're* on the committee. If you don't know, why would we?" Tony teased.

"I don't know who she is, but she sure has great legs," said Bill, staring.

Suzanne caught sight of an emerald bracelet. "Why, that's Marla!" She blurted.

Bill furrowed his eyebrows. "Who's Marla?"

"She's the girl who moved here from New York. She was here just our senior year."

"How could I have missed her?" Bill shook his head.

FALLING APART, FALLING FOR YOU

Suzanne shook her head, laughing. "That girl was always full of surprises. I was talking with her last night, and she never mentioned a thing about being Dolly today."

Rachel leaned in front of Tony, laughing, and said to Suzanne, "I guess she stores costumes in her purse too."

To quiet the crowd, Willie raised a hand. His fingers strummed a few chords as Dolly belted out a solo.

"She must have written those lyrics herself," Suzanne said to her tablemates. "The real Dolly sure never sang a song about Port Mariette or the nuns at St. Cyp's."

While Willie and Dolly sang, Suzanne leaned around Tony and tapped Rachel's shoulder. With one of those looks women give to one another when they can't say something in front of others, Suzanne jerked her head to the side. "How about a trip to the ladies' room?"

As Rachel gripped onto Suzanne's arm, they wended their way across the ballroom but bypassed the ladies' room. Suzanne whispered in Rachel's ear the whole way, then they disappeared behind the stage.

On Dolly's final note, the crowd burst into applause. A few people pushed up from their chairs, clapping, whistling, and laughing. Dolly beamed.

The second song, a raucous duet, earned Dolly and Willie a standing ovation. As the clapping diminished, Herbie pulled off his wig and spoke into the mic. "I'd like to get serious with you for a moment, if I might."

The room instantly turned quiet.

"You may have heard the State is constructing a new highway near Port Mariette." Heads nodded, and several people murmured. "Some of us have been working on a plan to revitalize the town so we can capitalize on the increased traffic that'll come here once our exit's completed. We thought tonight would be the perfect setting for a sneak preview." He scanned the room. "Maybe some of you will even want to move back to town once you see what's in the works."

Herbie turned sideways to wave some people onto the stage. "Here to present the plan are Suzanne, Rachel, and Dolly—I mean Marla." He put a hand on his hip, faking a fluster. "Well, it's an understandable gaffe. After all, she's still wearing her balloons."

Suzanne shook her head and laughed as she lifted the mic from its stand. Meanwhile, Rachel and Marla unfurled an immense roll of white paper, almost as tall as themselves, spreading it from one end of the stage to the other.

"I'd like to invite you all to take an imaginary walk with me." Drawing on her training experience, Suzanne lengthened her back and flashed a wide smile, capturing the crowd's full attention.

With flourish, she waved a hand toward the artwork unfurled behind her and read aloud some words she'd written in elegant calligraphy. "Welcome to Port Mariette—a Small Town with a Big History." She pointed toward Marla. "We can all thank marketing whiz Marla Galani for our town's new slogan."

As the crowd applauded, Walt rushed to a seat in the front of the room. He slapped a notepad and pen on the table and adjusted his camera lens.

New headline. Suzanne chuckled to herself as she clicked her heels across the stage. "I'd like to take you on a virtual tour of our town's future Main Street." She stepped toward her artwork. "Imagine a revitalized Port Mariette, with the new exit already in use. As we exit the highway southbound, our first stop is Rachel Baran's gas station, which she and her son Pete will renovate to look like a building from the Fifties."

Rachel waved to the audience and grinned.

"They'll serve to-go meals like Rachel's homemade pasta and pierogies, along with other convenience store items and fuel at the pumps."

Suzanne swayed her hips a tad as she continued her stroll along Main Street. "You probably know Herbie already owns several buildings on Main Street. He also

FALLING APART, FALLING FOR YOU

recently bought the empty one next to the bank, and he's going to turn it into a country store, complete with vintage toys, scented soaps, and penny candy."

"I'll be upgrading the pizza shop too." Herbie hollered to the crowd.

"And there's more," Suzanne continued. "The antique store will be expanded to include special collections for dolls, porcelain figurines, and local history memorabilia. In the empty storefront next to Herbie's pizza shop, my sister Andrea will sell her oil paintings, along with our mother's crocheted items, and my artwork too. It'll be a consignment shop. Maybe some of you would like to talk with Andrea about items you want to sell there."

The crowd buzzed as Suzanne continued the tour. "Along with all that, there are surely other businesses that might be renovated or established. For example, Mary Frances, I haven't had a chance to talk with you, but perhaps you'll want to expand your office once the revitalization spurs more real estate activity."

Mary Frances, sitting in front of the stage, made no reply as she tilted her head and squinted as if in thought.

"And here will be the new visitors' center, constructed by Mitch Mitchell and his team of craftsmen." Suzanne pointed to the end of Main Street. "Mitch plans to build a charming replica of one of the town's mansions."

The crowed oohed in support of the idea.

Mary Frances called out to Suzanne. "This is all wonderful—but who has the money to pay for it? Not me, for sure." She frowned and added, "And I hope our taxes won't be going up either."

"Glad you asked." Suzanne grinned. "We are blessed to have among our classmates someone who has been phenomenally successful, is incredibly generous, and has pledged to provide grant money—up to five million dollars—for the transformation of our town! Anyone who is starting or renovating a business can apply for a grant. No repayment will be required, ever."

Mary Frances's mouth dropped open.

"Who is it?" Several people called out in unison, as they looked around at one another. Many eyes fell on Bill, others on Herbie.

"Tell us, who is it?" Mary Frances blurted.

"It's Marla Galani." Suzanne stretched her hand toward Marla.

The audience came to its feet, clapping and cheering, as Marla beamed, radiating joy.

Walt snapped more photos and jotted notes.

"Now, don't mob Marla tonight." Suzanne raised a hand. "The details will be announced in Walt's paper in a day or two."

Walt gave Suzanne a snappy salute and a grin.

"But wait." She held up a finger. "There's still one more announcement, a big one. Mitch is going to create a small park next to the visitors' center with benches, a playground, and a water fountain where people can toss coins and make a wish." Suzanne's eyes drilled into someone at the back of the room. "It will be called 'Penny's Park.'"

People clapped once again, and Suzanne motioned to Penny. "C'mon up here, Mayor Frampton."

Penny hesitated, but Mitch nudged her forward with his palm, and she poked her way across the ballroom to the stage, eyes averted, a weak smile on her face.

"It's because of Penny that this plan can go forth." Suzanne spoke as the mayor ascended the steps. "Lately, there's been some confusion about whether or not we'll get our exit, but Penny has given us her word that we will get it." Suzanne held out the mic. "We are thankful we can count on our mayor."

With a quivering hand and a smile that looked more like a grimace, Penny accepted the mic. She thanked the

FALLING APART, FALLING FOR YOU

town for their support in two choppy sentences. "I—I don't deserve to have that park named after me but thank you. I, uh, look forward to the day when our exit is constructed."

"You feeling okay?" Mary Frances hollered from a table in front.

Penny nodded almost imperceptibly and shoved the mic back in Suzanne's hand.

Marla motioned for Herbie to come from the wing of the stage and for Mitch to come forward from the back of the room. As they neared, she leaned into Suzanne's microphone. "These two gentlemen—Mitch Mitchell and Herbie Herbinger—are the visionaries that got this ball rolling."

More applause and buzzing in the crowd.

Walt asked for some photos of the entire group, so they readied themselves to pose in front of Suzanne's illustrations. For her, it was a shining, if lonely, moment. Having read somewhere that smiling automatically improves your mood, she forced herself to grin as far as her lips could go.

Penny tried to leave the stage, but Herbie pulled her back to the group. "You're not going anywhere, little lady." He laughed as he slipped her hand into his.

Mitch shook his head as he looked at Suzanne and Marla. "I don't know how you pulled this off."

They burst into laughter, as Marla poked Suzanne in the arm. "You're both a Michelangelo and a mastermind!"

Rachel squeezed in between them. "Are you laughing because we're getting our picture in the *Port Mariette Gazette*? Didn't I tell you we would?"

Amid all the joy and a lengthy standing ovation, the group began their exit from the stage. Tony jumped from his seat to help Rachel down the stairs, and the rest followed.

Suzanne whispered to Marla. "I'm guessing that was Grace standing in the back of the room."

A smile washed across Marla's face. She nodded.

"She sure looks like you."

Marla grinned as her eyes darted around the ballroom in search of Grace. "Let's go find her. I'd like to introduce you two."

Donnie Blue began spinning oldies. A lively, upbeat tune drew a crowd to the dance floor.

With the crowd thinned out, Marla spotted Grace and introduced her to Suzanne.

"What a tremendous gift for you to find one another. I'm so happy for you." Suzanne gave Grace a hug. "I hope you'll sell some of your river rock jewelry at Andrea's shop. Marla tells me it's both unique and beautiful."

The music switched to a slow song, and Suzanne noticed Rachel and Tony dancing together closely, talking and laughing like they might have at a high school dance. *Good for her.* Spotting Bill walking toward her with a lecherous smile on his face, Suzanne excused herself from Marla and Grace. She slipped into the empty hallway, then darted onto a hidden corner of the veranda.

Looking out over the empty golf course, she focused on her breathing. In and out, deep and slow. She hadn't had time to process everything from Adam's visit yesterday, and now, tonight's events had added another layer of emotion.

With elbows resting on the rail of the veranda, she prayed out loud. "Lord, I surrendered it all to you, and obviously, you've heard that prayer, because you've taken it all away." She shook her head in disbelief. "No job, no income, no purpose, no husband. Not so much as a dinner date. You've cleared my decks." She gripped the cement railing and gazed into the star-filled sky. "Now, I pray for your guidance, and I willingly accept whatever you have planned for me."

She stayed on the veranda a while, gazing at the skies. Then, inspiration struck. She strode back into the ballroom and grabbed her clutch. As she passed Marla on the dance floor with Mitch, she whispered in her ear. "Tell everyone I had to leave."

FALLING APART, FALLING FOR YOU

Before Marla could respond, Suzanne had disappeared into the crowd.

CHAPTER 33

Six months later

Early Saturday morning, just as a sudden snowstorm hit town, Suzanne snagged a parking space in front of Andrea's art shop. Bundled in a knee-length down coat, she turned off the engine and stayed snug behind the wheel, waiting for the squall to blow past.

Today, she'd drop off another batch of artwork to sell on consignment—this time, mainly her popular watercolors. Her sister's oils also sold well, and their mother's crocheted items were a sensation—even generating a waiting list, thanks to a customer's Instagram posting of her baby adorned in a one-of-a-kind christening gown.

Right after the reunion, Suzanne had immersed herself in art, experimenting with watercolor and gouache, sculpture, charcoal, photography, collage, and even caricatures drawn with colored pencils. She found practically no medium uncongenial to her ability or interest.

As she worked she listened to music, often Christian, or songs from her high school days. Sometimes she sang along or prayed. Thoughts and revelations fluttered about in her mind—memories, realizations, plans for the future. She'd never experienced such a high and felt God's hand guiding her like never before.

Anytime she was back in Port Mariette with Rachel and Marla, they fed her advice and support. When the three were apart, they kept current over the phone and on video calls. Their renewed relationship grew stronger than ever.

Of course, there'd been challenges.

"You're behaving like a victim." Marla barked at Suzanne one night at Dom's when she was whining about the demands of her life. "You're the one who made the choices; face the consequences. If you don't like the outcome, figure out a way to change it." She crossed her arms. "Take it from me. I learned the hard way."

Rachel put it softer. "Your past is your past. Let it go. Make a new future, one that suits who you've become." She squeezed Suzanne's hand. "Remember when I told you about that porcelain figurine Joey Sowak broke when he hit a ball through my picture window?"

Suzanne nodded, even though she didn't remember the details.

"I kept the head of that figurine in my nightstand all these years. Every night, I'd open that drawer and get irritated all over again about Joey Sowak." She pursed her lips. "After the reunion, I went home and threw that thing in the garbage. I forgave Joey—and everyone else I held a grudge against. Such a freeing feeling!"

"But I don't hold grudges." Suzanne protested, her eyebrows furrowed.

"I know." Rachel patted Suzanne's hand. "I'm just telling you what I put behind me. We all have things we need to put behind us, otherwise they color our world, and not in pretty shades."

Despite paying close attention to the Lord and absorbing advice from others, it still took Suzanne time to see through the jumble in her mind. "Life's messy, after all," as she often said. Once she got clarity, though, she took swift action.

She wrote to Adam, thanking him for their time together and for lining up Drew's new job. She forgave his deception and wished him well in his life and career.

FALLING APART, FALLING FOR YOU

She called her ex-husband Mike and acknowledged her part in wrecking their marriage. Young and immature, she'd not chosen wisely and made mistakes of her own. She'd focused on her own priorities and ignored his needs.

As for Tony? Poor guy. Rachel said he had open-heart surgery a couple months after the reunion and had already lost twenty-eight pounds. Suzanne sent him a note thanking him for clearing the air about the prom, along with a gift card to a restaurant known for its healthy menus.

Rob? Oh yes, she talked with him too. Often. If she'd been a paying client, she would've had to land a high-level job to afford him. That man, he still sent a rippling through her every time they talked.

Right after the reunion, on a day when she felt particularly distraught about her life and her career, she'd poured out her heart to him. He asked her a question that led to the next chapter of her life. "What else is possible that you haven't considered?" Funny how a single question can right the direction of your ship. From that moment on, she decided her history is her history. She'd no longer be dragged down by it; she'd only face forward.

As abruptly as it had begun, the snow squall ended. Suzanne popped out of her car and dropped off her artwork, then scooted over to Marla's spa.

Rachel's car already sat in the parking lot. It figured. Rachel still raved about the spa day they'd had in Pittsburgh. She probably couldn't wait for her facial today.

Suzanne parked, then dashed up the steps, the icy wind whipping across her face.

Marla swung the front door open. "Welcome to our pre-grand opening." She waved her hand toward the reception room with great flourish. She'd suggested they meet at the spa since they'd all be in town for Christmas.

Rachel rose from the loveseat, recently reupholstered with luscious mauve velvet. "Group hug!" She laughed as she reached for the other two.

A moment later, Grace appeared in the foyer. "How about a tour before your facials?" She led them through the house, pointing out the changes she and Marla had made.

"What a fabulous renovation." Suzanne oozed with compliments as they wound their way through the rooms. "These furnishings are stunning. And I love your paint palette of rose and tan."

Marla beamed—whether it was because of Grace or the renovations, Suzanne couldn't tell. Probably both.

"Grace oversaw the restoration since I was often back in Manhattan. She did a masterful job." Marla's eyes glistened.

"The place is as transformed as we are!" Suzanne rested a hand on her chest.

Grace ended the tour in a large former bedroom, now outfitted with inviting spa chairs. "Hannah will be with you in a moment for your facials."

"Hannah from Herbie's pizza place?" Suzanne's eyes widened.

Marla chuckled. "One and the same. She's friends with Grace. When Hannah heard about the spa, she went to school to get her license. She'll do a beautiful job, I promise you."

Hannah walked in a minute later, a friendly smile spread across her face. "Hi, ladies, welcome to Victorian Spa." Her strong hands expertly cleaned and steamed their faces, then smoothed on the masks. "I'll be back to take them off in twenty minutes."

The door closed and they looked at themselves in the mirrored wall. Rachel giggled. "We look like creatures from the green lagoon."

"But soon, we'll be beauties." Suzanne laughed as she lifted a tendril of hair from her face and looked in the mirror at Marla. "I can't wait to meet Warren tonight." She'd heard all about Marla's former lawyer but had never met him. "Does he miss his law practice?"

FALLING APART, FALLING FOR YOU

"Not at all," Marla said. "Since he sold it, he's been incredibly busy dealing with my legal matters—and his own too."

"How come you never knew about all his real estate investments?" Rachel scrunched her face. "Didn't he ever mention it when you dated the first time around?"

"It was years ago when we dated, and back then, he hadn't bought anything yet. When he became my lawyer, we avoided discussing his personal life. Then, when he sold his practice, he'd just finished tying up the loose ends on the sale of my business. I was so immersed in finding Grace and all the issues with the spa and the town's highway exit—it wasn't until I got back to Manhattan that I learned why he wanted to meet for dinner."

"Aw, so romantic." Suzanne's eyes twinkled. "He harbored love in his heart for you all those years." Suzanne smiled the best her facial would allow. "Sounds like this could be headed somewhere serious."

Marla smiled. "It's going well. In fact, we've each decided to sell off some of our properties, so we'll have more time for other things."

"Like what?" Suzanne turned toward Marla.

"Remember how you told me you used to visit churches when you traveled?"

"Mm-hmm." Suzanne nodded.

"Warren and I did a little of that in Manhattan. We found a church we love. I—I guess you could say I discovered I've been chasing the wind." Marla looked up. "I'm not sure where all this searching will lead, but I can now see how both of you, and others like Mitch and Deanna, have helped me along this path."

"Spiritual growth—now that's a subject I can relate to." Rachel chuckled. "I've been throwing away old grudges left and right." She wagged her finger toward Marla. "You're the one who helped me most with that. I'll never forget those awful scenes I caused with you—and most of all, how ashamed I felt after you took care of me at the reunion." Tenderness filled Rachel's voice. "You were just like Jesus."

Marla put a hand on her chest. "How can I respond to a statement like that—except to say thank you." She touched her cheek as she looked in the mirror. "This mask feels almost done. Mine's cracking as I speak." She wiped her hand on a soft towel. "So, Rachel, where do you think things are heading for you and Frank?"

"We've agreed that a little companionship is right for both of us, probably nothing more." Rachel shrugged. "That trip to Poland with Sandy Roczinski was a turning point for me. I realized how much I enjoy my freedom. Being independent has been a new experience, and I'm not willing to give it up, at least not anytime soon. Besides, Frank and I have been friends and neighbors so long, it's hard to make that into anything more. A game of cards, a movie, a weekly dinner—that's plenty for me."

Suzanne glanced in the mirrored wall. "I'm glad he'll be at Dom's tonight. I want to get to know him better. Warren too." She touched her cheek. "Can't wait to see how much better our skin will look once this mud's washed off."

Hannah rapped at the door. "Time's up, ladies."

Everyone pulled into Dom's parking lot around the same time, filling the area with introductions, laughter, and hugs. Red lights twinkled in the evergreens, and an enormous blow-up Santa with a raised, white-gloved hand greeted them near the entrance.

The wind had calmed, but Suzanne shivered from the near-freezing temperature. "I should've worn more than this little wrap." She announced it with a giggle to anybody within hearing distance, and immediately, many arms enveloped her with warmth. Her heart overflowed with joy.

FALLING APART, FALLING FOR YOU

She'd always loved the Christmas season, and this year's might be the best ever.

Warren reached the door first and gallantly held it open for Marla, then for everyone else. Dom himself welcomed the group as they entered. "It's an honor to have you here tonight." He looked at the ladies and lowered his voice. "That highway exit is already such a boon to my business. I can't thank you enough." He paraded them under a stucco archway decorated with artificial holly and led them to a round table nestled in the back.

A powerful aroma of garlic, onion, and oregano wafted around them. Warren pulled out a chair for Marla. "I don't know how the food will taste, but this place sure smells delicious."

Marla faked a gasp and threw a hand on her chest. "Black linen tablecloths and candlelight centerpieces? Dom's not kidding, business must be booming."

Rachel tittered as Frank pulled out her chair. "Thank you." She slid her considerably lighter and firmer self onto the cushioned seat.

Suzanne glanced at the menu, then leaned to her right and whispered: "Get the red."

"A pinot noir? A Beaujolais?" Rob's eyes questioned her.

"You must think you're back in wine country, sweetie." Suzanne's eyes sparkled as she explained the inside joke. A tingle went through her just sitting beside the man. So comfortable, yet excited to even be near him.

A pony-tailed waitress bounced over, pen behind her ear. "Here's our new wine list."

"Joke's on you." Rob chuckled. He pulled out his reading glasses to scan the extensive list. "How about this pinot noir from New Zealand?" He arched an eyebrow at Suzanne, then his eyes followed her down as far as the tablecloth allowed.

Suzanne peered at the wine list, her mouth dropping open. "Wow. Dom has lifted the bar high."

Rob laughed, his face moving into those familiar smile lines that she'd grown to love so well.

"May I say, you look stunning in that red dress." His eyes twinkled. "Even though the shawl covers your lovely shoulders."

She preened in jest, then squeezed Rob's hand. He'd bought her the silver-gray cashmere wrap one chilly but romantic evening in Carmel. She slid it off her shoulders and Rob hung it on the back of her chair.

The server pulled the pen from behind her ear as Rob ordered a bottle of something red.

Was it the one from New Zealand? Who cares? She looked him over—that perfect profile of a face, that amazing mind, that gentle spirit. *Thank God for this man.*

The night of the reunion, standing on the veranda, praying, and looking out over the golf course, she'd pondered the stars and the moon. God put them there and kept them there, right where they belonged. Everything in this world is in God's hands. *Including my future.* In a flash, she'd known she should accept Rob's offer to stay for a while in his pastor's casita. It'd be the perfect place to figure out what that future would be.

After leaving the country club, she'd called Rob to make sure the offer still stood, then caught a plane a few days later—perfect timing for Jill and Drew to use her condo until they moved into a home.

She and Rob found time to walk the beach, drive along Highway 1 through Big Sur, and wander the charming streets of Carmel-by-the-Sea. The astounding beauty unleashed in her a desire to paint, draw, and sculpt. She set up a temporary studio in Rob's garage and turned out pieces like a prisoner set free after a long sentence.

Their conversations covered all the bases—happy topics like when Suzanne turned down a job offer in order to become a full-time artist, and sad ones, like the pneumonia that led to Meg's death. Through it all, they vowed to be honest with one another. While that sometimes made Suzanne uncomfortable, she finally broke her long-standing habit of keeping men at a distance.

She continued to surrender herself more and more to the Lord, finding it the key to true freedom. Surrender washed away her need for control, along with her stress and anxiety, even blessed her with a clear mind. To her great relief, she now rarely misplaced her keys or cellphone.

Flying back and forth to the West Coast didn't come cheap, but she'd accumulated a reasonable retirement fund and was earning income from the pieces she sold at Andrea's. Besides, spending time in three vastly different places—Carmel, Pittsburgh, and Port Mariette—stimulated her. It resulted in a range of artistic pursuits—a collage made from Carmel Beach driftwood, a pen and ink drawing of downtown Pittsburgh, a watercolor of Port Mariette's mansions.

And now, she glanced around Dom's, imagining how she might compose an ink drawing of the six of them sitting here tonight. Maybe a caricature? Even thinking about what she might create from tonight's experience excited her. Soaking in her emotions, Suzanne leaned her body against Rob's firm shoulder.

He nuzzled her hair and lifted her hand, giving it a quick kiss.

They remained still for a moment, bodies pressing into one another.

Rob lifted her chin and gazed into her eyes, saying nothing, saying everything.

Warren, looking up from his menu, interrupted the silence by asking Rachel and Frank a question. "So, what do you two locals recommend?"

Rachel looked at Frank and giggled. "We usually eat here on Friday nights. We've never tried the osso buco, but we've enjoyed everything else."

"Rachel's being humble." Frank leaned forward. "The reason the food's so delicious is because Dom buys his pasta dishes from her now. Everything but the veal and poultry comes from Rachel's commercial kitchen at the service station."

"It's Pete's place too," Rachel said. "He's now fifty-one percent owner. All I do is cook. He does everything else, even the paperwork." She smoothed her napkin. "But don't tell anyone where the pasta dishes come from. Dom's funny about them being made in a gas station, as he says."

Marla tapped her menu. "No osso buco for me. I think I'll try your famous sausage lasagna." Her emerald jewelry shimmered under the dim lighting, and her smile shone even brighter.

Suzanne had never seen her friend so alive. "You look terrific, Marla. And I think it's more than those spa treatments." Suzanne chuckled.

"Thanks." Marla smiled.

Suzanne flipped to the next page of her menu. "How's your aunt doing?"

"She's aging in reverse. That swimming pool has changed her life."

Warren draped his arm on the back of Marla's chair. "Adele said to tell you all hello."

"She adores Warren." Marla touched his cheek then looked at Suzanne. "She'd like you and Rob to visit if you have time."

"We fly back two days after Christmas. We'll be sure to stop over." Suzanne set the menu down. "I think I'll order that lasagna too."

The server took an order for six sausage lasagnas and glanced at Rachel. "You should be in sales." She pivoted and headed to the kitchen.

Warren lifted his elbows onto the table and folded his hands. Arching a thick eyebrow, he turned to Suzanne. "I've never heard the full story about Penny. Marla said you're the only one who knows all the details."

"Probably true." Suzanne sat up straight, hands on her lap. "It still amazes me how everything fell into place. Now

FALLING APART, FALLING FOR YOU

that it's over, I see it was all God's doing." Her eyes misted, and she blinked. "I'll tell you how it all happened."

"The night before the reunion, I ended up at a casino with my friend Barbara. She wanted to lift my mood—I'd had an awful day." Suzanne held up her hand. "Don't even ask." She rolled her eyes. "Anyway, Penny happened to be at the craps table, losing big time. Barbara took my cellphone and managed to sneak a video of Penny at the moment she lost ten thousand dollars."

"Talk about being in the right place at the right time." Warren chuckled.

"I led Penny to believe I'd show others the video. Believe me, I had no intention of doing that." Suzanne laid a hand on her chest. "But she was terrified I might, so she agreed to throw her support behind the exit."

"Okay, I get that." Warren lifted a hand, palm up. "But how about the rest of the story?"

"The night of the reunion, Penny was acting funny. I thought she was upset she had to publicly commit to the exit—or maybe she thought I might renege on my promise to keep her gambling secret."

"That would be understandable." Warren rubbed his chin.

"Anyway, I had a lot on my mind that night, so I left the reunion early. As I walked through the foyer, Penny came up behind me and grabbed my arm. She said, 'Come into my office. We need to talk.' What else could I do? I followed her into the room. She burst into tears, said she was in big trouble. After we talked a while, she admitted she was a gambler like her father and deceitful like her mother."

"Such a heartbreaking confession." Marla took a sip of ginger ale.

Suzanne nodded. "She told me she was deep in debt and had made a deal with some legislator in Harrisburg—Penny would get the Port Mariette council to agree to forego the exit, and she'd get grant money from the State for her business, along with some extra cash for her personal pocketbook."

"Boy, you read about things like that in the newspaper, but you never expect it to happen with your own mayor." Rachel frowned.

"The woman saw no way out." Suzanne shrugged. "She was so distraught, I thought she might do something crazy like jump off the bridge down at the river. I didn't know what to do. Finally, I asked her if she wanted to pray about it.

"She agreed, so I prayed aloud, asking God to guide us. We sat in silence for a while, then Penny said she needed to admit to others that she's addicted to gambling. She promised she'd go to either therapy or Gamblers Anonymous.

"I congratulated her on her decision, and I thought we were done, but then she told me she was in a financial hole—she needed to declare bankruptcy. We prayed again. Eventually, Herbie and Mitch came to my mind, and I suggested she sell the country club and golf course to one of them.

"Her eyes lit up, and she ran into the hall to get them. We explained the situation.

"Herbie asked Penny how much she owed, then he and Mitch went into the hall to talk. When they came back, Mitch made an offer for the country club, and Herbie for the golf course. The total amount covered Penny's entire debt. The next day, she resigned as mayor and went public with her gambling problem."

"I remember reading it in the paper." Frank shook his head. "I'd just taken my first swig of coffee. I choked. Splattered it all over the front page. Had to run next door for Rachel's paper to read the entire article."

Rachel nodded. "Talk about a shock. Nothing like that's ever happened in Port Mariette."

Marla blew a kiss across the table to Suzanne. "We all thank you for what you did."

FALLING APART, FALLING FOR YOU

"Thanks, but I think you all know I didn't do it. I just made myself available for God to use me." Suzanne looked down at her lap, touched by how God had moved in her own life, as well as in the lives of everyone at the table.

Breaking the silence, two servers arrived with round trays jammed with steaming hot lasagnas, filling their table with scents of garlic and spices. Rachel looked the meals over and gave a smile of approval.

They all bowed their heads as Rob said the blessing.

The six of them ate, drank, talked, and laughed, not even realizing that, over time, every one of the other tables had cleared.

Eventually, Warren motioned the server for the bill. When the others objected, he waved his hand. "It was worth it to meet all of you and to hear Suzanne's story."

Frank patted his stomach. "Best sausage lasagna in the world."

"Thank you." Rachel looked around. "I guess we'd better get moving."

Rachel and Frank sauntered out first, followed by Marla and Warren, arm in arm.

"We're going to finish our wine," Rob explained, as he and Suzanne stayed behind.

The restaurant fell silent except for some distant voices and the clanging of pans. Candlelight flickered as Rob took Suzanne's hand, engulfing it completely. They sat in a comfortable, satisfied silence.

He kissed her hand then looked up. "You're a woman of tremendous beauty, Suzanne. On the inside as well as the outside. I love learning about you and all the things you've spent your lifetime doing and becoming."

"That is so touching." Suzanne tilted her head. "Thank you, Rob."

"I knew there was something special the first time I laid eyes on you in that hotel hallway in Phoenix, something beyond the physical thrill you gave me. Something deep in my bones, deep in my spirit, told me you were the one for me." He kissed her hand again. "You're a treasure."

"You're making me blush!" She touched her cheek.

"I love making you blush." Rob chuckled as he caressed her face, then glanced around the empty room. "I guess we should leave before they throw us out." He draped her shawl over her shoulders and gave her a quick squeeze.

Hand in hand, they stepped away from the table. As they reached the archway, Rob pointed to something above them. "I believe that's mistletoe."

Suzanne wasn't sure what it was, but she smiled as Rob wrapped his arms around her waist and pulled her close.

They shared a long and gentle kiss, then gazed into each other's eyes.

She longed for this man. He'd seen something in her she hadn't even known herself, and he allowed her the space to discover it. How many men would do that? None—except for this remarkable man. Who was now kissing her neck. *Oh my.*

Rob searched deep in her eyes. "You are the woman I want to learn with, play with, zip zippers for, and make love to the rest of my life. Suzanne, will you marry me?"

Her hand flew to her lips as Rob opened a black velvet box to display a dazzling solitaire engagement ring. The shock of the moment stunned her into silence. Although they'd discussed the possibility of marriage, she hadn't expected it so soon, and definitely not tonight. The logistics of their families, coupled with the uncertainty of her income, were more than most men would take on.

Yet Rob was not like most men.

Anytime they discussed the possibility of marriage, he'd promised they'd spend time back east to see Jill and Drew and precious grandbaby Elizabeth, as well as Suzanne's mom and Rachel in Port Mariette. "You could even coordinate trips for times when Marla's back in town." He'd thought it all out. "Everything will fall into place,"

FALLING APART, FALLING FOR YOU

he'd say with confidence. "Remember, with God, all things are possible."

She drew in a breath. Tears filled her eyes and her chest heaved with emotion.

He nuzzled her ear, then whispered with a smile in his voice, "Stop analyzing it, honey—just feel it."

She wrapped her arms around his neck and laughed. The man knew her so well. She met his lips for a loving kiss.

He caressed her face and broke into a grin. "Are you going to give me an answer?"

A joyful laugh escaped Suzanne's lips as a smile spread wide across her face. "Yes, Rob. Oh, yes!"

ABOUT THE AUTHOR

Chris Posti began her writing career at age eight, when she gave her mother a book of poems she'd written in pencil on a lined yellow tablet.

Since then, Chris has authored two nonfiction books, a workbook, and dozens of articles. For twenty-two years, she was a Sunday columnist for the *Pittsburgh Tribune-Review*. Self-employed as an executive coach, job search consultant, and public speaker, she also wrote scores of proposals, presentations, résumés, and cover letters.

Chris is an active member of American Christian Fiction Writers (ACFW) and Women's Fiction Writers Association (WFWA). She lives in southwestern Pennsylvania with her marvelous husband, Dave, and is only a half-hour away from her beautiful daughter, brilliant son-in-law, and two outstanding grandsons.

DEAR READERS—

Thank you for reading *Falling Apart, Falling for You*. If you enjoyed it, please consider leaving an Amazon or Goodreads review so other readers might enjoy it too. Just a couple sentences will do. That would mean so much!

You're welcome to contact me with your comments and questions at chris@chrisposti.com.

You can sign up for my newsletter at chrisposti.com to receive updates on future releases as well as topics you'll find of interest. When you sign up, I'll send you something I think you'll get a kick out of!

QUESTIONS FOR DISCUSSION

1. In the first chapter, Suzanne asked her boss if she was being fired because she was too old. Shocked and upset, Suzanne's mouth somehow got ahead of her brain. Have you ever said something you know you shouldn't have, then tried to justify it? Or heard someone else do so? What tends to trigger saying something you didn't mean to say, and how can you avoid it in the future? How did Herbie's long-ago comment to Marla that she was a "classy gal" affect her life? What does Chapter 3 of James say about the power of the tongue?

2. At her husband's wake, Rachel is emotionally in control, attributing it to knowing the drill from the deaths of her youngest son, her dad, and her in-laws. Sometimes we're tempted to rein in our grief instead of allowing it to run its natural course. Why might someone do that? If you've suffered the loss of a loved one, how did you cope? What advice would you have for others?

3. Marla wondered if she was being short-sighted about selling her business or if her decision was just an expedient one. Suzanne had lived for many years as a single, independent woman and then felt a stirring in her soul to settle down—but had her doubts about with whom. Have you ever second-guessed yourself when making a major decision? What might you do to feel more comfortable with making such a decision?

4. Rachel kept a broken porcelain head in her nightstand drawer for many years, which helped her harbor her irritation with Frank's son, Joey. What does the Bible (Hebrews 12:15) say about bitterness? What's so bad about holding onto a little anger or irritation? Rachel's porcelain head might seem ridiculous to you, but what bitterness might you be holding onto that would seem equally ridiculous to anyone but you? If you've overcome a grudge or bitterness, what would you suggest to help someone else going through a similar situation?

5. The relationship between Suzanne and her daughter Jill was affected by something Suzanne could control (keeping her opinions to herself) and by something she could not control (Jill's husband Drew). Many parents struggle to maintain healthy, positive relationships with their grown children. What lessons have you learned about doing that well? What mistakes have you seen others make? What could you do to strengthen your relationship with your grown children or other family members, especially those you find difficult or unreasonable?

6. Mayor Penny Frampton's behavior was less than admirable. She gambled, didn't manage the golf course and country club well, and apparently was willing to accept a bribe from someone in her state government. Could someone like Penny ever get into heaven?

7. Suzanne accepted the video recorded (by someone else) against the rules of the casino, then gave Penny the impression she'd use it to expose her. Suzanne's scheme brought about the intended effect, but was she right in what she did? Does the end sometimes justify the means? If you were Suzanne, what would you have done to persuade Penny to support the highway exit?

8. Have you experienced a "second-chance" relationship or marriage, or do you know others who have? What

FALLING APART, FALLING FOR YOU

advice—both good and bad—have you given/been given? Or have you just kept your opinion to yourself? How did Deanna and Mitch show themselves to be evangelists? What ways have you used to point others to Christ?

9. You've seen how Suzanne, Rachel, and Marla have each grown spiritually. How would you describe their journey to date? Whose journey can you best relate to? What do you expect will happen in their journeys in the next book of this series? What do you expect your future to be like, based on where you are in your spiritual journey today? If you're not satisfied with your answer, what can you commit to now to change it?

Made in the USA
Monee, IL
21 May 2022